THE POWERS SPEAK

The Voice returned, wonderfully compelling my trance.

"XARAF FIREBRIDGE, YOU MUST PAY CLOSE HEED."

"My Lord, I am listening."

"LISTEN WELL, FOR THE FATE OF THE WORLD AND YOUR OWN MAY HANG IN THE BALANCE. YOU WILL RETURN TO YOUR OWN TIME ... ONCE THERE, YOU ARE TO SEEK OUT AND DESTROY THOSE SORCERERS WHO ARE TAMPERING WITH THE WORK OF THE POWERS ...

"THE CREATURES YOU OPPOSE HAVE FORFEITED ALL RIGHT TO HUMANE CONSIDERATION ... UNLESS THEY ARE THWARTED, YOUR WORLD WILL SHUDDER IN DARKNESS FOR A HUNDRED THOUSAND YEARS ..."

The Black Grail

Damien Broderick

AVON
PUBLISHERS OF BARD, CAMELOT, DISCUS AND FLARE BOOKS

AVON BOOKS
A division of
The Hearst Corporation
1790 Broadway
New York, New York 10019

First Avon Printing: September 1986

AVON TRADEMARK REG. U.S. PAT. OFF. AND IN OTHER COUNTRIES, MARCA REGISTRADA, HECHO EN U.S.A.

Printed in the U.S.A.

K-R 10 9 8 7 6 5 4 3 2 1

For my mother and father
these new revised syllables

ACKNOWLEDGMENTS

LIFE:

Bertrand Russell, *A History of Western Philosophy*
Ernst Kris, *Psychoanalytic Exploration in Art*

SLEEP:

Sir Fred Hoyle, *Ice*
Nigel Calder, *The Weather Machine*

DEATH:

John Gribbin, *The Climatic Threat*
John Gribbin, *Genesis*

REBIRTH:

C.W. Nicol, *Moving Zen*
Otto Rank, "The Double as Immortal Self"
Plotinus, *Enneads*

The Black Grail

LIFE

::Rationality, in the sense of a universal and impersonal standard of truth, is of supreme importance, not only in ages in which it easily prevails, but also, and even more, in the less fortunate times in which it is despised and rejected as the vain dream of men who lack the virility to kill when they cannot agree::

—Bertrand Russell

::It would seem as well demonstrated as any conclusion in the social sciences that the struggle against incestuous impulses, dependency, guilt and aggression has remained a recurrent topic . . . ::

—Ernst Kris

ONE

Once, Darkbloom asked me which animal I was.

"Animal?" I looked at him stupidly.

"Each of us has an inner creature," he told me, with that infuriating blissful smile which made me want to beat his face. I was ten years old. "It walks with our legs when we fail to pay attention. It can be cowed, or tamed, or befriended. So again I ask you, Xaraf: Which animal are you?"

"I am not an animal," I said angrily. I walked away from his meager fire and its stink of herbs and belly fat. The sun had not gone down but ice winds were blowing from the glacier. I slapped my hands on my biceps. "You fool, old fool, ugly man, I am a warrior."

"It certainly begins to look that way," Darkbloom said with a sigh. "Have I wasted my time with you, boy? I should take myself off and sleep in a hole in the ground."

The sun was cold and terribly bright across the peaks, putting long shadows on the ground and making my eyes blur.

"How can a man be an animal?" I said stubbornly, staring back at him and blinking. "It is a contradiction."

That made the shaman laugh. "Well, at least my instructions in logic have not failed to leave an impression." He cuffed me on the shoulder. "I think perhaps you are a dumb, clumsy bear cub, Xaraf." He got to his feet and went away into his squalid hut, leaving me to bite my lip and wonder how he had managed once again to insult and badger me and leave me feeling hungry for his company.

That wasn't the end of his witless, profound paradoxes.

"Which garment are you, little warrior?" he asked me,

5

much later, after he had shown me the bitter truth of the Open Hand.

"Garment?" I was speechless with indignation. A man is not his garb. A man is his station in the tribe.

"What food, Xaraf? Which drink, which tree, which weapon, which dream?" Nodding half-asleep by his rancid fire, he asked *me* these questions, a warrior he had disabled with his beautiful guile.

Which dream was I?

It was unfair of him, and unnecessary, to ask which dream I was. Most of the dreams in my head he had placed there himself, like the unhatched eggs of some bird, marooned in a lonely nest. He left it up to me to warm them into life.

A bird was not, though, the animal I chose to be when he tried his quiz on me again. I was something stronger and faster and leaner and hungrier and more cunning than any bird.

(The weapon, of course, was a battlesword, but I told him it was the Open Hand. He looked hard at me, reproachfully, no fool.)

Nor was this the dream, though it was one of his:

In a place brilliant and dazing as the secret interior of a jewel, light flares up from torches wrought in copper-green with verdigris.

At the polished room's focus, cupped in the gaping jaws of a black stone skull, cushioned by gold and emerald pillows on a pallet sprung by ivory fillets, a man like a toad squats in the pouches of his own pallid flesh.

A pair of horrendous warriors glare forth at me from the deep pits of the skull's eyes. Their skin is dull green, inhuman, scaled as a reptile's. From their slit mouths ferocious tusks jut, gleaming with spittle. I regard them with dread, and at last oblige myself to return my gaze to the terrible creature they guard.

He is motionless. Against his bulging, crinkled flab is pressed a lovely woman whose features seem demented with disgust. Heavy with gems, his right hand grips her pale, uncovered thigh.

The worst of it, of course, is that I know her. She is the companion of my dreams.

The flames of the torches swoop and flutter in some impalpable wind. Nothing else moves. Trapped in the dream, every muscle of my paralyzed body straining to leap forward, I can only watch my lost love with a despair physical as an amputation.

When I first dreamed the beautiful child, the gold and bronze fire of her hair, her eyes green as the sky's first momentary ignition before dawn and her wonderfully smooth flesh like a warmer, paler gold, I was hardly more than an infant, perhaps two or three years old.

Her image swam upward again and again from the muzzy pools of my sleep in all the years that followed. She was perfectly real, even if I did not know her name.

It seemed to me that we spoke, at first without understanding, inventing speech as we went; later with chattering fluency in a language I had never heard.

When I was six, we built forts and wells together from the clay and sand of our dreamscape. At eight, I climbed unknown trees to chase her into their frondy boughs, and her knees were as scabbed as my own. There was no ice in our secret world. I told no one about her, not even Darkbloom.

In those years when boys go together like raucous apes, in bands, despising girls and all they stand for, I kept my faith and rambled with her through long shivery winter nights, until at last even that failing faith was stolen by new urgencies in my tough stringy body. The swaggering of adolescence brought me scorn for dreams and soft things, along with mucky bubblings and oily pittings in my swarthy skin.

So I drove her out of my sleep with the advent of those first dark hairs at my chin and crotch, the ripening of my manhood.

I kicked her out and invited in the berry-breasted girlets of the clans and the timid bruised creatures from the towns whom I learned to coax or wrestle into the young men's hut.

My brothers wasted their energies in boisterous taunts and rivalries: fights with those sharp bone knives that pared and pierced flesh and could lose you an eye if you weren't quick; breakneck races along the grass-flattened tracks beside the winter valley rivers. . . . I relished these contests no less than my kindred did—but within reason. And reason told me there was more juice to be drawn from life than the sweaty and crack-voiced jostlings of bucks' games.

So for a time she was lost to me, driven from my dreams, that lovely child who kept match with my growing until she and I were at the lip of adulthood. With her going I was diminished, coarsened, and left rudderless (though that metaphor would not have occurred to me in our mountain homeland) until my mentor Darkbloom fetched her back to me, in sleep, in that slipping moment of awakening, and in truth.

From the outset, so I gathered in late childhood, my father had deemed me a bastard, no true seed of his warrior lineage.

Probably he'd have had me put down at birth (or done it with his own blade, more likely, or snapped my neck with his large-knuckled hands) if it hadn't been for the noisy *ooh*'s and *ahh*'s from all his clucking wives as they peered into my swaddling cloths.

They, at least, found no difficulty in spying out, in my dark, squashed, and bawling face, those grubs of nose, mouth, and jaw which were destined at adolescence to burst forth into a quite comical parody of his own hawkish features.

It might be supposed that my father's irritable qualms were perfectly understandable. Cuckoldry is not unknown when a man has as many wives as my father. Still, his suspicions about my legitimacy were odd, since the man he seemed to suspect most adamantly was a scrawny outland priest whom Father had gelded with his own hunting knife the day the fellow arrived at camp.

My mother could hardly warrant the truth of the matter convincingly (if you allow the absurd: that a docked shaman might somehow recover his maimed manly function), for she spent nearly every spare moment in Darkbloom's grubby humpy at the outskirts of camp.

There, under the chilly pressing sky of winter, she lay in trance, drugged into grinning hallucination on his herbs.

The superstitious (and that was all of them, of course) kept their distance, dreading sorcery. They construed their own cowardice as sensible caution. Still, more than once some flush-cheeked nagger must have gone scuttling to the fire with news that the outland shaman lay stretched that very moment full-length upon my mother's naked, unconscious body.

Only in the most attenuated, garbled form could this word have reached my father, or Darkbloom certainly would have forfeited life as well as balls.

Yet the reports were true enough, as I learned when I was far advanced in Darkbloom's tutelage.

The shaman had indeed played his part in my mother's condition. It was scarcely the part any jealous, ignorant husband of that squalid tribe might have envisaged.

In my mother's womb, I clung like an aquatic lizard while his magic searched my unformed organs.

It beat through my mother's swelling belly like drumbeats of light and pummeled me.

That magic muttered to my inner ear in tongues alien to my people.

It painted images within my skull.

Mysteriously, it strengthened my growing.

In simple truth, the magic of Darkbloom made me the god-child of a . . .

Of course I hesitate. Well, how better to express it?

. . . of a god.

Despite my father's relish for butchery, I disgraced myself, as I say, by embracing an outland creed. At its core was a fervent faith in the Forceless Way, the Open Hand. To my father's shocked and disbelieving shame, I had sworn an oath never to take a human life.

When in turn I broke that vow it was for no better cause than to please him, the father of my body. Some confused and lamentable sense insisted that after all I had betrayed the central truth of my kin and myself. Yet, in the event, hacking a man's sneering head from its neck sickened and excited me nearly to the point of delirium.

* * *

It is a vile day to recall . . .

. . . the slap of leather on hide, my own bitter yells and
taunts, thunder of baluchitherium hooves (those glorious giant
Miocene animals, genetic restructs from the Black Time, that
I shall never again ride), the dry haze of dust in eyes and
throat—

The air pressed down. I felt it through the thick saliva in
my throat, the blood raging in my muffled ears. All the eager
world leaned on my shoulders, like a pantheon of godlets
holding their breath.

Above the distant mountains, the whole great valley, vast
banks of snow cloud towered. Above and through it all—clang
and clash of our poor metal blades, stones flung from hooves
spitting sparks, throats opened in rage and pain, blood spurting, my warriors pressing hard on the wheeling Rokhmun
thieves—those ponderous heavens tipped into the valley's bowl
an offering of gentle flakes of white.

What *I* most wanted, in the midst of this wonderful carnage,
was simply a share of the righteous conviction my men took
as much for granted as the air they breathed, while their blades
ripped into flesh, as their companions and foes lurched and
tumbled from their mounts, eyes staring, mouths afroth.

In that whirling melee I hung back, paralyzed for all my
yelling, my untainted sword in its scabbard banging at my
back.

Right and duty. Courage and manliness. Truth. And the
noisy snow-thickened pushing and striking and the Rokhmi
dying two or three to every buck of mine. Yet my own fell
too, fell in blood and filth.

A moment earlier the dust had gritted my nostrils. Now it
churned to slippery mud as our enormous mounts lashed the
snow. A mud-fouled animal broke through, pressed to my
right hand. I heard the thieves' battle cry bray in my ear, and
spittle or snowflakes struck my face.

The icy wind came into me, then.

My blade was in my hand, freed, roaring.

I knew well enough how to use it. It was not my competence that was at issue.

Back jerked the jeering Rokhm. Our mounts were huge, slow. He slewed his beast about. My blade went into the animal's neck.

Three times the height of a man, the baluchitherium rose in panic and pain. It bellowed, lashing without aim. It stumbled. The bandit went howling into mud among trampling limbs huge as boles.

In all that blurry white, blood streamed along my virgin blade.

I tasted my own sputum like blood. The pressure in my head was like the thick whirring of a blow to the base of the nose, when there's the tang of metal at the back of the tongue and a kind of stupidity enters the brain.

I was drifting away from it all. But the anger and confusion roared in my body, drove my heels into my beast's sides.

The snow rushed, an obscuring blanket.

With no warning it was instantly evident that all the Rokhm were accounted for—all but the leader. Four of my warriors were missing: dead or mutilated. I stared around me, wrenching from side to side. The intruder realized how matters stood in that same moment and wheeled with hysterical speed, and was gone into the white fury.

Yes, four were lost and the rest battered and exhausted. I was the only one still with the strength for pursuit. My reserves had been husbanded at a cost I measured now in an access of shame.

"Go back," I cried to them. My voice was lost in the rising wind. I tugged ferociously at my mount's reins, put my mouth next to Yharugh's ear. Flakes were melting in his filthy beard. He was afraid of me, but I did not like the sidelong look he gave me. "Take our victory to camp," I said, slapping his armored shoulder. "Tell Golan that I shall fetch him a trophy."

Yharugh said nothing. Not one of them spoke. I returned my bloody sword to its scabbard.

I spun away then from those soaked, tired warriors. It was cold and wet and the light was almost gone, but I hardly noticed.

Vengefully I rode after the man I desired, suddenly, with all my heart, to kill.

I remember perfectly, to this day, the jolt of the blow going into my arm, into my clumsily braced body, all the virtue and grace of balance, of physical poise which Darkbloom had labored to instill in me, lost in that foul instant, and the blood gouting in its bright, diminishing pulse.

The flurry of churned snow, its white slushed with mud and red.

I leaped from my high saddle, whooping, anything to keep my sanity, and scooped up the thing which had been the cage for a mind and was now a filthy mockery.

I grasped its greasy hair and swung it aloft. It weighed so little that it carried my arm up and over my shoulder, and emotions I did not wish to acknowledge roared in me. I grinned, laughed out loud. I shrieked with sick joy, brandishing my trophy though no one else was there to witness my triumph.

I looped the braided hair of it into my belt and spurred my monstrous lumbering baluchitherium toward my father's snow-shrouded tent.

And became lost.

And fell into endless time.

I realize that what I am saying is difficult to understand, let alone give credence. Never fear. I shall explain this mad detour, in its turn.

Where I am now, people frown on murder. It makes me feel as if I'm wandering in a dream.

They don't approve of killing other people for revenge, profit, or whim. They settle their scores by the methods I once imagined my old teacher had invented.

I never for a moment really believed those stories. Darkbloom told them to me when I was restless, chafing at my exercises. He gazed into his own emptiness and told me the stories he saw there. His brooding, wistful fantasies of a different world.

How was I to know his ridiculous tales were true?

Can they really live without honor and mayhem? I used to provoke poor Darkbloom with my scorn. Now I see he was correct, but I still don't pretend to understand it.

They know rage and lust, like the men and women (and the mocking children, for that matter) of my own tribe, of my tribe's enemies. How do they manage without killing?

They contain themselves.

Believe it or not, that's the answer.

They hold their tongues. They back down. Conciliate. Smile. Offer gifts to those they despise. Somehow they deal with their most powerful impulses without losing themselves in a tempest of screaming, chanting, leaping, hacking ruin.

Often they seem merely pallid to me.

At other times, when I watch their cool restraint, I am awed by their courage.

Surely it takes bravery to trust individuals you have never met. These people don't give it a second thought, as far as I can tell.

They place themselves in the hands of those whose names are a mystery to them.

Outside your own tent, who is reliable? How can you gauge the intentions of a man whose ways might well be as alien as the way of the reptile to the cat?

Or as sinister and dangerous as your own reflections in a lying pool.

A pool, or a mirror, shows you your own face, but reverses it. That is something Darkbloom showed me when I was very small. (The pool, I mean. We had no artifact as sophisticated as a mirror, there in the tribe.) To this day, I treasure that frightening, still knowledge.

There are criminals here, as everywhere. Are they slow to kill? It seems so. I don't know what stays their hand. Is it merely the fear of consequences, if they are apprehended? Even dogs, even yapping curs, are richer in spirit than that.

Still, it must be admitted. The criminals are reluctant to murder their opponents.

And for the rest, those governed by custom and law—yes, certain exceptions are allowed.

The truly wicked are put down by the State, formally executed, though it's rare.

Limited military actions are permitted, against a declared enemy.

So is self-defense on the part of the civil police.

There are lists written down in books. That is how they are. They like to refer to the records before they do anything irreversible.

So the spontaneity is taken out of killing. There's no zest in the act. The deliberate infliction of death always provokes a lot of heart-searching and ethical debate.

Amazing. I feel as though I've come into the company of a nation of gentle lunatics.

Not that such tender-mindedness is in itself strange to me. As I say, Darkbloom had long since inserted such odd notions into my mind. I just never expected to see them put into practice on a larger scale.

What I find in this place is my own guilty eccentricity writ large. The man or god who trained and guided me in the brawling tents and huts of my people held similar beliefs in the sanctity of life. If anything, Darkbloom was even more obsessed about it than these people.

Maybe that was just in contrast to what he saw all around him. It must have driven him to distraction.

Now I see his philosophy acted out on every hand—empty hands, yes, weapon-free. How strange it is to recall the sick fascination and unbelieving shock I felt when first he alleged the wickedness of murder, the sinfulness of rapine, the injustice of my father's tribe's random bloody raids on the property and persons of our vile neighbors.

Once I had a dream with which I taxed Darkbloom, for it filled me with a curious disquiet.

"Can the images of sleep truly be read?"

"As your village shamans read the entrails of chickens and new lambs? Hardly."

"No. As written runes are interpreted by those who can figure them."

He ruffled up my hair, though I shrugged off his hand. "Tell me your dream, little Xaraf, and let us see what we can do with it."

"I was coming down from a great height. It was at night, and firebugs flew about my face. I climbed down a strangely constructed palisade, like something the filthy townsfolk might use to keep our goats out of their crops, and the fences were made of wattling in small squares tied together into large panels. It was not meant for climbing, and I had trouble finding purchase for my feet, though I skimmed lightly as a bird, my shirt billowing up about my chest. In my hand I held a big branch, though it was more like a small tree covered in red blossoms, branching and spread out. They were bright as cherry blossoms. As I descended I had one of these trees, then two, then one again. I came to the end of the palisades and already the lower blossoms were faded. A tall young man was standing in the garden, a stranger, I think, though it seemed that I knew him. He used a rake to comb out thick tufts of hair from the branches of a tree similar to mine. I approached him and asked if trees of that kind could be transplanted into my garden. He hugged me in a brotherly fashion, but I struggled against him. He insisted that this was allowed, and promised to show me how the planting was done in another garden. It was his claim that though he was to receive some advantage, I would not suffer by it."

I fell silent then, troubled.

"Did he show you the planting?" Darkbloom asked finally.

"I do not remember."

He glanced at me. "Did a wetness wake you from this dream?"

I blinked, then saw what he meant. It made me laugh.

"No, old fool, it was not such a dream. He was not a girl."

"Did not you and your cousin Yharugh once play such games?"

Now I became angry.

"You make everything filthy. It was not such a dream. I

wished to kill him.'' Then I blinked again, for I had forgotten that.

"Ah." Nodding wisely, Darkbloom added another thin stick to his poor fire. "Who was this young man, then?"

In a very low voice I said, "I think he was my enemy, whom I wish with all my heart to kill."

Darkbloom rose, drew his tattered cloak about him, stalked away shaking with rage into the night, and stared up, like a deeper shadow under the shadow of his hut, at the bright stars. When his voice came to me from that blackness it was remote, and crueler than I had ever heard it.

"Yes, Xaraf. That was your enemy. That was your brother. That was the stranger you will wish with all your heart to kill. Instead you must master him by another means. He will throw down his hot blossoms from heaven and scorch your garden, and you must not strike in return." Suddenly, with not the slightest sound to betray his movement, he stood at my shoulder and his rotten-tooth stinking breath was chokingly in my nostrils. "Do you hear me, Xaraf? You must swear again, swear and swear upon the womb of your mother and the staff of your father that you will keep to the Open Hand." His hand gripped my upper arm with a fierce, demented strength. "Swear that once more, Xaraf. Swear, I say!"

When I was thirteen or fourteen years old, I trembled with terrified delight to hear these extraordinary opinions.

I was enraptured by his moral sensitivity.

Of course I doubt I'd have listened all that long to him if he hadn't shown me, in endless, painful, and exultant lessons, how to beat the tripes out of anyone who looked sideways at me.

The paradox of rational pacificism, yes.

To my father, of course, such ideas would not have been so much anathema as unthinkable. He was unable, literally, to frame the concept of nonviolence in his great bearish tempestuous head.

My defection was incomprehensible to him. It pointed to some tragedy, perhaps even some guilt in himself—or, more likely, the infestation of a demon, an unmanly weakness from my mother's lineage. Certainly, as I have mentioned, she was strange enough in her behavior since before my birth.

Even so, at last I chose deliberately to enter into adulthood, in accordance with the cruel laws of my people, by slaying another human being.

On that same day I lost my way in time.

You could say I took a wrong turning, and tumbled a million years into the lovely and terrible evening of the world.

TWO

The severed head bounced at my knee, looped to my belt by its filthy braided hair. In the gray gloom of the storm it seemed to mock my guilt with its grin. Dark streaks and clots of blood stained my leggings, the stains frozen by rime.

I felt certain that I was about to die.

"No," I muttered, gasping for breath in the freezing wind. "I will not die. No, I will not die." To my surprise the words came louder, defiant, howling at last from my throat. Eyes slit and stinging, I tried uselessly to penetrate the gusting snow.

Turmoil. I screamed to the screaming wind, "Lords of Light and Death, give me your guidance!" No answer came; I had expected none. Somehow, though, the numbing cold and the ritual of invocation kindled a warm fire of imagination. I built around me a picture of the safe, despised city of childhood, the defended trading city Berb-Kisheh. On market days I had scampered there amid raucous throngs, through the bazaars and granaries. Bright fabrics were spread in the sun; I breathed in the rich riot of tangs and tastes, kebabs turning over charcoal, lamb blackened but red and bursting with juice within, slices of onions and fat chunks of vegetables we never saw from season to season except on our visits to the city, and all the cries of peddlers and merchants shouting to outdo each other, mats and tables piled to overflowing in the warm protective bustle of the enclosing stone walls. . . .

Sleet whipped me. Cupped by the hard flaps of my hide helmet, my ears caught the dream-boom and hiss of an ocean I'd never known. The fury of the storm tore at my soaked, clinging clothing. Its clamminess disgusted and infuriated me.

Snow, blinding as sand, howled about the unprotected legs of my baluchitherium, picked like the beaks of carrion birds at his eyes. It hammered my own face, layered my cheeks with a crust of ice.

I hugged the saddle with stiff thighs, jolting as we blundered without vision. My fists clung to the reins but felt nothing.

In all this gray desolation only the jarring motion of my mount broke through the confusion which knotted my instincts, my senses.

It was not impossible that I had been blundering, in these hours of the storm, through great stupid circles.

"Keep moving, don't stop," I heard my mouth saying. My face pressed the baluchitherium's huge neck, and my eyes were closed tight again. "You fool, you thrice-damned fool." Wind ripped the words away. It was true, though. Only a fool would lose himself like this, not three hours' ride from home. I shivered in a racking tremor. My father's scorn. And the others, the scarred elders. I heard their derision. It made my belly cramp.

In the sightless pall, my numb hand fell from the rein and struck something icy, hairy, knobby. His head, my murdered foe. I let my fingers rest on his eyeballs, and laughed at the horror of it. Let them scoff. My party had routed the enemy. That was enough. There would be no scorn from the elders when I flung my trophy at their feet.

His eyeballs were frozen, like small round stones of ice.

I snatched my hand back, pounded it on the animal's neck. He cried out, tossed his head. He was ready to lie down in the snow and sleep. I brushed clumsily at my own eyes. The darkness was night falling. How pitiful. How Darkbloom would relish the pointless loss of grace in this moment. So nothing now remained but the ride into the frozen dark until my animal collapsed under me. For my dirge I would hear the ignorant shrieking of the wind.

I nursed the fake warmths of memory: of gorges wild with life, the roaming bears and nests of snow geese; of Berb-Kishen, the Green City in whose shadow I'd been born, and its smug townsfolk of whom my own nomadic people were so stubbornly contemptuous. The sweet scents of the Rezot-Azer valley seemed to brush my face, though I knew that my face was frozen, the spring breath of tulip and rose blowing in profusion, the meadows of clover far from the desert, where we love to rest. . . .

I slipped in my saddle, was falling forward, struck something hard with my forehead.

The baluchitherium floundered in a drift of snow, churning enormously to his own disadvantage. A crust of ice broke beneath one hoof as the other foreleg slid, twisting like a tree trunk broken by wind, across a shattered boulder. His head swung from side to side, and his mouth foamed as he shrilled.

All my reflexes were gone. I slid face downward. Some convulsion of the animal's huge shoulders threw me clear. I sank into deep-piled whiteness. A pastern snapped. The beast screamed, flailed.

"Damn you to hell, you hell-damned Gods!" I shrieked, hearing my death. Legs churning slush, I dragged myself into a standing position, holding the broken edge of the shelf of rock which had been our undoing. The sword came easily enough from its scabbard across my back. The injured animal, already passive in the deep embrace of the snow, rolled brown glazed eyes at me.

I slashed his throat.

He kicked and died, and his cooling blood gouted to seep dark into the dark ground. It was the fullest irony of my submission to my father's scorn. This dismal skirling chaos seemed to me the final price, now paid, for the renunciation of my vow. Sighing, I turned away from the dead beast into the blast of the wind.

Light glinted.

I stared in astonished hope.

Through the slapping, swirling flakes, light.

Now I heard its song as well, through the howling wind.

"No bright, there!" I yelled, fallen back to the argot of the campfire thieves. I checked my impulse to stagger forward. "Demons!" I cried. "Soul-eaters!" All of Darkbloom's skepticism was gone. I was a barbarian facing something worse than death by freezing; none of the shaman's instilled sophistication remained in that instant.

For surely only spirits could carry flame in such a storm.

There were no demons. There was no light. This was merely a fancy, a trick of wind and snow and desperation. I could run into the voices of the storm forever, and they would retreat like shadows of light before me.

Not forever.

That burst of sardonic clarity woke me up, I suppose. There was a light, now gleaming, now blotted out by some flurry of snow. With a sheer effort of will I dismissed my terror. At least the light provided a line of direction. I would go to it.

I leaned over my dead animal and wrenched the Rokhm's head from the saddle. Bitterly, I twined the bloody hair around my ornamental belt. I shed the weight of bow and quiver, kept only my new-blooded sword. A growl came from deep within my heart, an invocation to the Death Lords, nearer to blasphemy than prayer.

My feet sank into mush. I closed my raw eyes. Night became a hail of sparks.

Yet the light beckoned when I forced my eyes open, and its high crazy song drew me on.

What could this brilliance be, if not witchcraft? Terror circled and circled like a vulture in the vault of a desert sky.

My feet sank, skidded.

With a jolting shock the earth broke open under me. My arms wheeled, as I toppled into light.

Hurled back by the snow, it cut into eyes and soul like a sun fallen into the heart of the cup of night.

Voices sang from a dream of lunatics, into ears deafened by the storm.

I fell into that cold brilliance, arms and legs lashing uselessly, scabbard slipping under my arm so that blade slapped belly, my throat raw in a hoarse, hopeless yell, and all the while the bouncing Rokhm head grinned insane dead vengeance from my blood-black belt.

I cannot say when I lost consciousness. In that fall toward the cold sun I had no means but my delirium to measure distance or the passage of time. How long is a fever? Once I watched my brother Jopher tumble from the high edge of a cliff where

we goaded a rhino to its doom. I watched with dread and
excitement as Jopher's flailing limbs caught at jutting bushes,
twigs, watched as he struck ledges which slowed his plunge
but failed to halt it. He hit the ground hard, moments later,
and walked afterward always with a gimp leg and an awry
grin.

It was not like that, my fall. Searing light and nausea. There
was not even the rushing of wind. My mouth filled with sour
bile and overflowed. I suppose the light swallowed me complete.

When I woke the light was gone.

I lay crumpled in my own rank liquids in a dim and humming place of black metal. I pushed myself up on my hands;
they were clammy, but sensation had returned. The black metal
was hard and warm, vibrating slightly.

Swaying with fatigue I got to my feet. I was still only half-
aware that this was not some foolish nightmare dreamed by a
man freezing to his death. My discomfort soon corrected that
dazed surmise. Water trickled down my back, squelched in
my boots as rime and snow melted in the warm, oil-tainted
air. Grimacing with distaste, I wiped vomit and mud from my
face and peered cautiously about me.

The seasoned warriors who taught me and my brothers the
use of beasts and weapons spoke sometimes, guardedly and
with all due care for their manliness, of the terrors of combat.
Only a fool relishes the prospect of a blade through the belly,
a jaw hacked away, a limb's meat slashed open to the bone.
The few imaginative youths among us suffered badly in our
dreams, for a while after that.

But here is my point: It is the very clash and thunder of
battle, our teachers assured us, which holds the warrior's bowels in place, insulates him against terror.

Just so, the shock of waking into this dark cavern touched
my brain to a kind of detached curiosity. My breathing eased.
Slowly my eyes grew accustomed to the dim violet illumination. I was standing in the centre of one inner face of a vast
cube of the ebon metal.

The faint light had no obvious source. It seemed to pervade

the place like some subtle liquid. I turned carefully, surveying each wall in turn, found neither entrance nor window. I walked across the dark surface to examine the nearest wall in detail.

Metallic echoes boomed as the hard soles of my boots struck the floor. I stilled, poised on the ball of one foot, thinking to detect in that echo a sound not of my own making.

Silence only, behind that constant hum.

I cleared my throat. The grating sound rebounded in a muffled growl. No other voice. Sweat or melted rime ran down into my eyes. I went on toward the looming blackness of the wall.

My heart quickened when I reached it. Unlike the bland extent of the floor, this wall bore the direct marks of some skillful artificer. Finally, I thought I knew where I was. It ought to have been obvious.

Before they destroyed themselves in the Holocaust, the mad men of the Black Time had built places all of metals, glass, strange stuff without names. Some they had raised into the sky, and these had melted in the fires of the Holocaust. We would not approach those poisoned craters. Other places of their construction had been sunk deep into the face of the world; vast tunnels, shafts, pipelines now corroded and dangerous beyond use. I had fallen, it now seemed evident, into one of those forbidden places.

This realization reawakened my dread. I shivered, clutching my arms about me. Demons ruled those places, that much was clear. Even Darkbloom had never denied so fundamental a truth. And those demons had lured me in here, with their wicked piping, their cold light. I shuddered and ground my teeth together, and waited for I knew not what.

I heard some tiny sound. Reflex brought my blade shivering to my hand. I spun about, gazed intently into the chamber's gloom. Nothing stirred. Now that I had grown accustomed to it, even the droning hum was fading from my awareness. Heart pounding, I turned back to the great metal tapestry.

So far as I could determine in the frustrating twilight, the entire surface of the wall was scored by alien glyphs. Their swirls and curlicues quivered with illusory motion, sent my

eye skating. The esoteric nature of the markings eluded interpretation. They filled me with foreboding.

I paced slowly to the nearest corner, walked on. Engravings
covered each wall of the cube. They hid no opening. At in-
tervals, I probed with my fingers into the reliefs and hiero-
glyphs. I let my fingertips trace the unknown patterns in the
darkness, and felt a nape-stirring sense of familiarity. I brought
out my sword and sought leverage in minute projections and
failed to gain it, thwarted by the astonishing temper and tough-
ness of the black metal.

In a burst of rage, I battered at the metal. The chamber
clanged with echoes, deafening me. When my fury was spent,
I found to my chagrin that my blunted blade's edge had failed
utterly even to mark the wall.

By the end of my futile circuit of the chamber, I knew that
I was close to collapse from hunger, fatigue, unrelenting stress.

I sagged against the rampart at my starting place. Nothing
made sense, least of all my presence here. The men of the
Black Time were dead and gone, ash a thousand years ago.
They had not lured me here. That was superstition and folly.
Despite the warmth of the place, I found myself shivering. My garments were damp and fouled and stuck to the
gooseflesh of my body. Behind hot lids my eyes itched with
exhaustion. Without warning my legs gave way. In semistu-
por, I slid to the floor.

When that brief instant of unconsciousness had passed, I
had abandoned the last vestiges of caution. Even in a hall of
the damned, a man at the point of death has little enough to
risk. I forced myself to my feet, and cried out as loudly as I
could.

"Speak to me, demons!"

It was laughable. My challenge came out as a croak. I lifted
my head, despite that, and yelled into the emptiness of the
black vault.

"Answer me, you vile old spirits. Why have you brought
me to this forbidden place?"

I got no reply. Yet some instinct insisted that creatures heard
me, sniggering.

With fingers so numb they could barely clutch the heavy

hilt, I flung up my sword once more and sent the blade crashing flat against the wall.

Through the rolling echoes, from no fixed position within the huge chamber, someone offered a delicate cough.

"Flowers?" a voice called, in a language I had never heard yet comprehended instantly. "Is it not rather early for your return?"

THREE

I whirled. In the cage of my chest I could feel my swollen heart hammering.

Dusklit though it was, I could see well enough that I stood alone within the room. The words had been uttered out of the very air.

Even as I filled my bruised lungs for a final challenge, the voice sharpened.

"Well, well, not Flowers of Evening after all. What *have* we here? Extraordinary."

"Light and Death," I cried in my own tongue, baffled and scared and not taking time to think it out, "show yourself, demon." I braced myself hard against the engraved wall and glared wildly in every direction. My breath rasped. "Where are you, cowardly spirit?"

"Creid! Balmorq! Come hither, pay heed to this entrancing phenomenon."

"My good Jesrilban." A second voice spoke chidingly, its deep sourceless timber resonant in the chamber. "Do contain your zeal. After the rigors of that last energy transfer, Eis and I are quite spent."

The language was the language of dream. Distantly I understood that, if nothing else. All the joyful, careless dreams of childhood. And that dream in which my nameless companion suffered under the hand of her dreadful captor.

With vicious mimicry, the first voice said, "My good Ah! I am hardly in the habit of crying wolf."

He did not say that, of course, but it was the significance of his metaphor, and I knew his meaning, as light shafts

26

through clear glass, even though I grasped nothing of the image he expressed it in.

(All this, naturally, is something I have pondered upon at my leisure, with the fright and confusion of that moment far behind me. At the time I was a beast in a toothed trap, struggling for sanity and survival merely.)

"Now, now," broke in a third voice, wheezy and sententious, "let there be no bickering, my dears. Doubtless the Power Jesrilban Julix has some matter of grave import to bring before us." I was abruptly bathed in harsh blue light. I could see it on my wet clothes, reflected from my skin like moonlight from the flesh of a corpse, sparkling from the sword in my hand. "Oh, bless my soul, Jesrilban."

I bared my chattering teeth and hunched my bunched shoulders into the warm unyielding metal at my back, cast about uselessly for my disembodied antagonists. Darkbloom's skepticism was quite fled. Thick tongue moved over dry lips. I waited for murder to flame from the air.

The first voice purred. "Just so, Eis. A trifling wonder, is it not?"

"And how in the Failing Sun did it get inside *there*? Or is it an 'it'? Jesrilban, you don't believe it might be human, do you?"

"It carries artifacts, if I'm not mistaken," said the third.

"Of course he's human, my dear Balmorq," the first voice cut in. "He called out earlier and caught my notice. Here, I have it in my crystal."

Then I heard perhaps the strangest, simplest, and most truly disheartening words I could ever have imagined hearing—my own, trapped from those moments in the immediate past when I had let them slip free of my lips; my cries, my taunts, my terrified howls. I knew I was listening to the genuine echo of my own words because I recalled speaking them, shouting them. Yet the voice was not the voice I hear in my own head when I speak. It was lighter, somehow, though deep and graveled enough to alarm a band of fleeing Rokhm thieves.

"Remarkably primitive semantically, but recognizably intelligent."

"I concur entirely," added the querulous tones of the third

demon. "The somatic and psychic lineaments of this unhappy oddity are essentially identical with those of certain regressed human communities beyond the Keep."

"Those lotus-eaters? Implausible, surely, that one of their number should have penetrated our defensive wards."

"Leave paradox aside," rapped the first voice. "Attend to the self-evident, despite its offensiveness. I should have thought the explanation to be obvious."

"Julix, we are tired. The clarity of our insights is doubtless marred by the not negligible effort of guiding a good portion of the sun's energy output across a time differential of some six thousand million years. Spare us your adolescent—" The voice broke off. "No, it's not possible!"

"Possible or not, the brute stands at this moment in the very nexus of our Primary Transference Matrix."

In consternation, the old voice cried: "Ah! Jesrilban! Surely you do not imply that this uncouth lout has been drawn here along a temporal wormline from a million years in the past! The scholium denies the very possibility. Here, consider the equation under—"

The invisible demons bickered, and I found no meaning in any of it. Blackness mottled the edges of vision. The weight of my sword pulled my arm down against my thigh.

Condescending and angry by turns, sardonic and tentative, the voices blathered their nonsense. I blinked open my stinging eyes, found myself crouched on my haunches, blade lying on the ebon surface where it had slipped out of my fingers.

"Demons," I croaked. There was a moment of silence. "Strike or be done," I told them. "Slay me, eat my soul—or let me sleep."

The silence lengthened. Incredulously, from the air, the deep voice said, "By the Failing Orb, my Powers! The brute can hear us."

Even the spirit named Jesrilban Julix faltered in urbanity.

"Remarkable," it ventured finally. "A seventh-order mentality, at least, for all the rudeness of the fellow's aspect. The affair takes on a different hue."

"Look you then, my peers." Briskness firmed the uneasy note of the third voice. "It seems we fail in our hospitality and grace. The stranger languishes for want of food and rest. Let us see to this matter first; colloquy may wait.''

One last curious vision presented itself to me before I sank into billowing sleep. A dancing net of tiny glowing stars flashed into sight all about me. I felt my body lifted up from the warm black metal, as an autumn leaf wafts in a breeze. The soft web of bright specks bore me to the very centre of the vast chamber. I was held there for an instant, and the sparks shone more brightly still.

I woke to the sweetness of a harp and the pinprick tinkle of windblown chimes. A flush of rose-gold bloomed on the silken walls of my tent. My waking was as languid as my sleeping had been innocent, refreshing as a child's. I stretched my limbs, fancying myself a great cat; like a cat I watched the morning world through half-closed lashes, and listened in charmed delight to the harmony which stroked the perfumed air.

Then I sat up with a jolt and a cry, like a man with his throat cut.

I hurled the covers off me and came to my feet. My toes went deep into thick carpet white and soft as snow but warm as living fur. Cool air brushed my naked body.

I was alone. My panic began to subside.

Three paces away, my blade rested on a polished trestle of beautifully grained timber. None of my own filthy garments was in evidence. I wanted very badly to get dressed. I crossed to my sword, found an open booth containing a variety of richly colored and decorated vestments.

Before I tried them on, however, I prowled the exquisite room with my blade in my hand. I found no explicit sign of the demons who had borne me here.

One fact I swiftly established. Unlike the disembodied voices in the black chamber, the sweet music possessed a definite source: a conch of chased silver. I peered into its mouth, put my ear to it. Certainly it was a magical contrivance, for its strings sang of their own accord and the tiny brass bells hidden within it chimed without breath of breeze.

You can see how sophisticated I was.

Its melody was pretty, but I turned away from the arcane thing with a kind of horror.

Dawn light flooded the room through a pair of sealed opalescent windows. Something about that coral light began to chafe at my attention.

I rubbed my rasping chin.

What could keep the sun from its rising? I considered shattering one of the embrasures with my blade. On reflection, there seemed no gain likely in such delinquency. The Black Time wizards had shown me, after all, no overt animosity.

Indeed, their provision of this sleeping chamber gave evidence of goodwill. Troubled and thoughtful, I turned from the enigmatic sky-glow and looked for a door.

None was to be found. Craning back my neck, I searched the ceiling. Lustily ornamented with a riot of mythic and human figures wrought in a delicate pale blue line, it too seemed all of a piece.

Puzzled, I went back to the silk-rumpled couch and brooded on my plight.

How long had I slept? I felt strong and wide-awake, after a restorative sleep which must have been the equal of a full winter's night from sundown to sunrise. What's more, my monstrous hunger had abated. I was not even thirsty.

So. My captors had granted me magical nourishment and splendid quarters. They had left me in peace to recover from my debility. Had they meant me ill, surely they'd have vented their hostility while I lay at my lowest ebb.

I found myself scowling. Each question unanswered hinted at a hundred more.

Darkbloom had insisted, always, that thought must precede deed, or a fool would carry out that deed. Yet now action, not contemplation, was required.

I rose, crossed the deep-piled fleece, drew out a handful of the garments, a Kishehm merchant's fantasy, which hung invitingly within the alcove.

The lustrous fabrics delighted my eye. They hung from some undetectable support but came away easily enough when I tugged at them. I stared with a child's enthusiasm. They were wondrously light and finely woven, soft and delicate to the touch. My father would have spurned them as woman's stuff, yet this was clearly meant as garb for a man, and a man of action, at that.

I let the lovely things fall at my feet as I viewed and discarded various items. At length I found apparel to satisfy me: a silken, snow-bright blouse with sleeves flaring at the wrists; breeches of some multicolored velvet which was to the pantaloons of Kishehm princelings as the peacock's raiment is to the owl's; soft warm undergarments; stockings of woolen weave; doeskin buskins. I'd have clapped a broad-brimmed hat on my wild hair if I had found one.

Nor was there cuirass, or scabbard for my blade. I contented myself with a high-collared suede jerkin and a wide striped leather belt, through which I thrust my sword.

I buckled the belt tight and wondered where my own befouled, bloody belt had gone, and with it the gory head of my enemy.

A shadow touched the pale wall. An instant earlier, nothing had been there to throw a shadow. My nostrils twitched. The heavy musk of a wild animal cut the room's floral perfume.

My new belt was half-slashed from my waist, so swiftly did my blade leap to my hand as I whirled, crouching.

In the centre of the room, watching me with gold feral eyes, a monster stood.

Shock poised me on the balls of my feet for a heart-cramped moment.

The beast widened its wicked beak. Golden wings flared from its back, lifting, each feather graved with a jeweler's perfection. It eased back on powerful limbs; sinews stretched, muscles flowed. . . .

I was hurling myself across the room, sword point rigid for its open throat.

The monster's wings cracked out and down like a thunderclap. Smeared lightning was the blade's flat catching and spinning light, as a forepaw struck upward, took my weapon from me. The shock of it went down my arm, hurled me to the furthest wall with a bruising impact. My sword arm, when I tried to flex my fingers, was numb to the elbow. My brain was dazed with disbelief.

I shook my head, eyes wide. The creature waited.

I feinted, threw myself to the nearest corner, rolled across the silken couch, and caught its frame left-handed.

My hip dropped. I lifted the couch, took its weight on my rising hip, and hurled it up in the way Darkbloom had shown me.

It teetered, hung in the air between us. Then it crashed, wreathed in sliding light, across the huge body of the fantastic beast.

There was no time for me to regain my sword. I followed the ponderous fall of the couch, hands thrust out in claws. I sought the gryphon's neck.

Wood splintered. The couch bounced on the carpet, shuddered. Betrayed, my leap slammed me to the floor's thick fur.

The beast had vanished.

Literally. It was no longer in the room.

I lifted my face from the white pile. The air sparkled, flickering. The gryphon stood there again, at the other side of the room.

Sweat ran into my eyes.

I tensed, glancing at the fallen sword not two steps distant. My right arm ached, but I could clench my fist. Feathers rippled green and gold on the lion's back of the creature.

At the window, through our gasps for breath, the silver conch sang its gentle harmonies.

The monster opened its mouth again, showing me its red tongue. As I leapt to grasp the sword it stared at me in astonishment, and backed away past the broken bed. I crouched and moved forward, lips tight, eyes narrowed. A growl came up from deep in me.

In the language of dream, the language used by the three disembodied Powers, I heard it say in an aggrieved tone: "Relax, boy. There's really no need to go on like this."

The gryphon was staring reproachfully at me. It backed away a little more, let itself down on its haunches. "Just put your knife away like a good chap, and we'll go and fix you some lunch, what do you say to that, eh?"

I stumbled in murderous mid-step.

My blade dropped. I threw my head back and the rigid bubble of breath pent in my chest exploded to my throat.

I realized after a second that my convulsive roar was laughter. A great gale of mirth rocked me on my heels, my heels that were shod so nicely in borrowed doeskin buskins. I clutched at my new, ruined belt and laughed like a fool until it hurt my ribs and left me weak and trembling with relief.

"A restruct," I said, in my own tongue. "A made-beast from the Black Time." I was all laughed out. "Nice pussy," I said.

The gryphon observed me with mild and curious caution, head cocked to one side like a giant bird.

"My thanks to your masters," I said, in the speech of dream. It came easily to my tongue. I wiped the last tears of laughter from my eyes, unbuckled the ruined belt. "I'm not really hungry, but a mug of ale would be welcome." I buckled a new belt about me, sheathed my sword once more.

The gryphon yawned (or was it a smile?) and padded past the wrecked couch.

"I believe we have a cask or three in the cellar. Look, allow me to apologize for coming in without announcing myself." He looked at me sidelong. "I must have given you a nasty scare."

I regarded the couch. "I seem to have, uh, broken it."

"Don't give it another thought. Plenty more where that came from. Perfectly understandable, under the circumstances." He proffered a paw. "Look, let's get on first-name terms and I'll take you down for a snack and a draught of that ale. Then we'll see about an audience with the Powers. My name's Goldspur."

Glinting razor-honed talons were tucked up genteelly within leathery pads. I took the paw uncertainly. "I am called Xaraf, of the Firebridge Tribe."

"Splendid, lad! Well met!" The eagle head nodded heartily. "I must confess, Xaraf, your tribe is one I'm unacquainted with. Ah, yes, the world is wonderful in its width and diversity, even to one placed, as I am, so close to the seat of the All-Knowing Ones."

He made a pass with his right paw. Specks of light like tiny stars glittered about us. There was a dizzy instant of blindness.

Then the pale sleeping chamber, with its scent of blossoms, its tinkling song, its smashed bedding, was gone.

We stood in an expansive flag-floored room walled in ancient sandstone and ceramic tile. A great hand-hewn table of oak, inlaid with austere, obscure patterns of polished obsidian, stood where the broken couch would be if this were still the sleeping chamber.

I gaped.

Benches against the walls were piled with fruits and vegetables I had never seen before, pale tubers and yellow-leafed plant hearts, purple cones, beans, long green fronded things, red balls, all of it suffused with sweet tangs and harsh herbal bites in the soft inner tissues of my nose, more wonderful than anything I'd seen in all the market days of the Green City. Meats lay exposed as well, and none of the white and the bloody dark cuts crawled with insects, as you would expect; hares and fowl hung from rafters. A sideboard held crystal flagons of spirits and wines.

My hunger came back in a rush. I gazed about wildly, in amazement and delight.

"Find yourself a stool." Goldspur padded through coral sunlight shafting from a high, glazed window. "I'll whistle up a bite to eat."

"This is the most wonderful dream," I muttered, and perched myself obediently on a sturdy wooden tripod.

It was an explanation which failed to satisfy me. Could one truly know, while dreaming, that one dreamed? Darkbloom claimed to have mastery of such a discipline, I recalled: He termed it "lucid dreaming," and had it on my agenda for advanced studies. Well, it seemed a speculation of doubtful merit here.

I rubbed my bruised shoulder ruefully. No dream had any right to be this realistic.

Could this be the afterland preached by the Kishehm priests? The nomadic hereafter of my own wandering people? Perhaps the godworld of Darkbloom? A scent of braised steak reached my nose, wet my tongue with hungry saliva. No. Unless cagey

Darkbloom had been hiding the important things from me, in all my experience no doctrine ever postulated such a life-beyond-death as this.

All my experience. It makes me laugh now, thinking of that raw, astonished boy.

In my naïveté and innocence, I put speculation aside. With a shrug of my wide, bruised shoulders, I gazed happily from smoke-stained rafters to shelves bright with crockery of gold and porcelain translucent as the sky.

I heard the gryphon's voice behind me.

"Quaff this down, my boy." Goldspur seemed more at ease, as I was, now that the formalities were done.

It had not occurred to me to wonder how an animal with wings and paws could provide me with sustenance. When the world whirls and sparks with magic, what is a little extra? Still, my eyes bugged to see a foaming tankard precede him, smoothly aloft in the air, skimming at bench height.

"Spit me for a rogue if this fails to hit the spot," the gryphon cried heartily.

The tankard slipped itself neatly onto the table at my right hand, and made way for a huge dish of gravy-drenched chunks of beef and two lesser side dishes of green salad, peppers, fat yellow fruits with the pungency of olives.

I could find no words to match this display. I hefted the pewter mug and drank deep of its warm ale, wiped froth on my forearm, belched with pleasure. It amused me to see the gryphon sink on haunches to the flags like a gigantic, grotesque watchdog.

Belatedly, a variety of chased silver utensils swarmed into the kitchen and sailed across to me, nudging either side of the large plate. These curious tongs and silver spears puzzled me for a moment. I glanced at my host. Politely, he looked away. Forgoing delicacy, I plunged my fingers into the steaming repast.

"Your masters," I said, my mouth full, "enjoy a fine table."

Goldspur gave a throaty caw.

"Good Xaraf, what distant land do you come from to suggest such a thing? Surely you appreciate that the Powers are far too spiritually evolved to suffer temptations of the flesh.''

''Indeed?'' I could not conceive such a condition. ''Who, then, are the gourmets served by this splendid kitchen?''

''Why, there's nothing here but plain, simple nourishment, provender for us servants of the Powers.'' Goldspur was candid. ''The fare is pleasant enough, but hardly lavish.''

Swilling the last of the ale, I hooded my eyes. I recalled without difficulty month on dreary month of grim sparse meals as my nomad people drove our herds from alpine summer to winter pasture. Even in the despised crop-raising towns like Berb-Kisheh, where the irrigation-fattened grain surpluses overflowed for home consumption and trade, where orchards brought forth rare delicacies and we came to barter our cheese and meat for metal and the wares of visiting merchants, even in those towns such plenty as this kitchen evidenced would be deemed lavish indeed.

Yet the gryphon's tone had been sincere, even self-deprecating.

''Tell me one thing, Goldspur.'' Restlessly, I left the table and paced back and forth before the winged beast. ''Who are these Powers of whom you speak? It seems to me that I heard their voices echoing in some great black chamber, before I slept. And yet—''

''If you have heard Them speak, you are more fortunate than the great majority of your race.''

The gryphon spoke with solemnity, tinged at the edges with touchy pride. His eagle head swung to follow my pacing. Without a word or a gesture, he caused the empty plates and bowls to speed on their way through the air to a hidden scullery. Vicarious arrogance entered his voice. ''The Powers do not often deign to deal with mortals.''

I found myself grinning. ''Be that as it may, they have fetched me here and put me in your hands. Your, ah . . .'' I cleared my throat in a marked manner. ''Sorry.''

''That is quite all right, human. I need no clumsy fingers to make the brute world do my bidding.''

''No,'' I said. I picked a piece of meat from my teeth with

a sliver of wood left in a bowl on the table. "Presumably these Powers wish to treat with me. I would know more of them."

The gryphon drew up his massive frame in quiet dignity.

"The Powers are the wise, hidden, good Lords of this world. In a short time They will call you to Them, and you will commune with Them and learn of Them face-to-face, and you will tremble at Their might. You will not 'treat' with Them. Learn humility, human, while you have time for the lesson. They are masters of this Keep, gods among those of us who remain to walk this dying world."

My jocular, simple mood collapsed. The made-beast was totally serious. A fist seemed to clench my bowels and heart, hard. I felt ill with fright, the same fright I had known in the place of warm dark metal. The pleasant charm of couch and table was dispelled in a moment. All that remained, chilling my face, was the awful majesty of this demons' Hall.

I made myself speak.

"If we must go, let us go now."

"Wait." Goldspur flurried his great glossy wings, clashed talons on the flags. "I will crave audience."

Some inaudible resonance shook the air.

A gong cried deep metallic thunder.

"Prepare yourself," the gryphon growled. In the back of his eyes, catching the rose-red of the high window's suspended dawn light, a spot of crimson glowed. "The Powers will receive you."

Flashing sparks leapt up to clothe me.

"Farewell," the gryphon said, with renewed kindliness, as blackness fell on me. I heard him say to himself, reflectively: "It's a shame you won't remember any of this, my boy."

FOUR

I stood under the naked sky on a chiseled mountaintop, or so it seemed in that first awful moment.

Magenta clouds, torn to tatters of scarlet, saffron, pink, streamed before a silent wind in the purple sky.

The wind should have lifted me from my feet like a twig, tossed me into the abyss which fell from the lip of the plateau. I stayed where I was, stock-still, not daring to move.

Pinpoints of blinding light, two in the west and two at the eastern horizon, blazed bright as boiling iron. I blinked my shocked gaze away from them, and for a moment saw only the pinpoint images of blackness which clung to my eyes. Still I heard no wind. I understood then that I was protected from that high fury by a colossal crystal dome which soared above the plateau.

And I forced myself to look finally at the quadrant of the heavens between those high, fierce chariots of light.

I had not recognized what I saw, not at once. Now I did.

Midday-high, vast as a cartwheel, sullen as an ancient god flecked with black cancer, loomed the coal-red ember of the dying sun.

I knew it, at last, by the melancholy which gusted through me. From a great distance, a voice intruded on my grief.

Once more the cool voice spoke.

"Moving as this vista is, Master Xaraf, one might almost be led to believe that you had never seen the sky before."

"No." It was loneliness I felt, bitter and apt. Everything I knew had been taken from me. I waited for the choking in my breast to ease. "No, never such a doomed hell-sky as this."

I lowered my gaze from the crimson dome, turned, and looked on the Powers where They sat.

And my misery fumed over into rage. "Rot blight you, damn you, why am I here? Is this hell?" My sword was in my hand. "I have broken my vow once. Nothing restrains me now. I will slay you all."

Soothing, like an old ostler calming a frightened, skittish foal, one of them told me, "Xaraf, you have nothing to fear. Put up your sword." This was the voice half-remembered from the black place as fretful, querulous. "Come, take your seat. Let us talk together."

Trembling, sweat clammy from my pores, I stayed where I was. I stared up at the wizards mounted on their gorgeous thrones.

One was younger even than me, to look at him, a pale exquisite youth with eyes gray as winter desolation, eyes that might have seen mountains crumble and oceans drain away to salt, seasons beyond recall. Settling his priceless robes more comfortably, this youth spoke with chilling hauteur. "Welcome, Master Xaraf. I am the Power Jesrilban Julix."

One was hard and grizzled. Beneath his gemmed cloak he was broad-shouldered as a warrior. And he was old, old as Time despite his burly strength. "I am the Power Ah Balmorq."

One was white and bald as the years he bore, frail as puckered parchment, veins beneath his wrinkled ancient's visage like a tangle of blue threads. "Do sit down, lad." A gleam of rings; his hands crept together in his lap. "You may address me as the Power Eis Creid."

A sweet pungency of incense chafed my nostrils. Smoke coiled slowly from chain-hung vessels, swirled gracefully in placid mockery of the scarlet hell beyond the crystal dome, ripped by the silent winds. My voice was rough. "What do you want with me?"

"We want"—Balmorq considered for a moment—"your trust." The bluff calm face held no hint of cynicism.

"How can I trust you? You have done nothing to earn trust. I ask one final time: Why am I here?"

The beautiful face of the Power Jesrilban Julix darkened.

"It is for you, Master Xaraf, to explain your presence. We have dealt with you fairly. Think! We have healed your hurt, succored you, permitted you to rest within this Keep where no other human has trespassed in a hundred thousand years."

"Jesrilban." Creid, the ancient, turned slightly in his marble throne, held up a cautionary hand. "By your own hypothesis, this young man is not merely innocent of culpable trespass, but doubtless thoroughly bewildered. Go gently, my dear."

Grudgingly, the youth admitted, "That is so." He looked down at me. "Master Xaraf, you present us with a peculiar problem."

"Send me home," I said.

"The matter is complex. We of the Keep have long isolated ourselves from the world of humans. Our privacy is sacrosanct, that we might pursue our studies without interruption from mortals."

Julix rose, slim, handsome, proud. "More than ever, we must now preserve our privacy. The very survival of this world depends on the successful completion of our work." He raised his arm, so that one pale finger pointed to the huge dim orb brooding in the crimson sky. "Look at the sun."

I stared at the flickering nightmare.

"The star is dying," Julix said. "Its energy is almost spent. Soon the last flames of its furnace will fail." His features were vehement. "This green world, the very fountainhead and spring of intelligence and sensibility, will die with it."

His arm had fallen to his side. He regarded me with ice-gray eyes. "We have taken up the task of healing that dying star. If we chose, we could leave this world once more and take with us the last of its pathetic creatures. It would not be so grave a dereliction. Thousands upon thousands of generations have already departed to the dark void and its brighter suns. We do not, however, wish to do so. This earth is our home, that sun its failing life-source."

The thrumming of my pulse beat in my temples. My heart drummed in sympathy to the beat of the Power's awesome words. I did not follow more than a quarter of what he told me, but I felt the grandeur and the purpose, the fine soaring passion which impelled the ancient youth.

Julix tightened the thongs of meaning about my mind: "When the sun swelled in its terminal convulsions, we shifted the world to a cooler orbit. We stripped the system's gas giants of their fuel and ignited them. Yet the sunlets we have hung above the world are palliative only, thwarting the symptoms, finally irrelevant to the fatal course of the disease."

I turned away from those freezing eyes, found with one hand the empty leather-cushioned chair at my side, slowly let myself down into it.

"I do not understand your words, wizard," I growled, "but I would listen further. Tell me what you want of me in this enormous undertaking."

Balmorq leaned forward. "You insist on asking the wrong questions. We did not bring you here. We want nothing of you but an explanation of how you entered the Keep."

I could only shake my head.

"If my coming here was not by your enchantment, it was the work of some other necromancer. I had thought it the doing of the demons of the Black Time."

Creid raised his old white eyebrows in interest. "Give us an account of your activities immediately before you appeared in the Solar Matrix."

"The metal chamber?"

"Just so."

"Why, I was lost in a blizzard. There was a fiery sphere of light. Cold, but terribly bright. I fell—"

Jesrilban sighed. "Then we were correct, Ah. Extraordinary!"

"We must ascertain the nodal point at which he entered," Balmorq said in his powerful bass. "Unless we return him to that precise space-time juncture, the continuum will be damaged."

"Consider," Creid said. "Might it not be the very fact of this young man's temporal transposition which has been interfering with our energy shifts?"

My attention became diffuse. Little of the Powers' discourse conveyed anything I could make use of, so I ignored it. At best, I learned that they genuinely were as puzzled by my presence as I was.

I let my gaze roam the chamber, lingering to scrutinize cryptic devices of bright metal and whirling light, tapestries which altered with stately grace as I watched, conveying formal tales I could not quite follow. Curious sculptures stood here and there, worked in milky stuff soft and entrancing as some flower's petal.

The stinging poignance of my dispossession eased. The Keep was terrifying but wonderful. Darkbloom had instilled in me an inquisitive and intransigent spirit which even when I was a child had left me unhappy with the doltish certitudes of my kinsmen. I discovered quickening within me an ambition to explore this place I had been fetched to, this world with its bloated sun and its miniature sunlets, its made-beast gryphon and its demon princes. I moved impatiently in the deep chair, and my blade struck cold and heavy against my leg. The Powers paid no attention at all.

At length, seething with restlessness, I heard Creid call me. "Young man, it is imperative that we locate your place of origin and return you speedily."

Now, by a paradox, I found myself cheated and annoyed that these insouciant wonder-workers should be so eager to have rid of me.

"Simple enough," I muttered ungraciously. "The Firebridge clan are presently encamped in the high pastures of the Rezot-Azer valley, in the lee of the Long Glacier."

The graybeard smiled, indulgently I thought. "I fear the matter is more complex than that, my dear. We already know *where;* what we must elicit is the *when.* You must convey to us the disposition of the stars as you remember them."

Nonsense, I told myself peevishly. All nonsense. Every time they begin to clarify themselves they lapse immediately into cryptic inanities. "The stars? Of all things in nature," I said, perhaps a little cuttingly, enumerating them, "—desert, ice, seasons, birds, beasts, the fishes in the river—only the stars remain constant."

Jesrilban Julix spoke then, and his voice seemed to partake

of the dry and weary winds of eternity, the winds of the open desert.

"You are wrong, Xaraf," he said. "Even the stars change, in time. Observe the star we call the sun."

Time.

I had not thought. I had looked at a sun exploded to cover a quarter of the sky, and had not dared to think. I cried out.

"Time? How much time could burn the sun down to an ember?"

Julix showed a face carved from pale marble, too young and old to remember grief.

"A thousand thousand years, Master Xaraf. Your people and your world have been dust for a million years."

They rose then, the three of them in their gorgeous raiment, and in silent file descended from their dais.

I recall only blurred images:

Balmorq went to a bank of colored lights which rose from the floor.

Julix, lithe and proud as the scion of some Northern potentate (Gone! I told myself. Gone, dead, crushed to ash and dust!), stepped to a complex thing all of gleaming wheels and polished tubes, where beads of green and yellow jostled, lofted, and sank.

Creid, bent by antiquity, trod carefully to a covered reliquary of silver and jade.

Light spun and sucked at me, a rainbow bent into a whirlpool.

Songs enticed me, shrill as bats' cries.

My limbs went to water. I struggled to get out of the chair's cushioning embrace, but my nostrils ran with an odor like pepper, and the Power Creid, his face all wrinkles and bright hard eyes, leaned over me, bringing from the open reliquary that which I had sought when I awakened and, to my relief, found missing: He held out into my face, by its filthy braided hair, the leering, mud-caked, blood-caked severed Rokhm head. . . .

—The jolt of the blow going into my arm . . .

Blood gouting in its bright, diminishing pulse . . .

Gray, churned snow, muddy slush stained red, my enormous rearing baluchitherium and the toppling headless body of my enemy . . .

—I was screaming with hatred and betrayal.

A Voice, a soothing ostler's voice, came with calm insistence: "REST NOW, XARAF. IT IS NOTHING BUT A BAD DREAM, A MERE MEMORY . . . RELAX, PERMIT YOURSELF TO FLOAT ON GENTLE WAVES OF WARMTH . . . SEE, NOW IT IS SUN-KISSED SUMMER, SWEET AND FRAGRANT . . . IT IS NIGHT, CLEAR AND CALM AND WARM, A NIGHT WITHOUT CLOUD . . . LIE BACK NOW AT YOUR EASE IN THE SIGHING SUMMER GRASSES, GAZE ON A SKY ALIGHT WITH STARS, BLAZING ABOVE YOU WITH ITS FAMILIAR CONSTELLATIONS . . . TELL ME NOW, XARAF, WHERE IS THE BRIGHTEST STAR IN THAT WARM SWEET SKY . . . ?"

And indeed I was lying in the sweet soughing grasses of spring turning to summer, right arm relaxed and warm about the saucy Berb-Kishehm girl I had lured from her brick redoubt to share a night with me while I watched the flocks in the pastures above the city, in the blossom-blowing night. With languid confidence I showed her the stars she had never bothered, in her city ignorance, to notice: the fierce bright eyes of the Great Auk, the cleft skull of the Fallen Warrior (she shivered and squealed in mock fright, so that I must tighten my arm around her, squeeze her breasts against me, kiss her flushed face), the wild wide wings of the Hawk and the dumpy long-necked shape of the Snow Goose, the far faint battle of Boar and Bear, so dim even in this crystal sky that I must teach her how to look *beside* rather than *at* them, until she fell to giggling and tugging at me, drawing my rough shirt up out of my baggy trousers and sending her exploratory hands high and low, while I yelled with laughter and lust and the animals drowsed in the musky night . . .

"The calculations are complete, Eis. He describes the sky as it stood nearly a million years ago."

"It seems he was caught at the penultimate nodal point."

"How could he have retained psychosomatic integrity during transition?"

"A mystery."

"This is an insufficient answer."

"What answer do you want? I do not know. It is a mystery."

"One thing is clear—he is a most unusual specimen, Ah. Remember, his provenance is a period of prehistory when *Homo sapiens* had only recently emerged from the condition of speechless brutes. The coordination of cortical and limbic structures in the brain remained incomplete."

"Could he be a mutation?"

"Phylogenetically the situation was extremely fluid. The concept of a specific mutation therefore serves no explanatory function."

"All this is true, yet it does not account for the unexpected drains on our energy shifts. I am convinced the fellow's presence is no mere coincidence."

"The logical tidiness of your conviction in this regard, Jesrilban, is flawless. As a causal explanation, it is worthless."

"Now, now, my dears. The scan on his life history is almost complete. We must correlate what we find there."

I floated in euphoric hallucination, someone's voice babbling from my own mouth, the Voice ceaselessly asking, probing, goading. . . .

Memories joyous and sour.

My cousin Lleehn tasted of salt, of liquors harsher than melted snow: new sweat from the slithery heat of our bodies, old sweat rewarmed, dried piss, all the creams and honeys and pungencies of that place where our bodies joined and jolted. I licked the salt from her small dark breasts, licked her eyes, licked her waxy small ears, licked her throat, and her hard-muscled legs pressed into my buttocks, her heels bruised me, her teeth came at me nipping and laughing, and every portion of my skin and bowels and senses and brain were connected as Darkbloom had taught me they were connected, a skein of delirious pleasure and mirth, and Lleehn began to lose control, her body convulsing, her voice rising, a hooting song fit to bring a baluchitherium stallion rearing and snorting to stud.

A hard hand fell on my shoulder.

Dazed, I lost my moment; I turned my head in the shadow of the tent, right hand lifted to strike the intruder. Lleehn's song broke to a shriek of alarm as she scrabbled from under me, and my father's face, angry and perplexed, loomed before me.

At the last moment I held the force of my arm which had been already to strike like an arrow from a hard-drawn bow. It would have killed him.

I wanted to kill him.

I shuddered at the impulse.

"Pull your robe about you!" Golan shouted. He was furious. "You shame me, Xaraf. You shame yourself." I had seen his bluster before; he used rage like a honed tool at the men's meetings, to cow and bully and have his way. This was more than bluster. "Do you find leather and metal so despicable that you must loll like a woman, day as well as night, in silk?"

Frightened, Lleehn cowered into the back of the tent.

"Is the meat of our warriors so vile that you must stuff your soft belly with the fruit of Kishehmun orchards?" A sweeping blow sent wooden platters crashing, spilled melons, purple grapes, apricots, costly morsels preserved from decay in a cave cut into the living glacier. I tightened the banded muscles of my belly. Soft? I would show the old blowhard! But I said nothing as he raged. A peeled fruit rolled across the dusty floor.

"You're subtle in chess, I hear," Golan told me with venom. "How do you fare in combat, my son? When are we to see your courage proved iron against iron with the desert thieves?" His fist clutched my gown, dragged me against his own broad, filthy breast.

Belatedly, he recalled my huddled, whimpering cousin. "Out, slut!" he roared. "This is the business of men." He cuffed her head as she shrank past, not without kindness. "In future, keep your tits covered and your legs together, at least until the sun sets.'' When she was gone he turned back to me, face coloring once more.

"Just a moment, Father.'' My face must have shown my emotion; I was cold as the glacier high above our camp, and my skin pressed hard against my bones. "You know of my vow—''

"Shut up.'' Golan spat into the dust. "I have no interest in hearing—''

"I will not keep silent!'' I was shaken by a passion I could not recognize. Tears of wrath made my father's image waver. "Is it necessary for the chief of Firebridge Tribe to humiliate his last-born son as a peasant shrew might shrill at a cur?''

There was nothing counterfeit now in my father's emotion. He roared with a kind of puzzled grief.

"Piss and shit on your stinking vow! Was it for such a puling, fainting pledge that your great-great-grandfather embraced the bloody and holy standard of the Wanderers? Did the Death Lords seek from your ancestor such a woman's pledge? Was it for cowardice and malice that your grandfather achieved leadership of all the horde?''

"It is not cowardice, Father,'' I said wretchedly. "I vowed reverence for life. Enough ruin has been done to the world by the demons of the Black Time—''

The old man snorted. With bitter scorn he bent, tore up my damp, rumpled bedding, brandished the silks in my face. "At least your effete vow has not weakened your manhood entirely.'' He stared at me with his bloody eyes, like a bird of prey. "Or has it? I hear you have a taste for the sluts of the city. How soon will it be before you despise our nubile girls and fill your damned bed with lisping Kishehmun boys?''

His mocking words ceased then, because my fist smashed like a rock into his mouth. He fell like a tree into the dust and lay there.

For an appalled, heart-stopped moment I crouched over him. My bleeding fist was still raised. I stepped back, blankly, and found to my horror that hot tears were running down my cheeks.

The fallen man moved, shook his head, pushed himself up onto his hands. He did not look at me. I was sick with terror.

And a joyous bellow shook the tent's brocaded hangings. Golan came to his feet with difficulty, wiping his bleeding mouth with one hand. He grasped me by the shoulder, while his victorious mirth rocked through my head, and pounded me on the back with his other hairy paw. . . .

Now, hearing my own voice tell of this moment, I felt neither distressed nor elated. The vortex whirled, I floated, all was warm and comforting, the voices from my mouth were a burr of insects moving over breeze-tossed grass.

"This explains much about the young man, but nothing of why he is here."

"Patience, Jesrilban. Little of his short life remains to be examined."

"Press on, then." Was it regret or pity I heard in his chill, elegant tones? "Poor mortal creatures. I had forgotten. I had quite forgotten."

I sat that same night by a glowing brazier in the centre of the chief's great hide tent.

"Responsibility is mine, when the reckoning is done," my father growled gloomily. He took up an urn of bloody wine and sloshed it into a goblet, ornate plunder of some heroic sortie. Almost as an afterthought, he reached across the coals to fill my own plain goblet.

"I have been too often away from camp," Golan mused. "I should not have allowed the upbringing of my sons to fall into the hands of others. Even so," he said, a rasp at the edge of his tongue, glancing toward me with a flash of his firelit eyes, "my other sons have grown into fine men. Not one of them but is a warrior fit and proud to bear the name Firebridge."

"I no less," I said instantly, "according to my lights."

The moment the words left my lips I heard how lame and pompous they were. Yet I was driven by an impulse of self-justification. Something in Golan's somber face stilled the impulse. I turned toward the crackling coals and was silent.

My father too remained silent. One massive hand slapped absently against the gem-encrusted goblet. At length he rose, paced slowly to the entrance of his tent, thrust back one flap to peer into the darkness of the sleeping camp. I rose, too. Only the very young and the infirm would dare infringe propriety by doing otherwise.

Here and there, beyond the open flap, watchfires glowed. Faintly, on the chill desert breeze, came an intermittent murmur of animals and men not yet at rest. An owl screeched. Over everything arched the clear, hard stars.

A guard turned a shadowed inquiring face. Golan curtly dismissed him, let the flap fall back into place. The sounds of night became muted.

"Sit, sit." He considered me sardonically as I attempted once more to accommodate my large frame to one of his hide-and-bamboo seats. "At least your ludicrous vow has not stunted your stature."

It was true, and perhaps the main reason why I had gone unmolested by my kinsmen for so long, despite my refusal to fight beside them in their skirmishes.

I had reached an accommodation with the shaman: He permitted me, within the limits of my vow, to drill at their side. Like them I learned the arts of sword and bow. I outfought any of them in practice bouts.

Since the onset of adolescence I had been the tallest and most powerfully built of all the bucks in the Firebridge encampment. For good or ill, like all my most singular characteristics, this was the work of Darkbloom. Each day he took me aside, riding with me into the woods or sitting beside me as I watched the herds, and drilled me through a regimen of arcane exercises unknown to my brawling, sloppy brothers and cousins.

"Physical power is a delusion," he would tell me, as I strained with all my force against a huge rock, my body bulging with muscles I had never known existed, the sweat bursting from my pores.

"Why, then, are you killing me?" I'd complain. "Let me sleep. It is too hot for this nonsense."

"Crouch before you lift so much weight, you stupid boy. That's right. Now, smoothly rising. Breathe deeply, hold your wind before the moment of maximum exertion, exhale as the power flows through you. Excellent. But that is only a small stone. Here, try once more with this one.''

I huffed and panted, eyes stinging. ''I will not. Physical power is a mere illusion. Why waste my efforts?''

Darkbloom did not reply. He stood before the rock he wished me to lift, a boulder massive as two men, and with serene grace had it on his back. He carried it to me, breathing smoothly, face as clear as a child's. Then he set it down in utter silence.

''An illusion, you see?'' Compared to me, after my years of such exercise, Darkbloom was a reed. He struck at me blindingly with one foot that rose from the ground and blurred at my left eye. Before it could contact me I had shifted my weight; my arm deflected the blow; I was behind the boulder. ''Try once more, Xaraf.''

I lifted the rock to my shoulders, grunting like a boar.

''Quite nicely done, my boy. Now I want to see you squat and rise twenty times before you put it back down. Quadriceps and gluteals, Xaraf. Not forgetting your hamstrings. What else?''

I grunted and heaved. ''Deltoids. Ten, Darkbloom.''

''Twenty. You could do thirty if you weren't so damned lazy. What other muscle groups?''

''You pitiless eunuch.''

''Abdominals. You'll need a strong belly, Xaraf, if you're to fulfill your vow. They'll try to cut you down to size. They'll mock you and question your manhood.''

''Eunuch!'' I squatted, stood for the twentieth time. I placed the boulder noiselessly on the ground, and collapsed beside it.

''Spinal erectors,'' Darkbloom told me. ''Physical power is an illusion. Knowledge is not. Knowledge is the Way.''

I thought of this in the gloom of my father's tent, stung by his jeering.

''There is no reason why the blessed doctrines of Darkbloom should stunt my stature, Father. Mind and body are a harmony which—''

''Syphilis on his ring! It's bad enough that the heathen's unmanly opinions should have corrupted the son of my loins, without them being given advocacy in my own tent. If that creature were not uncommonly acute in his predictive wizardry . . .'' Golan spat into the flames; the spittle hissed. ''But it is wizardry of a darker kind I must speak of, my son.''

I blinked. Golan was a warrior of a doggedly practical bent. His councils held their share of shamans and priests, superstitious babblers and time-servers, but I had supposed that my father was sufficiently the pragmatist not to listen with overmuch attention to their cryptic advice. Only Darkbloom's reviled advice gained his notice, though he rarely admitted as much.

''Wizardry, Father?''

''Sorcery is brewing in the Northern tropics, my son. Lands where ice and snow is never seen, where rains fall endlessly into hot mud, and trees cover the world. Word has come from that place of demonic sorcery so vile that those who carry its rumor are like madmen in their fright.''

Darkbloom had instilled a brash skepticism in me. Madmen indeed, I thought. Yet my father's seriousness touched me with a breath of raw fright. I leaned forward.

''Father, I had heard nothing of—''

''No, you have not.'' Golan was still bitter. ''We have not given this news into the common gossip of the harem sluts.'' He grimaced, washed down his chagrin with another great draught of wine. ''Enough of that. I have fetched you here, one man to another, that you might listen to what none of your warrior kin have thus far learned.''

This was extraordinary. I was taken aback, and regarded him with fascinated curiosity.

''You should have been my favorite son,'' Golan said. ''Even now I judge that you bear within you the spirit of a mighty slayer. I know that you have a readier wit than most of them.'' Ruefully, perhaps, he touched the bruise half-hidden in the darkness.

''I have always pledged you my loyalty, Father.''

''The pig-shit loyalty of a eunuch's flunky,'' Golan said angrily. ''Listen to me! For all the glory of the Firebridge Tribe we are far from the largest among the Wanderers. The time is coming when our strength must be at its height, when we face this Northern threat.''

"Who are these necromancers, Father?" Curiosity and skepticism vied within me. Could this tale of distant sorcery be nothing more than a ruse to trick me from my oath? I recalled eye-rolling visits to the charlatans in the temples of the Walled Green City, with their stinking fumes and booming voices, flashes of violet and red, loud bangs and fraudulent miracles. "Do their powers exceed those of the priests of Berb-Kisheh?"

Golan's fury burst from him in an instant. It seemed that he would rise and strike me to the ground. "Have you not heeded a word I spoke?" he cried. "These sorcerers fly among the clouds like the demons of the Black Time. They send fire and storm. Do you think that the chief of the Firebridge Tribe would pander to a son corrupted by heresy and cravenness," my father roared, shaking with emotion, "if his only enemy were a gaggle of painted harlequins?"

I was abashed. Heat rushed to my face, then shocking coolness. The muscles of my abdomen cramped. Those at jaw and throat tightened, so words milled in confusion behind my tongue. "My chieftain—"

Golan's choler changed in that moment to the contained fury which served him so well in battle, if half the tales of the old men were true.

"The days of prophecy are upon us." He sat down, waved me back to my seat. "Why the Dark Lords have chosen this hour to manifest their wrath with mankind I cannot guess. Yet it is clear enough that this wizardry which lays waste the Northern lands has not been seen among men since the Black Time."

"The North is so distant," I said. "The glaciers protect us—"

"That has always been true in the past. It is not too distant for those in the service of demons." I saw that my father was profoundly frightened, for all his courage in battle. "They will rip us without counting cost, for life is what they hate."

My own cynicism dispersed like the frail vapor it was, and my mood chilled to match my father's intensity. Red coal light glinted within the bowl I held in my hands, ran blue and green from the gems set in my father's goblet. The softness of my voice amazed me:

"What would you have me do, Father?"

And Golan, iron and leather, bombast and resolution, leaned far back in his chair; he threw his head forward, gaze burning into me, and made a sound like laughter.

"I would have you do what we all must do, my strange son. Prepare for the clash of blade against madness. Whet sword and blood it. Make ready to confront those who would shatter the shape of the world. That is all I want—that you should give up your foolishness, that you should spit on the mean, womanish creed of Darkbloom the outlander."

With the impressive grace of some wise, tough old desert wolf, my father moved past the brazier in the gloom and placed on my shoulder his great paw of a hand, all scarred and stiff from a hundred slashes and tendon-bruising blows.

"You know that I could order your obedience under pain of banishment or death. I will not: I will *ask* it." His bearded face was no longer harsh with anger. "Golan Firebridge would have his son by his shoulder in the demon battle."

All Darkbloom's knowledge was an illusion, powerless against this appeal. The glad, sad confusion in my head did not abate. I felt tears once more in my eyes, twice in a day, and used that excuse to withdraw my gaze. Something breaking—

"I shall do as you ask, my father," I told him.

Calm, calm, floating womb-warm, womb-happy.

" 'Darkbloom'? Is this possible? Can he mean Flowers of Evening?"

"I fear this is our key, my brothers. By the Failing Sun, what have we wrought in our tampering?"

"A coincidental play on words, nothing more. Flowers of Evening stands with his machines at the dawn of the solar system, six billion years before Xaraf's birth."

"Can we be sure? Some disaster may have overtaken him. I shiver, I shudder, I groan to think on it! Can Flowers of Evening be lost to us, penned in the age of early humans?"

"Impossible. He is immortal, true, but not even one of us

could retain life and sanity during such exile. There must be some other explanation.

"How else does the brute come here, then, if not through Flowers of Evening's wormline?"

"One of us must go in search of our brother."

"This is out of the question. Three must stand here as anchor, while one works to harvest the core of the primordial sun. Any alternative is unstable. All would be lost."

"Perhaps all is lost even as we speak. It seems apparent to me that catastrophe is upon us. Some other agency has gained entry to our wormlines—these 'sorcerers' Xaraf fears."

"Ah, you are overemotional. What is done is done. Everything the lout describes has been dust for a million years."

"For *him* it has not passed: The worst of it lies ahead. And it is of our doing. Whoever these supposed sorcerers were, it is our energy they are drawing on."

"Ah is right, my impetuous Jesrilban. Moreover, the matter is of stringent cogency. If creatures in the remote past are tapping into our energy transmissions from the sun, it is possible that the drain will increase. What then of our plans to revive the sun?"

"I apologize. What you both say is true. Indeed, worse is possible. Consider: If this youth can stumble into a nodal Transfer Matrix, what is to stop his enemies from storming through?"

"It is more likely that Flowers of Evening led Xaraf to the gateway. He could scarcely 'stumble through' unaided."

"Yet on this conjecture our brother ought simply to have employed the gateway for his own return to us. I fear that the sorcerers themselves might be responsible."

"If so, and if Golan Firebridge was correct, they were insane. They could ravage our failing world."

"We must close down the Solar Matrix immediately!"

"And strand our brother in antiquity? Shameful madness!"

"Besides, we dare not. Better a potential doom than a certain one."

"One ploy is available, hazardous but fascinating. Since we can neither cease our operations nor confront the problem in person, Xaraf must serve as our creature."

"Implausible."

"Immoral!"

"Indubitable, on both counts. But necessary."

" . . . Yes."

"Reluctantly, I agree."

"Therefore let us begin at once. The boy has much to learn before we can return him to his own time."

The Voice returned, wonderfully compelling in my trance.

"XARAF FIREBRIDGE, YOU MUST PAY CLOSE HEED."

"My Lord, I am listening."

"LISTEN WELL, CHILD, FOR THE FATE OF THIS WORLD AND YOUR OWN MAY HANG IN THE BALANCE. YOU WILL BE RETURNED TO YOUR OWN ANCIENT TIME, THOUGH NOT IMMEDIATELY. ONCE THERE, YOU ARE TO SEEK OUT AND DESTROY THOSE SORCERERS WHO ARE TAMPERING WITH THE WORK OF THE POWERS."

"I am . . . reluctant to kill. Already my vow has been shamed with blood."

"XARAF, YOUR AVERSION TO SLAUGHTER IS BOTH NOBLE AND ADMIRABLE. BUT THE CREATURES YOU MUST OPPOSE HAVE FORFEITED ALL RIGHT TO HUMANE CONSIDERATION. THEY ARE CORRUPT. UNLESS THEY ARE THWARTED, YOUR WORLD COULD SHUDDER IN DARKNESS FOR A HUNDRED THOUSAND YEARS, AND OURS WILL PERISH WITH ITS RUINED SUN."

"I am one man alone, powerless against wizards and armies."

"YOU WILL NOT BE WITHOUT RESOURCES. ALTHOUGH THE POWERS CANNOT ACCOMPANY YOU INTO THE FRAY, THEY CAN AND WILL PREPARE YOU TO ENTER IT."

"You will teach me enchantments to pit against those of the demons?"

"XARAF, THE POWERS WILL TEACH YOU NOTHING, AND FOR TWO REASONS. THE FIRST IS THAT THE SPECIFIC ATTRIBUTES OF THE ANCIENT SORCERERS ARE UNKNOWN EVEN TO THE POWERS. HENCE, THEIR AID MUST BE OF A GENERAL NATURE.

"SECOND, AND MORE IMPORTANT, KNOWLEDGE OBTAINED

WITHOUT EFFORT IS MORALLY WORTHLESS. YOU MUST SEEK LEARNING FORGED IN THE CRUCIBLE OF EXPERIENCE."

I felt a shadow smile pass across my lips. "So says my mentor Darkbloom. Yet where am I to gain experience in fighting sorcerers?"

"BEYOND THE PROTECTED WALLS OF THIS KEEP EXTENDS A WORLD AS VAST AS YOUR OWN, YET ALIEN TO YOURS IN EVERY RESPECT. YOU WILL BE PLACED THERE WITH NO CONSCIOUS RECOLLECTION OF WHAT HAS PASSED HERE. IT WILL BE SCHOOL ENOUGH. WHEN THE TIME IS RIPE, YOU WILL RETURN TO THE KEEP AND THE POWERS WILL SEND YOU BACK TO YOUR OWN ERA. THERE YOU WILL PROSECUTE YOUR MISSION.

"NOW FOR THE MOMENT, SLEEP.

"AND FORGET . . ."

SLEEP

::Albert Einstein's generally accepted theory of gravitation holds that the energy output of the Sun has slowly increased, by about 30 per cent, since the Lower Archean [4.5 billion years ago], and yet no glacial epochs are known until 2300 million BP. If a drop of 30 per cent in the energy output of the Sun were to occur today, all the oceans [would] freeze solid. [Yet] the temperature of the ocean of 3000 million BP was 50 degrees C—that is, about 30 degrees C hotter than the modern ocean::

—Sir Fred Hoyle

::Some astronomers want to say that the core of the Sun is stirring itself and cooling down for a few million years, like a fire being restoked. Series of ice ages would then be due to the peculiar stirring in the Sun every few hundred million years::

—Nigel Calder

FIVE

How long is a fever? I fell and fell. Searing light and nausea, a fall that lacked even the rushing of wind. The light, at last, swallowed me complete.

When I opened my eyes it was cloudy night. I sprawled in thick tufts of grass. The sphere of light was gone.

The endless fall was somehow a memory of a memory. I experienced a jolt of illness, but it was a phantom sickness. My ears rang but I did not vomit. I sat up, leaning one hand in the grass.

Grass.

The jagged, snow-covered terrain through which I had been stumbling, after my steed broke his leg and I was obliged to slay him, had been bare and rocky, scoured by the elements. In that denuded landscape, high above the Rezot-Azer valley, only thorny scrub could eke out a meager existence. Given that I truly was still alive, I ought to have been lying exhausted and filthy in mud and melting snow.

Half-blind in the moonless night, I got to my feet. Grass. The night was moderately warm.

I've been rescued, I told myself, finding it difficult to believe. Someone has removed me from the place of light to this more hospitable haven.

For what reason? I could think of none. To enslave me? I was free of shackles. Simple gratuitous decency? Or the hope of reward? Either was feasible—but where, then, was my benefactor?

I reached for my blade, strapped across my back. And caught my breath.

My sword hung in its scabbard, hilt ready to my hand. I did not draw it. My arm had rustled a sleeve of rich silk. I had been clad in soaked, foul battle order; now I was arrayed all in a prince's raiment of silk and suedes.

My eyes were adjusting to the gloom. I stared about me, rigid with consternation, breathing shallowly. Surely there must be some sign of life—a fire, a tent, a tethered steed.

The cool breeze brought me only the chitter of strange birds, a distant grunt of beasts I could not place: nothing human, nothing I knew.

Other than the darker shadows of a few trees, and the far-off edge of a forest, I stood in the midst of an aching loneliness.

Shrugging, I took my hand from my sword's hilt. As my arm fell my fingers brushed something matted and vile. I grimaced. It was the Rokhmun chieftain's head, faintly reeking, tied by its brained hair to my new belt. So my benefactor was not without a bizarre humor. Or perhaps merely a dogged sense of honor.

I ran my tongue about my mouth. It was clean enough and moist. I was neither hungry nor thirsty, yet I knew that this was a circumstance which time would alter. How far was I from home? Impossible to judge. I needed to make what provision I might while my strength remained. The distant forest offered the best hope of water. I set off across springy grass toward it.

Small creatures scurried in alarm as my luxuriously shod feet paced the gently declining plain. From what I could see of it in the dark, the countryside was rich grazing land. I kicked about as I walked and quickly encountered indubitable evidence of herding.

The cow pats were dried, old. I bent to examine them, letting my fingers trace indentations where the animals had trodden in their own fresh ordure. Weather had virtually obliterated the hoof marks. The few I found were oddly shaped: three-toed, more like those of preposterous birds than of cattle.

A cold wind sprang up, shouldering aside the breeze. I shivered, wishing my unknown savior had bequeathed me a cloak to cover the soft, light clothing I now wore. Admittedly, this wind was not so cold as the howling blizzard which less than an hour earlier, if my memory was any judge, had chilled me to the bone. But exhaustion and the very chill itself had then numbed my nerves to the bite of the wind.

I turned these considerations in my mind. By rights I ought to have been raveningly hungry, frostbitten, half-blind. All these deficits had vanished with my ruined garments. Grateful as I was for these transformations, I could not for the life of me recall the meanest detail of their occurrence.

The first question, perhaps, was this: What had become of that flameless, burning sphere into which I had fallen?

I cast an automatic glance over my shoulder. Rolling savanna stretched behind me, dim and featureless, as I had known it would. The wind blew my long hair into my eyes; I pushed it aside, wishing for a helm or even a soft leather Kishehm hat. Like the cliff over which I had stumbled, like that roaring snowstorm, that enigmatic globe of light might never have existed.

I trudged on. Meager as the information was which my senses brought me, I was not bored, not precisely; but after a time I strode in a state of remote abstraction, the mood of a desert nomad used to a landscape of endless minor variation on a theme of endless identity.

Eventually I was near enough the dark mass of gnarled shadows to ascertain that it was in fact the outskirts of a woods. I caught myself glancing at the sky with a frown, without quite knowing why. From the wood I heard cries of night predators. I knew perfectly the songs, the harsh hunting cries, the yells of warning, the stirring hoots and howls of courtship kept in their repertoire by the birds of my people's annual traverse. These were none of them. I shivered again. Gusts whipped my flowing sleeves like fluttering pennants.

I slipped into the shadows of trees like another shadow.

Undergrowth quickly tangled itself before me.

I could hack my own path through, but that is a laborious means of making one's way. Cursing, I struck across it at an angle.

Twigs and fallen branches crackled under my feet. I hardly

dared let my thoughts rest on this evidence that I was pushing through country at the end of its high summer, when hours before I had nearly perished in the early storms of winter.

Thirst started to annoy me. I found a small dry stone to suck. Faint trills of running water, real or imagined, taunted me as the rising wind veered and muttered in the tops of the trees. I prowled on.

As I got further into the stand of huge knotted trees, the ground became less littered with brush. Even in daylight this section of the woods was likely to be a dull, protected place. Webs hung and looped between the great dry boles; I struck them aside with distaste. It was the penalty I must pay for the easier going. And here, at least, some of the day's warmth was still trapped, some of the wind's chill deflected by ample trunks.

I saw a gleam of yellow eyes in the dark. I waited with my hand on my hilt. The eyes blinked, withdrew.

The slope fell away more rapidly now, and the gurgle of water across stone came more distinctly. I descended.

Here, of course, would be correspondingly greater danger. Those flashing eyes would not be alone. As dawn approached, night-prowling carnivores would also be making their way toward water. I hoped that they had all fed satisfactorily.

I saw a clearing through the trees. As carefully as I might, I slipped through dimness. The wind was falling. The stream's rushing made my heart quicken. I wished to slake my thirst, but more crucially the watercourse would lead me (perhaps via a river and a tiring slog, but eventually it *would* take me) to some human habitation.

With luck and the bleak aid of the Lords of Light and Death, I told myself, I'd then at last be in a position to determine my location. Once I knew where I was, I could make preparations for the trek back to the Firebridge encampment.

I watched a moment longer at the edge of the clearing. The clouds had cleared while I marched beneath the trees, and the seeing was slightly better.

Wary of how vulnerable I was in this place I knew nothing of, I stepped into starlight. And I drew my sword.

Shock stilled me.

I looked at the open sky, then at the sword in my hand.

It was not my sword. It was not my sky.

The blade, we are taught, is the sword. Grip, pommel, and guard, no matter how ingeniously or expensively decorated, are subordinate.

My battlesword was no prize, hardly the stuff of legend. Firebridge had scooped it up as booty, no doubt, in some raid on a walled settlement where they made such things in their forges and beat them with hammers and lacked the singleness of mind to employ them well enough to keep them from the likes of us.

Still, I knew it intimately. Yes, Darkbloom made me swear never to use it against a man, as, to my bitter regret, I had done, but he never refused me the right to learn its exercise. My right hand—and my left too, for it was a massive piece of iron—had memorized its heft, its slightly sour balance, the nudge of thumb and forefinger in their proper place.

Half of those familiar details were unchanged. Only the blade was new.

It shone like light under the stars. Both edges were ground to a wondrous bite. A sigil I could not read was graven into the flat.

Like light, it shone, under the . . . stars.

The clearing was empty of life, rocky as it fell to the stream I heard babbling like my babbling mind. On the farther side the trees were small and shadow-dark. The sky was turning from black to deepest blue, and tatters of cloud went fast before the cold wind, showing the stars.

Some god had wrenched the stars from their places.

He had juggled them, then hurled them back in absurd patterns.

So might jewels be ripped from a priceless setting and strewn in sand by an imbecile.

Swaying, leaning on the sword which was and was not mine, I sought for even the least of the constellations I had always known.

And from some guarded place deep within me, I seemed to recollect a Voice which soothed and reassured my fears in just such a moment. I could not quite grasp the words, or even be sure I had once heard them, yet my fright diminished to a kind of head-shaking astonishment.

I do not know how long I stood there like that, deaf and blind to everything except the disordered sky. I do know that my baffled torpor almost cost me my life.

In the tongue of the nomad tribesmen, a person I could not see said urgently: "Danger, Xaraf! Draw your sword."

I whirled, brought up my blade.

Something very large gave a coughing roar.

I was staring into the large glowing eyes of a crouching beast. The eyes were slit, and filled the world.

There was no further warning, from either the voice or the tremendous cat. The animal sprang at me, ears flat against its tawny head, claws scything from the black pads of its paws.

Men have fought lions and not died. Men have fought everything that lives, except perhaps some of the monstrous creatures of the deep, and survived the encounter. Those, though, are the exceptions.

Fewer men still have had such a mentor as I. Darkbloom had prepared me well. No thought. I acted with clean, perfect, instant reflex.

Eyes, flattened ears, ripping claws: I had thrown myself away from them, convulsing like a tumbler with firebrands in both hands. I went backward down the slope, came cleanly on my feet as the beast twisted in flight, let my momentum carry me to a crouch which jammed the hilt of my long-bladed battlesword into the soil.

Lashing blows ripped space where I stood no longer, though I had occupied it an instant earlier. Fangs like spittled daggers closed on air.

For all its agility, the beast could do nothing to alter the path of its leap. The heavy body slammed with a shattering jolt into the poised blade.

Breast bone cracked, splintered.

Blood cascaded from the great rent.

Even while the animal died, foam-flecked jaws tried to take my face off. I moved with the spirit of Death, as if blown like a leaf by its stinking breath; I felt the whiskers of its snout scratch my cheek as I slid past its murder, and I took the hilt I knew and, two-handed, jerked up the exquisite blade I did not know, so it sheared the very heart and lungs of the creature free within its body.

I was gone with my dripping sword when the animal fell on its side, blood going out like a black river from its sundered heart.

Tail lashed flanks, and it was still.

Then I sat down. I was gasping like a man who has run for a watch without cease. Both hands still gripped the sword's hilt from guard to pommel, gripped it with white-knuckled intensity. I forced one hand free with an effort of will. I wanted to cry with relief and triumph. Salt sweat beaded my lips. My eyes darted hysterically, but I could see no other predator in the brooding darkness of the wood. Nor could I find that man who'd given me warning.

"That was well done, Xaraf," said my sword. "Yes, you carried that off very neatly."

During the Black Time, legend insists, there was no commonplace tool but had its own voice.

In those demonic days a thousand years prior to my birth, before the sky went red with fire and men's flesh peeled away, before the sky went dark with poisoned soot and screaming winds, before the sky cleared on a world scoured and almost emptied forever of life, and the glaciers came up from the South, and the high melted cities flickered at night in their craters and ill gets were thrown of cancerous mothers, before all that had come to pass, in the terrible days of the pride of the Black Time, people flew through the air in vehicles which governed themselves, they dressed and ate and amused themselves with the products of man-made instruments which thought with small, quick, stupid brains.

That was what legend held. Darkbloom had confirmed this to me, so I was perfectly prepared to believe it.

Seeing and hearing the proof is entirely another matter.

I howled with fright.

A sword which spoke was a pent demon, or a tool from the

Black Time. Either way it was an evil thing, a thing of power, a cause for dismay and an alluring, awful temptation.

I threw it on the ground with a shriek and skidded away down the scree into the cold creek.

Froth and gore matted the dead cat's muzzle. I looked it over carefully in the early predawn light. My head still rang from the chilly water I'd splashed into my face, down my neck. The sword lay in the grass, bloody and silent.

A rancid feline stink came from the cat: It had voided its bowels as it died. That made me frown. If the beast had fed already this night, why its ferocious attack? Not hunger. Its glazed, staring eyes were the eyes of a hunting cat. Often enough, such animals hunt in the company of others. I tensed, refusing to look for the comfort and protection of my bloody sword.

I got down on my haunches and nudged the warm, massive body, gauged the weight of bone and muscles beneath the coarse pelt. I had never heard of a cat such as this. It was neither leopard nor lion, jaguar nor cheetah, nor any other of the breeds of great hunters which roamed the countryside beyond the boundaries set by men.

Even using both hands I was scarcely able to move the stiffening corpse. The jutting legs shifted slightly. Starlight glinted from something bound low on one hind leg.

I grunted. The gleaming object, when I'd wiped away the shit which matted the animal's leg, was a band of silvery fabric. I tugged hard. It would not tear. Somehow it combined metallic strength with the flexibility of cloth. I looked more closely. This was the remnant of no broken shackle; a pair of esoteric symbols were etched into the fabric, the sign of ownership.

So where were the master workmen whose creature this beast obviously had been?

My fingers rubbed at the curious soft fabric of the garments I now wore. Had they been provided by those same beast-masters? If so, I had repaid them poorly by slaughtering one of their animals. Yet I was justified: The beast had attacked me without provocation.

Once more, the desolating awareness of my ignorance in this strange land boiled up like a poisoned fog.

How, after all, had I got here from the storm? I clamped my teeth together and lifted my face, in an access of defiance, to the jumbled stars. At the far side of the stream, streaks of dawn lightened the darkness behind the trees. Animals were stirring, and birds.

I slapped my hands together. Nothing more was to be gained by staying here, and considerable merit in departing before the arrival of any additional carnivores—branded or wild.

The sword lay where I had dropped it. Holding it away from me, I took it up and wiped clean its bloody blade with fronds ripped from the creek bank. I stared at it sourly.

"Speak to me."

"You're quite sure?" the sword said testily. "You wouldn't care to take another dip first with all your clothes on? Xaraf," it said sorrowfully, as I held it at arm's length in my trembling grasp, "you're a bundle of nerves."

"That's enough," I shouted.

"I thought it might be. Speak, don't speak. No consistency. I save your life and what do I get in return? Thrown holus-bolus on the hard ground. Left there all mucky—"

"Hold your tongue!" I cried. I lifted the thing and jammed it into its scabbard.

"Tongue," it said derisively, faintly muffled. "I suppose I see what you mean." It fell silent.

I made my way downstream. Brush and fern closed in as I progressed: tree roots, thorns, undergrowth knotted in confusion, parasitic vines overhanging the banks of the rushing stream. This was the price exacted by my decision to avoid the game trails I crossed, stamped flat and unprotected by untold generations of the wood's inhabitants. Instead, I pushed my way as best I could, although finally I was obliged to draw sword and hew the more offensive impediments from my path.

"Xaraf."

"What is it?"

"I've been thinking. You remember that metal band?"

"Of course I do."

"I think we should go back and get it."

"No."

I hacked on.

"I really think it would be a good idea."

A flock of birds, waking noisily as saffron brightened the sky to my right, launched themselves across the water with a flurry of wings. Their plumage was somber—dark green as the leaves about me—while legs and beaks were russet as their bodies. "Why?"

"There's a substantial chance that you'll encounter the animal's owners, you know. It would help if you had the band."

"It would be an open admission of guilt."

"Trust me."

I laughed. The sword said, "Have I steered you wrong so far? I warned you that the cat was about to attack, didn't I?"

"You took your time," I said savagely.

Cawing, the birds wheeled high overhead, then fled in arrow formation toward the hidden sun. I followed their passage absently, trying to assess the sword's reliability. I did not wish to waste time and energy returning through the scrub to the dead cat.

"I'm here in an advisory role only," the weapon said haughtily.

I ignored it. Some peculiarity in the sky made me push finger and thumb into my eyes.

Abruptly, brilliance speared from a cleft between two silhouetted trees in the east. I blinked against scalding light. I staggered; it was much brighter than the rising sun had any right to be. Thorns ripped my sleeve, stung my arm.

Squinting, I glanced again at that intolerable point of brilliance. It rose between the trees, white-hot and glaring, small as a star. It was neither the sun nor any star I knew.

"Relax, Xaraf," my sword said, "it's just one of the sunlets, it won't hurt you."

Full of dread, I'd turned and scrambled up the slope. A huge brown trunk blocked my panic-stricken retreat. I fell against it, pressed my sweating forehead into its rough, reassuringly solid bark.

I turned, when my heart had slowed a little, and faced the incredible star.

"Here we go again," the sword muttered sardonically behind my ear.

Upstream, a second point of blazing light was rising from behind a stand of taller, heavier trees. Majestic as some solemn nightmare, the two pseudosuns brought a kind of morning to the world.

I pushed myself away from the bole. "You knew about this?"

"Naturally I knew about the sunlets. They've always been there."

"You're lying or you're wrong. Where's the sun?"

"The sun'll be up in a little while. Not much there to stay up all night for. There're four of them," it added.

I sat down on the ground and rubbed my eyes. I was getting hungry, on the verge of losing my temper. "Four suns," I said flatly.

"Four *sunlets*, Xaraf. The Powers put them there thousands of years ago."

I stood up again abruptly. "Let's go and get that bracelet."

"Oh, good," the sword said happily. It whistled a martial air as we struggled back the way we'd come.

A small feral beast with six legs was gnawing on the cat's extruded tongue when we found the body. It withdrew, hissing, but darted back to its breakfast when it saw that we—that I—posed no competition.

Something was amiss. After a moment I had it. There were no buzzing, stinging insects in the usual irritating cloud around the corpse.

I bent over the stiff leg, tried once again to wrest the soft metal band from the limb. While I managed easily enough to work it down the thick fur to the splayed paw, I could tease it no further.

"You'll have to cut it free."

"I can see that."

Scowling, I drew my garrulous weapon and hacked the paw away. I drew the circlet from the oozing stump.

Now that I had the cryptic thing in my hand I wondered again what use it might serve—except, as I'd suggested, to enrage the dead beast's owners if they found me with it. I forbore to question the sword further on the matter. Shrugging, I looped the thing to my belt, alongside my other odorous trophy, and started off once more in search of a human voice from a human throat. I did not look again at the twin sunlets. I forged ahead, drinking from the widening stream to allay my hunger, pushing with stolid determination through bracken and scrub.

The sword sang melancholy folk songs when it tired of marching tunes.

"What is your name?" I asked it finally.

"I have no name," it said. "I'm just a simple machine. They don't give us names."

"I can't just call you 'Hey you!' "

"You mean you'll consider *gifting* me with a name?" the sword asked, pathetically eager.

"It'd be easier all around." For a time I mused on possible names. It took my mind off my belly.

After about twenty breaths of peace the sword said, "Give me a hint."

"Shut up or I'll name you Shit-a-breeks."

"You wouldn't!" it shrieked. But I noticed that it was remarkably subdued until I next gave it leave to speak.

None of the wildlife I encountered offered me threat, nor, despite my growing desire to break my fast, did I them. I stumped on, and creatures out of a fevered dream scurried warily from my path.

A purple-red serpent clad in shiny crimson spikes coiled back into a hole in the side of the hill I climbed, and watched me lazily with dull black eyes. Rodents with six tiny legs and great flat feet chittered from the grass. A gilled, grease-slicked beast plopped up in the middle of the stream onto a half-submerged log. It lacked eyes; pale delicate tendrils probed lightly from its face, swung tenderly to follow my path.

Birds screamed down from leafy branches.

"I'll call you Alamogordo," I said suddenly.

That is a name from the depths of the Black Time, a curse and anathema which even a thousand years after the time of ruin we recalled with respect. I do not know what it means, except that it represents the weapon which all but burnt up the world. I needed something bleak and sacred, a touch of black blasphemy.

"Alamogordo." The sword tested the sound approvingly. "I like it. What does it mean?"

I explained.

"Thank you, Xaraf," Alamogordo said quietly. "You are a friend." It reflected for a while, then spoke in a pleased tone. "I believe you've been getting peckish, am I right?"

"The thought of breakfast had occurred to me," I confessed.

"Observe the glossy blue berries on yonder thorny bush."

"They look poisonous." I had been eyeing them doubtfully for some minutes.

"Far from it. They will purge your pangs, refresh the whites of your eyes, scrub the plaque from your teeth, and put power in your pizzle."

I cleared my throat in a menacing manner. "Thank you, Al. You remind me of a Berb-Kisheh merchant who once sold me a silken gown with the grubs still in it."

There was a strangled silence. Faintly, the sword said: "Al?"

"Al's friendlier," I explained, plucking some of the berries without slowing my pace. Ripe yellow fruit, oblate and tempting, hung from several trees which favored the edge of the stream. I pulled several loose. "Are these safe?"

"Practically *everything* is safe," Alamogordo told me sulkily.

I bit cautiously into the soft flesh. As with the berries, the taste was unfamiliar but enjoyable, as if it had been bred by a skilled gardener for the human palate. I found my dazed mood improving as the immediate pangs of hunger eased.

"It's shorter, too. Less formal. More forthright. Trips swiftly from the tongue during battle."

"All right, all right," Al said. It settled down to a display of bird imitations and spurious animal bellows which fetched a mixed brigade of inquisitive and incredulous animals out of the brush until I put a stop to it.

SIX

The stream deepened and widened as it was joined by several tributaries. Twice I was obliged to detour somewhat in order to ford these creeks. By the time the sunlets had climbed a third of the way into the sky I felt sure that human habitation could not be far off.

Alamogordo was useless as a guide. It professed ignorance of geography. "I'm a specialist in tactics and interpersonal relations," it told me. "If you want a gazetteer, look elsewhere."

Increasingly the forest gave way to lush breeze-rippled grass, perfect for pasture. The foliage covering scattered trees to the northwest threw back tints of gold, now somehow bloodied to bronze.

Hair stirred at my neck.

I drew Alamogordo. The bright blade glinted red. Slowly, I looked over my shoulder to the east.

In that moment I knew somehow that I had been waiting for a dreadful thing which I could not specify. The fact of it, the actuality, was cramping and bitter as a blow to the groin.

On the tree-choked horizon hung a maimed, failing, violet sun.

It was huge as a cartwheel, but I knew it for what it was. Not the desert sun rising, nor the mountain sun, rich and potent in scarlet. This sick bloated orb would never put on the strength and majesty of noonday splendor. Like a bruise, like clotted blood unleeched, it came into the sky and hung there, a harbinger.

I looked away in grief.

And a kind of clarity emerged. An insight presented itself to me, as clean and certain as iron ringing on iron.

"This is why they brought me here," I said aloud.

"Who?"

I had forgotten the sentient sword. "My benefactors. The demons who fetched me to this place."

Alamogordo was uninterested. "I'll take your word for it."

"Because the sun is dying," I said, marveling. "Because of the threat my father fears. There is some connection." I looked at the black-scarred sun. "I am meant to help return the sun to life."

"No one can say you lack ambition," the sword said. "Look, Xaraf, talk sense. The sun has been dying ever since greedy humans discovered the wormline principle and gutted its core. The whole system is on its last legs. Nothing remains but to drain the last of the wine to the dregs and smash the bowl."

Was it possible that a man might intercede in the death of a god? Assuming that the sun was a god. My heart was lifted by a surge of purpose.

If it *were* so, my presence in this appalling landscape was not void of meaning; was indeed urgent, momentous, perhaps even central.

The sun came up above the trees, laboring at the start of its doomed journey to the far horizon: brave, perhaps, in its infirmity, refusing the exhaustion which sucked it toward unlit night.

Garments and limbs aflame in the light of the dying sun, I raised my sword in salute. A sort of exultation burst up in me. I threw back my head in a roar of furious, defiant laughter.

"Very romantic." My sword was caustic. "If you've quite finished, it might interest you to know that we've attracted some more livestock."

Two of the great catlike beasts stood in my path an arrowshot away, their smoldering eyes expectant.

I stood stock-still, both hands clenching the sword's hilt.

One cat padded delicately in a wide curve to cut off my retreat. Mouth dry, crotch painfully tight, I searched from the sides of my eyes at the ground near me. A substantial branch lay in the grass near my feet. I freed one hand, sank with infinite care to a half-crouch, took up the broken stick, rose slowly. It was heavy but brittle; it had been too long in the grass, was a dead thing without sap. It would have to serve.

The beast behind me started forward, herding me toward its waiting companion.

A shriek came from the forest as some creature fed its natural enemy.

Bubbles burst on the stream's surface: A fish had leapt and caught a hovering insect.

Leaves sighed in the faint breeze.

I edged forward, perceiving everything in the open net of my senses without prejudice and seeing only the cats, branch, and blade in my hands. My eyes darted from one animal to the other.

Now both cats were on the move, tongues wet and red between white fangs. Inexorably, they forced me crabwise back into the heavier timber. I maintained sufficient distance that a single lunge would not reach me, but found myself stumbling through undergrowth that crackled and dragged at me.

It struck me suddenly that the beasts were herding me, not for the kill, but in an ordained direction.

We came out into a clearing which marked the junction of several game trails. They took no advantage of their opportunity. Long moments passed and they did nothing more menacing (though it was menacing enough to soak my armpits with sweat) than force me back along the trail.

"They're droving me," I muttered incredulously.

"So it seems," Alamogordo said softly. "Take no precipitate action, Xaraf."

Dappled light ran red-gold in their tawny hides, glinted in silver flashes from the bands at their hind legs.

If they are indeed governed by a plan, I thought, they will drive me back to the track if I attempt to leave it.

Testing this notion, I feinted several times into the brush. Both beasts instantly tensed. Their relaxed gait hardened into postures of teeth-baring threat. Alamogordo hissed peevishly.

I swallowed against the hard knot in my throat and continued my slow, directed retreat along the game trail.

"Have they been sent for me?"

"It is entirely possible that their masters have by now discovered the dead animal," the sword said. "And you didn't exactly leave it looking as if it had died peacefully of old age."

Patently, the cats were not themselves of markedly high intelligence. Why, then, had they failed to attack me on sight with the instinctive ferocity of their predecessor?

I glanced down at the piece of shiny fabric wound about my belt. Was this the factor behind their extraordinary behavior? The creatures continued to press me. I tried to place myself inside those sleek skulls, tried to mimic the limited mental processes of the powerful half-tamed cats.

"This is why you urged me to carry off the anklet," I surmised aloud.

"I'm not prescient, if that's what you mean," Alamogordo said. "It just seemed reasonable."

"But you think that the band communicates somehow that I am not to be harmed?"

"Certainly it is a means of identification."

"Yet I am clearly not a cat," I said, "as a cat would be the first to notice."

"Nor, I conjecture, are you much like their masters. Otherwise you would be permitted your freedom."

I hissed, as the sword had done, in aggravation. The beasts must be more discriminating than I had first credited.

"In short," I said, "I represent an unknown to them, and must be taken to their overlords for inspection."

Alamogordo was direct. "Better than being eaten on the spot."

At length the trail opened into another clearing. A guttural shout made me jump.

I had time for only the quickest glimpse of five or six luridly accoutred men squatting around a massive dead animal whose gray and black mottled hide they were skinning off with sharp knives.

My feline attendants growled, a deep poignant rumble which snatched my attention back to present danger.

The big cats closed in, fangs glossy with spittle. It seemed almost as if they were eager for a definitive assessment by their masters of the paradox I represented.

I maintained my nerve, though every instinct pressed me to strike now, or turn and run for quarter to the men. I did neither. Gooseflesh pinching my spine, I strode with a display of confidence into the clearing.

By now the hunters were on their feet. Blood-dripping knives at the ready, they eyed me suspiciously, talking among themselves in low grunting tones. They fanned out in front of their kill.

"Bugger," said Alamogordo. "You're on your own, friend."

"What?" I muttered without moving my lips, approaching step by slow step. I had let the heavy stick fall to the ground, and kept my hands open and well away from the sword.

"I don't know that language. I took it for granted that I'd be able to translate for you, but my programming seems to have been less than exhaustive."

"Your what?"

"My . . . teachers must want to keep you on your toes. Sorry. I recommend maximum politeness."

One of the hunters, smaller and more fantastically fur-draped than the rest, cupped hands to mouth and uttered a weirdly mewing cry. The sound made my ears itch and my skin prickle. It had a galvanic effect upon the huge cats treading lightly at my flanks.

That to my right slipped closer, voicing unmistakable warning. I stopped dead.

That to my left bounded with terrifying speed to the mewing man. He kept his two smallest fingers in the corners of his mouth, stretching it wide, and continued with his eerie mewing song. The animal fawned at his feet as though listening studiously. When its master fell silent it growled a response.

The small man addressed his companions in the ugly grunting tongue of the hunters. They glanced meaningfully at the silver band wound at my belt.

"They speak with beasts," I said weakly.

"So?"

"With dumb animals!"

"The cats are not dumb," Alamogordo pointed out, puzzled. "You heard that one speak."

I shook my head in dismay. "Animals cannot speak. They have no souls."

"A curiously bigoted notion," the sword said chillingly. "I counsel you to retain such opinions in the secret of your bosom. Not everyone is as generous and forgiving as I."

This persiflage annoyed me, but I paid it scant notice, for voices were rasping in angry cacophony. Pale hairless faces darkened with emotion.

A fellow with broad flat features gestured impatiently. He roared out an order which brought several more hunters gliding from among the trees into the clearing. He spoke sharply to the beast-master, who lifted his wizened face to the sky and howled a piercing cat-cry.

Undergrowth rustled. Dry twigs and fallen branches crackled as five more of the beasts crashed out of the forest. In turn, each presented itself to the small man, growling a brutish report. That done, they took up positions at the shoulders of selected hunters.

In the laden silence, I examined my captors more closely.

Garish splashes of dye stained their fur garments yellow, crimson, purple, grass-green. Bone and ivory fastenings of bold, barbaric design looped thongs to hold tight the jackets and boots.

Most remarkable of all was their utter lack of hair, a trait common to them all, young as well as old. They ranged in age from the elderly cat-master to a fresh-faced scowler not far into adolescence; the rest were men just short of their middle years.

This silence lasted no more than ten heartbeats.

The leader stepped forward, shouted a question in a manner which suggested that I might do well to answer humbly and swiftly.

I shrugged, shook my head, stared back impassively. The fellow's mouth twisted. Brandishing a knife still gory from butchering, he hectored me again.

"Since I fail to understand your words," I said reasonably,

"it seems less than likely that you will understand mine. Can you speak the tongue of the Wanderers of the desert?"

They looked blankly at one another. The flat-featured man frowned, stepped three or four paces closer. It came to me that these hunters were more afraid of me alone than I was of all their group, fierce cats included.

"They take me for another," I said quietly.

"Plausible," Alamogordo whispered to my ear. "Of course your clothing is distinctive. How are they to know it is not your own?"

At the end of his patience, the leader abruptly yelled something across his shoulder. He stepped back.

The little beast-master mewed a sharp command.

Tensing, I drew my sword. The cats before me stood trembling where they were.

I had no chance to defend myself. A tremendously powerful blow struck my right arm from behind. Alamogordo fell from my paralyzed fingers.

Claws still sheathed, the great cat which had come like a thunderbolt from the forest at my back struck again. A stunning blow smashed the side of my head. I gasped, dropping like a stone, conscious of nothing in that final moment but the filthy, overwhelming stench of the creature's breath.

Cramp strangled me, from the tendons in my legs to my hunched shoulders.

I lay on my side in musty gloom, knees pressed hard against my chin, forearms bound against shins and lashed tightly to my ankles by strips of the metallic cloth.

I could breathe only in short rasping inhalations. It took all my energy to concentrate on forcing air into my compressed lungs and out again, while the throbbing agony in my bruised shoulder and cheek seemed likely to overwhelm me utterly.

Cat stink stifled me, like a putrid cloth draped over my head. Evidently the customary use for this rush-floored hut was as a kennel for the great hunting animals. It seemed likely that they fetched in with them their choicest morsels to gnaw in the boring stretches of the night when they could find no stranger to molest.

There were indications, as well, that the adage declaring against the fouling of one's own nest had never had much currency among these beasts.

I was in a loathsome mood.

Reddish light filtered weakly through chinks in the mud-caked thatch of the room, but it did little to illuminate my featureless cell. Thin cracks of orange daylight framed the doorway. Trussed as I was, I tried to jerk myself closer to it to gain a view of what lay beyond.

By a catastrophic burst of effort I succeeded in throwing myself on my right side. The pain was excruciating. It drove me once more to the brink of unconsciousness.

I lay gasping and sick, the damaged tissues of my face scratched by the rough, evil flooring, and there waited for the hunters to return. There was no telling what they would do to me. The only favorable aspect of the affair thus far was that they had declined to kill me out-of-hand.

In my misery, I found myself longing for the company of Alamogordo. Naturally, they had taken my sword, and I doubted I would ever again have the opportunity to speak with that peculiar intelligence.

Darkbloom had instilled into me, even when I was a child, a variety of disciplines for the conquest of pain, but I had never been so severely hurt before. With difficulty I found the word he had given me, its three meaningless syllables, and began to repeat them endlessly, muttering them to the beat of my hoarse, quick breaths.

The mind cannot long sustain a concentrated effort of attention on a single thought, a sole object, an unmodulated hum. It shucks off the object of its tedium and returns to its own pain and boredom. It was Darkbloom's special trick to deceive the mind by this very process into neglecting its own suffering: to run around and around that loop of weary dreariness and so forget itself.

After a time of this enforced meditation, I found a strange lassitude ebbing and flowing in warm waves through my distressed body. I sent myself afloat with it, severed the nerves of agony, projected the blurred focus of my awareness beyond myself.

Orange light flickered rhythmically. One of the cats paced up and down outside my prison.

Murmurs of women's high voices came and went. Shouts and wails of running children.

Another of the cats drowsed in the sun not far away. Its heavy purring made a relaxed drone which almost seemed to vibrate the adobe walls.

Wind shook leaves somewhere, gusted in cool draughts under the door.

Birds sang unfamiliar melodies; I distracted myself from my pain with their tunes, placing them carefully in my memory.

Water trickled in a creek nearby.

A scent of roasting meat wafted to my nostrils, returning my attention, against my will, to my own hungry, ill-used flesh.

I groaned and redoubled my efforts to break the bonds. All my twisting and rolling served merely to exacerbate my hurt. The metal thongs were irresistibly secure.

Over the next few hours, with the aid of Darkbloom's remedy, I kept the pain at a tolerable level. To my surprise I even managed to sleep.

A commotion woke me. Light was fading outside the hut. Men's gruff tones boomed. Women and children called and laughed. I heard the inhuman mew of beast-masters. Growling animals made the grass rustle as they stalked obediently into the settlement.

The wooden door flew open with a crash. Two brawny figures stood against ruby dusk; a cat behind them lashed its tail. I caught a flash of red from its huge hooded eyes.

I struggled to sit up.

The hunters strode into the hut, leaned across me, touched the bands in some obscure pattern. My arms and legs fell away from their cramped embrace, and fire surged along them as the muscles stretched. Even if I had been given the chance to escape, I was in no condition to attempt it.

One of the shadowed figures dragged my arms behind my back, snagged the metallic bands tight once more about my numb wrists. They jerked me to my feet and half carried me into the large paddock outside.

Dim as the evening's twilight was, I blinked a little. Circulation slowly revived in my limbs, and as it did so I walked on spear points.

I saw twenty or thirty rude dwellings. A considerable gathering moved to and fro among them. The inhabitants were uniformly pale and quite free of hair, and I do not exclude the women and toddlers.

That fact baffled me for a moment, until I learned to distinguish the females by their generally lesser stature and characteristic postures. Even so, by comparison with my own people, there was little distinction between the sexes: It was a matter of nuance. Like the men, the village women wore trappings of bright-stained fur.

Children and cat-cubs tumbled merrily together, until their racket grew so raucous that parents of both species cuffed them quiet, gazing stolidly at me as I stumbled by on aching legs. I must have seemed, to them, an outlandish sight.

My escort, I found, was dragging me to a wide, peak-roofed building at the end of a lane of packed dirt. The place smelled like any semipermanent gathering of my Wanderer nomads: sweat, food cooking, furs tanned and untanned; here there was cat piss instead of the dung of baluchitheriums and goats. I could not locate the jakes with my nose, though, and that surprised me.

I wrenched my neck around, searching. Something else I could not smell was smoke.

How, I asked myself, can meat cook without a fire? In all the clearing there was no campfire.

Light shone without flicker from within the big hut. An alcohol lamp, burning clean and steady? Yet that was not the answer to the secret of the ovens; my nose was acute enough to know that these people were braising their food without benefit of fuel. An absurdity, and it frightened me more, in its way, than my bondage.

The leader stood at the hut's opening, big arms folded across his big chest. His shadowed face looked as if it had been crushed flat in infancy: slab cheeks, nose splayed and wide.

My arms were released from their thongs. A bravo shoved me in the back. I fell on my face and lay there for a moment in great pain. A crowd of muttering, hostile shadows gathered behind me. Cats prowled here and there.

I struggled to my knees, and would have risen, but a boot nudged me warningly in the kidney. In fury and pain, I stared up at the chief. "Since we cannot understand each other, this seems an exercise in futility, you thrice-damned bald ape."

My recalcitrance, at least, survived the lack of translation. His thick hairless eyelids narrowed; he spat out an interrogative stream of gibberish.

When he saw that I was not able to answer, he turned with decision and went into the building. A moment later he returned with a large container wrought from the silvery metal. Yelling to the crowd, he drew from it my belt, still adorned with the stolen band. I guessed with a fatalistic plunge of my belly what the other hand must offer.

Those gathered at my back roared. It was a sound mingling reproof and a sort of sanctimonious bloodlust.

I stared up at the sunken eyes and idiot leer of the dead Rokhmun chieftain. The skin of the murdered man's face had shrunk slightly, tightening, like a mask of pale leather. He stank.

In a grotesque tableau, rich with some ritualistic or legal significance, the hunter stood for a moment of pent silence with his arms, and their evidence of my crimes, lifted above his head. The unflickering light at his back cut all humanity from his form, made him seem to me an icon of legendary vengeance.

He let his arms fall. Immediately, everyone began babbling and shrilling, all talking at once. I imagine that they were proposing suitable vexations for me.

Uncertain of the mood of the company, one cat-beast whined, scratching at the dirt.

Heated, sweating bodies moved closer to me. I felt their pressure, keeping my eyes fixed on the leader's naked features. The fellow glanced down at me in candid speculation. Throwing my belt back into his mesh bag, he swung the severed head by its braid, at arm's length, and rapped out an accusatory, hysterical demand. The crowd growled its approval.

I knew that words were useless, but I could not contain myself.

"The dead man is no concern of yours. Set me free! I would have asked your aid, in friendship. Now I demand my freedom, or you will know the wrath of my people!" Empty bombast, and foolish, but a man must speak while he has breath.

Before my words were done they had me by the arms, hoisted to my feet. For a pendulum beat the grisly trophy swung at the end of its braid. Contemptuously, the chieftain then released it, so that it flew to roll like a misshapen ball nearly to my feet.

"Return my sword," I shouted, "and you'll have a fight to send Darkbloom cowering in despair, you miserable grunting cat lovers."

The sky was quite dark now. Strangely, soft sources of light made themselves known in the high branches of certain trees, casting down over the assembly a mellow illumination like a dozen harvest moons caught up in the deep green foliage.

There was a stir behind me.

An old woman came out from the hut. She carried a great cloak of feathers, green and cinnabar, stitched in unpleasant emblems on a sheet of soft leather.

With full ceremony, the hunter chief received this vestment from her, draped it on his shoulders. His countenance became grave, the mask of a priest-king. He advanced from the yellow-lit doorway with slow, portentous steps.

My guards wrenched me about to face the gathering. They were not careful of my injuries. Pain blossomed at my bruised shoulder, threatened what remained of my self-control. I lost my legs for a moment, caught myself with my last reserves of dignity. Faces danced before me, white ovals in the spilling light from the temple.

A low rumble rose from the prowling cats, which seemed almost as numerous and engaged as the human hunters.

My moment, if ever there had been one, was gone. Judgment had been passed. It was a bitter discovery. I still had no clear idea of my transgression. There seemed not the slightest doubt, though, that summary justice was at hand.

"Alamogordo," I cried at the top of my voice, shameless in the face of death. "They are going to kill me! Advise me!"

I did not know where they had sequestered my blade, but it seemed likely that it was within the temple. It should have heard me. Had it spoken, I would certainly have heard its voice. My whirling mind told me that sound of an unknown voice from within their sacred building might be enough in itself to give the hunters pause.

Silence.

It seemed certain to me then, as it had in that penultimate moment of the storm with my baluchitherium dead at my feet, that I was about to die.

I found no comfort in the irony that I had tricked death on that occasion. My entrails squirmed. I was cold inside and out. Moisture began to burst out on my face and chest.

They were dragging me through patches of darkness and mild light to a huge old tree which towered at the clearing's edge. Its topmost leaves glimmered with a butter-yellow glow.

How could I act? I was surrounded by tough, brave men and women who patently wanted to see me dispatched. Beasts neither tigers nor jaguars, yet like both in their lethal capabilities, padded and snarled on every side.

Even if I could break my bonds, even if by some miracle I could overcome and evade my human captors, those beasts would hunt me down and tear my flesh from my bones before I was ten paces into the forest.

A bugle sounded, clear and haunting as the cry of a brass-throated bird.

I thought for a moment that it was some crazed trick of my sword's. But the sound had floated from beyond the nearest trees of the forest.

Its effect on the crowd was dramatic, all that could possibly be asked in a last-moment rescue. Everyone stopped in his tracks, looked at his neighbor in confusion and, I thought, trepidation.

Solemn in holy plumage, the leader broke step and turned his face to the west.

Stars shone bright above gnarled and leafy trees. Again the

bugle called, lofting across the intervening forest with its beautiful imperative.

Fingers slightly unsteady, the chief unhooked the thongs at his throat, let the gorgeous cloak slip from his shoulders. His elderly acolyte darted forward for it. The rest of them waited expectantly while he debated some somber issue deep within his breast.

Abruptly, with a quick sidelong glance at me, he rapped out an instruction to the beast-master and strode back to the big hut after a curt signal to my guards. The little fellow mewed softly to his cats, gathered them around him, several times repeating a brief message in their simple tongue.

The crowd dispersed, at once disappointed and animated. One of the women gave a stricken cry which transcended all language barriers. I found myself grinning broadly, no doubt from the rush of relief which loosened the fist-sized knot in my diaphragm. Like the woman, I had detected the pungent smoke of burning meat. She ran across the flat grass to attend to that practical task.

I caught one last view of proceedings at the edge of the forest before I was yanked around and directed back to my prison:

Straining in their impatience, three of the giant cats growled a response to their master. He clapped his hands briskly and let them go. They sprang like golden wraiths into the forest, lovely and formidable, bodies rippling, and in a moment had vanished in the direction of the unseen bugler.

SEVEN

Clatter of hooves woke me from a fitful doze; that, and the nervous whinny of a horse paced by large carnivores.

This time the hunters had refrained from trussing me like a plucked fowl, contenting themselves with a sturdy band at my ankles. My arms remained tied behind my back. I jackknifed across the unpleasant floor, pressed my face to the crack which edged the door.

The illumination in the tops of the trees had been quenched. Light still swathed a strip of clearing outside the entrance to the big hut. A number of fur-wrapped hunters stepped from shadow and strode toward the approaching rider.

Here was a curious and provocative fact: When they shouted wary greeting, they were answered by a low sonorous call in quite a different, more melodious tongue. Further exchanges took the same form, without any obstacle to mutual comprehension. Yet I felt sure that few if any of these insular, prickly folk would feel at ease in the argot, let alone the language, of another. This was, of course, no more than a fleeting and inconclusive perception.

The steed halted outside my narrow field of vision. His rider dismounted with a jangle of metal, a creak of leather.

I cursed and hitched myself higher, pushing my cheek beside a slightly wider crack. Unavoidably, my bruised shoulder scraped rough-hewn timber; stabbing pain made me wince. All my body was protesting. My belly grumbled. I badly needed to evacuate my bowels. I tried to ignore these internal messages and peered from the side of my eye into the clearing.

A tall person in elegant but sturdy equestrian apparel crossed

89

the long bar of light, leading a horned milk-white steed. I looked more carefully.

Yes. My inadvertent rescuer was a woman.

Several hunters escorted her, showing every courtesy. Their group was flanked by the three watchful cat-beasts. The stranger took these attentions diffidently. It was only after they passed from view that I realized how weary she had looked.

Hope rekindled in a rush.

Beyond doubt, the horsewoman's garb was far closer in style and make to mine, bequeathed me by my unknown benefactor, than to the garish furs of my captors. Was she therefore the agent of the wizard or demon who had fetched me here from my own wintry country?

In my innocence, it did not even occur to me that the sword Alamogordo might have summoned her on my behalf. My sentiment toward that gifted artifact would have been more cordial had I guessed.

Voices lost definition. Light winked out as the door of the chief's hut closed.

Wind gusted high above, shaking the forest to its somber song. Over the rest of the camp, silence prevailed. No human guards made their turns in the empty clearing.

I let my eyes close in the darkness, listening to my stomach whine. Several handfuls of berries and fruit had been my last meal, and I was more than a little thirsty.

Above all, I was desperate to be free of my bonds.

The guards had released the thongs from my wrists by pressing at a sequence of distinct points. A hazy physical image began to form, constituted more by memories of touch than of sight.

Under normal conditions it should have been the work of a moment to bring my feet up to my hands, pent behind my back. Now, though, I was severely bruised, my limbs were stiff and wooden from the ill effects of restricted circulation, my fingers clumsy.

I maneuvered across the rushes, got the soles of my feet against one wall. Squirming backward, I reached without much feeling for my heels. I panted and grunted, snared the heel of my right buskin.

Almost at once, cramp began to stiffen my legs, forcing my toes together in a spasm of agony. I contracted muscles one by one, pushing blood into the constricted tissues as Darkbloom had taught me. My fingers curled into the awkward positions necessary to reach the pressure points of my bonds.

The cool fabric was marked by slight depressions, where symbols were stamped; I had seen these on the cat's brand. It was these the hunters had caressed to release me. I loosened my mind, gave over my fingers into a mimicry of memory.

Cramps again and again. I ceased my experiments but would not relinquish the painful posture. Breathing in a slow, careful rhythm, I quieted the pulse beating at my temples. The cramps eased. I probed once more at the thong.

This cycle of pain and semirelaxation grew more and more oppressive. There is a kind of tense frustration, akin to the claustrophobia of being trapped in tight confinement, which is more galling and unendurable than the cruel pangs of a wound; this, I understand, is the basis for most successful torture. I was almost at the point of abandoning my efforts, with a scream of rage, when the band went slack. My legs were free.

And where had this achievement got me, in all honesty?

I lay on my back and stared at the dark roof, while blood tingled and burned in my limbs. Still my hands were of no use to me. At length I rose to my haunches, stood and examined my prison as best I could without light.

The walls were solid timber, chinked here and there but sturdy nonetheless. Given time, I might kick loose a board from the wall; obviously there was no way to accomplish this without waking the entire camp.

Nothing could be gained in the direction of the door; it was fastened on the other side by a stout drop-bar.

Only the mud-and-grass-thatched roof offered any hope, and with arms bound as they were I could discern no way to reach it.

I picked out a spot near the door and sat down there. The next pair of hunters who came arrogantly through it would pay a poignant price for their cavalier treatment; this resolve made me grin wolfishly.

My mentor Darkbloom had not been a pacifist. I had learned

from him a variety of tricks by which an armed attacker might be immobilized by an unarmed man. Now I was literally un-armed, but I vowed that if these hunters offered me further threat at least one or two of them would never again hear a woman cry out in passion.

The darkness of prison is no time for such gruesome night thoughts. This vivid fantasy stirred me to a pitch of ven-geance, and then left me to fall into despair and self-accusa-tion.

What had become of Darkbloom's persuasive teachings, that I was eager, and so quickly eager, to delight in the prospect of injuring a fellow human?

It was true that I had shamed my vow with blood. Was a single transgression sufficient to make me forget all my ideals?

I lowered my chin to my breast, shivering, and brooded in the dark. Whether or not I tried to deny it, I felt that some wicked heritage had been wakened within me. It was that ele-ment which my father had rightly recognized: the spirit, as he had dubbed it, of a mighty slayer.

The door of the long hut opened to a mutter of dissenting voices. The visitor's firm contralto cut through the dispute. I got quickly to my feet. One or two of the hunters made for my cell.

Troubled by doubts, I waited tensely for them to open the door.

The factor of surprise would be in my favor. The prospect of revenge beguiled me still; I dismissed it, for two reasons. Beyond its unworthiness was its irrelevance to my overriding concern, freedom and escape. Maiming and emasculating sev-eral of the lesser troops would hardly help me avoid the larger threat, the great cats.

In contrast, a display of passive cooperation would earn me time, perhaps, to enlist the visitor's support—and to get back my sword.

This logic irked me. Even so, I stepped back from the door-way and waited cautiously against the farther wall.

The bar-lock slid free. Two men stepped inside. One of them bore a small light-emitting crystal.

Their jaws dropped comically when they saw me partly free. Shrugging, I stepped forward and waited.

The guard with the magical light gave his companion an impressed glance and grunted a command at me, with more respect in his tone than I'd yet heard. He gestured his intentions with a jerk of his bald head.

Seeing the door open before me, I was nearly overwhelmed by the impulse to strike and run. Instead, I did as I was urged. Flanked by the hunters I stepped into the fresher air of the night and walked slowly back to the chief's hut.

Its interior was bright with yellow artificial light. I frowned, blinking against it.

Simple, strikingly vivid tapestries hung on the rough-hewn walls. Skins of exotic beasts lay scattered on the floor. Of all the furs I saw among these people, the rugs alone were splendid in their own muted natural hues and markings.

Benches and trestles were laden with the scraps of a feast on handsome stoneware plate. They stood to the sides of the structure, leaving the centre of the main room clear.

Here were gathered the hunter chief, a handful of his subordinates, and the elegantly attired visitor. With a shock of irrational relief and pleasure I saw that unlike the rest she was not bald and hairless. Red hair fell thick and straight to her shoulders from a parted line which crossed the crown, leaving a fringe to curve forward above her tanned forehead. It was almost a shock to look into blue eyes darkly lashed, lightly browed. I found her face plain, intelligent, calm: an encouraging face in such circumstances.

The escort made a show of bravado as they thrust me forward into the circle, then took themselves off to stand by the door.

I regarded the remainder with no show of emotion, studying them.

As yet, the patterns of deference were unclear. By his slightly stiff posture, I judged that the flat-featured leader was no longer wholly in command of the situation. Of course, that had been implicit from the start. The very blare of the horse-woman's bugle had been enough to call a halt to my execution. Still, a subtle tension in the visitor's insouciance revealed that when all was said and done, she was equally unsure of her authority.

I relaxed fractionally. This unspoken strain promised me advantage, if I proved astute enough to grasp it.

A scowl brought the leader's hairless brows together. In an unthinking parody of my own constrained stance, he clasped his hands behind his back and leaned forward, rapping out a question in his guttural tongue. I sighed.

"We have already established that we cannot understand each other's words." The visitor watched my response with interest. I met her stare. "What of you, rider of the horned steed? Do you know the Wanderers' argot? Or perhaps," and I shifted to that patois, "the trade lingo of Berb-Kisheh?"

She pursed her lips in a silent whistle of surprise. Evidently she intuited the drift of my question, for she shrugged, smiling. In the melodic tongue I had heard her use in the clearing, she addressed several words to the chief. His eyes moved to a device resting near us on a dark-stained trestle: ovoid, inert, dully gleaming. Grudgingly, he gave her leave.

She stepped quickly to the table, scooped up the device. It sent a shiver through me. Even though the thing had no obvious function, it had the look of a tool from the Black Time.

The rider brought it close to my face. I flinched away despite myself, but submitted sullenly when it did me no immediate harm.

Suddenly my sight blurred. I thought I was falling, and my bound arms tried to reach for support. My ears roared with a screaming babble of voices which were not in the room, a torrent of sounds which might have been the crashing of a high waterfall.

When the room came once more into focus, the visitor was carefully replacing the instrument.

"His speech represents a different language group entirely," the woman was saying in her soft, implacable voice. "It is as different from yours and mine as ours are one from the other."

"Then where is he from? Unlike you, he had no steed."

"As I suggested, Oak-is-Strong, he is obviously from some very distant land, borne here by one of the ancient transportation devices. It is not impossible that he is from beyond the sky itself.''

"That's as may be," grunted the chief, and to my amazement I understood what he said even though he continued to speak in his own narrow language; "he must nevertheless face the Test of Hunters, in satisfaction for his trespass. I had thought him one of your people, under your protection. For this reason alone have we postponed his rigors.''

"Oak-is-Strong, the fellow was acting in ignorance! Look at him. How could he know of your prohibitions when he was unprepared in this most elementary matter of the translation of speech?''

I could scarcely believe what was happening. Her language, too, was unaltered, its melody as gracious as before. Yet I followed her words, I knew what she was saying, as if I had conversed in her tongue since infancy.

"He has dared enter the Forest of the People without seeking our permission." Oak-is-Strong was adamant. "He profanes the ground where no stranger may walk without escort—''

"Your Law cannot hold him to account for a crime he did not know he was committing." The woman was keeping her temper in check, but this was clearly no matter of idle debate with her.

"We did not slay him when we might have done," Oak-is-Strong said in a growl. "The purpose of the Test is precisely to determine his degree of culpability. In any event, his simple presence within the Forest is not the whole of our complaint. You forget the murdered hunting cat.''

"I took it for a wild beast," I burst out. "The animal gave me no opportunity to do other than defend myself.''

"There!" the woman cried. "You see? To the ignorant, your cat would indeed seem a wild beast, ferocious and frightening, to be avoided if possible, slain if necessary." She glanced at me from the side of her eye, warning me to hold my tongue. "Indeed, his courage in tackling such a terrible creature with only a sword is estimable.''

Maintaining her reserve, she moved to my side; she no longer smiled. "But as you see, the fellow is now capable of responding to your questions. Ask him. If his answers are unsatisfactory, proceed with the Test. But mark you, Oak-is-Strong''—she locked eyes with the hunger—''I would have him safe and whole if your Law will allow it. He may be an appropriate object of my quest.''

I had been listening to this, I confess, through a mist of incredulity. One lesson I have learned in my peculiar wanderings is that one astounding wonder does not mitigate the shocking impact of the next.

"Explain this marvel," I insisted. "I hear your true words and they are no more than noise to me, and yet—"

"Yet your mind takes up our meaning," the horsewoman said. "Naturally. Until now, the communication field was not attuned to your linguistic matrix, only to my own and that of the People. I have attended to that detail, and thus you hear and speak through its medium." She fell silent, searching my face. "Surely one who comes from . . . far away . . . should be familiar with the device? Or have you other and more sophisticated means to deal with strangers, now removed from your possession?"

She could only mean my sword, but how was she to know of its sentience? Discretion rather than candor was indicated. I glowered at the floor.

Oak-is-Strong took this for insolence.

"Answer when you are addressed, criminal! Where are you from? Why do you come skulking through the forbidden Forest of the People?"

I raised my eyes, felt my quick temper flare. There was no reply I might give which would not betray me. The rules of this interrogation eluded me. I let my anger speak.

"Release me instantly!" My voice carried a sharper note, now I knew that what I said would be understood. "My name is Xaraf Golan's son, lastborn of Golan, who is chief of the Firebridge Tribe in Kravaard." I turned deliberately away from Oak-is-Strong to the coolly smiling visitor. "I have given my name freely. I would know yours."

The hunters shifted uneasily. Clearly I had slighted their leader's dignity. Oak-is-Strong made to move, lifting a fist, his face a study in controlled emotion. He hesitated as the woman reached out and placed her hand on my left shoulder.

"You are correct, Xaraf. Our host here is Chief Oak-is-Strong, lord of the Forest People. I am Glade Month/Five Day/Eight Resilience, always trader and latterly quester, from the Plains city Asuliun the Gray." She refrained from naming the other hunters; circumstances were, after all, hardly those of a social gathering. She looked piercingly at me. "Although we have not met before, Xaraf, I believe we share an acquaintance."

I could not credit such a thing. Only one name came to mind. "Might this be Darkbloom, my teacher and adviser?" It seemed just remotely possible.

"This is not a name I recognize," Glade said. "No, I was thinking of our friend Alamogordo." I stared at her. "In fact, he and I were engaged in a rather diverting conversation just before I entered the Forest to make my usual trading call on the People."

"Rather ahead of time," Oak-is-Strong grumbled, happy to have some cause on which to vent his spleen. "You would be advised to keep to the agreed timetable."

"What is a day or two between friends?" Glade asked airily. "Doubtless," she added plausibly, to me, "your presence in the Forest can be explained without offense to our hosts."

Oak-is-Strong was unmoved by these pleasantries. "The intruder's presence is itself the offense."

He pulled a bench to him and sat down. The rest of us were left standing, leaving him, as he had intended, the advantage. His pale features made a severe contrast to Glade's sunburned countenance. Where hers showed a temperament at once wry and sensitive, the hunter was uncompromisingly stolid, inflexible, and blunt.

"If my presence is what concerns you," I shouted back at Oak-is-Strong, "the condition is easily remedied. Release me and I shall depart."

"Not without expiation, if then!" roared Oak-is-Strong. "You have slain Mraowla the Swift, and must be punished for that blasphemy."

"The beast attacked me without warning. I had no recourse but to defend myself."

"Naturally Mraowla attacked you. He saw that you were a criminal and acted accordingly."

The unreason of Oak-is-Strong's indictment made the skin creep on my back. "You know nothing of me. By what logic did your animal discern what is not the case, that I am a criminal?"

The hunter lost his temper. "Are you mentally deficient? Your intrusion into the Forest was your crime." He stood up, curtly signaled the guards at the door. "Take him back to his cell. The fool's insolence galls me."

Glade stepped hastily into the path of the guards. She held up a hand. "My friend Oak-is-Strong—reconsider. Do you not see that if Xaraf is indeed a visitor from another world, both his attitude and crimes can be forgiven as the understandable defect of one deprived of knowledge of your customs?" The room crackled. "Shall we not probe the matter more deeply?"

Muscles at Oak-is-Strong's jaw stood out.

"Lady Glade," he said, with alarming softness, "you risk your prerogatives in interfering thus. Our most sacred laws have been infringed. The administration of justice in such a case is the privilege and duty of the People alone. Still . . ." He sat down again, rubbing his jaw. "Your objection might conceivably be relevant." To the guards he said, "Return for the moment to your posts."

My own patience was very nearly exhausted. The metal mesh bonds, flexible as they were, rubbed my wrists raw. I was light-headed with hunger, my bowels pressed, my injuries pained me.

"I will answer no further questions," I said clearly, "unless I am accorded the minimum decencies. Untie me, direct me to your jakes, fetch me food and drink. Or you can search in Black Hell for your answers."

Unexpectedly, Oak-is-Strong gave me a hard smile. "Very well; we would not have you thwart justice by fainting during the Test. Do not consider this leniency an opportunity for escape, however; you would be cut down at once like a dog."

A hunter released me, led me outside to a small structure

wherein stood a seatlike bowl into which, I was made to understand, I should defecate. I did so, to my enormous and noisy relief, and received a rude shock a moment later when my bare arse was flooded with a jet of warm water. I leapt from the seat, britches tangled around my knees, and was brought out into the night, wet and cross, by a hooting hunter.

Viands awaited me. I sat at a bench, rubbing at my wrists, and looked at the fragrant meats and vegetables before me. None were remotely familiar.

"I can recommend the pale wine," Glade told me. "It sets off the fowl nicely."

"Thank you." I set to. The fare was excellent, if strangely spiced.

The wizened beast-master regarded me with antagonism.

"Oh my Chief," he said, "it pains me to see this lout fed at our table. Let us bandy no more words with the impertinent creature. He must explain instantly the odious purpose behind his intrusion, and then be returned to confinement."

"I shall be the judge of correct procedure," Oak-is-Strong told him in some irritation. "We owe the Lady Glade a debt. Granting her the chance to interrogate this fellow will discharge it at no vital cost to the People."

"You are generous." The horsewoman inclined her head, and I thought her expression more than faintly sardonic. Perhaps, though, that was merely the trader's weariness. From her drawn countenance it seemed that she must have traveled for an extended period without rest. Called through some occult means by my sword?

If so, Alamogordo must have sent out its summons at the moment we made contact with the hunters poised over their kill, if not before. A prudent intelligence for a lethal weapon.

I ate hungrily, musing in this manner, lingering over the fine wine.

At last I pushed my plates aside. "Ask your questions."

Glade was containing some excited emotion. Anticipation? But of what? "Xaraf," she said, "I would advise probity and directness in your answers."

"This is my invariable practice," I told her, "when I am among friends."

"Despite appearances, we are not your enemies. Very well. In the first place: Are you a native of this world, or do you come from some other?"

The question struck me as absurd. There was *the* world and no other, unless one gave credence to an afterlife.

And yet . . . I could not forget those dislocated constellations, those burning miniature sunlets, that sullen dying sun. If this was *the world,* it had been changed monstrously in the span of a night.

I gripped the edge of the bench with a hand that still prickled slightly from its ill-treatment. Glade's question was, in truth, the vital one. It slipped past my defenses, caused me to reply more openly than I had intended.

"I do not know. My world has one sun only, and that a fierce bright orb. The stars in this sky are differently disposed. Many of the beasts are unfamiliar. How this can be is beyond me."

All trace of weariness was now gone from the horsewoman's face. Her strong intentness stood in contrast to Oak-is-Strong's uncertainty. With the exception of the beastmaster, who pretended disbelief, the other hunters glanced at one another in fear and fascination.

"You cannot remember the method of your coming to this world?" asked Glade. "What of your craft, your companions? Surely you recall some detail, no matter how minor."

"I had no—craft." What hell boat could traverse the metaphysical gulfs between worlds? I did not take her meaning. "There was a storm," I said, honestly searching my clouded memory. "In its midst I found a white sphere of flameless light. It sang to me with a high, unearthly hum. I was near death from exposure. I tumbled from a cliff, fell into it, awoke just beyond this forest." I said nothing about those intervening hours I could not recapture, when my wet garments had been replaced.

The horsewoman's whisper was barely audible: "An interstellar gate. Oh, you lovely man, what riches have you brought us? That secret has been lost from Earth for a hundred thousand years." She seemed ready to embrace me.

Oak-is-Strong showed grudging interest. "What secret is that?"

Glade Month/Five Day/Eight Resilience sank down onto an uncushioned bench, drew a flagon of wine to her, sloshed the pale green liquid into a goblet of worked metal, drained it. Her eyes shone.

"The transference gate, Chief Oak-is-Strong. Do your legends not speak of it?"

"We are concerned only with our sacred Forest," the beastmaster told her sententiously. "With our cats to guard us we have no need of gates."

"No, no," Glade said. "I speak of a system of transport whereby one might be taken in the twinkling of an eye from one place to another far distant."

Not to be outdone in piety, Oak-is-Strong growled, "The People of the Forest have no call to leave their own domain. Such a device would possess no attractions for us."

"Ah, well." Glade sat back, hugging one leather-clad knee. "Even among folk less aloof than you Forest hunters, the device is remembered only as a thing of fable." She looked at me with a measure of eagerness unfitting in a canny merchant. But then, there was no risk to her in tipping her hand; I was marked for chastisement in any event. "Fable no longer! Now we have evidence of its existence. More: We have a man who can take us to it, show us a path from this exhausted planet."

I shook my head. "The sphere is gone. Indeed, when I awoke—"

The cat-master cut me short with a hysterical outburst. "Unholy! Blasphemy!" He was a fanatic, the worst of men, as Darkbloom had taught me. "O Chief, these outlanders tempt us with seeds of destruction. If what they say is not malicious falsehood, as seems likely . . ."

"Why should I mislead you, Oak-is-Strong?" Glade cried indignantly.

" . . . the danger is worsened a thousandfold," the wizened creature went on triumphantly. "They beguile us with change, disruption, the cursed alteration of true and ancient custom."

He seemed set on a full-scale denunciation. His leader cut him short.

"Enough, Winter-is-Chill! We are well aware of the hazards of change. I seek to know of this device solely to determine the criminal's origin. Justice must be served."

"The integrity of the People and our customs is a preemptive value."

"By the nature of things, justice and custom cannot conflict."

Winter-is-Chill muttered, "Once already you have put tradition in jeopardy."

One of the lieutenants spoke icily. "Hunter, you forget your station." Oak-is-Strong's face was wrathful. "Our liaison with Asuliun the Gray is essential to the People. Would you have us break the ancient commandment by lighting fire? Without fresh power cells, how would we eat? Light our homes? Maintain warmth in winter? For shame!"

The chief stood, raised his white, thick-fingered hands.

"There is no need for justification. If Winter-is-Chill questions my leadership, he must feel ready to challenge my leadership." His voice cracked like a lash. "Eh? Speak, hunter! Declare yourself."

The fanatic cringed away from this ferocity.

"O Chief, such heresy is furthest from my mind. I spoke merely from an excess of zeal."

"Your zeal is praiseworthy." Oak-is-Strong resumed his seat. "The excess provokes you to offense. Sit. Let there be no repetition of this performance." He dismissed the matter coldly, turned to me. "Is the Lady Glade correct? Did you travel here in a transference device?"

"I have told you what I know, which is little enough. Certainly that would account for what occurred."

"If you came to this world by accident," prompted Glade, "you could have had no improper intention in entering the Forest of the People."

I tasted a gourd containing a bitter intoxicant, put it aside with a grimace. "I have already stated my innocence. The sphere of light deposited me in the midst of an open field. I was without food or drink. I came to the forest to find running water. Naturally, my purpose was to seek out the closest settlement, request aid, and do what I could to find my way home."

"Mother of Cats!" Oak-is-Strong sucked at his lip. "Your defense is novel, criminal. What you claim is so implausible it might well be true, else your audacity is unprecedented." These people were deficient as well, I decided, in skilled tale-tellers. Every night around the fire I had heard and relished more ludicrous accounts than mine, among the drolls and jongleurs of the Wanderers. Oak-is-Strong mused, and his flat face innocently reflected the contrary sentiments which tugged at him.

"I judge that he speaks truly," said Glade. "If so, my quest is here fulfilled."

"How so? He is our prisoner."

"My proposal is this." Now Glade's professional manner returned to her. Diffidently, putting her drinking vessel aside with a negligent hand, she told Oak-is-Strong, "If your tradition allows a pardon for inadvertent trespass, I will personally make good the loss of the hunting cat."

"What are your terms for this restitution?"

Glade was magnanimous. "Let this man go with me and you shall have one season's supply of power cells in exchange."

"Two seasons' supply," rapped the Chief.

The beast-master leaped up, face mottled. "Mraowla was no filthy item of commerce to be bartered for a carton of batteries!"

Oak-is-Strong bunched his shoulders; the deltoids stood out like blocks carved from wood. He swung his squat head in a slow survey of his men's reactions to the proposal. What he saw was not encouraging. He fixed his gaze on me. I looked back as levelly as I might, but I knew I was a dead man.

"Winter-is-Chill is right," he told Glade. "This Xaraf must face the Test of the Hunters." He paused. "Of course if the criminal survives the ordeal, he will be banished from the forest. In such an eventuality, you may make your own arrangements with him. Provisionally, however, your offer is accepted. If Xaraf lives, you will forfeit a year's exchange value."

Glade swallowed, tightened her lips.

Oak-is-Strong stood, now impassive. The rest rose with him. The horsewoman said nothing. Her sun-darkened face was flushed. The trader had been so effortlessly bested at her own art that I nearly laughed aloud at the gallows humor of it.

"Take the criminal to his cell," Oak-is-Strong ordered. "He will face the Test at dawn. See this time that he is provided with the amenities."

I was marched without ceremony back to the stinking hut. Two of the great cats were stationed at the door.

The guards brought me a pile of sleeping furs, water in a wide shallow dish shaped from a huge gourd. They loosened my bonds, stood over me while I performed my ablutions. The water was chilly and refreshing, tart with minerals. A tiny light-crystal threw distorted shadows on the rough walls.

When I was done the hunters bound me securely, arms folded across my chest. One of them placed the gourd in one corner, presumably for me to lap from if thirst took me uncontrollably. Perhaps by the same token I was meant to piss into my boots. They went away.

The cats groaned ominously beyond the locked door. My shoulder ached. I lay on the soft furs, eyes open and sleepless, staring into the unhelping dark.

EIGHT

A phosphorescent insect buzzed insistently about my face, which was peculiar since I had seen no other insect in this world. I tried to raise my hand to brush it away, but my arm would not move. With a jolt I woke, opened my eyes.

Someone was whispering my name. A narrow beam of light shone on my face through a chink in the wall.

"Who calls?"

"Sit up if you can," said a soft contralto. "Bring your mouth to the chink and keep your voice low. It is Glade Resilience."

I moved without notable noise across the pile of furs. The trader masked the light with her fingers; a red glow now indicated the gap in the timbers.

"Do you plan to release me?"

"Impossible. The cats watch your cell. Even in this area, at the rear of the kennels, I am far from safe. I cannot linger."

"The roof."

"Too noisy. Listen carefully. You are shortly to undergo a species of divination. Unaided, your chances of survival are negligible."

"What is its nature?"

The trader gave a terse hiss. "You will learn soon enough. Suffice that I shall attempt to rescue you. The risk will still be great. You must stand ready for my intervention."

I interrupted her. "The hunters hold my sword. I am reluctant to lose it. Can you obtain it for me before we depart?"

Glade laughed softly. "Our mutual friend? I'll do what I can. Pay attention now, here is the crucial element. I am about to thrust a small phial through this aperture. Place your lips against the wall and catch the phial as I drop it. Do you understand?''

The notion seemed to smack of farce, but I had no choice. "Yes."

"Whatever happens, you must not break the phial until I give the word." Her whispered voice was intent, strained. "It contains vapors which, by themselves, are toxic in the extreme. At the appropriate time, on my instruction, fracture the capsule with your teeth, inhale the gas, spit out the broken shell. If swallowed, the fragments will rupture your internal organs. Now, put your mouth to the chink.''

A warm slick object touched my lips. My nose and chin struck the rough boards unhandily, making it difficult for me to maneuver the capsule into my mouth.

I probed at it with my tongue. Sweat sprang out on my forehead. The object slid to the edge of my mouth, teetered. I eased my face down the wall. A splinter entered my cheek.

Beyond the door a cat stirred, groaning. Wind blew through the chink, making my eyes water. I drew my head away from the timbers. The phial hung between my lips, slipped free, fell into the darkness.

Glade heard my curse. "Do you have it?" she asked anxiously.

"Play your light through the hole. The damned thing has fallen among my sleeping furs."

The trader added her own curse. "Do you smell a sharp bitter odor? If so, move at once to the farthest corner of the cell and hold your breath."

I tested the air. "Nothing but cats. Can you brighten the light?"

"Our danger is correspondingly enhanced. Still . . ." The beam intensified, cast a bar of gold which splashed a circle in the center of the hut. I bent with excruciating delicacy, found the phial nestling in a fold of shadowed fur.

I crept backward on my knees, leaned over until I had the thing in my mouth. My shoulder throbbed. The phial slipped under my tongue and stayed there. "I have it," I mumbled.

"Say nothing more. I fear the beasts grow suspicious. I

shall look to Alamogordo if the opportunity is right. Until the ceremony, Xaraf, farewell.''

The light vanished. Glade slipped away with a stealth equal that of the great hunting cats she sought to elude.

I lay back in the soft, faintly dusty furs and attempted to relax. The exercises taught me by Darkbloom would quickly have returned me to sleep, but with this poisonous thing squeezed under my tongue that was the last thing I wished to do.

So I sought instead that state of profound restfulness once readily evoked in me by contemplation of the Oneness of Life. This too I failed to achieve; my betrayal of that principle haunted me, caused me to wonder whether this entire extraordinary situation was perhaps my punishment, decreed by the powers of life and darkness.

In my fitful state the memory of a dream stole over me, a dream from my young manhood.

Above the nest of a bird of God, matted and shit-slimed, a huge droop-feathered creature hovered, beating at the air with molting wings. Down it settled, cruel claws closing under its belly, and warmed to life the egg beneath its breast. I swam within that egg, yet two fish moved there, identical, passing and curving in the sluggish waves of the egg's curdled yellowish soup. One fish turned, teeth bared, and rent the other, eating its scaled silver flesh. This first fish grew powerfully while its brother bled, and disdained the wormed hook which dangled invitingly to their pool. A great black hooded hunter sat beyond the boundaries of the stream, sending down his line again and again. The lesser fish, fleeing in dread, tangled itself in the line. Its hook pierced me. I cried out, and my words were bubbles of useless blood in the dark soil all grown about with fleshy flowers hungry for the light.

''How did he escape?'' I had mumbled, waking after that terrible dream with my hair in the cold ashes of Darkbloom's fire.

''None escape,'' my wakeful mentor said with a sepulchral laugh. He rolled his eyes. ''Have you been dreaming again, warrior?''

"A fish," I said.

He lost his arch grin and peered at me seriously.

"Who is this fish, Xaraf?"

"Tell me."

"Where do they swim?"

"In the egg, of course." Then I halted, baffled and foolish. "I mentioned one fish only, Darkbloom. Is this dream one of your sendings?"

He touched my hand lightly. There was gooseflesh at its back.

"Attend to it, boy. What does the fish say?"

" 'I would kill you and have what is in your guts for my supper.' "

"Which fish is this?"

"Why, the stronger. The elder brother."

"Which fish are you, Xaraf?"

I glanced at him slyly. "This is a trap you cannot lure me into. Is it not your teaching that I am both fishes, and the water, and the black fisher, and—" My tongue stumbled. *"You are the fisher, and the bird."*

"Some dreams point to those things beyond us," Darkbloom said, munching his words. He was busy boiling up some water over his rekindled fire, and chewed on a dried strip of meat to break his fast. "Perhaps I am in your dream. Or perhaps it is merely a bird of God."

I shuddered. "So I am the fish which failed to get away."

"Here you are. You may leave at any moment. I am just a smelly old eunuch, after all."

"And the greater fish is my enemy."

"Do you have an enemy, Xaraf?"

My eyes lost their focus, and I looked into the crackling morning flames.

"You know I have an enemy, Darkbloom. This is your dream. I know your dreams, now. He is my great foe, whom you made me swear not to kill. He is my brother." Tears, suddenly and unexpectedly, forced themselves through my hard-blinked eyes. "He has escaped the hook, and I must kill him."

Darkbloom seized my jaw with his hard fingers, turned my

face to his. His hair was matted and thin, like the stinking feathers of a molting bird.

"We are each of us on a hook. Even the immortal gods are impaled, twisting on a thread dangled by the stars. He has not escaped it. And you must not kill him. Disarm him, yes, that will be your duty. Cast him from the sky. Hurl him from the waters that he breathes. Do you hear me, warrior?"

I could hardly fail to hear him. He was bellowing fit to wake all Firebridge, where they stirred in the camp well beyond his dirty humpy. But I did not understand him. Even after his dream had come to me again and again, so that I woke choking with the yolky waters of that battleground, even then I knew only that my enemy waited and circled and avoided the line from which he had slipped free, upon which I was bloodily gaffed.

Dawn had not yet washed away the stars when my door was thrown open. Bald-headed men entered with the solemnity of nightmare to remove the thongs from my legs, though not from my arms, and lead me into the cold clearing.

Cats prowled, blinking and yawning. Yellow light glowed from the chief's building. By a paradox, I found this a heart-warming sight.

A hairless, naked child ventured from one of the huts and stared at me with great eyes before pulling her thumb from her mouth and running squealing back inside. Perhaps her mother was one of the women who shuffled between dwellings with gourds of river water perched on their pale skulls.

The phial pressed the pouch of my cheek, lethal as a pluto; and as huge, to the amplifying touch of my tongue, as an auk's egg.

The sunlets rose, their blinding force diminished by the heavy foliage of the trees. Oak-is-Strong emerged from his temple-dwelling, gorgeous in the cloak of plumes. He cried out in a deep voice, priestly, authoritative. Without fuss the hunters gathered before him on the packed-dirt lane.

I looked around surreptitiously for Glade. There was no sign of her. Perhaps custom, I thought, excluded strangers from the Test. All, of course, but the stranger waiting to be tested.

This time I was able to follow the proceedings. Oak-is-Strong looked down at me, and his flat face might have been a bas-relief cut from marble by some ascetic. "Attend, criminal!"

"Do not call me criminal. I deny your accusations," I said. This earned me a buffet I could have done without.

"Know that you have offended custom and the Law of the People. We proceed now to the Test of the Hunters. If you survive this mortification, it will be seen that justice acquits you. In the case of guilt, failure carries its own sanction. Let it begin!"

Instantly I was seized and frog-marched, as on the previous evening, toward the vast old tree at the clearing's edge. Ritual was, it seemed, among these hunters brief and to the point.

Oak-is-Strong led the procession, his green and cinnabar cloak magnificent in the early light. The crowd pressed my heels. Cats roamed ahead, their tawny fur glossy over gliding muscle.

Where it could be seen, the tremendous trunk was gray and ridged, roots rising from the soil like buttresses. It wore a mossy coat of blooming lichens which lent it a velvet sheen of purple, ocher, and amber. It was a beautiful, formidable thing, a god of the forest. Vastly high overhead its branches spread mantling arms; leaves like platters shredded the post-dawn light to flashes of gold and blue.

My guards stepped with care over the gnarled roots, working quickly, averting their faces from the lichens. I was trussed to the base of the giant tree by chains of silver metal looped about its girth. I leaned at an uncomfortable angle, head and shoulders pressed into the soft embrace of the mosses. My mouth seemed swollen; I fought an impulse to swallow the capsule, stared malevolently instead at the bright-clad gathering.

Now an acolyte scurried to the chief's side and handed him a huge crested helmet. Oak-is-Strong settled it over his head, drew the feathered cloak about him, and was revealed as a terrible bird of prey. I found my thoughts drifting, my attention diffused. The helmet was the head of a fantastic eagle. Eyes flashed ruby flame; beak curved dreadfully, all of gold;

crest rose in spurs of hyacinthine zircon. I giggled, sagging against the chains, thinking of Alamogordo's birdsong imitations. The eagle form was shimmering like a gaudy shadow, the crowd at its back swirling into muttering daubs of color as oil moves in rainbow shapes on water.

I started to close my eyes, nodding off into delightful sleep. A sweet scent floated in the air, caressing my nostrils, a rapture. I slipped downward.

Wrenching pain shot through my shoulder. It stabbed my mind awake. Confused, alarmed, I jerked up. The capsule's cool bulge rested against the inner surfaces of my lower teeth.

I closed my fists hard, pushed my fingernails into my palms, made the chain bite into my wrists.

When my vision had cleared a little, I found Oak-is-Strong leaning far backward, the beak of his mask open and directed to the branches high above. The seductive odor crept into my brain again, lulling me, stealing my mind. . . .

"Lichens," I muttered aloud to myself. "Poison. Kill you." Haunting as a demon lover's kiss, the perfume urged me to sleep. "Glade," I said, though there seemed to be something in my mouth. "Help me, Glade." In my moments of clarity I knew that I could not for long resist so insidious a foe.

A piercing shriek, like the cry of a bird of prey, slashed through my sweet muffling fog.

Oak-is-Strong was howling to the sky. His cloak spread from his shoulders like wings. It was the magic of invocation through effigy. And it worked, worked most horribly.

An echo of his cry fell down from the green leafy canopy.

The crowd murmured. I heard, or seemed in my drunkenness to hear, a screaming of great birds.

Black shadows settled in the branches high above my head.

My chin touched my chest, and I jumped in that small convulsion which is the warning that we are at the verge of sleep when we should not be. Strength was draining out of my limbs, flowing in waves. I opened my heavy eyes. Everything shimmered, danced, blurred.

Two young bleating animals had been dragged to the base of the tree. Oak-is-Strong took a dish from the old woman, wrinkled and sexless as an ancient bald man. He bent over the woolly creatures, tore out their throats with a curved knife. Blood gushed in bright streams.

I forced the phial into my cheek, breathing in shuddering gasps. My body was a traitor.

I was waiting, that was it. Yes. Waiting for what? Waiting for a signal. Ah. I clung on.

The bodies had stopped kicking. It seemed that a very large bird was moving over them. Entrails and dark, slick organs tumbled on the grass. Shrieks came from above. Shadows flapped terrible wings. A cat-beast mewed hungrily, slipped forward. A small wizened figure jumped up, Winter-is-Chill, growled a warning in the tongue the beast understood. The cat bared its fangs but slunk back.

Sweetness blurred into rainbows.

Down from the green firmament, shrieking like devils, the birds fell. Their faces were gold and ruby. Their talons and spurs rent the bloody corpses.

A figured moved before me. I was splashed. Head and shoulders were wet. Warm sticky shock. The stink woke me. Salty blood ran into my half-open mouth. Roaring and screaming. Wind crashed at my eyes. A huge body fled through air to tear my breast with fire. Pain a melody of flame. Gold seared my arm.

"Now is the time, Xaraf!"

A voice crying out to me, hooves like thunder in the midst of that storm of wings, shadows scattering and furious, Glade's beautiful deep voice, men and cats in uproar. "Bite into the phial!"

My teeth cracked the brittle capsule.

Choking, horrid stench filled my throat. I wanted to cough explosively, and did not cough. I drew the foul stuff far into my lungs, spat out the shattered husk. I could not distinguish the blood on my face from any possible cuts in my mouth.

The real world, free of languid reveries, burst upon me as lightning strikes a dry tree.

Glade Resilience rode through an emerald-gold haze of great birds, laying about her with a hissing lance of pure light. Where it struck it burned. There was a reek of burning feathers.

Her milk-white horned horse reared and snorted as huge birds, wounded and whole, threshed in the air. Hunters and their beasts milled in stunned confusion, not yet mobilized to counter the trader's sacrilegious intervention.

Vigor surged back into my muscles as the acrid vapors worked to nullify the perfume of the lichens.

"Are you alert, Xaraf?" The horsewoman's blade sizzled, clean and lovely as a bar of metal roasted to white-heat. She cut birds from the air; the dismembered bodies slammed into the ground; the wounded tore savagely at one another, or themselves.

"Get me loose." I was heaving at my bonds without effect. Now the hunters were running forward, urging their cats to the attack. Glade jostled nearer. Her leather-clad shoulders were ripped and bleeding, but her swordarm swung tirelessly, her lance shrieking and spitting with hot sparks.

The gallantry was hopeless. When the cats reached her, it was inevitable that she and her beautiful steed would fall almost at once.

"Save yourself, Glade," I cried. "There is little gain in adding your death to mine."

The trader made no reply. Her lance cut off suddenly, extinguished as if it had never existed. She released her reins, clinging to the saddle with her thighs, reached into a pouch.

With dazzling speed and agility, then, she turned her horse to face the angry hunters. She held a squat glass container. She hurled the thing into their midst.

It exploded with a dull, unimpressive sound. Clouds of pale violet gas rose up where it had struck the ground.

The stuff was vitriolic. Men and women reeled as it caught their throats, coughing, clutching their garish furs to their faces. Children darted blindly for their parents, or stayed stock-still in attitudes of terror and panic, screaming.

A streamer blew across to me. I recoiled, eyes smarting.

Glade hummed a bright tune. Her lance wove a shield around her, an aura. She spurred back to me through the cawing, air-filling maze of maddened birds.

If the gas disconcerted the hunters, it had a still more marked impact on their cats. The beasts seemed stricken. Eyes rolling, flanks twitching, they turned their great heads this way and that without purpose.

Heedless of personal discomfort, Winter-is-Chill ran to his favorites, mewed encouragement in their ears. Foam flecked their fangs. They snarled at him, flattening their ears. Frightened, he backed away. No place existed for his retreat; the beasts surrounded him.

Glade reached me, held her fuming radiant weapon against my silver chains. Heat ran like lightning, scorched my wrists and ankles, burned through the chains a moment later. The bonds fell away.

A rasp of unbelieving horror entered the cat-master's voice. He pointed to the trader, who was reaching into her saddle pack. Out came Alamogordo, gleaming and hard-edged and beautiful. My heart lifted. I took the sword from her and sent it whirring above my head. A bird dashed to the bloody ground, headless.

Another of the infuriated creatures made for Glade's eyes. Her strange weapon crackled. "Any moment now," she said with a gasp. "My key is working a rusted lock."

Convulsion, then, and roaring, roaring.

Everywhere at once, the cats turned, like killing machines. The pair nearest Winter-is-Chill mauled him with savage joy. They and several of their fellows lunged at every human they could see, remorseless as the wild monsters which were their remotest ancestors.

I watched aghast. These people had tried to murder me, but this carnage was horrible and disproportionate to their crime.

By a stroke of fortune and quick wit, the children and many of the women had been hastily evacuated to the rear of the group when the flask of gas exploded. Now they ran howling for their huts, while the warriors fought with splendid courage to maintain a line against their own rebellious cats.

Sweet lichen scents probed again for my mind. Metal jangled at my wrists and ankles. Blood ran from gouges and cuts in every exposed part of my body. I slashed and slashed at my aerial attackers, expecting the cats to find us at any moment. Strangely, though, I saw that most of the cats were neglecting their human rivals.

Some instinct, shackled until now by the hunters' training, had burst up throbbing and vital in them. Perhaps it was the animosity of cat for bird, like a tale from mythology. Roaring with primeval joy, they threw themselves upon the strident sacred birds.

"This buys us our chance." Glade was in no better shape than I. She flicked red wet hair out of her eyes, reached down and hauled me up behind her on the horned horse.

The clearing was a pageant of carnage, a parable of viciousness. Feathers darkened the brightening sky. Cats blinded by wicked beaks tore their own kind hysterically. The forest rang with brutal cries; the grass steamed with blood.

"Fine sport," Alamogordo said laconically as I sheathed the blade.

Glade looked at me quickly over her shoulder. She wheeled past the vast tree, spurring away from the slaughter.

"Your friend has no grasp of economics, Xaraf," she muttered. "The certainty is now somewhat diminished that these customers will renew my contract."

The crimson sun was up. We rode out of the forest into rose-tinged grassland.

"The violet gas will quickly dissipate," Glade had commented. "Its influence will diminish. We cannot tarry."

Hardly a word passed between us after this. We pressed desperately through trees and undergrowth, fording creeks and streams with a splash. Under its unaccustomed burden, the horned horse tired rapidly. Glade urged it on without pity.

With the forest behind us, the trader permitted her mount to slacken its pace.

"They will not pursue us beyond their boundaries."

"Are you sure? They are strongly motivated."

"It is an aspect of their creed," she said crisply. In matters of specialist knowledge, I saw, I was not to question her judgment. My hackles lifted for a moment, but I was too tired and injured to fight with one who had saved my life. Besides, I could see her point. Arguably, I was reacting this way for no reason except that she was a woman and I was a man: a form of bigotry Darkbloom had labored wearily, and with limited success, to disabuse me of.

We breasted a slight rise, came into a minor dale sprinkled with yellow-brown flowers. At a little distance a colorful tent stood pitched.

Several horned horses browsed in the grass. I saw a second person dressed in trader's garb. He leaned on one elbow in the grass, observing the sky with stoic patience. He rose when he saw the pair of us approaching, giving us a languid wave.

"My companion," Glade told me. Spouse? Lover? Colleague? Hireling? All was left unexplained. It made me nervous. Among the Wanderers, station is everything. I itched to know but felt disinclined to ask, if my patron felt no impulse to declare herself.

We dismounted and walked the rest of the way through thick, rippling grass. My limbs were trembling with belated reaction. Cuts and bites stung my face and arms. My lungs wheezed, laboring still from the onslaught of the lichen and the capsule's bitter antidote.

"How went it, Glade?" the waiting man called.

"Ambiguously." She made a sardonic gesture at her battered condition. "We must find a new client for our surplus power cells."

She handed the reins to the fellow, let herself down into the sweet-smelling grass, leaned back with a sigh. "A mug of wine, if you please, Vanden, for my friend and myself. And this splendid steed would appreciate a good rubdown."

The man brought a cut-glass flagon from the tent, filled three mugs.

"My companion lacks refinement," he told me, handing over a mug. "I am Vanden Month/Nine Day/Fourteen Tenderness."

I grinned at this barb, gave my own name and station. "Her daring and resource are ample compensation."

"Derision from the one, flattery from the other!" Glade said, laughing. "Neither affects me. In a month I shall be able to chastise the first and demand the second."

"Glade!" Vanden was enthralled. "You have already found the object of your quest?"

"You stand beside him," she said with lazy satisfaction. "Be humble, Vanden. We attend on history. Xaraf of Firebridge is a visitor from the stars."

The second trader seemed genuinely taken aback. "Astounding! I congratulate you both. Still, it is common knowledge that history ceased a hundred thousand years ago. If you will pardon me, the steed must be seen to."

I let warm mellow wine run down my parched throat. The conversation had been obscure, but the goodwill of the two traders seemed established. I sat in the grass beside my deliverer and closed my eyes.

How could I possibly be connected with Glade's quest? Presumably the answer must lie in her speculations about my origin. I found myself frowning. Could I indeed be on a different world? Nothing in my experience, not even the endless parables and half-grasped tales of Darkbloom, prepared me for this notion. I finished my wine.

Glade roused herself. "Come, Xaraf. We must look to our injuries before they become septic. I have ointments and sterile water within."

The tent was all of some translucent material which admitted sufficient light by which to see adequately; it was closed by a soft seamed curtain which sealed itself behind us. To my astonishment a breeze, soft and clean, blew within the place.

Glade carefully placed her saddlebags beside a pile of sleeping furs, unbuckled the carved hilt of her mysterious bladeless light lance, found a deep copper bowl and filled it from an amphora. Without any trace of self-consciousness or coquetry she shucked off her clothes, laved the congealed blood and dust from her body. I watched her with admiration; she was strong and lean, and every movement she made was direct, economical, graceful.

She caught my eye. "There is another bowl in the corner. Use it." I found it, but could not cause water to flow from the container. With a grunt, Glade took it from me, filled it, set it at my feet.

My feelings were confused. In the tents of my people I should have accepted this service from a woman as my due. Here, I felt clumsy, ignorant, humiliated. I turned away without thanking her, threw off my own clothing.

The water was astringent. I hissed as it burned my cuts.

"Xaraf!" The trader was shocked. She put aside a tube of pink ointment she had been rubbing into her abrasions. "You should have told me."

"Honorable wounds," I mumbled. "Why complain? Nothing can be done about it, after all."

"Your medical science must be as rudimentary as your transportations are advanced." Glade examined my shoulder. A tremendous purple stain, flecked through with green and mottled black, stood out above trapezius and deltoid; as her fingers palpated my back, the great latissimus dorsi muscle contracted away from her touch and I gave an involuntary cry.

"I don't understand how you can still be conscious," Glade said, less in sympathy than rebuke. "This is atrocious." On my breast and forearms deep rents oozed blood; the giant birds of the forest had not been gentle. "Sit down," she told me sternly. "I have medicaments which will ease the pain and facilitate healing."

I slouched on a stool, head swimming. Still naked, careless of her own hurts, Glade Resilience cleaned my wounds with brisk, stinging strokes, coated them in unguents of various hues, covered the deepest with strips of some colorless substance which clung to the skin as if it were skin itself.

Gently, with a kindness which reminded me less of my poor demented mother than of Darkbloom, she massaged liniment into the purple bruises. I pressed my teeth together and would not groan.

"An ugly injury," she said at last. She rummaged, tossed me a shirt of silk. "Here, this is Vanden's. Too narrow for you across the shoulders, but it will serve." She helped me on with it. "I am impressed at the vigor with which you nevertheless fought once your chains were removed."

"I was too confused to reckon the odds." I slumped back into the furs and stared at the sullen sun through the veiling roof of the tent. Fatigue was blurring my thoughts. Already, though, the ointments were at work; my aches faded. "Tell me, Glade. Why did you risk your life to save me?"

She finished repairing her own wounds and pulled a handsome shirt down over her breasts, retained her dusty leather breeches. "A distress call from your associate interrupted Vanden and me as we pitched camp here last night. What else was I to do?" A leather jerkin went over her shirt. She sat down across from me.

"Alamogordo." I had forgotten the role of my bewitched sword. It lay beneath my piled, tattered clothing, where I had dropped it, still in its scabbard. I did not pick it up. "Sword, do you hear us?"

"I do," a muffled voice said.

"You have means to speak across great distances?"

"To those suitably equipped for reception, certainly."

"Why did you not tell me this?"

"In the first place, it seemed self-evident. I am not responsible for your deplorable ignorance of this world."

I raised my voice. "I did not ask—"

"In the second place," the sword said as if I had not spoken, without raising its voice one whit, "it was my task to protect you by every means at my disposal. Naturally I sent out a distress call. In the third place, if you recall, we were separated before the nature of your predicament was clear to either of us. Shall I go on?"

"Oh." Abashed, I looked at the floor. "Alamogordo."

"I haven't gone anywhere."

"Permit me to apologize."

"Machines do not require apology. Machines are built to serve."

"Nevertheless, I do apologize."

The sword's tone became sunny. "Xaraf, that's very handsome. I accept, gladly."

"And I thank you. Now, if you'd just go back to sleep—"

"Whatever you say, my lord."

Glade was looking back and forth between us with delight. "You are a remarkable man, Xaraf."

"You are a remarkable woman, Glade, which is the point

I was making. It was obviously to your advantage to refrain from interference, despite Alamogordo's plea for help. I am grateful, very grateful, but I must say this: I do not judge you to be an impulsive altruist.''

The trader offered me a look of mock grievance. "Why, your assessment is unjust! My friends know me for a romantic fool, given to wild acts of generos—"

Laughter cut her short. Vanden touched the curtain; it skinned open, sealed itself behind him. He was sweating slightly from his exertions. "A fool, perhaps, Glade; a romantic, in some respects. But generous? Absurd!"

He threw himself down beside me, refilled the wine mugs, still chuckling. "Xaraf, this woman has become the leading trader of Asuliun the Gray due to one trait only: an innate cynicism worthy of an entire convocation of priests."

Glade shrieked with laughter; a moment later she frowned, tremendously serious. "Your appraisal is guilty of inconsistency," she stated, with the mien of a scholar. "How may cynic and romantic coexist within a single breast?"

"Not easily, I'll warrant!" Vanden broke open a parcel of rations. "You see," he told me, "our friend here grows easily bored with the time-honoured perfidies of merchanting. Not content with extorting a handsome profit from the outlying regions, she has let her gaze linger on the very crown of our fair city. Thence, her poetic impulse—which has, if I am not mistaken, cost us heavily this day."

"One year's furs," Glade admitted, "if not our total concession in the Forest." She reached into the open parcel, took a handful of figs, black bread, hard chunks of cheese, and passed it on to me.

The other trader raised his eyebrows, whistled softly.

"Well, Glade, it appears I have misjudged you. Your quixotic qualities have evidently overwhelmed your previous detachment. Let us trust you remember your old friend and impoverished partner when you come into your kingdom."

Glade stood up. In the rosy light her face was now authentically solemn. She put her hand on his shoulder.

"I swear to you, Vanden, this man from the stars will bring my quest to glory. The cool Lady Aniera is as good as supplanted. When the Episcopal in Asuliun lowers the crown on my head, you shall sit at my right hand as Chancellor in the city."

Her companion stared back in silence for a moment. He chuckled then. "First win the crown," he advised. "You cannot be certain that your rivals will not produce some still more astonishing wonder."

I munched the heavy food and said nothing. If traveling with the two traders would take me closer to Kravaard and my Tribe, travel with them I would. How, though, might a man return from one world to another? It remained, to me, a concept suited to wild shamans and lunatics.

On the other hand, until I gained a clearer idea of the methods by which I might tackle that primary problem, I owed Glade Resilience an obligation that might be discharged most easily by attending them for a time.

"You speak of a quest," I said. "What is its precise nature?"

"The rule of our city Asuliun the Gray shortly falls vacant," Glade explained. "The crown now rests with the Lady Aniera Arina Argaet, but she is weary of the task. Invoking an ancient tradition, she has declared a quest of ninety-nine days' duration."

"You are ruled by a woman?" I asked incredulously.

"In this cycle." Vanden pursed his lips. "If Glade is successful, in our next as well."

"And she is without issue?"

"She has heirs," Glade said. "Is this relevant?"

"Surely her sons—her daughters too, if it comes to that—must now tussle among themselves for priority?"

The traders stared at me in perplexity, then at one another. Vanden said slowly, "You posit a hereditary authority? A royal lineage?"

"How else might matters be arranged without endless bloodshed and disorder?" I asked, equally baffled.

"Alternative methods have been suggested, you know," Glade said dryly. "No, our method of governance is by thaumatocratic contention."

The translating device quite failed this test, or perhaps it was the limits of my own mind and narrow experience. I struggled with the concept. "You . . . strive for the production of—wonders?"

"Their discovery, rather," Vanden said. "The world is far too old for innovation."

"The sun, as you see, is dying," Glade said. "Boldness and initiative are slowly vanishing among our people; despair saps our vitality. Declaration of a quest is, if you'll forgive the pun, a sovereign means to detect those equipped with these rare qualities."

I frowned. It seemed an arbitrary procedure, and yet there was a kind of logic to it.

"In my land," I said, "there is never any dearth of bravos and contenders."

Vanden Tenderness smiled. "Our way of life, on the whole, is formal and restrained. The women of Asuliun are cool, the men characteristically unmoved by passion of the more violent sort."

"You are, then, exceptional in this regard?"

The trader sighed. "Not I. Glade is the one gnawed by unspeakable ambitions. I suspect that she would return with you to the stars if she had the opportunity."

"Perhaps I shall." The woman's plain face was transfigured by a kind of yearning; she gazed speculatively at the vast ember in the sky. She shook her head. "But you are too modest," she rebuked her friend. "Who suggested as the goal of my quest that we seek out the lost towers of Treet Hoown?"

Vanden coughed ostentatiously. "I grant my complicity. Still, without your impetuosity I should now be relaxing in my stalls behind the gray ramparts of Asuliun."

"Set your mind at ease. Now that Xaraf joins us, that dangerous trek is unnecessary."

My skin prickled. "In what way may I help you fulfill the terms of your quest?" I asked cautiously.

The wine was gone; Glade found more, of a lighter hue, pleasantly effervescent. She poured for all of us. I became warier.

"Five principals, I among them, set out seventeen days ago. Our duty is to fetch back the most striking novelty we encounter in our travels. The Lady Aniera Arina Argaet will herself adjudicate which of these rarities is the most diverting.'' Glade shrugged. ''Vanden and I had planned to examine the haunted towers of Treet Hoown, a place from which none but madmen have returned since it became deserted a hundred thousand years ago. You, of course, represent an even more entrancing *divertissement*—and spare us the risk of our sanity.''

I had been wary; now I was abruptly filled with consternation.

Perhaps I may justly ascribe this affliction to the sum of every bogey, every threat, every shock to my certainties which had deluged over my naïve head since I woke the second time, thinking it the first.

Memories came to me like a voice of warning, memories of the pits at Berb-Kisheh, and other such centres of advanced civilization, where animals were skinned alive and baited, all for the mirth and coin of fat townsfolk and wall-eyed desert miscreants. I recalled the cripples and limbless who eked a living from the artful presentation of their ailments; bulb-headed creatures a hair away from stillbirth who by mischance had lived and now paid their parents' way by gumming and gawping hilariously, masturbating without cease; adults, by contrast, with tiny heads topped with knots of hair, foolish and great-handed, raped in back alleys by the crookbacks who kept them for sport and show. Oh, the world was full of mountebanks ready to show off the freaks of nature, ready as well to manufacture them if none came to hand, gouging the eyes, say, from snot-nosed orphans so the pious might see, and seeing weep, and weeping toss a coin.

All this in a moment. My face filled with blood. I crossed the tent in a leap; my blade was out of its scabbard, in my hand, high across my chest, while I poised and looked slit-eyed from one to the other. I must have been slightly mad.

''You plan to put me on show?''

The traders were agog. They stared at me, speechless.

''Is that your plan? You mean to present me as a shackled grotesque?'' As I said this I wavered, struck by its inanity, yet boiling with apprehension.

Glade indicated revulsion. "Nothing of that sort! Xaraf, you will be received with all due celebration and pomp. It is a myriad of years since any of those who abdicated from this world have chosen to visit us. Under any circumstances, you would create a sensation. With the secret of the transference device in addition . . ."

I replaced my sword, feeling sheepish. And guilty. My heart sank further when I realized what Glade was telling me.

"You have put your life in danger for no gain," I said in a low voice. None of us mentioned my raised sword; it was never brought up later. These were a cool people, not easily roused or disturbed. "If I knew the secret of that magical device I would never have ventured into the forest—I would have returned at once to my own world."

Glade dismissed the difficulty. "This much I have already gathered. We have simply to locate the machine, however, and learn how to manipulate it. Concentrated study must reveal what you, in a condition of shock, failed to discover."

"You fail to understand." There was nothing for it but honesty. I explained how my garments had been replaced while I slept, that doubtless I had been removed from my point of origin. "It seems a likely ploy, meant to thwart just such a search as you propose."

With inordinate care, Glade placed her mug of wine on the tent's smooth floor. Her satisfied grin faded into a parody of a smile. She turned her eyes slowly to meet the sardonic inspection of Vanden Tenderness.

"A year's furs," she remarked in a toneless voice.

Her companion shook his head. "A totally alienated clientele," he said.

A thin sound emerged from her throat as Glade leaned her head, eyes closed, against the yielding wall of the tent. For a moment I thought she was weeping. The sobs broke into the air, were guffaws. Vanden began to laugh. They fell on each other with great peals of silly mirth. I felt my own solemn expression give way to a smile, a grin, and then I was laughing as well. We fell about in the furs, bellies heaving, and roared.

Finally the quester wiped the tears from her blue eyes. She

hoisted her wine mug, staggered to her feet, raised the potation into the air.

"Onward!" she cried. "On to the mad towers of lost Treet Hoown!"

NINE

Camp was struck only after we had spent several hours poring over mold-grimed fragments of ancient maps. These told us nothing salient, hardly to my surprise.

Somewhat more sober, but still curiously buoyant, Glade Resilience proposed an exploratory circuit of the forest's rim lest, against all probability, the transference mechanism might yet be available for inspection.

I shrugged. "Where are we in relation to the region where I entered the forest? We do not know. That is bad enough. As well, I doubt my competence to lead you to the spot where I woke. It was night, cloudy, the constellations were awry when they finally broke through."

"No matter. We lose at most a day; we stand to gain a kingdom. Moreover, Vanden and I are not unfamiliar with the locale. Together, we should have little difficulty in discovering the general area."

The other trader nodded. "Any unusual installation or activity should stand out plainly against this pastoral country-side. Now, if you would be good enough to step outside, I shall collapse this tent and accelerate our departure."

Everything was packed with dizzying speed, and made an unbelievably modest load. When all was ready I mounted a sturdy horned chestnut which previously had served as a pack horse.

"I fear we have no spare saddle, Xaraf," Vanden told me apologetically.

"Unimportant." I vaulted to the animal's back. After my usual mounts, the giant restruct baluchitheriums, my perch seemed perilously close to the ground. I dug in my knees and boasted a little. "My people delight in bareback escapades. We are the terror of the plains of Kravaard."

My new mount and I proved this was so in a series of dashes and turns, flashy, exhilarating. Although I nearly came off during one of these preposterous evolutions, Glade forbore to comment.

Still, I was becoming aware of the differences in mood and attitude which separated us, never more than in our horsemanship. My own manner was zestful. No doubt Glade viewed it as barbaric. Compared with the careful, competent riding craft of the city-bred traders, I might have been literally an extension of my horned steed. It pleased me to be superior to them in this one thing, if in nothing else.

By the time we set off, two more brilliant luminaries had risen, chasing the bitter ruined sun toward the west. By this time I was beyond astonishment.

"How many such sunlets does this world possess? Although my world has a moon to brighten the night, these phenomena are unknown."

I understood as I spoke that my doubts had been resolved. This was, indeed, an alien world. Unquestionably, I had been transported to it across some unthinkable gulf. It is a limitation of my imagination that I did not consider the possibility that the gulf was an abyss in time rather than space.

"You do not have them," Vanden said with a smile, "because you do not need them."

"You argue a divine Providence which compensates for human needs?"

"Perhaps," the trader said. "The sunlets have not always shone. They made their appearance only when our sun entered its terminal agonies. There were tremendous dislocations in those days." He was silent for a time, meditating on the proportions of his proposition. "Whether they are the work of a metaphysical agency, or the artifice of an advanced if benign science, it is impossible to judge."

Glade brought her mount closer to me. "Vanden neglects a common superstition. It has been held as an important truth in certain communities that a consortium of gods or supermen created the sunlets from an unknown mountain fastness."

I stared at her. "Do they have a name, these gods?"

"They are known variously. The Lords of the Evening, the Last Scientists, the Powers. Why, Xaraf! What troubles you?"

A pang passed through me, constricting my heart so that momentarily I swayed. The faintness went as quickly as it had come. I recovered myself, baffled, and shook my head.

"It is nothing. For an instant it seemed . . . No matter."

The traders exchanged a glance of concern.

"Perhaps your injuries are graver than we suspected," Vanden said. "Let us rest a little longer."

Brusquely, I insisted: "It was nothing. Proceed."

"Very well." The man shrugged.

We rode for a space without words. To our left hand the forest chattered with life. Grassland rolled to our right, rising and falling in gentle undulations, one league barely distinguishable from the last. In the distance we spied herds of quietly grazing cattle, or perhaps large shaggy birds, and the wind brought us the off-key singing of their herdsmen.

"Tell me, Glade," I said at last, awkwardly, "what was the trick you employed to facilitate our escape?"

The quester pursed her lips. "The details are known only to my apothecary. In brief, most citizens of Asuliun the Gray are reluctant to venture beyond the city walls. Those of us sufficiently atavistic to perform the exchange of goods necessary to the city's economy retain, in some degree, that sense of caution."

"You were not cautious when you cut your way to me through a throng of murderous birds."

"Oh, we can rise to the occasion. But you see, we go well prepared. The cultures with which we do business are uniformly defensive and insular—as is, if I am honest, my own."

"The People of the Forest, in particular, are noted for their hostility to strangers," Vanden added. "It is a mark of Glade's diplomacy that she initiated contact with them despite their paranoia."

"As it chanced," she said, demurring, "I was fortunate enough some years ago to find Chief Oakstrong's second child, a baby boy, wandering lost beyond the perimeter of the Forest. Well, the circumstances are unimportant—''

"Give her half a chance and she will talk your leg off about it.''

"The result being a pact," Glade continued resolutely, "granting me exclusive trading rights with the People. Despite strong opposition from Winter-is-Chill and his toadies, I managed to introduce power cells into their culture, replacing a grossly inefficient alchemic system they had until then employed.''

Again, our discourse pressed to its limits the powers of the translating device. Intent, I frowned, and made do.

"Conscious of this dissension," the quester went on, "I took what covert precautions I might. The People exist in a virtually symbiotic relation with their Forest. Since this has been achieved in the main by redirecting the instincts of such creatures as the cats and the sacred birds of prey, I carried on my person preparations designed to disrupt the effects of that training, to provoke the thwarted tendencies.'' She laughed. "A simple plan, but one dependent on the doubtful skills of my mountebank apothecary. In this case, however, his accomplishments matched his boasts.''

"What of the phial you gave me?''

Glade looked surprised. "Surely your world has natural opiates? The lichens are merely one of numerous soporific and hallucination-inducing agents growing freely in every region. Many, it is claimed, originate beyond the sky, introduced here in the days when star-venturers still visited us.''

I was put in mind of Darkbloom's pharmacopoeia, the stock of disturbing specifics and simples which sent him reeling into trance, as he ingested and burned and introduced them into his scrawny body. "All these substances require lengthy and arcane preparation before their potency is realized," I said doubtfully.

"Not in this case. The People utilize the lichen during religious displays; it seemed prudent to carry an antidote lest I find myself the unwilling focus of such a ceremony. Despite Vanden's mockery, my nature is essentially neither cynical nor romantic—merely provident.''

The place we rode through now seemed familiar. At my suggestion we reined in our mounts, turned to examine the area.

No signs of human habitation were in evidence. We went on slowly through swaying grass, watching warily for any threat. Every tree and bush had three shadows. My trained hunter's eye had difficulty matching the weird landscape with that dark terrifying memory of my awakening. Even so, I thought to discern a gnarled trunk here, an oddly shaped bush there.

I raised my hand. "This cannot be far from my starting point. As you see, there is definitely no building or artifact anywhere here."

Vanden rubbed his smooth chin. "We do not know, of course, what a transference device would look like. Perhaps it is immaterial, a mere stress in space. Or perhaps its operative parts lie buried away from the elements."

"That is likely," agreed Glade. "Otherwise it should infallibly have been discovered long ago by wandering herdsmen." She threw up her hands and groaned. "How *can* one search for that which the resources of a lost science have conspired to keep hidden?"

"What's this?" cried Vanden. "Words of discouragement from Glade Month/Five Day/Eight Resilience?"

The quester smiled sourly. "When the obstacles to progress in a given quarter prove insurmountable, turn elsewhere. Before we do so, though, let us at least subject the region to the closest scrutiny."

We each systematically and fruitlessly scoured a zone incorporating a third of the area. After an hour we gloomily met. The bloody roof of the sky had tilted into cloud on the horizon; the hindmost sunlets followed it.

Wind tossed my hair, lifted my mount's mane. My thighs ached. I was sagging into a mood of futility and depression.

Where was the purpose in this indefinite search for a device which might well not exist? Yet if I failed to locate the wizards or gods who had brought me here, how was I to return to Kravaard? The fact is, I was bitterly homesick and did not

recognize the emotion. I had never been away from my own
territory before, except in the company of my raucous kinfolk.

And it was imperative that I return. I thought of my father's
warnings. Sorcery and terror to match anything I had experienced were marching down from the north, in that world, my
world, toward the homeland of my people. My place was at
my father's side in the hour of reckoning.

Rain was threatening. We ate a hurried meal of cheese and
dried fruits. I drew a borrowed cloak about me, brooded as
the others climbed into their saddles.

"We will ride south," Glade decided. "A tributary not far
distant runs down into the forest; there we can fill our amphorae. Waterfowl should provide a pleasant addition to our
diet, which is boring me to screaming point. Then we ride
southwest until night overtakes us. Such maps as we have hint
that Treet Hoown lies in that direction."

Darkness had fallen when we pitched camp in a clearing illuminated by crystals which Vanden affixed to convenient
trees. He was a cunning outdoorsman, and had captured two
fine birds during our brief halt at the stream.

I was fascinated by his method: Using only his concentrated
breath, he impelled drugged darts with great force and accu-
racy through a narrow metal tube. To my chagrin, when I tried
my own aim was poor and the impulse of my breath insufficient. Vanden corrected my aim, explained with a sympathetic
laugh that the art required prolonged and dedicated practice.

This hardly mollified me. I felt a fool once more, inept and
unschooled. I stumped away with the ducklike birds and
cleaned them by the stream, scattering feathers and bloody
guts in a temper.

Glade, though clearly the leader of the expedition, took a
share of the toil; she cooked the game within a curious contrivance that delivered a controlled intensity of heat without
fire. I sat outside the tent, watching the scarlet and blue of
dusk, sniffing appreciatively.

"This simplifies the task of the cook," I called to her.

"As you will confirm when your turn comes by," she said tartly.

I went inside and watched her manipulate the device. "I await instruction. It functions by applied magic, I take it?"

Glade could not believe that a man from the stars could be ignorant of such a commonplace.

"The oven operates from power cells. Fire is, of course, forbidden; only the insane would risk a conflagration."

"You fought with a lance of fire," I reminded her.

"Not fire. The principle involved is different in kind." She said a number of things which the translating device left incomprehensible to me. "Fire cannot be controlled," she finished. "The effects of wild fire upon nature's delicate balance might take generations to heal. We are all the world's custodians."

I detected an earnest note of piety here, and quickly changed the subject. "These power cells are your stock in trade?"

Ruefully, Glade said, "Supplying cells for illumination and cookery was my main commercial activity among the People of the Forest."

"Where do you obtain them? Surely they are priceless." Magic for sale! I thought of Darkbloom's pretensions and sniggered to myself.

"Created automatically by an unbelievably ancient machine in Asuliun," Glade confessed. "The machine serves as our principal resource; it draws on the deepest heat of the world's core."

Since I knew that the world was shaped like the arch of a bow, the idea of its owning a core seemed to me an amusing superstition, but I was too taken by the machine she described to be distracted. "It does this with no human hand to guide it?"

"Of course." Glade looked askance. "Few though they are, nearly all machines from the lost days are of this kind."

I made no further comment. If I could master the principles of this demonic force, I reflected, I might be able to carry it back with me to Kravaard, might help meet the invading wizards on their own terms. The thought made my flesh prickle with excitement. I left the tent and watched the sunlets set amid purple glory.

Vanden had been tending to the horned animals. He joined me.

"An old and capricious world," the trader remarked. The first stars were igniting in the east. "What wonders does your young world hold that ours has not seen a thousand times and forgotten?"

"I do not know. The marvels you take for granted would astound my people. Perhaps, however, there is a spontaneity in my world which has been lost here."

"Very likely." Vanden rose. "We are waiting for the end of the world, and the prospect does not greatly alarm us. You, it seems, have a firmer claim on the future. I do not think I envy you."

His words drummed an echo in mind, but of what I could not say. And it was true. When my unmarried sister Babinya had died of a lingering flux, wasting from day to day while the women came and went, and the small children loitered beyond her tent flap to hear her groans and coughs and to peer wide-eyed at one another until they were chased away by mothers frightened of contagion, that was a piercing sadness, and her death and burial in the traditional wastes at the high place above the valley sent stinging tears down my cheeks, all her strong young beauty spoiled, desecrated, thrown away: The restless night she had spun me a haunting story about the girl I met only and always in sleep, whom I had revealed to Babinya and no other; the day she saw a chieftain from the Ironsmith Tribe and fell crazily in love, and her despair when the councils of the family forbade the match; seeing her, happy and glad and crotchety and *there,* and now gone, gone away, not returning ever. . . . That was mourning. I knew it well enough.

Death for an entire world was too large a tragedy for grief or terror to encompass; only a melancholy mood of resignation could encompass it. Babinya's loss was more poignant, more compelling somehow, than the cosmic doom of a world.

Somewhere between the two were the threatening storm clouds rising above Kravaard: the demon hordes my father said were riding their wizardry from the North. I shivered, filled with foreboding.

And went in to my meal.

Being the age I was, distraction came easily. Roast fowl was set before me, tangy and succulent in an herbal sauce. My gloom quickly dissipated. The dry, amusing banter of my two companions completed this improvement of mood. When nothing remained of the birds but tender memories and a scatter of bones, Glade handed around a bowl of soft brown nuts.

"Chew them slowly," she told me. "They contain a mild intoxicant which frees mind and body from stress. A pleasant sleep is ensured, enlivened by delightful dreams."

"Which of us shall stand the first watch?" I asked, seeing that both the traders already made free with these soporifics. "Allow me to volunteer." I pushed the bowl back.

"No need," Vanden told me. "Thank you, though. If you will excuse me, I will set up the wards for the night." He took a number of polyhedral objects from a bag and went out.

"The fauna of the grasslands are typically harmless," Glade explained, "but the wards will protect us from any which are not, as well as deter the random large herbivore which otherwise might trample us while foraging for food."

"This world is tame," I said, somewhat boastful. "In my world, we must always remain alert against the depredations of feral beasts, not to mention the schemes of our enemies."

Glade's expression clouded. "No world is entirely tame. My spouse perished thus, before the attack of a wild creature."

I held a soporific at my lips, inhaling its odors. "You were married?"

"Indeed, most happily. To Vanden's twin, Hahn." Her eyes lost focus as the drug moved upward through her mind, soothing and easing her memories of hurt. "Sometimes you remind me of our son, when he was younger."

The meaning of her words skimmed by; I caught it with an outstretched hand, as it were, and drew it back to my sight, not certain that I believed what she had said.

"I? Glade, you can only be four or five years older than me."

"So I suppose," she agreed. "Time enough for family; for grandchildren, if it comes to that."

I gaped at her. "What lunacy are you uttering? Do you throw children like kittens? Glade, how old *are* you?"

"Why, a little more than six years."

"Six? Six?" I was hurt, for she mocked my credulity. "Twenty-six, at least."

Her eyes sprang open at that, as if I had accused her of immortality. "Do I seem such a hag, Xaraf?"

"Even then," I said doggedly, "you must after all have borne your child at the age of six, to have a son as old as me."

Abruptly she was laughing, a silly bubbling laugh that made my scowl vanish. She raised her fingers, counting.

"I think I see, Xaraf. Your world and mine have different years."

This was too much for me. I chewed a nut and watched her.

"How old are you, Xaraf?"

I told her. She calculated. "Then by my accounting you are barely two years old, my dear. My son and Hahn's, Ren Orthodoxy, is nearly three; the celebrations are due within the month."

This was growing too metaphysical. It was not until much later that I recalled this conversation and performed some calculations of my own. According to the seasons I was used to, Glade had been born somewhat more than seventy years earlier. She was old enough to be a great-grandparent.

I changed the subject. The pungent flavor of the nuts filled me with an agreeable glow. "Your larder is as wonderful as your mechanisms."

Glade smiled acquiescently. "How are your injuries?"

To my surprise, and truthfully, I told her: "No pain."

"Fine. So my medications are as wonderful as my larder." Her jaw moved dreamily. "Speaking of mechanisms—" Nodding, she caught herself with a small jolt of the neck. "Do we speak of mechanisms?"

My tongue felt numb and uncooperative. "We spoke of larders, as I recall."

We both giggled.

"Speaking of mechanisms," Glade said with owlish determination, "I shall adjust the communication field before we sleep. It has limited range. To remedy this deficit, we shall abandon the process of continuous translation."

I found myself laughing helplessly. "Everything will take twice as long if we are reduced to sign language."

"No, no." Vanden returned. "Explain to him, sir. You are the technician."

"What topic?"

Glade had been throwing off her clothes. Now she rolled herself into her furs and closed her eyes, muttering drowsily. "Never mind. Xaraf, attend: It will induce in your linguistic centres a working vocabulary and grammar of our language." I had no idea what she meant, but by then she was asleep and a moment later so was I.

"Who are you?" I ask, for his features are dark and powerful and terrible to behold.

"Horus, you know me," he says. How gentle is his voice. I look upon him with love and pity.

"Osiris," I recall, for Darkbloom has told me this tale, this mystery, this magic, this wonderful foolishness.

"Is your mother well, my son?"

"Surely you know that your sister Isis grows fruitful with your inundation, Father Nile?"

He is sad, as a man might be sad who has suffered the ultimate betrayal at the hands of his brother. "And Set?"

I hang my head. "He holds your heritage, Father. He ruins your fertile soil, making it desert."

"You do not avenge me?"

I look into those ancient, pained eyes. "I swore to kill him, Father, yet my mother, Isis, begs me to spare him."

"Spare him?" The rage of dead Osiris towers like lightning.

"While he is your murderer, is he not also your brother, and hers?" I shudder at the shock of those emotions which course in me.

Then he shows me once again, as his rebuke, in a whirl and crack of smoke, the murder done by Set:

With his cunning my father he traps in mortality.

With his treachery my father's flesh he hews into fourteen vivid, bloody pieces.

With his vile servant Oxyrhynchid my father's manhood he devours.

I cry out. From the gloom, tearing her garment, runs my mother to scrabble up the poor broken fragments of my murdered father. With mud from the great river she joins them, all but the part which has been stolen, and over his body she stretches herself, until his spirit rises up and enters her waiting, moist, aching body and finds a place within her womb, and I am made, I, Har-end-yotef, protector of my father, I, Hartomes, lancer and piercer of my enemies and his.

Everything changes, then.

Again I cry out, in uttermost dread.

. . . I, Set, killer of my brother . . .

The others were snoring lightly in the warm darkness when I awoke, covered in sweat.

Out of habit I drew my sword, pushed through the tent's curtain with ingrained caution. A spatter of rain caught me in the face. I stepped silently into the blowing night.

"What are we doing out here?" Alamogordo asked softly. "There's nothing interesting for leagues."

"Hush," I mumbled, still half asleep. "Just need to take a leak."

I did so, turned back to the tent.

"Oh," the sword said. "Oh, oh, oh."

A cascade of sparks burned in the darkness.

The great beast stood there then, feathers glistening as rain danced on his furled wings. He swung his imposing head toward me and spoke a single word.

Memory opened like a casket of riches.

I was two men grafted into a single skull. I clapped my hands to my temples, too distraught to scream. Alamogordo whimpered.

"Goldspur," I said.

"Good morning, Xaraf," the gryphon said gravely.

"Have you come to send me home to Kravaard?"

"Not yet."

"The Powers insisted that no aid was forthcoming until I found my own way back to them."

Drizzle was a dancing veil between us.

"The situation has altered." Goldspur lowered himself to his haunches, like some old stone temple guardian.

"We ride to Treet Hoown. Does this displease the Powers?"

"Quite the reverse. However, the traders' maps are inaccurate. I bring you the correct information."

I was troubled. "These are good people, and they have been misled in a more important way. They believe me to be a star-traveler."

"This is without significance. Do not concern yourself. The Powers are the wise Lords of this world."

My throat felt raw; I laughed. "Your conviction is touching." I lifted my sword across my breast. "Take me back to the Keep. I would return to my people."

"The moment is not yet ripe." A force seized the blade, twisted it out of my hand. Alamogordo hung in the air, a cross of bright metal. Sparks streamed from Goldspur's raised talons, struck the blade like liquid fire, spat, pouring and looping, leaving traces on my night-sensitized eyeballs. It seemed like a stylus of red and gold radiance etching a message into the naked metal of the blade. A high thin screeching came from the sword.

It fell back into my hand. Warmth came off it. I ran my fingers down the steel of its flat. It had been inscribed with symbols I could not read in the night.

"A potency has been instilled within it," Goldspur said. "You will find it necessary when you enter the city of madness."

"Am I to retain my memory this time?"

"No. That would defeat the purpose of your journey. Farewell."

Sparks glowed about him. He spoke one final word and was gone.

* * *

I walked through light rain to the tent. Vanden stood at the curtain staring suspiciously at me.

"I heard voices. The wards remain unbreached. To whom have you been talking?"

I drew back my head. "Voices? I heard nothing. Perhaps a dream—"

"Why are you bearing arms?"

"My sword? It seemed prudent." I hefted the blade to sheathe it. A patchwork of lines and sigils was etched into the flat where, a moment before, the metal had been smooth, unmarked. I almost dropped its considerable weight on my foot.

"What now, Xaraf?"

I pushed past the scowling trader into the tent's subdued night light. "Can you account for this, Vanden? I know that I cannot."

His expression altered. "A diagram, annotated in the script of Asuliun the Gray."

"You can read it?"

Vanden reached down, shook Glade awake. I repeated what I knew, which was nothing: that I had left the tent, relieved myself, returned. Rain drummed the sides of the tent, wind thuttered the roof. I looked wild-eyed from one to the other.

"Xaraf, we are being guided." Glade seemed exultant. "What we have here is a description of the path we must follow to attain Treet Hoown. And see, this map shows that city in relation to our present position." Her blue eyes shone. "Not merely the Forest of the People—this very spot where we are encamped."

"How could such a chart be made?"

Vanden shrugged. "Some agency has an interest in our movements."

"The wizard who brought me to this world."

"Perhaps not," Vanden said. "The quest for Treet Hoown was undertaken by Glade and me many days before we encountered you."

"Yet it was to me that the message was given."

"True. The affair has its disturbing aspects. We must decide at once whether to trust this unknown agency."

"It is possessed of manifest power," Glade mused. "I judge that we *must* trust it; this intervention cannot be frivolous. Had it been malign, the agency could have destroyed us as we slept."

The realization was growing in me that I was being manipulated like a toy or a slave for ends of which I had no inkling. "It has been devious enough," I said roughly. "We may be acting out some grisly farce for the delectation of these arrogant wizards."

Vanden smiled. "Calm yourself. You are not of our world. A certain caution colors the acts of every conscious being on this doomed world. Perhaps those who guide us to Treet Hoown are simply reluctant to reveal themselves."

"The test of the map's veracity is simple," Glade said decisively. "We need only follow it. Who knows, Vanden? Perhaps the Fates themselves would have me ruler in Asuliun."

We returned to our sleeping furs. The wind led itself a chase, with our wild thoughts, through what remained of the night.

DEATH

::Just about every new test applied to the study of the sun came up with a 'wrong' answer according to the standard picture. The first cracks . . . came with the search for solar neutrinos, particles that should be produced in copious quantities by nuclear reactions going on in the centre of the sun. . . . The neutrinos have not yet been found after years of searching, and the only sensible explanation is that they are not being produced in the sun, that it has gone 'off the boil' temporarily and cooled down in the middle by perhaps 10 percent . . . ::

::It is, in fact, just possible that the Sun is not being maintained by nuclear burning at present. . . . This is borne out by the dramatic discovery . . . that the Sun may be shrinking at a slow rate today. This is exactly what we would expect of a star if nuclear burning were switched off—the star starts to collapse under gravity, but maintains its brightness as gravitational energy is converted into heat . . . unlike the situation at the end of the Paleozoic [225 million years BP] . . . changing terrestrial factors alone cannot easily account for the greatest of these extinctions, when at the end of the Cretaceous so many dinosaur species were wiped out. . . . Something very dramatic happened a little over 65 million years ago, something which brought an end to the reign of the dinosaurs. . . . We owe our own origins directly to the events, whatever they were, that led to [their] demise. . . . Whatever happened overwhelmingly affected creatures on the surface of the Earth, especially large creatures, but had much less effect on anything below the surface of the sea—compelling evidence that the disaster struck the Earth from outside, from space::

—John Gribbin

TEN

The journey took twenty-seven days.

Grasslands extended on every side to the sky: a billowing infinity of copper in the first flush of dawn, yellow-green as the foremost sunlets came up, orange-russet under the somber eye of the dying sun, copper-gold once more as the later sunlets set in their own magnificence of rose and gray.

Even to one accustomed to the endless sequence of seasonal herding, with every year and portion of the year like its predecessor, the beauty of this cycle soon gave way before its monotony, grassy steppe flowing tediously into grassy steppe, a monotony which clenched down on our spirits like a mailed fist—and at last, by the mysterious return at a higher level of nuance (as dogged, placid Darkbloom would have insisted), its subtleties emerged, beautiful again, quiet, never repeated.

For the prairie had its muted splendors. Flowers bloomed in unexpected patches of crimson and gold ("Sunsorrow," Glade called these), blue and violet ("Heart's calm," said Vanden, reaching down to pluck a long-stemmed blossom for his hat).

They reminded me, for all their differences, of tulips, wild dark peonies, and hyacinths purple as the dusk; reminded me until my heart keened with homesickness.

Marmots burrowed under the matted soil, and their tunnels caused our horses to tread carefully. Six-legged rodents scurried underhoof, and creatures not altogether unlike antelopes browsed in the briefer grass and fled at our approach.

Even the grass itself was half-familiar, hardy feather cereals, needles blowing in the ceaseless wind, silvery gray and tossing like the surface of a vast lake in those stretches of the plain where rain had watered the soil.

As we crossed the map etched on Alamogordo's metal, though, rain was getting increasingly rare.

The long undulations of the earth sloped imperceptibly higher. Beyond the horizon, unseen mountains cast their shadow in the shape of thirsty, stunted grass. Wind now rushed chill across the night, dry, so barren of moisture that it stung the eyes and parched the lips.

Even those scattered trees which had clung at the lip of survival fell away. Saxaul scrub turned the air bitter with its breath; ghostly thickets barred our path. We went on, and saw no trace of human habitation beyond the rare scars of broken dwellings ruined a thousand years before, doleful, unwelcoming, abandoned.

In such country, creeks were rare, streams more so. It became essential to search out deep cisterns and old wells, fed from water tables far below the surface. Sometimes these had the appearance of natural oases: clusters of rich green rising from the thin ground cover. At other times, we had to forage uncomfortably among the smashed masonry and decaying pipes of those ruins we preferred, by reason of their macabre decrepitude, to avoid.

As a source of potable water this last left much to be desired. In my own world it would have been unthinkable, almost certainly lethal. The traders had a mechanism of cunning filters which purified the foulest water, taking in rusty stuff more like sludge than water and yielding up a sparkling liquid sweeter than anything I'd ever tasted.

"Minerals," Glade explained. "When the filter decontaminates this awful muck, it segregates and retains certain trace elements which the human body craves but cannot find in rainwater."

"So magic triumphs over nature."

"Not so. Nature made us with a taste for these additives. It made us, as well, with the wit to enhance our lives by a judicious employment of our knowledge of nature. So we complete the circle, Xaraf, and nature triumphs over the craft you choose to term 'magic.' ''

We smiled at one another, watching the amphorae fill with splashing water from the smooth, enigmatic filtration device. Our steeds cropped and meditated beyond the crumbling wall of this lost mansion. Vanden was not with us; it was his task to pitch our tent, some leagues away, and to butcher the large stringy herbivore which Glad had trapped and slain for us earlier in the day.

I must have been rubbing at the great lifting muscle of my right arm, for Glade frowned suddenly with concern, came to crouch beside me.

"How are your hurts, Xaraf?"

"Well enough." I looked at her, and my pulse quickened a little. In my own world, I could easily have been dead or horribly maimed by this time, having taken such wounds. Perhaps the remedies known to Darkbloom might have spared me, as Glade's had done, but his was knowledge outside the custom of my own people. Glade's eyes were blue, as I have said, blue and direct, and now somewhat misty, and she touched my aching arm with skillful fingers.

"There is a form of massage," she said, "a healing art . . ." and we were kissing one another, our hands touching lightly, moving from face to hair to waist to neck, while our wet mouths went in search of eyes, licking, tasting, went in search of nipple and navel, our clothes scattered all about us, went in search of the soft flesh behind the knee and the soft pungent places where man and woman join.

Glade broke away. "I have a mattress in my saddlepack. Wait for me."

"Here," I said, inflamed. "Now."

"Xaraf, dearest, I am uncomfortable, oh, oh you lovely boy, very well," and I came to her, there among the broken shards of a thousand years.

When we were done, slumped and shamelessly uncovered under the vast open sky, I found new scratches up and down my back and chest, some from the rubbley grass we lay amongst, some from Glade's nails. I pointed these out to her. "Massage," I said, reflectively. "A healing art."

She took me by the hair and shook my head until my vision lost its focus.

The amphora beneath the filter was flooded over. We took up the clarified water in our cupped hands and splashed each other, laughing with the chill of it, and I thought this the first moment of true happiness I had felt since my fall from the world.

"What of Vanden?" I asked, dressing.

"We are old companions," Glade said. "Certainly we have known physical joy together, but the men of Asuliun are unemphatic in love."

"He will not object?"

"It is not for him to object to anything I choose to do," Glade said, somewhat tersely. "Nor for you."

I went close to her. I put my arms about her strong shoulders. I touched her cheek. "I think I would be jealous if you made love to Vanden as you have just made love to me."

Glade made as if to speak, but was silent, pulling my face down to hers and kissing my mouth sweetly.

By the sixteenth day we were well into desert. Compared with the scorching wastes north of Kravaard it was a temperate place. The four sunlets seemed to produce more light than heat, and the failing sun was barely more than a dull coal. In compensation for this benefit, the nights were atrociously cold. Only the heating device carried by the traders saved us from freezing in our furs.

Game had grown scarce and timid. Our provisions were almost exhausted. One afternoon, after fruitless hours of hunting, Vanden and I returned empty-handed to the tent, coated with the dust which swirled in ceaseless eddies across the moribund plain.

Glade was gloomy. "I had hoped to postpone this expenditure of our resources." To my astonishment, she touched settings on the empty oven, placed an equally empty bowl within it, and activated the device. This was the sort of futile superstitious behavior which Darkbloom had taught me to despise in my own ignorant kinsfolk. I repressed an outburst.

Only seconds later, therefore, my astonishment was trebled.

A rich odor filled the tent. Out from the incredible machine came a steaming bowl of stew.

"A distressing drain on our power cells," Glade said. She glanced up at Vanden, who stood rubbing his hands together in happy anticipation. "How are our mounts? Should I constitute a bag or two of fodder?"

"I think not," he said matter-of-factly, as if the conjuring of food called for no comment. "The grass hereabouts is spread thin in tufts, but they ought to find sufficient for several days yet. I am more concerned about water." He sat down cross-legged and began hungrily scooping the hot meaty stew onto a plate.

I cleared my throat in a marked manner.

Glade looked at me. "I'm sorry, would you prefer to wash first? You looked so hungry—"

I stared at her, speechless.

"Come along, help yourself. It's quite palatable. The matrix is an old family favorite."

I uttered a strangled cry. "You conjured it! You made it out of thin air!"

Vanden snorted, began eating. "The people of your world have certainly been thoroughgoing in their repudiation of elementary machines." Was there a new edge to his voice, the rancor of a civilized man cuckolded and too decent to speak plainly? Or was that my guilty imagination?

"Air is precisely what I made it out of," Glade told me. She took a healthy serving on her own plate. "Of course a tremendous quantity of energy was required for the transmutation. Our power cells will be exhausted rapidly if we have to do this very often."

There was no succinct answer I could find to explain the total impossibility of what had just been done. Even the monstrous tyrants of the Black Time had never been credited with the power to create matter from energy—only, and bitterly, the reverse.

Nor, strictly speaking, had I witnessed magic. To achieve such a marvel, the sorcerers of fable required at least a scrap of bone, a feather, a dried thread of vegetable fiber, so they might summon up, by sympathy, their manifestation.

The prosaic way Glade did her wizardry outraged my sense of mystery no less than my reason.

Since there was, finally, nothing I could say to either of them on either score, I dipped my fingers into the bowl and ate with gusto.

Naked and aroused, I crept from my nest of sleeping furs to Glade's.

"Not now," she said sleepily.

"You are beautiful," I whispered in her ear, caressing her hair as it lay free. "I burn for you, it is the song of you I hear every day in my ears, your breasts haunt my dreams, my hands speak to me of your belly, your haunches; open to me, Glade, love me, most beautiful," and I insinuated myself into her furs and pressed myself to her.

"No," she said clearly.

"Glade, Glade," I hummed.

"Go to your bed."

"Tell me you do not want me, lovely Glade," I taunted her.

She sat up in the dim night light of the tent. Vanden snored faintly from his corner, face turned away. I had said all these things to Lleehn, my cousin, had sung and whispered them to a dozen girls of my own tribe and a score of women from the bordellos and markets of Berb-Kisheh, and the women had bloomed for me, had delighted in the flattery and poetry of it, had softened, giggled, bloomed, and opened—yes, like flowers. I, stupid boy that I was, meant no insult in spending on Glade old coin which had pleased all these others. She knew my tricks at once, of course, and resented my callowness. Besides, as she made plain with no words minced, she was deathly tired from our trek into this increasingly hostile country, and offended at my insensitivity for Vanden's feelings.

"He sleeps," I said sulkily. By now my ardor was lost, but I persisted out of childish pique.

"So do I, now, Xaraf," my friend told me, without the anger which would have spoiled her generous lesson, "and so, my dear, must you." She kissed me quickly on the mouth, then on the tip of my nose, and curled herself into her furs and was still.

I crept back to my own furs, puzzled but strangely happy, and slept.

On the evening of the twentieth day we reached the edge of the badlands.

Behind us the plain was virtually dead. Dun moss and lichen covered it, so dry it had cracked and powdered under our mounts' hooves.

Ahead, the ground erupted in jagged scarps, wild eroded landscapes of nightmare.

Wind piped and shrilled through the broken teeth of the earth's jaw. We hunched our shoulders before it and rode on.

The horned horses stumbled among shattered passes and crags. White glare and crimson splashed from the hard bright cliffs. The light dazzled us. We forced the reluctant beasts onward.

Had we lacked that device which took air and energy and made them into meager rations of victual and water for both species, the expedition would have faltered a dozen times. I do not doubt that we should then have died in the wilderness, unmarked, unrecorded.

There was no more talk of the delights of love.

In the midst of ruin late on the twenty-third day we pitched our tent, a frail illuminated egg scratched by scouring winds; and ate, drank, sponged ourselves half-clean, defecated, crept to our sleep and our nightmares:

Inferno blazes in the timbers of the bridge. No stream waters the dry gulch beneath its piers. I face my enemy through his smoke and flare, and his face is very terrible, though I see clearly only the eyes.

His eyes are stars. His eyes are suns. His eyes are stones set alight.

I cry out in my terror and raise my sword. It is a battlesword of finest steel. Its touch burns my hand, and I throw it from me. It tumbles, turning in air, falling to the depths of the lost river.

"Give to me that thing I desire," says my enemy.

"No."

His voice is sweet, and my dearest wish is to see him dead.

"Who are you?" I ask, trembling.

"Oh, you know my name. He has told you, I think."

"Never."

"Call me Gilgamesh."

That name booms and echoes in me. "And I?"

"Enkidu," he tells me, laughing cruelly. "Eabani. Look at your hairy dark pelt, ugly boy. Look at your shaggy hair, woman's hair."

"Yes," I say, and can be cruel, too. "Now I know you. You are the fool who won that thing you sought, and lost it—"

"Be silent!" Wroth, his golden face flushes with rage. Tall and beautiful he stands before me, and takes a step, and I know that he means to kill me, to take what I have won.

"Yes," I say, taunting him. "Its prickles stung you after you sank to the ocean's bottom, as you wrenched it from its hidden place, but you kept it in your hands, you swam up and up and placed it in your boat, and drew yourself within its safety and lay there gasping and heaving for breath, with immortality beside you in Urshanabi's boat, and then you lost it—"

"I shall kill you and have it again!" and he takes another step, while I quake with my terror and speak despite it, knowing no other way to defeat him than through the damage which his own pride has wrought upon him.

"The crocodile stole it," I cry. "The snake took it from you."

"Your life is forfeit," he tells me, banners of smoke wreathing his face, his eyes all glinting and flaring, and he comes on toward me like a god of doom.

I hold up my hands in the way Darkbloom had shown me, like the antennae of insects. Poised, weightless, swaying, I reach for his centre. I probe and touch, lightly, lightly as the drifting touch of cloud.

His hand catches my wrist. I scream at the flames, pivot to the pain, tiger rising to mountain, strike him with all his own terrible force.

I see his face, the face of my enemy. It is the face of Darkbloom. It is the face of my brother. It is my face.

The twenty-fifth day found us filthy, stinking, not speaking to one another, and on the far side of the badlands.

Mountains soared at the horizon.

Between us and the foothills of those colossal ramparts shone the golden dome of a great, lonely citadel.

"Your map has not deceived us, then." The acerbity which had for several days replaced Glade's placid tones was gone in its turn; I heard a hint of awe. "Legend has it that just such a tower marks the outskirts of Treet Hoown."

"It has more the look of a pleasure palace," Vanden said, "than of a fortress."

"And its position," I added, "is singularly exposed."

"You forget that the War Master of Treet Hoown was the last great warrior of this world." Glade wiped her face, left a smudge of greasy dust on her brow. "His instruments of defense included fearsome beams of naked flame, corrosive projectiles, waves of sound so terrible that an enemy would be shaken to dust at ten times the distance of an arrow-shot."

I considered this catalogue of menaces overfanciful, but said nothing. Those wonders I had already seen had blunted the edge of my cynicism.

Weary to our bones, we cantered toward the golden citadel. No matter how fraught with peril it might be, each of us was anxious for an end to our appalling trek.

At the world's edge, stark and desolate, the mountains loomed like great gray thunderclouds. The mingled light of sun and sunlets flashed from the snow on the loftiest peaks. Patches of purple and gray-green indicated rare tenacious stands of timber even on those arid slopes.

Of the city Treet Hoown itself, nothing was to be seen.

In sight of the golden fortress, we reined our steeds and went with daunted caution.

All the ground was scarred and pitted, nearly as barren as the badlands at our back. What growth did show was dispiriting: black moss, infrequent clumps of evil-smelling brush.

Boulders littered the place, blasted and split, piled in ugly heaps as if by some primordial catastrophe.

In the long shadow of the citadel even the moss failed. Raw spines of stone jutted from the banks of glassy, frozen rivulets; rock once molten, now hardened. The horned horses picked their way, some delicate equine genius taking them safely across the treacherous ground.

Glade raised her hand in a peremptory gesture. Under a mask of dust her features were gaunt and apprehensive.

"We have already ventured too near the citadel for good sense. Let us advance no further until we have tested whether its defenses are defunct or merely dormant."

Vanden shrugged. "Is this necessary? Handsome as the place is, it seems entirely derelict."

"When that impression has been confirmed we will proceed. Xaraf, a hand if you please."

The quester dismounted. She went to one of the pack beasts; we removed its load. The animal submitted passively, waited patiently for the bag of feed which usually accompanied such activities. To its considerable surprise, Glade led it several paces in the direction of the citadel. It stood there, looking over its shoulder at us.

With a loud yell, Glade struck it smartly on the rump.

The horned beast emitted an outraged neigh and cantered off.

The nearest wall loomed above it. The animal slowed to a trot, cast a wounded glance at its mistress. There was no response at all from the citadel.

Unharmed, evidently at a loss to know what was expected of it, the animal trotted back and forth at the foot of the wall. The citadel left it unmolested. It gave us a reproachful bleat. We burst into laughter and the tension left our taut muscles.

Glade pursed her lips in a piercing whistle. Relieved, the packhorse galloped back and was rewarded with a sweetmeat.

"Let us not grow sanguine," Glade warned. "We have not yet ascertained that a human may approach unharmed." Without another word she dug her heels into her mount's flanks and spurred swiftly for the fortress.

"Glade!" I cried, and made to follow; Vanden, more familiar with his companion's impulsive character, was quicker than I and had my reins tangled in his own.

"Wait, Xaraf. She is right. There is no gain in all three of us risking our lives." I was mutinous; he released my reins, put his hand on my right forearm. "It is her quest."

"Very well."

We watched her anxiously. Nothing untoward occurred. After a few minutes she rode back to us unscathed.

"The residents, if they exist, are subtle to the point of recklessness. Come, we will seek entry to the citadel."

Corroded but unbreached by time, the basalt walls curved in an unbroken bulwark. We rode around the structure, peering up at its impressive blankness. It was the biggest building I had ever seen.

The principal entrance, when we found it at the back of the fortress (that is, facing the distant mountains), proved an anticlimax. Two great pitted metal gates stood open to the scouring wind.

"Easy to see why we were not menaced by defenders," Vanden said.

We passed through these gates. They stood pushed back upon the paving stones of an empty courtyard, dunes of dust piled against them. A small measure of light slanted into the gloomy enclosure through the opening. On either side of that crimson swathe the shadows seemed twice as dark, but no less untenanted.

Nothing came to us but the echoes of our own steeds' hooves as we rode cautiously in to the mouth of the citadel.

The courtyard comprised virtually the whole of this lowest section. A flat ceiling of metal was suspended high above us, pierced in several places by thick pillars of stone which thrust upward from ground level.

The most imposing of these rose from the centre of the enclosure. It had a portal, and this portal was open. We gazed through it into blackness.

"No living creature has been here in hundreds of years,"

Vanden said. He indicated the dust of the courtyard, thick and matted, disturbed only by our own intrusion. "Come, let us depart. The place depresses me."

"It scarcely fills me with elation," Glade said dryly. "Still, we ought at least to examine the upper chambers."

I rode slowly forward to the central pillar, dismounted, put my head through the gloomy doorway.

"It is a shaft. I see neither stair nor ladder."

The traders joined me, bringing their light-crystals.

"An absurdity," Vanden said, venting a groan. "The walls of the shaft appear smooth as glass. Even with ropes I foresee little prospect of scaling it."

Glade paced to and fro before the portal, cracking her knuckles. "A ladder," she mused. "The surroundings are barren, true, but we can surely gather enough pieces of timber—"

This was wishful thinking, and I said as much. "In any event, why set ourselves unnecessary difficulties? I had thought the city itself to be our goal."

"So it is. Scrutiny of the citadel, however, may offer us some crucial advantage when we come to face the deranging effects of Treet Hoown."

I shrugged, bored by the place, finding little meaning in Glade's quest if the truth is to be told, and stepped inside the shaft to gain a more comprehensive view.

Blue light blazed about me. A portcullis slammed down without a sound, cutting me off from the startled traders. My knees buckled and my stomach surged. The walls seemed to plunge past my face into the ground.

A second portcullis slid downward into view. It stopped smoothly, silently, at the level of the floor. My belly rebounded, seemed eager to fly from my open yelling mouth.

Smooth as an oiled sword in a scabbard, the barrier retracted upward into the shiny material, neither metal nor stone, of the wall. Beyond this opening extended a vast blue-lit chamber.

Swallowing the taste of bile, with Alamogordo in my hand, I stepped from the shaft. The room was huge. There was a stink of corroded metal.

I did not really see half of what my eyes showed me. There

was no way for me to understand what I saw, so I did not truly see it.

Tremendous windows presented images of the surrounding desolation. But they were not windows; these views were amplified, and showed forth on shimmering oblongs of polished quartz.

Instruments alive with tiny stars crouched against the walls on every side. I had never seen anything like them, for they were bold and gargantuan, pitted by time, while the mechanisms carried by the traders were smooth, functional, cleanly elegant. These terrible things had the barbarous quality I associated with the legends and remains of the Black Time.

Overhead loomed the interior arch of the golden dome.

None of this was important, by comparison with what I saw directly in my path.

I raised my sword in front of me in an instinctive gesture: How futile that would have been, had it been necessary.

The gigantic figure of a man seated in the centre of the domed chamber made no response, for it was all of rotten metal.

It was in worse repair than the other instruments, its steel discolored, mottled with bruises of red rust and stains which might have been the sweat of an iron god, eaten by those moths which prey on the bones of the fallen cities of the Black Time.

I watched it, not breathing, and it sat motionless on its great throne, ruby eyes burning with an unblinking violet light, metal arms resting at its sides, metal fingers long and thick as my own forearms poised over embossed levers.

Not for an instant did I doubt that the giant was alive.

Pouring out from the ruined being I felt a manifest aura of chained power and purpose. The fixed ruby eyes stared with horrid intelligence, the metal hands awaited some cryptic command which might free them to seize, rend, tear the human mite who dared to despoil this sanctuary. . . .

A half-heard whisper made me whirl, too late.

The portcullis closed as I leapt toward it. I pressed my face to the bars. Blackness glimmered in the empty shaft. The moving floor was gone.

I was trapped by my own stupidity, alone, in blue nightmare, with the metal giant.

My eyes darted this way and that. Terrified, I crossed to the nearest of the contrivances. I put my hand near it. It was a squat box looped with bronze coils, old and ill with the ills of very ancient metals, but like the giant it retained its potency. The very air shuddered with a deep inaudible vibration. I did not dare tamper with the thing. A flaring muzzle pressed the rough stone wall. Plainly it was an engine of awful destruction.

I prowled on, covered in sweat.

None of the machines was remotely familiar. The heavy battlesword in my hand seemed suddenly as comforting as a brittle twig. I thought of old Darkbloom. How he would enjoy this veritable den of sorcery!

Now I stood closer to the immobile giant's throne, but at a cautious distance from it. The huge right hand hung above levers, a massive weight suspended at about the height of my head.

My gaze drifted along the titanic bulge of the being's arm from elbow to ridged, rust-gnawed shoulder, up to where the colossal head faced forward to the closed portal . . .

No. To where, now, it stared down across its shoulder, stared into my eyes.

ELEVEN

I went cold with a rush of icy sweat, the kind that bursts out on skin gone deathly white, and the same coldness seemed to grip my bowels, contract my muscles in shock.

The metal monster had swung its head to follow me. No expression showed on that stiff, immense visage, yet somehow it communicated a brooding malevolence more terrible than any contortion of rage or fury.

In that moment I was as helpless as a mouse trapped by the hypnotic hunger of a striking serpent. I stared back, paralyzed, into the ruby eyes.

Taking away my gaze required every reserve of will. My jaws ached. My neck creaked. I looked away, and cried out in a voice as puny and shaken as a child's, "Who are you?"

Shockingly, after the silence of the citadel's machines, there came a grating of metal on metal, a harsh roar like the violence of a rock-fall shaped to speech. It conveyed no sense at all.

"If you have the power of speech," I cried, gaining a measure of control over my own throat, "answer me."

The chamber's blue light dimmed, surged, steadied once more.

"For all your grandeur," I yelled, "I judge you impotent." I did think so, now. If it were not, surely by this time I would have been crushed like an ant. "Do not seek to intimidate me."

Ponderous and mocking, the being lifted its head toward the golden dome and laughed its brazen laugh.

"Had I my freedom, impudent mortal," it bawled in a flat,

toneless voice, "you would not live long to regret your impudence."

It was as I had suspected. Some intangible bond restricted the giant. The thunder in my pulses subsided. I felt the cold cramp in my bowels loosen, and with it my legs shook in reaction, but my terror was gone.

Coolly, therefore, I said: "I asked your name."

A splenetic rasping issued from the monster's throat.

"Death was long ago my name, pygmy. Then I wielded in my right hand Flame, and Fear in my left. Now I sit in bondage under the endless cycle of day and night, waiting for the sun to die." Its voice echoed with an appalling grief. "My name is Forever."

I had begun once more to examine the chamber during this oration, to signify exactly how unimpressed I was.

"Cease your rhetoric," I told the giant. I slid Alamogordo into its scabbard, placed my fists on my hips. "Tell me without further equivocation your purpose and history. Where are the ones who built you? What is your connection with this citadel and the lost city of Treet Hoown?"

"So many questions from a pygmy!"

He had done me no harm; I was now fairly well convinced that he could not. "I command you to reply."

"Listen then: I was the War Computer of that doomed city, arm and brain to the War Master of the world. He spoke, I obeyed; he chose his goal and I designed his strategy and tactics; he sounded the horn and I slew his foe."

I sneered as convincingly as I knew how. "You have not done well out of your triumphant generalship."

The giant said in its terrible voice: "At the end, as you see, I suffered defeat. There came those more puissant even than the War Master. For my services to him I was tried, judged, and restrained in my throne, and have sat here under the bite of rust and humiliation while the world passed ten hundred hundred times around the dimming sun, and will sit here when it chills to final frost."

A voice at my back said, "Elegiac, but obscure."

I spun on the ball of my right foot, hand on Alamogordo's hilt.

The portcullis had retracted once more. The two traders stood before the portal. Vanden glanced from the giant to me. "Your abrupt departure left us with a locked shaft. A tricky business of coded energies. Still, we are here at last. You appear to have a difficult situation well in hand."

I could not repress a smile. Vanden was quivering with fright, and there was a rattle to his banter. He jumped when the harsh metal voice burst out in its full force.

"More effrontery! Is not my confinement sufficiently galling, without the rude attentions of additional pygmies?"

It seemed prudent to ignore these outbursts. "The giant and I were discussing our antecedents," I told the traders. "Unhappily, it seems to abhor directness."

Glade crossed the wide floor, energy lance in her hand, eyes fixed on the immense figure.

"Mathketh," she said softly, almost to herself. "Astounding! Only the vaguest and least truthworthy legends—"

The giant cut short her musings. "You know my name? Know this, then, also. Imprisoned I am, yet I guard this fortress. Depart swiftly and live. Touch the smallest weapon in my armory and the flesh will fall from your frail bones."

Vanden snatched back an inquisitive hand. Ruffled, he sought to feign a continued insouciance.

"Mathketh?" He was skeptical, raised an eyebrow at Glade. "I recall that when my brother Hahn and I scampered too far from home, our nurse frightened us with that name. I have always considered the monster a mere bogey."

Glade gave him a tight grin. "Evidently not." She declined to lend the creature any respect, however, turning her back on it. "Yet I wonder if the robot speaks the literal truth. One of these death machines would make a fine trophy to lay before the Lady Aniera."

"It would save us a further trek to Treet Hoown," her companion agreed, "not to speak of the consequent risk to our sanity."

"Doubt my warning if you will," bawled the giant, not to be ignored. "The defensive relays are poised. Your obliteration will at least rid my citadel of your accursed blather."

I had been assessing the situation. "While I do not believe

the creature," I growled, "the risk involved in such a test outweighs the advantages." I stared up at the hulking robot. "You thwart us in this particular, but we shall certainly not depart until you tell us plainly what has become of the city and its inhabitants."

"Foolish mortal. If I misled you in one instance, how can you place credence in anything else I say? Enough. Go now and leave me to my doom."

"Mathketh, you have lost none of your legendary cunning," Glade said quietly. "We will not go until you have satisfied us." She placed a hand on my arm, and I felt a surge of fellow-feeling for her, part sexual, part simple comradeship. "Xaraf, you are mistaken in doubting the robot."

"Its interest is to lie," I said, covering her hand with my own.

"Such robots must speak the truth," she informed me. "As a very minimum, they must avoid outright falsehood. Their makers rightly feared the power and intelligence of their creations."

"Can we be certain?" Vanden asked dubiously. "Do the constraints of rationality obtain with so perverse a mentality as the War Master of Treet Hoown?"

"All the more reason to expect this precaution. The paranoid leave no chink for their real and fancied enemies to crawl through." She caught my look and explained further. "Against the risk of their own robots turning on them, the ancients invariably incorporated into their artificial intellects a series of ineradicable directives. The imperative to truth was one of these."

"If so, the creature is adept in evasion."

A gloating note seemed to enter the robot's rasping voice.

"Each of these conjectures is correct, including the last. My patience is exhausted. Take your ephemeral follies hence."

I leapt forward, vehement, suddenly furious.

"My patience too wears thin. Humans have built you piece by piece from the melted rock and, by the gods, humans will tear you down again unless you answer us." Raging, I drew Alamogordo once more from its scabbard, held the blade high above my head so that the engraved map faced the robot. "We have followed this chart across lands desolate as Hell. We shall not be frustrated by your insolence."

To everyone's surprise, then, the clear voice of the sword rang out into the broad curve of the chamber, hard and biting as its true steel edge.

"Mathketh, you will obey this man. Understand who speaks to you."

The robot's dreadful cry, full-throated, unrestrained, crashed from the blue-lit walls with the clashing anguish of a hundred discordant trumpets.

"Now I know you. I do not know your name," the giant roared, and for a moment I was unsure if he spoke to the mind of my sword or to me, "nor have your feet stood until now within my citadel, yet I know you. Those Powers Who bound me have sent you." A terrible yearning entered the metal voice. "Give me my freedom, I implore you. Ask what you will and I shall answer. Set me loose from my travail and I shall serve—"

"Be quiet!" I cried. Hands pressed against my ears, I shuddered under the impact of that intolerable passion. Vanden had fallen to his knees, face blanched, eyes staring white and contracted. Glade reeled. "You deafen us!"

Instantly, silence.

Head ringing, I bent and helped Vanden to his feet. The chamber's illumination shifted to gold, to white bright as spring noon in my own world.

"Moderate your tone," I said, "and speak." I returned my astonishing sword to its home. The traders, I saw, stood now to each side of me, close, as if seeking my protection.

"Of the city I once guarded, I know nothing," the robot told us. "I am prohibited from such surveillance by Those Whose talisman you bear. My belvedere screens display only the immediately surrounding district."

"Give us your best estimate," Glade said, with a glance to me.

"My surmise is that all who inhabit Treet Hoown maintain the same condition they sought a thousand centuries ago."

"Their descendants, you mean?"

"I do not. I refer to those who left me to face the Powers alone."

I frowned. "Do you imply that those very individuals are still alive, after all these scores of millennia?"

"Alive—and not alive. They exist in a condition of abeyance, awaiting their liberation to true vitality." Mathketh paused. While its vast decayed body remained motionless, it seemed as if the shoulders shrugged. "Doubtless, of course, they may be truly dead, lost to dust. Unless this is so, however, they remain in the twilight sleep, their lives merely adjourned. Had they been revived, I should have been visited by the War Master."

I could make nothing of this. Glade's face, though, was vivid with profound excitement.

Addressing the robot, she cried: "There are tales of a catastrophe termed the Final War. Describe the events of that disaster."

Mathketh turned its great ruby eyes on the quester, hesitated.

"Do so," I ordered.

"Before I was created," the giant began, "wave after uncountable wave of humans had left this world for other celestial bodies. Earth's sun, they foresaw, was on the verge of death. Its energies had been drained by the wormlines of extravagant cultures long dead. In the normal course of things, a star of your sun's kind ought to have burned brightly for five or six billion years more; this poor ember had been vandalized, its furies stolen and wasted."

"Humans had the power to work these changes on the sun?" I asked, incredulously.

"At one time," Mathketh said in its tolling voice. "No longer, unless we consider as human Those Beings Who imprison me here."

Vanden said: "Would the mere extinction of the sun bother such godlike creatures?"

"Perhaps not," Mathketh admitted. "More significantly, they were weary of this planet of their birth. They had made it over a hundred times, built fresh mountains to replace those which use had reduced to sand, filled the exhausted oceans with water, seeded its forests with animals and flora of their own devising. Now they were bored.''

"The weariness of gods," I murmured. "My mentor has posited such a condition. It is a thought more distressing than the emptiness beyond an atheist's grave."

"There were compensations. The remainder of the universe awaited them. So they left, they took their science and their spirit. Only the most sedentary remained."

"Even among the placid," Glade said in her strong voice, "some are born who hunger for more than mere survival. I am one; why should there have been none in the past?"

"You are correct," Mathketh told her. "After aeons of slow decay, a culture quickened once more which yearned for conquest. More precisely, a man was born who burned with that ambition. He drew together the last scraps of science which had not been lost, and he built a city from which to launch his empire. He was the War Master of Treet Hoown, creator of the greatest empire in all history."

"No such empire exists today," Vanden remarked dismissively.

"It flourished for a thousand years," the robot said with pride. "Only as the War Master aged did its glory wane."

I felt Glade shudder, and realized that her shoulder pressed mine. "The curse of immortality is a curse against the weak by the strong. Thankfully, it no longer exists on Earth."

"Nor then. For all his knowledge, and with my might to stand beside him and enforce his rule, he could not stave off that final enemy forever. He became obsessed with life, and with his impending death. He sought the secret of eternal youth, that prize of which you speak disparagingly, known once among those who had fled this planet—"

"And failed to find it," Glade said. "To our infinite gratitude."

"On the contrary. It is here on Earth."

I gave a derisive snort. "You speak in riddles. I do not see him here today. I fail to observe his empire. Or did the secret impel him to asceticism?"

Mathketh's horrid eyes seemed to brighten. He gazed down on me. "You should understand, bearer of the talisman."

From my back, scabbarded, Alamogordo said, "He speaks of the Powers."

Hairs stiffened, prickled at my nape. I reached up, took the sword's hilt.

"I did not say he gained the secret," Mathketh said, "merely that he found it. Four Beings of awful power had returned from the stars, summoned by nostalgia for the original home of humankind."

I swayed, tugged by the edge of some psychic maelstrom.

"They established Their Keep in the midst of his empire and They closed Themselves off from all contact with lesser men. Immortal and effectively omnipotent, They rejected every importunity on my Master's part. At length, driven to extremes by the onset of his terminal debility, the War Master mustered the legions of his global empire and declared war upon the Powers."

Cold as a block of ice, the hilt of the engraved sword dug into my clenched fist.

A calming ripple fled across my brain, and I was myself again.

Glade was saying, "It is held in legend that They placed the sunlets in the sky to stave off the final doom."

"Perhaps," Mathketh said. "Theirs is the only potency I know of which might be capable of such an act. Certainly They are still resident on this world, for it is Their puissance which constrains me here."

Vanden strolled among the engines of destruction which rimmed the citadel's war room. It was a formidable sight. "They repelled the War Master's assault by superior science?"

"Superior in such degree that his host fled before Their wrath. I threw the bolts of heaven at Them and They were unchecked. My stings annoyed Them, at last, and They lifted from Their fastness and stood before me; They girdled me with Their word and pent me to my throne."

Shaken, Glade asked: "What of Treet Hoown and its people? Are they too pent in punishment?"

"They are, and they are not."

"Do not anger me," I cried, and knew it for bluster, but the great machine took my command most seriously.

"I am not toying with words; rather, I convey a paradox. Observing the humiliation and collapse of his ultimate battle, the War Master retreated to the city with his newest bride and activated his last defense. It had been prepared as a measure of desperation lest his search for immortality prove unfruitful. Now he used it to block the vengeance of the Powers."

The quester drew in a quick, hard breath. "Stasis! Absolute suspension of change. He brought this condition upon the entire city?"

"Precisely."

"That was thousands of years ago, tens of thousands. What has occurred in the interim?"

"As I have explained, I do not know. The probability is high that Treet Hoown is yet confined in that twilight sleep."

Vanden stirred. "Protected as well by some dread influence which provokes derangement in intruders."

"As to that I cannot say. There appears scant distinction to me between sane and insane humans. Perhaps his technicians forged some such device in the last hours of the Final War." The robot's tone became remote. "I know this: I have been judged. I have been sentenced. I sit without hope, awaiting the sun's last convulsive flares." Red as blood in the tainted metal face, Mathketh's eyes held mine. "Or do you, emissary of The Ones Who punish me, come now to emancipate me?"

I drew forth Alamogordo, held its cruciform up before me, looking at the englyphed blade for some hint of the future. I could have sought the advice of the blade's intelligence, but declined to diminish my autonomy in this pivotal moment.

Mathketh considered me an agent from its jailers. Glade and Vanden thought me a visitor from the stars. On the basis of what I had just learned, both or neither might be correct. Should I free the robot? Was that part of my purpose in being here?

The traders had withdrawn from me, watching me intently, hardly breathing.

No, I thought abruptly. Treet Hoown was the goal stipulated on the map graved into Alamogordo. Nothing indicated the liberation of this giant. If I was to escape this preposterous world, if I was to go free so that I might fight beside my father against the wizards of my own world, I did not dare thwart the plans of my manipulators.

The logic irked me. It sapped my sense of integrity and self-esteem. No son of Golan Firebridge ought dance obligingly on marionette strings, even if those strings were wielded by the gods themselves. Yet, for the time being, I could find no alternative. I had no love for the robot. Mathketh's horrid intellect was best left chained.

I lifted my head.

"Your sentence remains unaltered. We go now to Treet Hoown. Do not think to attempt our detention; you know the fury of Those I represent."

For the veracity of this last claim I felt little conviction. Still, its effect upon Mathketh was evident. I had expected a repetition of its earlier demented outburst. Instead, the metal giant responded instantly with silence and total immobility. Tension left the air. The chamber's illumination slowly dimmed to its initial deep blue.

I clasped the hesitant traders by the arm and smiled, exhausted.

"Come. Our beasts will have grown fretful in our absence." We entered the shaft. "More crucially, I need my dinner."

With a hissing whisper, the portcullis descended. Through the astragals of the bars I caught a final glimpse of the robot. The ruby eyes were dull, brooding to an infinity of ennui. It was a pitiful thing to see, and I shall remember it to the end of my days.

Vanden Tenderness managed a sardonic smile as we fell. "You can think of dinner after such epoch-making conversation? Ah, Xaraf Firebridge, you are indeed a barbarian."

I chose to bait him.

"You deem it more perfect to meditate upon the moral of Mathketh's doom?"

The trader's smile grew broader. Stepping into the gloom

of the courtyard, he brushed fastidiously at the grime of travel which coated his face and garments.

"Not at all." He was lofty. "It is *our* condition which perturbs me. How might a gentleman entertain the notion of settling himself to a repast while his body reeks and his apparel is less than meticulous?"

Glade clapped a hand to her own smudged forehead. "Shocking! What shall we do to remedy your plight?"

"Bring me water, scented soap, laving attendants, and a tailor; then, perhaps, I will consider my stomach's needs."

Glade lost her sober expression. I roared, though it was not a joke my father and the old men of the tribe would have found amusing. The Wanderers are not notorious for the niceness of their hygiene. Darkbloom's influence over me in this regard was another stroke against him in my father's account.

In a mood of hilarious relief, we spun and romped in the dusty courtyard.

"Frankly, I doubt that metal robots have much use for baths," the quester said with a laugh, clipping Vanden's ear. She put on her most solemn face, cavorting. "Until we reach the fabled perfumed viaducts of Treet Hoown we must, I fear, pinch our nostrils and avoid the wind."

Vanden eagerly plucked down from the back of a patient animal the machine with which we would create our provisions. "Alas," he said, sighing. "I fear you are right." He had found a plum or two, left over from our last meal; these he happily plopped into his mouth. "Questing is simply not the occupation for a man of sensibility." Juice spurted.

"Your case for good manners would be more incisive, or at least more audible," Glade told him tartly, "if you refrained from speaking with your mouth full."

Only the feeblest light came through the open gates into the enclosure. Deepening mauve, the sky drained as the later sunlets, gone behind the mountains hours earlier, sank to the hidden horizon.

A frigid wind came down the slopes, sweeping dust across the glassy plain encircling the citadel. I heard its whine; it made me shiver. The prospect of spending the night within the grim walls of the fortress was bleak, but less dispiriting for all that than venturing at once into the cold night.

"Let us pitch camp here," I said.

"I suppose so," Glade said, looking depressed at the idea. There was little sensible alternative, however. The route to Treet Hoown led high into the craggy peaks beyond the walls. She acknowledged this fact: "Scant progress is feasible in any event after nightfall."

As soon as the device produced its menu we ate ferociously. There was something farcical about the three of us, filthy and tired, crouched on flagstones in a dusty yard, wolfing delicate soufflés, crisp-fried rings of some tentacled sea beast, fresh fruit dipped in a pungent yogurt. The glow of the heater, the internal warmth of our meal, renewed our spirits.

Vanden raised the tent behind the massive central column while Glade and I saw to the needs of the animals. Ripe and itching, we drank wine and sprawled on our furs in the warmth of the tent. Under the pale rose luminescence of light-crystals, we examined more closely the chart cut into my blade.

Subdued now in mood, we were each of us, I believe, preeminently conscious of the brooding presence in the blue chamber high above us.

"Mathketh is emblematic of the hazards we will confront in the city," Glade pointed out, "except in one respect, perhaps the most important: *His* malice has been disarmed." Probably she was unaware that her fingers played ceaselessly with a small sharp knife, splintering a fragment of wood until the floor at her elbow was littered with tiny chips.

Vanden grimaced. "Neither have we gained any insight which might help us avoid the risk of lunacy."

I stood up, took one of the light-crystals from its bracket.

"This discussion serves merely to weaken our resolve." I skinned open the curtain. Cold air entered, dust-laden and unfriendly. "Come, we are restless and overwrought. Let us explore the remainder of the citadel. With luck we will discover a pipe of running water for Vanden."

The trader raised only a token objection. "The robot cautioned us against tampering." I could see he was as avid as I for action, any action. Glade was already on her feet, pulling on her jacket.

"Only with reference to his weapons," I countered. "Surely we may examine more mundane contrivances with impunity."

It proved to be so. The lesser shafts were resistant to entry, but Vanden's cunning instruments swiftly found the codes which opened them.

Moving platforms wafted us into a variety of musty, pitch-dark rooms. To the delight of the city-bred traders, several of these were clearly designed for elite accommodation.

"The War Master himself must have loitered here," Vanden surmised, rubbing his hands together. He stood at the entrance to a lavish apartment decorated for sybaritic tastes. I followed him in. Shortly he was crying: "A bathroom! We have stumbled upon civilization!"

These rooms had been untenanted, by Mathketh's account, since before the time of the creation of the sunlets; to the traders that was a time to be sought in legend. Despite this immense antiquity, many of the facilities still functioned.

I looked down, hardly able to believe my senses, at a vast sunken bath of jade, encrusted with ornaments of chrysolite, sardonyx, mother-of-pearl, gems I had never seen in all the bazaars of Berb-Kisheh. Vanden activated it at once, yelling with uncharacteristic verve as it gushed steaming, brackish water.

"Wait," he said, when I laughed and held my nose at the bitter stink. He was right; the contaminants rapidly cleared, and the bath rushed with pure water, all aswirl. Heedless of his previous anxieties, Vanden delayed only long enough to throw off his leather and weapons; fully clad otherwise, he plunged into the filling pool.

"Ecstasy," he said with a sigh. "Ah, ah!" Clouds of warm mist went up into the air, beautifully scented, and muddy ripples spread out from Vanden's floating person. "Come on in, friends, there's room for all."

I hesitated, remembering Glade's rejection of my advances. That had been due, among other causes, to Vanden's presence; here, the situation was utterly different, yet I feared placing a foot wrong.

None of these inhibitions were evident in Glade's behavior, however. With a grin she put off her boots and belt, bangles and lance, and leaped into the deeper end of the bath, cut through the roiling water with the joy of a small child, a dirty wake whirling behind her.

"I shall stand guard a while," I growled. Vanden lifted his eyebrows, made as if to speak; water filled his mouth as Glade, creeping behind him, playfully ambushed him from below. He rose again spluttering and shouting in mock alarm. Clinging, sodden garments dragged at their limbs. Glade kicked, floating, and began to peel her skirt from her back. I turned away.

Their guileless laughter stung me. I roamed the dim chamber, leaving them to wash the dust of the badlands from their bodies and the considerable tensions of the day from their souls.

After all, I told myself, they had been lovers long before I met Glade. Or so I surmised. It was not my place to intrude. At that moment I caught an image of myself in a wall-swallowing mirror, and crouched from it in terror, tearing out my sword: the man I saw did the same. He was dark, fiercely glowering, abominably soiled from boots to greasy hair.

My heart slowed, after a time. I went closer to the mirror, saw its trick (the same trick Darkbloom had shown me long before, in a clear reflecting pool), turned away with a carefree, utterly unconvincing laugh.

The light-crystal I carried bobbed in my hand, throwing moving shadows.

It was odd. Musty as the apartment was, it remained impossibly clean and neat considering how long it must been empty. Unlike the courtyard below, there was no trace of dust, of cobwebs, and little enough of the marks of decay which scarred Mathketh's own great body.

My movements triggered some patient mechanism. Lights came up in the apartment, pearly and flattering. Quiet music began to play, strings and percussive instruments plucked and struck like hail falling into crystal and glass.

Enthusiastic cries met this success.

I called into the room which held the sporting traders: "I do not see how these devices continue to operate after an aeon of disuse."

"Xaraf, get your carcass into this pool."

I returned to them, crouched at the water's edge. Both were naked, clean as fish; their clothing was piled at the end of the bath.

"You are going to be uncomfortable when you dress," I said nastily.

"There will be a cabinet somewhere which vents warm air, meant to dry our bodies," Glade said. "We can adjust its setting to dry our clothes as well." With her hair plastered against her scalp, she looked plainer than ever. I decided that she was one of the least attractive women I had ever known. The tips of her breasts bobbed in the iridescent bubbles seething on the surface of the hot, lathery water. Her blue eyes shone. I looked down at my hands.

Vanden cleared his throat. "Not all of the support systems here have survived," he pointed out in a detached voice. "Still, many machines from the Age of Wonders are virtually indestructible. Our own industrial resource in Asuliun, the device which creates energized power cells, is a relic of that period."

As if he heard his own words with surprise, Vanden shook his head, rolled in the water. "Do you know, Glade, that's true. Here is an opportunity to replace our own depleted power cells." He stood up, water foaming at his hairless calves, stepped out of the pool. Glade remained where she was, suspended, luxuriating.

I pulled off my boots as Vanden took himself and their clothes to a recess where, somehow, he caused a gust of warm air to blow from the floor. "You plan to loot the apartment's devices?"

"If need be. That should not be necessary. There must be a store of power cells located in the vicinity." Miraculously, he was already dry. I dropped my odorous garments into the frothing water and stood naked at the pool's edge. Glade regarded me placidly. "While you make yourself human, Xaraf, I shall look through the remainder of the apartment for their location." He looked me squarely in the face, held my eyes, smiled, was gone.

The water was delicious. I lay in it like a child suspended in its mother's womb. Glade drifted nearby, humming almost inaudibly in counterpoint to the strange melody of the stringed instruments. The hard knots of my muscles eased.

Glade's breasts touched my chest. We glided across the skin of each other, opened into the moistness of our mouths, and then the buoyancy was a trap, we bobbed and jostled, cracking our elbows on the jade bottom of the bath, laughing, slipping and holding, gulping water, spitting, the natural lubricants of our bodies stolen by the foaming water so we skidded and scraped at each other but were together, then, together moving, our feet tangled in my shirt and one leg of my breeches working itself between our bellies, giggling and joyous, thrusting, Vanden long gone about his search for power cells, my hands holding Glade's hard buttocks, and her legs and arms trustingly about me while I drove us together, together, coming with cries, not with passion, no, not with obsession but with consolation and caring and, I don't know, perhaps with love.

When Vanden returned with his arms full of fresh power cells, we had dried ourselves in the wonderful scented artificial summer breeze, our clothing was ready, and if Glade and I were more languid, more pleased with ourselves than we had been when he left he did not draw attention to this fact. Vanden was, as he had earlier claimed in jest, a gentleman.

We went quickly down the shaft and through the chilly night to our tent.

"These cells are fundamentally identical to those created by our own master machine in Asuliun," Vanden confirmed. He and Glade cast aside the nearly exhausted cells from their own powered contrivances, packed the reminder against future need.

"I believe we can forgo the wards for the balance of this

night," Glade told him. She hugged him quickly, went to her sleeping furs. "Fortune obviously favors our survival."

"Tomorrow, the final march on Treet Hoown," Vanden announced with relish. He smiled, bent to clasp her hand, went to his own furs. "Sleep well, Glade, Xaraf."

For all its ambiguities, the evening's explorations had plainly been more than adequate in banishing the trader's apprehensive mood. I did not let my mind dwell on the question of what had passed between the two while I skulked through the apartment. I told myself I was not jealous, no more than Vanden might well be.

Certainly my dejection and homesickness were gone. I fell asleep, and for the first time in weeks my slumbers were undisturbed by images of dread and loss.

We rode out of the citadel at sunrise. By nightfall, we had climbed more than halfway up the rugged slopes. On the morning of the twenty-seventh day we continued our ascent, plodding beside our stolid animals.

No distinguishable trails remained. Precipitous scarps loomed to hinder us. Boulders overgrown with pungent moss blocked our path. Pebbles slipped and shifted dangerously beneath hooves.

Harsh winds howled down from the thin snow far above us. We wound makeshift scarves about our heads for protection. The air was thin and bitterly cold, so that we gasped for breath and every gasp was a knife blade.

We trudged on.

At midday, with the dying sun scowling from its bloody eminence, flanked by the searing sunlets, we emerged on a wide plateau as bare and desolate as a lake of rock.

"This is no work of nature." Glade wiped tears from her wind-reddened eyes. "Human hands have hewn the mountain level."

Vanden squatted, patting the flat, sheared rock.

"I had thought our journey near its end," he said plaintively. "Where are the ruins of the city which should stand on this plateau?"

We stared helplessly at the empty plain and then, in exhausted bafflement, at one another. I began to curse foully in my own tongue.

Treet Hoown and all its living-dead inhabitants was gone without trace, vanished from the world which once, for a thousand years, it had ruled.

TWELVE

I walked back to the edge of the plunging cliff, gazed down the tortuous declivity we had scaled with such effort.

The dome of Mathketh's citadel gleamed far below, bright in the wilderness as a yellow flower. White as parched bones, the badlands shimmered to the distant horizon.

Gusts buffeted me, stung my face, threatened to hurl me from the cliff. I hawked, spat phlegm into the hateful void.

At my back, Glade cursed vehemently.

"We cannot have mistaken the route! Neither can the city have disintegrated so thoroughly that not one stone of it remains. The War Master built for eternity. If Mathketh's fortress is still intact, so too much Treet Hoown be."

"Then we have strayed from the path," Vanden insisted with weary logic. "Either that, or the chart was meant after all to mislead us. Perhaps our original maps were correct. Xaraf," he called, loudly to defeat the wind, "bring forth your sword once more for our inspection."

Lines of disappointment and fatigue ran from Glade's eyes, cut outward from the edges of her mouth. "What use?" she asked sourly. "We have committed it to memory. There is no doubt that by its reckoning this is the plateau where Treet Hoown once stood." She pressed her forehead into her horned steed's neck; the animal whinnied softly. "I think we must assume that its Master's final experiment led to its total annihilation."

Vanden was suddenly furious. "You contradict both yourself and the known facts. Explain the madmen who through

177

the centuries have brought their garbled tales of horror from the city."

Glade threw up her hands. "Congenital lunatics and liars. Their tales were fabrications of their madness. My stupidity lay in trusting such a source."

"I do not think so." Vanden's tone lost its fierceness. He took her hand in a comradely gesture. "You neglect the peculiar agency which has gone out of its way to guide us here. Neither illusion nor caprice can explain that. I repeat: It is in our interests to examine the chart once more."

I shrugged, turning from the edge of the abyss. I grasped Alamogordo's hilt, drew the sword halfway from its scabbard. A chill passed through me as I did so, halting my hand. A flicker had danced at the corner of my eye. For the briefest instant I had glimpsed ghostly minarets, piles of crumbled masonry, massive palaces of red stone.

I uttered a cry.

"Xaraf?" The plateau at Glade's back mocked me in its absolute emptiness. "You look pale as death."

"I thought for a moment—" It was too foolish. "No matter."

"The altitude," Vanden hazarded.

"You wished to see the map," I said roughly, and brought Alamogordo gleaming into daylight.

Shock ran down my arm. I lifted the battlesword with one hand, muscles bulging along my upper arm, and a tingle like the burning of sherbet went across my scalp. The runes, the engraved map on the blade seemed to flare with light. I raised my eyes, looked past the bewildered traders, and gazed on the somber towers of lost Treet Hoown.

They rose in the midst of the plateau. The city was bold and barbaric, ancient as Mathketh's citadel.

A hundred millennia of scouring mountain winds had not been kind. Façades once bright with polished tile and metalwork were chipped and faded; spires of gray stone tilted; mounds of debris and rubble on the city's outskirts spoke bleakly of time and erosion.

Yet the Master of Treet Hoown had built well. Even now, a pair of gilded minarets soared brave against the scarlet sky.

Enormous wind-worn buildings stood intact, arched entrances closed with arabesqued metal doors pitted but untouched by rust. Noble marble friezes still topped basalt pilasters. Streets choked with dust and flakes of stone retained much of their original magnificence.

Over all of this, fluttering above stepped towers and blocky palaces, skeins and streamers of saffron luminescence trembled. The yellow glow confused my sight, distracted me, caused the lofty towers to waver on the brink of unreality whenever I moved my eyes.

Glade touched my left arm. With a jolt of surprise, I realized that I was standing with the great weight of the battlesword extended above my head, my right arm rigid and trembling.

"What troubles you, Xaraf?"

"The city," I said, taken aback. "What else? How is it that we have not seen it until this moment?"

Vanden took a step back. "The poor devil has taken leave of his senses," he murmured. "Glade, can the deranging influence have lingered, even though the city itself has gone?"

I shook off Glade's hand. "What are you saying? Here is the city." I pointed at the campaniles, the thoroughfares.

Glade followed the direction of my gesture. "Xaraf," she said quietly, "nothing is there but barren rock. Here, you must rest. Put down your sword. The thin air has distorted your perceptions."

An extraordinary surmise came to me. I held the blade up to my face.

"Alamogordo, do you hear me?"

"Of course. You are correct, the city is there."

Glade grunted; her head went back; she began to smile. "Ah."

"And if Glade were to take you in her hand . . ."

". . . she would see the city. That is part of my function."

I passed the sword to the quester. She took it in both hands, bunching her shoulders. The tingling at my scalp ceased the moment I relinquished the blade. The city vanished.

Although I was half-prepared for this, it sent a jolt of alarm into me. At the same moment Glade uttered an astonished yell.

"It *is* there!" Now I saw how bizarre and discomfiting this experience was for an onlooker, for her eyes roved and tracked across the empty plateau. "That yellow glow . . . It must be the corona of some mechanism which renders the towers invisible." She passed my blade on to Vanden, who had watched these proceedings with fascinated acuity. "Incredible! A perfect illusion of vacancy."

"Why did you keep this information to yourself, Alamogordo?" I asked with some testiness.

"Yours is a voyage of discovery," the sword told me. "The terms of reference of my commission include intervention only when your life is threatened, and then only when you seem unable to deal with the threat unaided."

"If you two are going to jabber away like this, I should not stand between you," Vanden said, grinning. He returned the blade to me; I saw the city flick back into reality. "An imposing metropolis," he commented. "I trust the shield does not operate within the city proper, or we shall be greatly inconvenienced in our search for Glade's trophy."

I regarded Treet'Hoown speculatively. Light flowed in subtle shades of yellow, saffron, orange. Dust whirled in small eddies. Nothing else moved.

If the inhabitants were not long dead, certainly they were still pent within their twilight sleep. I could see no obstacle to us entering the city immediately.

"Come," I said, sheathing my blade. "I will lead the way." I mounted.

Vanden was diffident. "Perhaps we should first send ahead one of the animals, as we did at the citadel."

Glade shook her head, foot in the stirrup. "Invisibility. Induced lunacy. Both methods point to a reliance by the War Master on psychological deterrence. Since we cannot test these defenses in advance, we must simply take our chances."

I reflected on the way Glade refused to allow me to take command of the expedition. It was not that I wished to do so, precisely; more that everything in the traditions of my people impelled me to seek mastery of any group I found myself among, especially one led by a woman. Darkbloom had mocked these habits as insular, suspect, unwarranted. For all my admiration of that extraordinary man, I did not invariably comply with his tutelage. Now I found that it was not a matter for me to decide. Glade did as she pleased. She was neither leader nor follower, nor did she impose such roles on Vanden or me. It was an unusual way to behave, uncomfortable and irritating. Day by day, however, I was becoming reconciled to it.

A short distance from the city's perimeter, Alamogordo began to vibrate against my spine, to sing a high keening note.

My steed balked, snapped its teeth in agitation. I urged it on with a sharp kick of my booted heel. The animal pawed at rock, moved forward no more than three or four hesitant steps.

"Draw me forth," Alamogordo said in a voice of pain.

I did so, held it forward.

A tremendous turquoise flash lit the air, a green-blue sheet of flame that leapt from the blade's tip with a thunderous crack and then was gone. Shocked witless, I dropped the sword on the ground.

My horse reared with a frenzied neigh. I battled it, regained control, swung to look behind me.

My companions were gone. Vanished utterly.

A dimple formed in the air, a ripple creasing the empty landscape, and Glade rode out of nowhere. Vanden followed her into existence. Their steeds' eyes were white and rolling.

"For a moment we judged you lost," the quester said, shaky.

"And I you." Heart thuttering, I dismounted and retrieved my sword. Alamogordo said nothing. The metal was slightly hot, transmitting this sensation to the hilt. I sheathed it. "Perhaps I should have left the cursed thing where it fell."

There was a muffled expostulation at my back.

"By no means." Vanden lent his voice to the sword's cause. "Alamogordo is a talisman of great power, as Mathketh recognized. We may yet call upon it to avoid the fate of our predecessors."

Treet Hoown had no bailey, no defensive city wall. Whether this fact reflected the awesome nature of the weapons with which the War Master had waged his battles, or his boastful arrogance, or simply that its mountainous altitude and inaccessibility rendered such a wall meaningless, Glade was unable to tell us.

In any event, this lack made strikingly manifest the artful and coherent design of the city's planners.

Grimy viaducts scummed with stagnant rainwater extended in an immense marble grid from the perimeter to the heart of the city, where the twin minarets rose golden to the sky.

We allowed our horses to follow the most direct roads toward that centre.

Warehouses, blocky and functional, gave way to residential towers, open markets, domed palaces surely once green with topiary and shrubs but surrounded now only by doleful blowing dust, crumbling terraces, sagging spires encrusted with gems and inlaid with precious metals, monumental statuary of warriors and creatures I had never heard of, even in the bestiaries of the imaginative. These, Vanden assured me, were valid representations of living beings from the worlds of other stars, fetched here to the Earth in the times of legend and now mostly vanished in their turn.

Nothing blocked our passage. That worried me.

Bridges took us across the canals. Thoroughfares stretched with military precision between the buildings. While I lacked my father's detestation of the urban way of life, I found myself shivering. My mother was a daughter of Berb-Kisheh; as I have noted, I had frolicked there often as a child. Still, this gigantic and regimented place made me yearn for open spaces and the friendly disorder of nature.

We cantered at last along the major esplanade leading to the city's core. Never in my life had I known any place so utterly, unforgivingly lifeless. In the desert reaches of my own world there had always been the chirring of locusts, the scurry of some burrowing marmot, the distant song or flutter of a flock of birds, the lonely wheeling of a vulture. Only the click of our mounts' hooves echoed now to fill the haunted silences of Treet Hoown.

"I do not like this," I said.

"I loathe it," Vanden said, candidly. "I want to go home."

"Better silence and universal death than a waiting army," Glade said, ever optimistic.

A broad plaza opened before us at the end of the esplanade, girded by the dusty, magnificent marble viaducts.

Heroic figures wrought in age-blackened metal glared from dry fountains. At the extremities of the square, temples stood, their porticos supported by thick serpentine pillars, decorated by repulsive gargoyles.

Directly before us, twin spires glowing like new copper in the slanting light of the crimson sun, brooded the massive palace of the War Master.

Glade reined in her steed at the base of the hundred steps leading up to the vast granite arches.

"We may expect the greatest threat to our well-being within the palace," she stated. "But here will also be the largest prize." She looked about her with teeth bared; her tremendous excitement was contagious.

I drew Alamogordo.

"Any last messages?" I asked sourly, and caught Vanden's smirk.

"You certainly have a way with words," the sword grumbled. "Go forward with bravery, Xaraf. You're going to need it."

Vanden roared. "Well, we have been warned." He turned back to his saddlebags, brought out an energy lance like Glade's. "Shall we go?"

Weapons in hand, we climbed the worn steps.

The shadows of the colonnade shrilled to the passage of bitter gusts. The air was thin, enervating; we gasped with the effort of our climb.

Huge, forbidding in its own gloomy darkness, the garish entrance hung above us like an iron cloud. The door itself was as high as four men standing one atop the next's shoulders. A grinning silver skull jutted at shoulder height from the embossed steel, as if meant for the easy grasp of giants.

The traders hung back. I hesitated myself, filled with foreboding. I reached up, then, and put my hand to the skull.

There was no time to grasp it, to turn it. The great door swung open instantly, though with a ghastly creaking groan.

I drew my hand back as if burned. The door had opened of its own accord.

Impenetrable darkness filled the space beyond the doorway. A putrid odor drifted through the opening.

Glade cursed. She tugged a light-crystal from the pouch at her belt. Its pale illumination probed weakly into the corpse-stinking void.

I heard a noise come from my throat, a noise an animal would make.

Still no assailant rushed at us, no ancient seneschal tottered forward to demand our business. Only shadows danced as the crystal juddered in Glade's hand.

Dust lay inches thick on the stone floor of the vestibule. The wind that followed us through the open door lifted it now, blowing up gray clouds to choke us as we paced cautiously forward.

Dull tapestries fluttered on the gaunt walls, woven of some indestructible fabric which had resisted time's hunger. Evidence of that ceaseless, uncaring destroyer lay all around us: metal fittings and jeweled ornaments from wooden furniture long since corrupted to powder.

With a shuddering squeal of hinges the great door swung behind us. I whirled, too late. It clanged shut.

A duplicate of the silver skull leered from this side of the door. I leapt to it, clamped my hands about it. Nothing happened. The door had locked itself.

Furious, I twisted at the grinning mask, putting all my massive weight into it. The door remained shut. Scowling, I turned back to the traders.

A putrefying corpse stood in the centre of the vestibule.

Rotted fabric, the remnants of a shroud, fell in tatters from its bony shoulders. It came toward us with shuffling steps, as though its decomposing limbs might collapse at any moment beneath it. The stench of the foul thing pressed in waves through the chamber with the fetor of a charnel house.

I have confessed several times already the fright I have felt when faced by something unprecedented and menacing. The cats of the People, at once feral and tamed, still sometimes pace through my dreams, fangs dripping. The ruby eyes of chained Mathketh made my stomach cramp with dread, until I took that creature's measure. This walking corpse, though, terrified me more than I can possibly express. Nor do I believe that this admission subtracts from my courage.

Was this fear merely my superstitious childhood revived within me? There are instants when all the gains of cynical adulthood are plucked from us, when we seem to plunge again into the estate of the child, seem to stand alone and lost in thin nightclothes on a rocky cliff, blown by a black wind, face averted from something appalling which snuffles at our trail.

Yet my consternation now was not so simply explained. Some mechanism of the War Master reached into our minds and found there the thing most demoralizing to each of us, and remade that thing to place in our path.

My jaw was rigid. Sweat poured like acid into my eyes, because what I saw was impossible unless the gates of hell had opened to my nemesis. I saw what I saw. In that moment, there was no leisure to reflect on the nature of illusion.

The face of the corpse, as it advanced on me, was eaten by decay. Folds and lumps of gray flesh hung from cheeks and jaw. It tried to move its lipless mouth, to speak, to bring forth its accusations. Fat white worms crawled in the slime of its sightless sockets, yet it saw me. It reached out to clutch me.

Its head had been clumsily stitched back to its neck, with the looping twine stitches of the tentmakers of the desert.

That head was the severed head of the Rokhmun thief, the man I had soiled my vow to kill.

"Go back," I screamed. Shadows swooped like bats as the crystal in Glade's hand shook. I swallowed bile and stalked forward on stiff, unfeeling legs. Alamogordo I held in my two hands, the great blade high before me. "Return to your hell, or I shall smash your rotting bones and feed your stinking flesh to the rats." I talked to him in the patois of the desert thieves, so that he might better understand my threats.

"Hahn," I half heard Vanden mutter, behind me, choking; and, "Oh, no, Father," cried Glade, and she dropped the crystal, spilling light as it rolled in the dust of the floor.

The dead man stopped and opened his mouth.

"Criminals, I am Death. Look upon me, for this is your

fate, you who dare encroach within the City of Night. Look carefully, before you die, for you know me well.''

Vanden stumbled backward into the musty gloom with a shrill scream. I glanced at him, and some part of me asked why the sight of the Rokhmun thief come back from hell should offend the trader so greatly. His skin was pulled tight as yellow parchment over the bones of his face. His eyes were wide and bulging; saliva dribbled from his gaping mouth.

''The stench! Stay away from me, Hahn. See, Brother, I recognize you. I know your thirst for vengeance, poor Hahn; oh, the chill from you, the wretched chill of the tomb—''

Glade was scrabbling in the dust for her light. She left it there, seized Vanden by the arm, pulled him brutally around to face her.

''This is not your twin, Vanden.''

''Yes.'' He shook and shook. ''See, are you blind, Glade? Look at him, oh, keep him away from me . . .''

''I thought it was my dead father, Vanden,'' Glade said fiercely. ''When I look at him that is what I see still. It is merely some ghoulish trick of the War Master's, conjured by our entry.''

I backed away to join them, holding my sword high. ''Glade, I see a man I killed in my own world.''

''Do not look at it,'' she told us both. ''Vanden, believe me. Hahn lies buried in the graveyard of Asuliun. Besides, his spirit bears you no grudge; the priests have long since deemed you guiltless.''

The trader's cheeks flushed with a rush of blood. He ceased his gibbering; in a tantrum, he flung aside Glade's hand from his arm.

''What can they know of my guilt? Had I lingered to face the beast which slew him—'' He fell silent, stared back at the corpse which waited in silence; shook his head as if puzzled. In the tones of a dubious child, he asked: ''Is this not Hahn, then?''

''No,'' I growled. ''It is a demon come to drain our spirits for the crime of venturing into this unholy place.''

The dead thing raised its arms. Shards of bone protruded from the decayed flesh.

"Foolish ones," it said in a voice like the slithering of slugs, "turn back now if you fear the grave. Death stands before you in the palace of Aji-suki-takahikone, Lord of Thunder between earth and heaven, War Master of Treet Hoown, potentate of the world. Unless you have conquered the spider Nothing, advance no further."

I leapt at the cadaver with a howl that drowned its slimy words. Alamogordo flashed in a hungry arc. Stench pierced my throat, the chill of the thing reached through my garments and my flesh to clench my thundering heart.

The blade sparkled with green witch-fire. I staggered, thrown off balance. There was no crunching of brittle bone, no spurt of sluggish ichor as Alamogordo cut through the horror. I might as effectively have slashed the wind.

Before I could recover, strike again, the corpse vanished like a candle flame blown out.

THIRTEEN

My superstitious heart gloated. I put my sword to rest.

"The touch of iron has driven the demon back to hell!"

Glade gave a shaky laugh. "I believe there is a less exotic explanation, Xaraf." She stooped, retrieved the light-crystal, blew dust from its shining surface. Vanden stared vacantly at the place where the apparition had stood. The quester went to him with anxious solicitude. "My friend, the thing was no more than an illusion. Do not let it trouble you."

The dregs of a nightmare can be shaken off; this clung, soiling the spirit, eating its guilt into closed rooms of the mind. Vanden blinked, brought his eyes into focus.

"An illusion . . . ." Grief and uncertainty disfigured his face. He nodded without conviction, not meeting our eyes. "Yes, perhaps. Had it been my brother he would have spoken to me of my guilt. Did he mention a name?"

"A long mouthful," I said. "I did not catch it."

"Aji-suki-takahikone," Glade said. "It is a very ancient name. The War Master took it in his pride."

"Yes," Vanden said. "An illusion . . . ."

I stared into the darkness of the large chamber. "Phantom or demon," I stated flatly, "the thing bodes us ill. Let us find our way out before it returns with more corporeal accomplices."

"There is no gain in retreat," Glade said vehemently. She directed the light this way and that. "Besides, we have already established that the entrance is locked. To escape we must go forward." Her grin was lopsided, wan. "Indeed, might we not yet capture some exotic treasure? Why else would the War

Master have rigged his palace with these abominable deterrents?''

I heard Vanden's teeth chatter. "I am afraid, Glade, deathly afraid." He pressed knuckles to his mouth. "The air stinks of old evil. We must go back. Xaraf is right. We place our souls at risk by lingering here."

Alamogordo spoke then.

It had said nothing during our explorations; I had forgotten that another voice might announce itself among us. My knees bent in readiness for assault, I whirled, the speaking voice whirled with me, I had the sword out and ready to strike before I understood that my weapon was the one I meant to smite with my weapon. I did not laugh.

"Xaraf is wrong," the sword was saying. "This chamber is sealed. In minutes it will begin to fill with poisonous vapors. I advise action."

By the end of this piece of unsolicited exhortation, I was aware of something I had been too busy to notice earlier: a shimmer of faint, indistinct radiance. I squinted past the glow of the light-crystal.

"Glade, douse the light."

"No!" Vanden was beside himself with terror. He clutched at the crystal. "We must have light! It will creep up on us in the dark."

"Shut your mouth. Do as I say, Glade."

She thrust the crystal back inside its leather pouch. The room was pitch-black, all but that part of it where a translucent sphere hung at the boundaries of visibility.

"I see nothing," Glade told me.

"Look again." I reached blindly in the darkness, found her hand, placed it in contact with the blade.

"Ah." She caught Vanden's hand in turn. "Presumably Alamogordo directs our attention to this object."

There was no further comment from my blade.

"A great bubble of some unearthly stuff, suspended a hand's breadth from the floor. Is that what you see?"

"Xaraf, it is a vehicle."

"But is it a trap?"

"Surely not," Glade said. "Evidently the thing is protected

by a screen like that which shields the city. Why hide a slaying device? That would be an excess of subtlety: intruders to this chamber are already sufficiently vulnerable.''

Vanden disagreed. ''There is danger in everything wrought by the hand of the War Master. He was insidious. Let us tread with caution, Glade, caution.'' His vision, whatever it was, had come close to unmanning him.

In the darkness we crossed the great dusty floor, clumsily, for each of us was obliged to retain some contact with the efficacy of the blade. All was quiet. Our steps were muffled in dust. Oppressive mustiness clogged our nostrils, but the charnel stench was gone. I detected a faint hissing from the doorway behind us, and with it the faintest fragrance of roses.

''We are safe,'' Vanden cried. ''The door opens.''

With controlled panic, Glade said: ''Quite the reverse. We must lose no time. That is the vapor Alamogordo warned us about. Can we get into the sphere, Xaraf?''

''Wait here.'' I circled away to the right, moving as fast as I could. The light reappeared; Glade had removed the crystal from its bag. My sword tingled slightly. Aided by its curious potency, I could now see both my huddled companions and the floating, luminous sphere.

No door opened into its smooth opalescence. Its purpose was obscure.

I smelled rose blossoms, and my attention slurred.

''Well?''

Scowling, I saw that I had circled it completely and learned nothing of value.

''No way in.''

''It awaits us, and in a locked room,'' Glade said. Her eyelids flickered, closed; she caught herself, gripped my arm fiercely. ''Xaraf, my father—I mean, the image, the thing you call a demon, it gave us a message. I construe it as a challenge to suitable recipients, as well as a warning.''

''I shall cut my way in if need be,'' I told her with abrupt, unmotivated anger. My head was thick with the fragrance. I imagined for a moment that I was chained once more to the tree in the Forest of the People. Cats. Killing birds. Alamogordo swung, blurring, above my head.

A flare of light. The hairs on the backs of my hands lifted. The blanket of invisibility was gone.

Like a solid convex sheet of ice, the sphere's hull curved toward us. Light danced in it. I felt a force dragging at my sword arm. The sphere was pulling at the blade.

"Sword and sphere have some affinity," I said. My anger was gone; now I felt ravenously hungry. The sword was lifted physically into the air by whatever force emanated from the sphere, swung to my left. "Should I release it?"

"By no means." Glade was staring at me with a lascivious expression quite at odds with her words. She began to unbuckle her breeches, stopped herself, looked at me in astonishment and chagrin. "Hurry, Xaraf. It is a map; perhaps it is a key also to this lock."

Vanden began to laugh foolishly. He sat down in the dust, tears of silly pleasure rolling down his cheeks.

Like a monstrous lodestone the sphere pulled at my sword. I went after it, my arms shaking with the effort of holding it. With a final quivering thrust, the point of the blade smashed itself into the featureless surface. It was almost torn from my grasp.

"Xaraf, I think we are dying. Please hurry," Glade cried. She was heaving at Vanden, who sat eating the dust.

I screamed in rage. "What can I do, you stupid whore?" The sphere cracked, opened. Light poured forth, brightened. The fissure extended to the width of a man's outstretched arms. At once, Alamogordo became inert, dropping heavily to my side.

If we stayed here we would certainly perish. I vaulted through the opening.

The interior of the device was warm and soft as human flesh. Bands of light ran endlessly around the bland concave surface. A faint musty odor tainted the air, but I smelled no roses and the curved floor was free of dust.

"Quickly," I called. I was half crouched, blade at the ready, eyes narrowed in the odd pulsing light. The sphere was void of life.

"Help me with Vanden," Glade called, gasping with effort. I turned. She had him half-hoisted on her back.

The sphere's entrance began to close.

I bounded forward, jammed my body between the advancing edges.

"Stand back!" Glade cried. "It will crush you."

I tensed, heaved. Some hidden mechanism, functional still after its epochal slumber, registered my presence. The valve cycled open. I reached down with one hand, helped pull the confused traders inside. We sprawled in a heap. The entrance closed.

Glade's breath rasped. The scent of flowers cleared from the air. It seemed that wasps hummed. The swirling bands of light muted. I found that I could see through the curve of the vehicle, as if its pearl were a clouded eye and we observers within the eye's chamber.

With wonderful grace, then, the bubble lofted up from the floor and drifted toward the great vestibule's farther wall.

I had not truly appreciated the size and grandeur of this palace, for the vestibule was prodigiously large. Through the wall of our bubble came blurred images of broken furnishings not entirely spoiled by decay, tortured fetishes of metal standing after an aeon of neglect, daises and pits half visible beneath the furry dust. These remnants glowed in the sphere's radiance, rendered by it into haunted, haunting shapes of dream.

Vanden gave a cry of fright. I looked ahead.

The wall was looming in front of us: dark, ominous, intractable. Instinctively I cringed from it, raised my arms before my face at the impending impact.

"We will be smashed like an eggshell," Vanden bleated.

"We will be safe!" Glade cried. "It would be utterly illogical—"

And then the wall was gone. We moved now through a different room entirely.

In an instant of shadow the bubble had curdled. I had hunched, chilled to the marrow. And we had flowed through the wall like smoke through a sleeping-net.

I had no time for hysteria, which was Vanden's response. This new room brightened with light of its own as we glided through it. Fantastic weapons stood everywhere racked, dulled by time but clearly similar to the devices poised in Mathketh's citadel.

"An armory?"

Sweat beaded Glade's face. She was hugging Vanden to her breast; the man was limp, weeping. "More likely a forward defense installation," she told me. "I think we will be immune. We ride, after all, in a device these weapons should have been programmed to ignore."

The room of death machines swept past. Another wall hung before us, indented with blank screens of quartz and multitudes of inactive indicators. Glade kept up a running commentary, her manner dry, taut with strain.

There was no faltering at the wall: The sphere went toward its destination, unstoppable, not to be deterred by mere material obstacles. Its leading edge seemed to sink into the wall ahead; shadow flickered; a shocking chill; we had passed once more without damage.

It was enough to unhinge the mind.

I gripped Alamogordo's hilt. The intelligence of the sword spoke no words of comfort or explanation. Inattentively I watched the rich, elaborate carving which decorated the pale golden walls of this chamber.

"How is this possible?" My own voice, like Glade's, was thin with stress. "Matter cannot penetrate matter. One would think the walls no more substantial than a cloud, than . . . than the demonic image which taunted us."

Unexpectedly, Vanden raised his red-rimmed eyes and spoke with careful rationality. "It is a forgotten art, but one commonly practiced in antiquity. Solids, liquids, plasmas, air—all are mere superficial aspects of an underlying principle of energy. This device possesses the capability to adjust the state of just these gross aspects, and ours as well, to a condition of permeability."

I swallowed hard. "You mean—" I had to stop. I slammed my fist into the yielding wall of the sphere. "It is we, and not the walls, which have become insubstantial?" I smote again. "See? Thus I refute you."

"Oh, Xaraf, you are naïve." Glade restrained my bunched arm, smiled at me with a strange, appealing sweetness. "We and our vehicle share the same state. How can that state be tested from within its own conditions? But do not be alarmed." She drew me down to squat on the curving floor. "The effect is only momentary. So long as the mechanism retains its functions, we stand in little danger of dissipating into particles smaller than dust."

We had been skimming through a minor room of excessive luxury, a bathing arena to gauge by the deep scallop in the floor and the lewd aquatic frolics displayed on the walls. Glade raised her eyebrows, gave me a secret smile. I touched her arm, her hand, squeezed her fingers. We penetrated a wall now, to drift in a gloomy corridor of vast length and height.

"What a comfort you are," Vanden told her sourly over his shoulder. He pressed his face to the bubble. "But what is this?"

All along either side of this dim hall, greenish ovoids marched in serried ranks. Each was almost twice the height of a big man. Within their unpleasant glow, human figures of conventional stature could be made out. Naked, eyes closed, they floated in some buoyant medium, hair streaming out from their scalps.

Glade drew in her breath.

"The people of Treet Hoown! Until this moment I did not quite believe—"

"Are they dead?" Undeniably they looked dead, looked, if the truth be told, like pickled fish in glass bowls.

"In a sense, perhaps. But I see no reason to suppose that they cannot be returned to life. They are locked in abeyance, safe from the corruption which has ruined the city."

In a harsh tone I asked, "How may they be released?" Down the endless, silent parade of living dead we went, watched them pent in that frozen instant which had lasted a hundred millennia, which could extend without change, if Mathketh spoke truly, until the very sun flickered and died.

"Only the Master would hold the key," Vanden said. He turned his face away from the citizens of the doomed city, mouth scarred with loathing. "A mind which could conceive such a plan was a monster indeed. To restore these unfortunates, we would have to risk his release." He looked from one of us to the other. "We must not do it. My soul cries out in shame as I say this, but we cannot hazard his global lunacy once more."

We lofted through dimness. Sleeping ranks passed like figures in a dream.

Now the character of the dormant citizens altered. Stern-faced military stood at attention in their time-stilled instant. These were fully appareled, polished armor turned murky by the green luminescence, decorated light-lances at their sides, bell-shaped weapons in their fists. If in its numbers it was not yet an army, I thought, it remained potentially formidable.

"The War Master's crack personal guard," Glade speculated.

The corridor ended then, and the sphere took us through a massive metal wall.

And we were in the throne room itself.

FOURTEEN

I had been in this place before. My skin itched with the recognition of it.

Brilliant and dazing as the secret interior of a jewel, light flared up from a dozen majestic torches wrought in copper green with verdigris. It leapt again and again in myriad reflections from the bright faceted steel of walls, floor, polished ceiling.

Smoke flapped, sulphurous. Surely the torches had been sparked by the arrival of our bubble. Not even the wondrous resources of this world, I told myself, could have maintained their flame endlessly while the very mountains wore away.

But my eye was not held by the fumes that fluttered and eddied, nor by the barbaric intaglios which slashed the mirrored floor with scarlet, bronze, amber.

At the polished room's focus, cupped in the gaping jaws of a great black stone skull, cushioned by gold and emerald pillows on a pallet sprung by ivory fillets, the War Master squatted in the pouches of his own pallid flesh.

My gorge rose. "The beast is more toad than man," I cried, knowing him, remembering him from nightmare. I raised my eyes in dread, sure of what I would see looming above him.

A pair of horrendous warriors glared forth at me from the deep pits of the skull's eyes. Their skin was dull green, inhuman, scaled as a reptile's. From their slit mouths ferocious tusks jutted, gleaming with spittle. Nostrils were sunk in horned folds between their eyes. They were appalling.

"Non-men," Glade whispered. "From what desolate experiment did they spring?"

At last I obliged myself to return my gaze to the terrible creature they guarded, and his prisoner.

He was motionless. Against his bulging, crinkled flab he pressed a lovely woman whose features seemed demented with disgust. Heavy with gems, his right hand gripped her pale, uncovered thigh.

I knew her, knew the gold and bronze fire of her hair, knew and loved her eyes green as the sky's first momentary ignition before dawn, knew the touch of her wonderfully smooth flesh, delicious, a warmer, paler gold.

And of course I had not been here before, not ever in my life.

I had dreamed this place. Or Darkbloom had dreamed it for me.

The shimmering bubble stilled its forward motion ten paces before the great throne.

A green, membranous ovoid surrounded and protected the skull and those within it, but every detail of the tableau was vivid in the dancing brilliance of the flares.

Aji-suki-takahikone leered his gross self-satisfaction, the very corporeal image of every bloated creature who has gorged and gorged on the cream of the world: Fat bulged in the pouches of his eyes, jowls, belly. He had eaten the world and the concupiscence of his greed distended his belly. It was a mockery of pregnancy. His flesh was pallid and ill. A loose, glossy gown of exquisite fabric covered his arms and shoulders, exposed the mounds of hairless flesh that tumbled from his breasts.

The valve of the bubble cycle opened without a sound. I hardly noticed. I was looking again at the woman I knew from my dreams. Her loveliness was disfigured by the terror and revulsion which opened her mouth in a held scream, lips thinned and drawn back over her teeth. Overwhelmed by feelings I could not name, I could not take my eyes from her. Her hair rushed like a mane about her bare shoulders. Everything in my life had pointed me to this moment. I was breathless. My hatred for Aji-suki-takahikone brought the blood to my temples like a bell struck again and again. Even in my dreams I had never learned her name.

I loved her so fiercely, so suddenly, after so long (all this storming together in my head and my choked breast) that I stood paralyzed, staring at her in her horrible captivity, uttering a deep terrible groan I did not hear. Glade touched my arm, and again; shook my shoulder.

"Xaraf. The sphere is open."

"What? What?" The woman whose name I did not know was pale as a daughter of Berb-Kisheh. All her tranquility and grace was lost, robbed from her by this vile beast. I would kill him. I would maim and unman him.

"We have entered the snare," Glade said. I looked at her, and she flinched from my expression. There was no way I could explain this thing to her, not now, not here. She said, "Let us see if we can turn the risk to our advantage."

"Yes," I agreed.

We stepped out onto mirror. Duplicates of ourselves, of the throne, of the ornaments and trophies that garnished the chamber, flung back from every facet to confuse us, diminishing in the false distances to crowds of images echoing our every step and gesture.

Here, at its destination, the sphere's shield of invisibility had been deactivated. It hovered above the floor like a soft bauble, a shell swimming with bands of shifting color. We ventured warily away from it.

Vanden uttered a tortured sound.

We stopped, waited for him. He stood still, looking broken and frail.

"Something in my spirit has been damaged," he said without embarrassment. His characteristic cynicism was absent; he held his fear tightly under control. "Perhaps it was the apparition, recalling to me guilt I have hidden too long from my conscience."

"Oh, Vanden, you are—"

"No, Glade, let me have my say." He rubbed his eyes with finger and thumb; deep bruises were there. "Perhaps my guilt is irrelevant. Perhaps it is the vile thing we see here before us, blatant as a running sore."

The air was perfectly still in the throne room, yet the flames snapped and flared. Everything had the likeness of illusion; none of it was. Vanden, I understood, had transcended his fear into a ruthless consecration.

"I find I am not interested in whether we gain booty and fame," he said. His voice was quite soft; it pierced, though, like a skewer. He looked with his bruised eyes into Glade's face. "Despite my love for you, my dearest friend, I no longer care whether or not your quest succeeds. I wish one thing: to see this filthy thing destroyed." He flung out his hand at Aji-suki-takahikone. "To see his crushed people released, to see the city of Treet Hoown returned to vigor, and at peace. Can you comprehend this?" He laughed. "I swear to you, Glade, *I* cannot, but it is so."

Vanden sighed then, a long exhalation of pain. He looked intently at Glade, at me, and then he sent his cold, zealot gaze once more to the tableau within the great grinning skull.

Glade, I saw, was very tired. Nodding, she lowered her eyes.

"You are right, of course, Vanden. Nothing seems to me more important than rescuing these unfortunates. Yet the obstacles in our way seem insuperable."

"We have been directed to this place," I reminded them. "Perhaps this is our intended task. Alamogordo," I added in a crisp tone, "is this so? Are we meant to wake the city?"

The sword kept its counsel. After an interval, Glade shrugged.

"As Vanden has already stated, we cannot risk unleashing this creature on our dying world. However, I think we shall experience difficulty in escaping from here with our lives, even if we leave everything as we find it. Have you not noticed the pitiful remains of our predecessors?" She gestured past the glowing curve of the sphere.

The position of the bubble, and the placement of the smoky flares, had conspired to hide in gloom one segment of the throne room. A pall of darkness hugged the region, casting back no reflection, troubling the eye.

All about this furtive realm, mordant as the leavings of a pack of wild dogs, lay the scattered bones of human skeletons.

"These carried away neither booty nor tales of madness," I murmured. I took a step toward the zone of shadows. How had these men and women died? Nothing moved to threaten us; indeed, nothing moved at all but the bright flames, casting up their wraiths of oily smoke. "Are we to be attacked by an automaton, another Mathketh?"

Vanden looked at the remains with abhorrence. "Perhaps this is the lair for some genetic construct like the non-men, with a taste for human flesh."

I did not know whether or not to take him seriously. I advanced another step. The flames guttered, as though a giant's breath had blasted across them, and us: the breath of a giant who had dined on ordure. I coughed, held my hand over my nose and mouth. The lights sank, sullen and red. In the reeking gloom, the corpse stood once more in our way.

It had not come alone.

Two naked youths clung to its putrid flesh. Youths? Perhaps children, for hair had not yet come out upon their bodies, not quite. They teetered at that place of balance between ignorance and knowledge; between, the War Master's illusion insisted, innocence and corruption. They were demonically beautiful.

The boy was white as marble, smooth, flax-haired, his pouting lips defined by a raised edge at the rims; and his blue-eyed gaze was sly, disconcertingly lewd. I had seen his like in the slave markets, where fat merchants bought their catamites. He fondled the corpse, grinning sidelong at us, and with his other hand, index finger wet with spittle, reached furtively to touch the budding breasts of his dark twin.

The girl was purple-black, her lips thin, eyes pale as high summer sky, piercing. If her twin's expression was indecent, hers was frankly ribald; she pressed her naked cleft into the sharded yellow bone of the leg of that thing to which she clung, like a dog in heat which mounts, in its confusion, an outstretched booted leg, rubbing herself in slow provocative gyrations. She closed her eyes to slits when her brother's fingers touched her, and she shivered, reaching behind the corpse to find the pale boy's buttocks.

A hint of perfume, of sweat and musk, came to us from their bodies, mingled with the charnel stench of the corpse.

The boy spoke with a voice sweet and seductive as a lyre made for melodies of lust. "Foolhardy mortals, do you persist? Leave this chamber and you shall know only ordinary death. Remain, and we shall have you for our games." He laughed, a trilling sound that broke, at the end, with the break a youth's voice makes in those months when he becomes a man. His eyes were knowing and he smiled, smiled.

Vanden spoke, in a voice that choked. "We will not leave." He stared past the three figures to the vault of shadows, turned in agitation to Glade and me. "They seek to distract us from that place where the others died. See, the bones—"

The corpse spoke then, foul and moist as before.

"You challenge the prohibition? Understand, then: Madness lies in that place. You will die in agony, and your mind will be crushed even as your body is torn. Do you stand here yet? Surely you fear Death. No man may conquer this domain unless he has first conquered the spider Nothing."

I did not understand what it was conveying, beyond my confused sense that taunts were mixed here with interdictions. The sight of the children at once aroused and sickened me. I roared out, as we had been trained to roar in the height of battle, "Stand aside! I have driven you off once with steel. Must I repeat the lesson?"

Glade said quietly, "Do not waste your strength. Again, it is merely an illusion. The War Master seeks to undermine us by stealth. We gain more by listening carefully to its every word."

The black girl smirked at us. She pressed her small breasts against the dead thing.

"Attend, then." Her voice was hoarse, sensual; it rasped my nerves. "You stand before the throne of Aji-suki-taka-hikone, potentate of the world. Within this tomb of darkness is life, for those with an abundance of it, and death for those who must die. Here is the city's key, which waits for one who has conquered death. This one alone may revive Treet Hoown."

Without the gloom in any way diminishing, it seemed that for the first time our gaze was able to penetrate the shadows.

A vessel stood there, within the heart of the darkness, carved from ebony, cool and lustrous as midnight, upon a slab of black marble.

Can there be black fire? A radiance one sees by the absence of light? If so, that was the color of the vessel. That was the means by which we saw it.

The youths fell back behind the dead creature, holding hands, and the terrible rotting face swung blindly toward the dark vessel.

"Go forward, then, if you are brave and deathless. The *Mysterium Coniunctionis* protects Treet Hoown's silence. Within it you will find destiny, riches, power to accompany your endless life. Step forward to claim it."

The copper-wrought torches blazed up again, dazzling in the darkness, making our eyes contract, water. I darted forward. Corpse and children were gone. Smoke curled where they had stood.

"Glade, what was that it said?" For the first time since the translation device had imprinted the grammar and vocabulary of the trader's tongue on my mind, I completely failed to understand a string of words.

"A defunct term."

"It has lapsed from general use?"

"Deliberately deleted, rather."

"Ah. A taboo phrase. Does it, perhaps, relate to those evil children?"

"Not precisely." My insistence was clearly a cause of pain to Glade. Reluctantly, she said, "From time to time, our legislators deem certain words mischievous. To permit their continued use would reinforce noxious patterns of thought and behavior."

"Can mere words yield such malign influence?" Darkbloom might have posed such a question of me, and now I posed it on his behalf, as it were, out of loyal habit; my own people, superstitious one and all, never doubted for an instant that words could heal or curse, damn or conjure wonders.

"Of course they can." Glade frowned, seeking examples for a proposition which seemed self-evident. "Suppose we were permitted to employ particles which automatically specified gender or physical characteristics, whether or not these attributes were relevant to what we discussed. Immediately, castes would be precipitated and validated. How might the damage then be undone? The employment of ordinary speech would seem to countenance atrocities.''

It was my turn to frown, mind racing. Gender? Physical characteristics? This was ludicrous. Was Glade suggesting the abolition of words like "he" and "she," "nigger" and "trasher," "child" and "adult"? Yet she herself used these terms constantly.

Something happened inside my mind then which made everything blur, as if I had been struck a soundless blow, as if my vision had gone double.

Glade had *never* used those words.

Nor had I, in speaking to her.

The machine which had reached inside my brain and written its rules for translation had done so at a level beyond my inspection. I thought in my own tongue, I suppose, and a genie within my mind took my ideas and found the best equivalent in Glade's tongue. And this "translation" was what I spoke, thinking it a perfect reflection of my meaning.

I was flabbergasted. In the middle of the throne room of Aji-suki-takahikone, another of the underpinnings of my world had been snatched away. Since that moment I think that I have not been the same man.

"Xaraf?"

"I . . . Another time, Glade. You have shocked me profoundly, and I doubt that I could easily explain exactly how." I tried to collect my thoughts, whatever verbal expression they were to be given. "This deleted term. Why was it deemed mischievous? Think carefully, Glade; your answer might be the clue to our safe conduct from this place."

"The damage occasioned by the term was philosophical."

"Everything you have said sounds like the rarest philosophy to me, Glade."

"Perhaps I should say 'metaphysical.' It proposes a condition infinitely desirable and absolutely unattainable, the mental equivalent of the quest for a perpetual motion machine. Oh, Xaraf, this is hardly the time to launch your education in physics and epistemology! The *Mysterium Coniunctionis* denotes a welding, indeed a wedding, of all opposites and principles."

I thought of the lascivious, endlessly youthful twins. "Male and female?" That dichotomy *was* translated, since the distinction was salient; how baffling to observe this happen now as I spoke, never to have noticed it before.

"I imagine so," Glade said doubtfully. "Sleep and Consciousness might be a better example."

A sharp, unpleasant taste filled my mouth. "Life and Death?" I thought I understood at last what the awful creature had been saying to us. "If Mathketh spoke truly, Aji-suki-takahikone valued immortality above all else. Do you suppose that this entire city could be a trap set for immortals? That he still hopes to win its secret, by guile now rather than by force of arms?"

Vanden paid us no attention. He stared into the dark flickering, his face transfigured by some unguessable emotion. But Glade was intrigued by the audacity of this speculation.

"Brilliant, Xaraf! And the *Mysterium Coniunctionis?* An apparatus, perhaps, for distinguishing immortals from their more fragile fellows—in a word, from us?"

The notion disturbed me profoundly. "It would explain a great deal. The ease with which we gained entry. The deliberate provocation of the specters. These bones of the mortals who have come before us."

Glade's shoulders sagged. "If so, discretion is the better part of wisdom. We cannot hope to satisfy such a test."

And then the time for philosophy, for judicious pondering and evaluation, was gone.

Vanden was running across the glittering metal floor, energy-lance in hand, running pell-mell for the zone of deepest shadow.

Glade shouted in dismay.

The trader reached the outer edges of shadow and stumbled. With a scream of agony, he fell forward as though something reached up and pulled at him, dragging him into the cold murky core of the place we could not see.

As he fell his screaming did not abate. He skidded on the slippery floor, hands splayed to slow him. And then I saw that he was not, after all, trying to escape from the zone. He was crawling deliberately into it.

"Burning," he shrieked in a high pitiful voice, dragging himself forward. "Burning, burning."

He went on hands and knees toward the marble slab and its ebon prize, and the shrill sound of pain and terror was torn from his throat like some bright and bloody organ.

"Vanden, stay where you are!" Glade halted at the outer limits of shadow. "The *Mysterium* will destroy you; that is its only purpose."

Her words had no effect. Vanden's mind was burning.

I stared helplessly. If I were faced by a savage beast, an armed opponent, even demon shapes out of Hellmouth—and I had confronted all of these—I might lay about me knowing that the contest was not impossible. But to enter this obscene snare would be futile self-destruction.

Glade was weeping, unable to go into shadow, incapable of retreating while her friend crawled to his death.

Shrouded by opaque shadow, Vanden gave one last scream of torment and did not move again. All around him, human bones lay like the discarded playthings of a giant carnivorous imbecile.

Glade was tearing off her heavy leather belt.

"Give me your jerkin and shirt," she told me, ripping her own garments into long tattered strips, twining the strips into a makeshift rope.

I pulled off scabbard, jerkin, silk shirt. My sword fell with a crash. As if woken from its sleep, the voice of Alamogordo spoke suddenly. "Xaraf, take me to him."

I think I had known that this was my task since I had first seen the lovely woman held in the grasp of the toad.

"Yes," I said. I seized the end of the rope Glade was still knotting together, wound it firmly through my own belt.

"No," Glade said angrily. "This risk is mine."

I drew Alamogordo. "You heard the talisman," I said. "Let us not make this a contest for glory, Glade."

"Glory?" Her fingers tore fabric, worked it, added to the rope, and her eyes burned with fury. "Do not be a fool, Xaraf.

My friend is dying. I am going in to get him. You cannot stop me.''

"Glade, you would die," the sword told her calmly. "I am permitted to lend Xaraf a limited potency to withstand this mortification."

"Mathketh took me for the agent of immortals," I added. "It was Alamogordo he recognized, Glade. Enough." I turned and hurled myself into shadow, the rope uncoiling at my heels.

Unexpectedly, the quality of the light did not deteriorate as I burst into the central zone of the *Mysterium Coniunctionis*. But a shaking chill went from my skin to my bones, to my deepest organs, as if I had plunged naked into a snow-swollen river.

While my entrails froze, a stinging rash of white-hot sparks seemed to pit and sear my hands and feet. My eyes misted at the double pang. Blisters swelled on the soles and sides of my feet, or so it seemed. I slowed to a hobbled lope.

Vanden lay ahead in congealed cloud. Beyond his body, the vessel glimmered with its black radiance.

A jerking tug at my waist, and then another as the rope caught in Glade's hands, linked me to safety, though every jolt sent a spasm of sickness through me. My head beat with illness, like the aftereffects of a day and night of drunkenness.

In my right hand, Alamogordo was beginning to glow, from red to hot white, like an unfinished sword on a smith's anvil. No heat came to me from the metal.

I stumbled toward Vanden. I seemed to get no closer. The nature of time had changed, as it changes during that poisoning of a hangover when a head propped on a pillow seems to swoop backward, falling and lurching, and dry tongue sweeps drier mouth, eyelids crust, night seems endless until day comes with its piercing light, and then its heat, its brightness, pushes and drags and labors through endless dreary retching misery.

And I knew that, like Vanden, I was dying.

Light flickered and reeled. I lay on a pallet of stinking furs holding closed a great wound in my belly, and my life's blood pulsed out through my wet fingers, shuddering waves of pain and blankness. I died.

I was dying. I ran howling down narrow clammy corridors of stone and oozing mortar, pursued in my claustrophobic terror by shapes that shrieked and had no face. Hands cold and tipped with claws fluttered about me, ripped me in freezing jabs I could not deflect. I bled and bled as they tore away my eyes, as I struck and rebounded from lacerating stone, bled as they gnawed me with their filed teeth.

I was dying. Voices whistled like the winds of a blizzard in the high pasturing places in Kravaard, explained their loathing and hatred, their cruel contempt. Laughter mocked into echoes as I died.

I fell into a pool of acids that seethed and hissed, and corrosion ate my flesh from my bones even as I screamed with a throat full of the tearing gases that foamed and licked me with lethal perfumes.

Flames leapt at me from darkness, explosive reds and yellows, roared up around me as I clutched my head, as my hair took fire, and I was plunging into inferno, burning, burning, powerless to extinguish the flames that charred my flesh as they killed me.

Alamogordo blazed in my hand.

"A dream, Xaraf," it cried. "Turn your mind aside from its tempting."

"I know," I whimpered.

A corona of sky-bright blue cascaded from the sword's englyphed blade.

Vanden lay immobile and twisted. The black slab held its treasure. I crawled toward it, dying.

Water sucked at my body, dragged my gasping, paralyzed corpse along the rasping drowned dunes of heavy sand at the ocean's floor. I choked, broke free, rose above the surface, took a breath full of water. Salt scoured my eyes. There was no land in any direction. A wave climbed toward me, broke, frothed, fell. I opened my choked throat to scream and the gushing torrent entered me, took me down, held me under until I died.

I was dead. Nothing moved. My pulse had stopped. I could not breathe. My lungs were in agony. My stilled heart convulsed, beat, caught, beat again. I clawed my way up from temporary death. Darkness everywhere, and stale dead air. Terrified, I lashed out my arms and struck wooden boards. Above, on either side, wood. The stale air was heavy with the stench of decay. My body had rotted. I knew suddenly, and with utter terror, where I was: wrapped in thick linen, suffocating in a Kishehmun casket, immured within the limestone of a burial cairn.

I shrieked, gasped.

I raised my face from the glistening facets of the mirrored floor. My belt was tight about my chest, choking me. I plucked feebly at it, to release myself from its murderous grip. Someone yelling.

Cold radiance, a brilliant blue, streamed from the object in my right hand, extended on the floor, its image doubled, doubly brilliant.

Someone lay without movement in a mirror.

My hand fluttered, struck a bone. The bone skittered and rolled into shadow.

A voice was screaming at me, faint, annoying. I was dead.

No. I was not yet dead, but death called to me, vile, desolate, hideously seductive.

Vanden stared up at me, out of the mirror. His eyes were glazed, but he blinked. I touched the trader's neck. Something pulsed there, dying, as I was dying.

I seemed to have risen to my feet. I put down my sword, tried to hoist the body onto my shoulders. I fell down. My arm twisted under me. Glade's voice, and another. Alamogordo's. I fell backward. Something had pulled me, was dragging me clumsily across the body I had been attempting to lift. Every jolt took precious breath from me. Furious, I caught the rope in my hands and gave a powerful heave. It sent me stumbling. I tripped over the sword's hilt, sent its blue radiance spinning. I held a slack snake of tattered cloth in my hands.

I cannot carry him, I thought.

I knew what I had to do.

"Alamogordo," I screamed, turning, looking for the talisman which would carry me safely through this ordeal.

The sword was gone. I could not find its light. Shadow and

pain. The black marble slab hung in the midst of shadow. I stumbled toward it.

Impossibly heavy. I summoned every last jot of will within me. My anger was gone. I threw myself toward the ebon bowl.

My fingers brushed it. It tipped. A cone of silver metal rolled from it, curved away across the slab. My fingers closed on it.

Weakness rolled across me in waves. Beside my left eye, where my face rested against the cold marble, I saw an indentation in the slab.

The *Mysterium Coniunctionis*. Yes. The wedding. Moon and sun. The Great King and His Bride. Death in Life. Oh, consummation.

My hand was inflamed with agony. I drew it and the key it held, by a series of slow, infinitely tiny movements, toward the keyhole.

The cone caught at the lip of the hole, wavered, slid into place with an almost inaudible click.

For an instant, then, I passed completely from consciousness.

I did not have time to slide to the floor. I woke again, ears ringing, shocked, heart pounding.

Trumpets blared. Their barbaric resonance shook the torches in their sconces. Flares leapt exultant to that bray, raw fumes roiling from white erupting solid flame. The brazen shout of the instruments crashed over my head.

I pushed myself away from the marble slab.

I was not dead, not dying. I was alive. I was *alive!*

And the throne room had awoken.

FIFTEEN

Tears streaked my eyes. I wiped them away.

Half a dozen paces distant, sprawled on the faceted steel floor, Vanden lay without movement.

The iridescent sphere hung like a weightless bubble behind Glade. Half-naked, glossy in her own sweat, she stood with her light-lance activated.

At her back, free now of the unpleasant green tints of the stasis field, the War Master stirred. He looked down at the three of us and he smiled, smirked with dawning triumph. Sprawled in his pillows, scratching the obscene folds of his belly, he tightened his possessive grip on the body of the woman who struggled awake, horrified, in his lap.

"So." Aji-suki-takahikone exhaled, languid and feral as one of Oak-is-Strong's hunting cats. His replusive obesity shivered, and it was a long moment before I understood that the War Master was laughing, wheezing with satisfied amusement. "So. The immortals have come." He spoke in the language of dream. It stirred the hairs at my nape to hear such syllables from his mouth.

Above Aji-suki-takahikone, the two tusked monsters scanned us from their weapons emplacements, animate now with a contained fury that seemed at once searching and mindless. They said nothing. Only the slow gliding of ridged muscles beneath their green hide proved that they too had emerged from timelessness.

Glade doused her energy-lance. Stepping boldly forward, she stared up into the jaws of the skull.

"You are correct," she cried. "We are the immortals who

210

have rescued you from oblivion. And now, I trust, you will spare no time in meeting our price for that service.''

The War Master lost his complacent smile in an instant. He was, I judged, a man of prodigious personal force, compelling, charismatic. That he had chosen the night side of his spiritual gifts was characteristic in an unchecked leader. It was a merit of the ways of the Wanderers that no one man might attain absolute dominion; the clans and tribes strained in endless contest for station, elevation, fame; the rigors of our life, the cycle of pasture and herd, the desert's glare and the shadow of the city, all these constrained the ambition of a hungry masterful man, and if not his ambition at least the implementation in practice of that ambition. Much of this, I freely admit, is Darkbloom's view of the case, conveyed to me over a hundred solitary meals out of earshot of the campfires, yet it seemed true to me then, and seemed profound as I faced this astonishing creature, this world-eater, whose jowls purpled at Glade's cool demand. The blood of anger rushed across his features. Our lives, I thought, hung on a breath.

Cunning asserted itself over passion then, and the War Master restrained his passion. His eyes closed slowly, masking his piercing gaze.

''My peers, I welcome you to Treet Hoown. Know that I am Aji-suki-takahikone, Potentate of the world. Your signal service shall not go unrewarded. Ask and it shall be yours.''

I was watching the woman. She seemed dazed, incapable of speech. In a rush, a kind of image made itself known to my sympathy, an echo of those dreams we had shared:

An instant before, to her, she and all those trapped in the city had faced annihilation from the Powers in Their battle with Aji-suki-takahikone; now, abruptly, she was once more awake, and three strangers stood within the inner sanctum of her captor. Little wonder that she waited, trembling, for clarity.

A note of derision had already entered the War Master's voice. He leaned forward slightly. ''But how shocking! I see that one of your number lies supine, unattended. What ails him? We must see at once to his condition.''

''There is no urgent necessity,'' Glade stated. I was astounded at the control she kept over her voice. She was fighting for Vanden's life in the best way she knew: by deceit, badinage, a trader's armamentarium. "The mild influence of your precautionary devices augmented a psychic strain in the Lord Vanden Tenderness, brought on by the peculiar rigors of interstellar travel."

The woman cried out at the word. Her eyes had come to rest on me, without belief, yet desperate and elated. Negligently, the War Master cuffed her, bruising her mouth with his jewel-ringed fingers. I tensed; Glade placed her hand on my arm. "You come, then," he asked, "from the high places between the stars?"

"Where else?" Glade said slyly. "To our discomfort, however, the vessel in which we voyaged became damaged when it entered the influence of this world's sunlets." Her lips quirked in self-disparagement.

"You suffered injury in this accident?"

"Certainly not." Glade waved this ludicrous conjecture aside. "Such a thing is not possible. No, our complaint is otherwise: None on this world, in its present degenerate state, are sufficiently skilled to repair our ship."

"Ah. You were unable to solicit aid from . . . certain parties?"

"Who would these be?"

"Perhaps they are known to you as the Powers."

Glade grimaced. "Long gone from this world. I doubt that you appreciate how many aeons you have loitered here in your condition of abeyance. Our instruments tell us that we are the sole star folk now on the whole world."

While Glade was about this hazardous game, I had gone to Vanden's side. I crouched, took his pulse. To my glad surprise, he lived yet, though the beat of his life's blood was feeble. I tore open his jerkin and shirt, massaged his breast and arms with vigor and prayed to the Lords of Life and Darkness.

"We languished for a time without hope," Glade was explaining. "At length we learned of this city which only the immortal could revive. Now we look to technical assistance with our repairs; failing that, an emolument which will assuage our alienation.''

"Understandable." Aji-suki-takahikone brushed at his scant hair. "You shall receive all that I can give. Ah, your friend is returning to his senses."

Vanden's eyes opened suddenly, and they were mad eyes, fixed and fierce. A hoarse cry broke from his lips. As abruptly, he turned back within his own ruptured mind. His eyes rolled up out of sight.

I wrestled him to his feet. Upright, Vanden stood like an automaton, lacking all the subtleties of consciousness.

With a show of disinterest that must have lacerated her heart, Glade said, "He shall recover momently. The strange air and customs of this world disorient him. Doubtless his peace of mind would be enhanced if your warriors relinquished their hostile stance."

The Master shrugged. "Unhappily, that is impossible. They are creatures bred and trained to eternal vigilance. Fortunately"—he smiled, with a charm which would have been disarming if it were not entirely and patently spurious—"they pose a threat only to the malign."

Suspicion and surmise crackled between us. I half carried Vanden to the foot of the throne, aware of nothing but the danger we were in. I had reached Glade's side before I realized that the ludicrous rope of torn fabric and knotted leather still trailed behind me across the light-startled floor.

As coolly as I could, I began to unravel it into its component parts, holding Vanden vertical with one fist snarled in the back of his shirt. Aji-suki-takahikone observed this procedure with a sardonic eye.

I returned Glade's belt; she picked up her pouch from the floor, whence the translation device interceded between her mind and the War Master's words, fastened it to its metal clips, buckled the belt about its waist. To my sharpened perceptions she seemed, with this done, appreciably more relaxed. I wondered what she carried there.

"A curious ritual," remarked the War Master, leaning back into his cushions. "But I grow uncomfortable; you have not yet honored me with your names."

"Your pardon, Potentate," Glade said. "This gentleman, the immediate savior of the city, is the Lord Xaraf Golan's son, of Firebridge in Kravaard. You will, I trust, forgive the Lord Vanden Month/Nine Day/Fourteen Tenderness; he continues to muse in a higher state of consciousness, as is our way on occasion. And I am known in my own world as Glade Month/Five Day/Eight Resilience. As to that other matter which caught your interest," she added smoothly, "the ceremonial rending of garments is of sacred significance to us, and I regret that I may not speak of it in detail without impiety."

The room's tension could be felt with those inner registers that know the tightness of belly and muscle, a tension threatening to detonate its repressed violence at any instant. Only Vanden seemed unaffected. He stood between us like a straw vermin-frightener propped in a field on sticks.

Aji-suki-takahikone was plainly impatient to gain our supposed secret and have us destroyed. The half-naked woman held by one imprisoning arm in his lap trembled with mutinous hatred. The War Master unobtrusively held one hand at the nerve cluster behind the hinge of her jaw; I saw his thumb press there against skin gone white, a jab of agony to hint at the torment he could inflict. I shuddered with rage, and had to stand there, no less curbed. He caressed her thigh with his other hand, and smiled.

"Welcome, then, Lady Glade. Now, if you will excuse me for a moment, I must set in train the machinery which will waken my lieutenants. I will then see to it that you are escorted to suitable apartments."

Glade's throat contracted.

"Lord," she said hastily, "there remains one matter which would best be dealt with, perhaps, while we still possess this ultimate privacy."

The War Master stiffened, took his hand from the woman's leg, reached toward a bank of switches sunk into the black stone at his side.

"And what is that?"

"Why," the quester said, ingenuously, "we desire to make you a gift of the substance which confers immortality." She paused artfully. "Or do I err? This attribute may already be commonplace in your inspiring metropolis."

An expression of such lust and immeasurable greed, a transfiguration I could never have conceived possible in a human face, seared all pretense from the War Master's countenance. The sophistication and authority of a thousand years vanished before the gluttonous hunger for eternity.

"Where is this substance?" He strained forward, heaving his great bulk from the pillows, lips literally flecked with foam. "At once! I must—"

And the woman I knew from dream dragged herself free, fell from his thighs to crash into the obsidian jaws of the throne. Belatedly, his jeweled fingers tore at her, but she was away, on her feet, running at us.

High above us all, squat and hideous as restruct lizards from the Black Time, the tusked warriors glared from their eye-socket emplacements in terrifying bafflement.

"You must not!" the woman screamed, hurling herself on Glade, who was delving at her pouch. "He must not have eternal life! Better that we all die!"

Blinding light scarred the air.

The raging energy bolt should have cut the woman in two. Perhaps the creature which aimed it tried to spare Glade and so perforce missed her assailant as well. A scorching spray of molten droplets erupted from the mirror facets of the floor.

Aji-suki-takahikone was on his knees, peering florid-faced across his shoulder.

"Desist, fools!" He howled vilely at his defenders, howled imprecations born of terror as he saw the precious secret of eternal life a hairbreadth from incineration. "The vats will have your stinking flesh! Every ganglion will be torn slowly from your bodies!"

And that terror of thwarted lust was the last thing Aji-suki-takahikone ever knew, the apex and nadir of his thousand years, for poor mad Vanden exploded from his apathy, spun away from my grip, pounced on Alamogordo, lying in the place where it had dropped from my hand in the depths of shadow's Hellmouth, and slammed with it in his two-fisted grip to vault into the grinning black jaws of the skull-throne.

The sword screamed in a great arc, screamed literally with the voice of a damned soul, and hacked the War Master's face to blood-flecked splinters. Vanden's arms caught a gush of bright blood from the severed arteries, rose and fell in hysterical hatred to butcher the obesity that lay already dead at his feet.

A second bolt of flame roared. Bright as lightning, scarlet incandescence cracked from the second non-man's weapon. Vanden was instantly a human pyre.

He blazed. His scream of agony died as it was born, as his larynx burned in his throat. A nauseating stink of charred hair and flesh filled the throne room.

I had no time for thought or grief. I leapt to the side of the throne, drew myself up the sheer polished rock toward the reptilian warriors. The death machine swiveled on its spheroid mounting.

Behind me, Glade struggled with the beautiful confused woman, blood welling from deep scratches in her face. "Xaraf, keep down," she cried.

A jagged firebolt singed my hair. The tip of my ear burned with its passage. From the corner of my eye I saw Glade hurl the woman to one side, pluck a gleaming capsule from her pouch.

"Cover your face!" she screamed. Her arm blurred.

All this in an instant:

I dropped back into the yielding cushioned jaws where Vanden's twisted bones glowed and flaked like coals. Aji-suki-takahikone's body leaked blood into the pit of his regal seat; the legs had been caught by the edge of the bolt. I looked away, gagging.

Glade's capsule reached its apogee just below the level where the non-men sat at their weapons, tore itself to shreds in a silent explosion of dense pale gas. The vapors boiled upward, shrouding the monsters.

"Your face, Xaraf!"

The folds of silk, when I pressed my face into them, were rich with musk. There were deep, brutal screams, as of animals mortally wounded. I could not prevent myself from looking.

The warriors were clutching their scaled heads, reeling and mewing in agony. Droplets of poison ate into their flesh. Huge pustules burst out in the green skin. I was appalled. I covered my face again, imagining that poison in my own eyes. Blindly, I felt for the throne's lower jaw, threw myself over, crabbed toward Glade.

"You can dispense with the cushion now," Glade told me in a bleak voice. I did so, looked back. The creatures were dead, slumped across their glossy machines. Aji-suki-taka-hikone lay like a carcass torn by dogs, Alamogordo buried halfway to the hilt in his belly.

Mildly, close to tears, Glade added, "My apothecary shall receive a special gratuity for that service." Delicately, she helped the young woman to her feet. "I am sorry, but there was no time for niceties."

Delayed grief shook her as she surveyed the turbid carnage. She released the woman's arm and walked carefully away into a smoky infinity of receding images, to commune alone with her bereavement.

I was weeping myself. The warriors of the Kravaard are not afraid of tears. Vanden had been my friend, and I mourned him. I raised my wet downcast eyes to the woman from the dreams of my childhood. We embraced, at once strangers and lovers, familiar and unknown. Her hair was an exotic flower of the sun. I heard her sob, felt the tremor through her body; she too had cause enough for sorrow, for consternation, for all the racking emotions which break our hearts.

"How terrible it must be," she said, "for an immortal to die."

How magical *that* was, that her first words were for Vanden, not for us, less for herself. Like balm, her compassion flowed over me. I drew a shuddering breath, tightened my arms about her.

"Vanden was not immortal. He was merely . . . human." I closed my eyes on stinging salt. "There are no immortals, except perhaps the cryptic beings who long ago defeated Aji-suki-takahikone."

Words caught in her throat; she held them there, astonished. I devoured with my eyes every detail of her face, and she of mine. I shook with the passion of my fear relieved, my grief lanced opened and purged, my appalling happiness in her presence and safety.

She said, "Your name is Xaraf?"

"Yes."

"In our dreams we did not use names."

"In our . . . dreams."

"They were not dreams, Xaraf."

"I am sure they were dreams, but we walked together in them."

"Walked?" She laughed softly. "Cast sand and snow at each other, rather. Climbed trees and built castles, fought and argued and told secrets and fell in love. We were children and adults. Can all that happen in a dream, and be true?"

I cupped her face, kissed her mouth. She was, yes, my other self. I was overwhelmed by her. "It must be so." Her being seemed to diffuse into me, as our hands touched, our mouths, the scraping roughness of my cheek against her neck. "These dreams—they came to you here, in your green sleep?"

"Of course."

"Not when you were a child?"

"How could they?"

"I see." My pain, my loss, diminished to a pulse in the centre of this strange serenity. Hidden from our sight, in what small privacy she might discover behind the curve of the suspended bubble, Glade was weeping quietly. I would have gone to her, taken her hand, held her in my arms as a friend and a lover, but the reality of what she was to me became lost in this enormous heart-filled joy. "You have not told me your name."

The chamber was chill. She shivered, holding me tightly.

"Yes. We know everything about each other and nothing, Xaraf. I am Comhria Chtain, of the Dow sept in Wyhnja Kareba."

It was beautiful, as she was beautiful, and I said her name back to her, and again, smiling and holding her against me in that terrible place which stank of burnt meat and blood.

"Everything," I said, voraciously. "Tell me everything."

"At the Great Gatherings I was Tribune to the Song Guild.

But Aji-suki-takahikone's mad vision of glory corrupted even our peaceful town. His machines found my image and caused me to be fetched to Treet Hoown at the height of his useless battle with the Powers."

"Fetched you? As concubine?"

"I wish it had been so. No. There were great Bridal Ceremonies. I pleaded for exemption but the sept conveners were obdurate. The choice of a bride from Wyhnja Kareba endowed cachet on our town." Comhria sighed. "Now, perhaps, all my foolish people are old. I had dreamed of going back to them. Dreams—" She broke off. "Tell me, Xaraf, how long has the city been held in abeyance? A score of years? A hundred?"

My own loneliness echoed hers, constricting my chest. I turned my eyes away into the silver depths of the chamber.

"Longer than that, Comhria. Beyond this building, the city is decayed by time's erosion. It has been many thousands of years, tens of thousands perhaps, since the end of the Final War."

She made a forlorn little sound, and her fingers bit into mine. Acrid fumes from the glaring torches curdled the air. A shadow crossed the floor; Glade stood at her shoulder, looking from one of us to the other. Her face was hard, etched; I reached out my hand to her arm, hesitated.

"My lady," she said, "is there easy egress from this chamber? I cannot tarry long, and I must—" Her voice broke; she cleared her throat. "I must see to the interment of my friend's remains."

Comhria was dismayed.

"Lady Glade, he should have a hero's funeral," she said, very softly. "Stay with me while I rouse the city. Lend me your strength and wisdom. We shall lay Lord Vanden to his rest with all fitting pomp and dignity."

Harsh, Glade cried: "He was a trader, merely a trader. Give us no titles." Haggard and distressed, she caught herself. "Vanden would not have wished grand obsequies. Thank you, my lady, but I cannot remain here."

"He must have burial," I said, my own voice like rocks grinding together in a torrent.

"If it were possible, I would have taken his remains to

Asuliun, there to be interred with his brother Hahn and those others of his kindred who have enriched our heritage. Since this cannot be, I shall myself perform the simple rites of consignment."

"Asuliun the Gray? That ancient town still thrives?" Comhria was baffled. "Yet I thought you to be visitors from the stars?"

"A ruse. We came for booty," I admitted. "But Vanden was snared by the War Master's trap, dying. Now he is dead in truth, and must be taken home."

Her hands reached up to my face.

"I have no right to say this; I can only ask your forgiveness if my words seem impertinent—"

Glade turned away. I felt my mouth tighten. "Speak, Comhria, please."

"Many deaths are worthless," she said carefully, hesitant. "The deaths imposed by Aji-suki-takahikone in his war with the Powers were so. Your friend's death was the opposite of worthless. It has won this city's freedom from the beast. His death, your resource, the lady—" Comhria hesitated, corrected her form of address. "Glade's presence of mind. You have purchased our manumission." She lowered her hands, stood back. "Treet Hoown is yours."

The quester laughed scornfully. "I doubt that the city is yours to surrender so glibly, madam."

"Perhaps not." Comhria Chtain's look was swift, close to angry. "It was never my wish to marry Aji-suki-takahikone, to be his consort. Nevertheless that role was thrust upon me. I am no expert in constitutional precedent, trader, but it strikes me as likely that I am now *de jure* and *de facto* mistress of this sleeping nation."

Such directness in one apparently submissive shamed Glade, I think. She considered Comhria carefully; not, it seemed to me, as a woman of my people would appraise another woman, but as a man would weigh the worth and temper of a rival in the men's councils of power.

"Comhria, I suspect you are correct. I apologize. Even so, I for one am in no case to accept delivery of a moribund city." She smiled a slightly strained smile. "As a man from the stars, it would seem that Xaraf is still less appropriate for this charge. Sadly, it could be that you must shoulder all alone the burden of your curious inheritance.''

Comhria was doubly baffled now, switching her gaze from one of us to the other. ''Just as Xaraf assures me that your claim of stellar provenance was a ruse merely, you repeat the assertion when nothing hangs on it. Which is it to be?''

''She believes—''

''His appearance in—''

We broke off, tangled. Glade shrugged, too deeply distraught to find much merriment in the confusion. As for me, conflict worked to my disadvantage: loyalty to Glade, my friend and lover; enchantment, heart-trapping and mind-whirling, with this poignant woman I had loved, somehow, since childhood.

''Glade believes that I have come from the stars,'' I said slowly. Of their own accord my hands went out to find Comhria's, sparking with shivery quivering at the touch of her, closed on her fingers, and my heart jumped like a boy's at the returning pressure.

''I know only that this world is not my own,'' I went on with difficulty. ''We needed to disarm the War Master's suspicions; Glade cleverly advanced this convenient speculation.''

''I see.'' Acutely, Comhria said, ''So you seek repatriation to your own world, whether that might be in the heavens or some distant corner of this one.''

I pressed her fingers to my lips.

''How often does the truth of a dream fall like a lightning bolt into waking life? Until now, yes, you are right: I have wanted only that one thing. By no wish of my own I was fetched here from Kravaard and the tents of my father. So I thought. Yet now I think it was to find you, Comhria. No other explanation makes the faintest sense.''

Now it was Glade's turn to stare from one to the other, totally nonplussed. I realized how little she understood of this situation. Certainly I had never told her of my dreams, even in those long days and nights trekking with poor Vanden through the ghastly wastes of the Bad Lands; who would bore his companions with tales of childhood dreams?

In every way, this instantaneous, this fervent, this plainly besotted liaison was a reproach to Glade's natural decorum, unseemly in the context of Vanden's savage death, an affront to the sweet dealings Glade and I had known. How was she to perceive that Comhria and I were closer than lovers, were dreamers of each other?

"Glade, I should have made this clear. Comhria and I are not strangers."

"Absurd! How could you know each other? Or is this some further delusion of the *Mysterium?*"

"Do not be angry," Comhria said, pleadingly, letting go my hand and reaching out for Glade's. The quester hesitated, stiff, more disturbed than aggrieved; then took the proffered hand.

"Hardly angry." Tears once again were leaking unnoticed down her face. "I am bitterly tired, my lady. Is there some place we might go which does not stink of the burnt meat of my friend?"

"Oh, Glade! I am thoughtless." Thoughtless? She had been plucked up and thrown down a hundred millennia later. Her captor-spouse was slain in the midst of his inhuman guard. Her city was revealed all corrupt with age, and the child of her dream stood before her as a man. I loved her in that moment for her generosity of spirit. "Come," she said.

And led us around the perimeter of the throne's gaping jaws, found a panel of jewels softly lit, struck several of them by pattern. Chimes sounded. A doorway opened, spilling soft creamy light from a ducted way descending out of the mirrored room.

"Wait," I said. I returned to the jaws, vaulted high, stood in blood and ash. Above me, the poisoned bodies of the non-men sprawled across their wicked mechanisms. Aji-suki-taka-hikone, hideously disfigured, slumped in red-soaked silks and cushions. Even the barbaric scent of the torches could not hide the reek of bowels knife-opened to the air. I took Alamogordo in two hands and dragged the blade out of the creature's guts.

The sword shrieked horribly, coming out of him, shrieked like a damned soul.

I shuddered, nearly dropped its massive weight.

"Quiet!" I snarled. "We can do without your whimsies at this unhappy moment." I wiped the blade clean on heavy silk, lifted it, sheathed it at my back.

"You have taken me to Hell, Xaraf," the blade said in a quiet, terrible voice. I had not heard it speak in this way before, as if from its true centre. There was something peculiarly distraught in that voice, perhaps deranged. "I am no more than a tool, Xaraf. Do not speak to me of whimsies and unhappiness, you apish halfwit. You have killed me and taken me to Hell, and here I am, in Hell still, nor am I out of it." Alamogordo gave a groan so deep and woeful that the hair rose at my neck, and my superstitious soul curdled with the horror of it.

"Quiet, I told you, and I meant it." I forced anger, to put a better face on my shudders. "You will not speak thus to me."

"I will not speak to you again in any wise," Alamogordo said, as if pronouncing an anathema, and fell silent.

I turned away from the foulness and ruin all at my feet, belly crawling with dread, and climbed back down to where two living human beings waited to dice—as suddenly, preposterously, it seemed to me—for my soul.

Sweet-breathed as a fig, her kiss woke me.

"Stay with me," she said.

White morning light touched the scalloped ceiling. I smiled, rolled to meet her, saw the pale blue sky in the high window, the clouds streaking in white feathers. Somewhere out of sight the sun was surely a brilliant circle of hot white light, and it was all wrong, the wrong sun in the wrong sky.

"What? Comhria, where—" The silken sheets rucked beneath my bunched fists, tangled my legs, and her smile gave way to confusion. I leapt at the lintel of the window, pulled myself high, stared down at fields and streams and the city of Treet Hoown all alive in a spring day. "What have you—"

"Oh, Xaraf, I am so sorry. It is an illusion, my dear, only

an illusion." The window smeared in front of my nose, went gray. A world lost in antiquity had gone back to its tomb.

I dropped heavily to the carpet, naked, sweating.

"An image," I said. "Then we are still below ground?"

"Of course," Comhria said. She opened her arms, and I sat gingerly beside her on the huge bed, one hand tangling her hair. "It is called a window. Do you not have such images in your world? How drab life would be!" And she laughed delightedly at the conceit.

I glowered at the floor and thought of the crystal screens in Mathketh's belvedere, and then of the dreams where Comhria and I had spent so many of our night hours: false screens of true adventures together, if the frolics of childhood can be granted so ambitious a title. Or was it true screens for the projection of false memories?

I turned to her then, gave back her sweet-mouthed kiss with a bristly one of my own. "How could I leave you, beautiful songbird?"

"We are both strays in worlds not our own, Xaraf."

"Yours will be revived."

"What a task that will be." She frowned. "Many of the citizens of Treet Hoown are, were, damn it, how can one say this—will again be?—mad beasts in the image of their happily dead Master. I have no yearning to revive them."

"Better we slit their throats while they hang in their green slimy capsules."

I had come to that, yes. I heard my own words and recoiled in revulsion.

"That is a solution which one such as Aji-suki-takahikone would find," Comhria said in quiet, penetrating reproof. "We must discover some better way to deal with the wicked than by duplicating their own crafts."

"You shame me," I said, and bowed my head. "The habit of killing is easily acquired, less easily abandoned." She made to speak; I covered her lips with a finger. "When I was a child, all the young men around me learned the arts of slaughter and defense, and I with them. Among my people one alone stood against this way of life, and he became my teacher, under the protective shadow of my poor mad mother, whose client he was.''

I pillowed my head in Comhria's arm, gazing at her strong young face, and told her all I could remember of Darkbloom: the tales of his shambling arrival, half-dead of privation, in our camp, his gelding at my father's hand, those shamanistic tricks which won him his life as camp mascot and eccentric. At last I told her of my vow, its rupture, the threat my father had revealed to me of the wizards who menaced the Kravaard.

Comhria withdrew her numb arm, smiled ruefully at me as she rubbed it back to life. ''You have an obligation, then, to return, if you can find your way home.''

''I have no higher wish at this moment than to linger here with you, sweet Comhria.''

''Beyond this moment are other moments. They will speak in your ear the call to honorable action.''

''How wise you are.'' I was giddy with love for her. I kissed her mouth, her eyes, her throat; I drew her to me and all my body burned with the touch of her. ''You must know that I cannot long stay away from you.''

''Nor I from you. Yet I too have my duty.'' She shuddered with our joining, cried out. Through all our lovemaking our conversation never ceased; it seemed that words and acts, mind and body were elements of a song for voices and musics, now this aspect predominating, now that: always, though, the harmony, the twining of our thoughts and our flesh. ''I must rouse these sleepers,'' she said a little later, and I grinned at her, pulled her ear, said: ''Cry so loudly, songbird, and they will be roused even as they sleep.'' She snorted, slapped at me. ''You are noisy enough yourself, Xaraf, to awaken all the kine and bring the bulls bursting through to plough the soil.''

We napped, woke, ate delicacies which our clever bed fetched us, drank juices tangy and soothing, and I hugged Comhria to me, bent into the curve of me so I pressed her buttocks and cupped her breasts and said into her ear where the hair fell back all damp and tangled: ''First, before all these things, my lovely love, I have a duty to my friend.''

''Glade?'' Who slept in an adjoining chamber, or prowled it in her grieving.

"The trek to Asuliun is no task for one alone," I said. "I will accompany Glade to her home, and when I have seen her safe, return to stand by you."

"Yes. You could do nothing less. Come, now, let us give each other a scrubbing, and we shall find your friend and make our plans."

A door where none had been took us to a cavernous place of blues and greens, where pools bubbled and small waves ebbed in rock, lapped sand fine as powdered salt. Comhria went into the water like an aquatic bird after a fish; I, less confident in an element I had never learned, hung at the edge and laved myself, taking good care to keep my head above the surface.

Glade was dressed in clean garments from her room's services when we announced ourselves at her door. Lines crossed her forehead and ran from nose to mouth where I had never seen them until now. I took her hands spontaneously, hugged her to me when she held back.

"Oh Glade, Glade, what a fine and terrible time this has been. I have not known such joy and sorrow intermixed."

The quester made a careless gesture. "What is done is done. Comhria, how might I find exit from this place? It bothers me that my pack animals have stood beyond the palace now for the best part of a day and night without care or provisions."

"This is easily remedied. Have you yourself breakfasted?"

"The machines here are admirable. Yes, thank you. I must make preparations, however, for my return to Asuliun."

"Glade, surely you do not imagine that I would let you go unaccompanied?"

"No, Xaraf," she growled, "I thank you, but it is not necessary. My fuel cells are fully charged, thanks to Vanden's discovery in Mathketh's citadel. My route back to Asuliun is now correctly charted. Remain here—the Lady Comhria will be in sore need of a companion at her side when the city is revived."

Comhria said, "Glade, I would not hold him here if I could. Happily, I have a gift for you both which will speed your trip to Asuliun and Xaraf's return to Treet Hoown. The vessel which brought you into the throne room can traverse immense distances in less than a day.''

"We have no command over its movements,'' Glade objected, with a look of quickened interest.

"It is guided by mental instruction,'' Comhria told us. "Until now it has been keyed to the War Master's brain; I believe the machines of the city can make it available to another.''

I was watching Glade, worried by her depression; now I felt a grin spread across my face. "You see? I must come with you, to guide the vessel home to Comhria. Who knows, my friend. Perhaps your quest may yet be fulfilled, and you crowned sovereign in Asuliun!''

Glade knotted her hands. "Poor, honest Vanden,'' she said mournfully. "Would that he had not missed this triumph.'' Sighing, she looked at me, and nodded. "Thank you, Xaraf, I will have your company gladly. If nothing else comes of the voyage, we can at least bear his remains back to the keeping of his kin.''

We all three sat down, then, I think as friends, to plan the awakening of the dead city.

REBIRTH

::With the acquisition of fighting skills, a potentially violent man becomes potentially more dangerous; but at the same time, the actual process of training gives release to his violence. Eventually the discipline and release of the fighting art will bring him through the full circle to true gentleness, not merely the repression and false control of his violent nature::

—C. W. Nicol

::What we really have in common with our remote ancestors is a *spiritual,* not a primitive self::

—Otto Rank

::All teems with symbol; the wise man is the man who in any one thing can read another::

—Plotinus

SIXTEEN

Treet Hoown dropped away below us. Shockingly, then, it blinked out of existence, leaving only its vast sheared plateau at our feet to dwindle into the bleak perspective.

Mathketh's golden dome slipped away, a bauble, its citadel foreshortened to nothing by our height. And the aching, pitted void of the badlands was rushing beneath us, dry and yellow as the bones which littered the *Mysterium*.

Impelled by some principle long forgotten, the bubble fled silently across the changing face of the world, found silky, gleaming wisps of cloud that were mere fog when we passed through them; this told me nothing of the nature of clouds, I thought gloomily, for the bubble treated all matter so.

Up we lofted, ever higher, crossing the slow westering path of the bruised, monumental sun.

This effortless flight mocked the exhausting trek forced on Glade, Vanden, and me when we crossed the badlands. Already we were flying over veld and silvery streams, a gorgeous tapestry neither of us had ever seen.

"A splendid mode of transport," Glade said, "if a trifle disconcerting."

Her spirits had lifted a little. No doubt this was largely due to the sheer distracting stress and effort involved in helping Comhria revive a dozen suitable citizens, preparatory to a general awakening of the city. A certain unforced glee entered her expression now as she peered downward through the translucent hull.

"Xaraf, without this vessel, it is doubtful that I could hope to reach Asuliun within the stipulated ninety-nine days of the quest. Yet I think we shall arrive with more than a tenth-year to spare.''

I grunted only. As Glade's spirits rose, mine fell. I sat brooding at the sky, leaning against the piled-up belongings of the traders, dwelling on the piquancy of Comhria's mouth, the taste and texture of her kisses. She had tumbled away behind me, gazing upward, her arm lifted; then her lovely features were lost; her limbs smudged; the city itself was gone as we passed the upper bounds of the invisibility shield. I slapped my hand against a saddlebag.

The quester glanced at me, and seemed to be holding back a smile. ''Never fear, my dear friend. I've no doubt the sweet lady is gazing even now into the sky where we vanished, pining for your return.''

No kindness in me, I said, ''Keep your consolations.'' The hint of a smile left Glade's face and she turned aside. I wanted to apologize, but my head rang with the vertigo of our aerial flight, the greater flight it seemed to encapsulate. My memories of Kravaard, family, the tents and cooking pots and fighting rings of Firebridge and the Wanderers, Darkbloom's caring, taunting parables and buffets, all my world seemed now nothing better than the faded fragments of dream.

Am I mad? I asked myself. Is this the real, the only world? What of Golan's allegations, the threatened onslaught of wizards from the North? Could any wizard in my world hurl himself into the sky? Fly by command of thought, without spells, drugs, hallucination?

Is that other world, I sugggested to myself, merely fantasy? False memory?

And which reality did *this* meditation betray?

''Glade,'' I said.

She did not look up, toyed with the collapsed hard rim of her folded tent.

''I am sorry, Glade. Hear me, please. It is not Comhria's fidelity I mistrust; it is my own prospects of returning to Treet Hoown.''

''You are master of this vessel. I will be sad to see you leave, Xaraf, as you must know, but I cannot hold you,''

Glade said, casting a sidelong glance at me, "nor would I do so, against your will."

I got to my feet, not easy in that clutter, went to her side, sat and leaned against the hull there. Cloud thickened, white as milk, thinned again to vapor, to sky. "You wonder why I came with you?"

"A captain is required to fetch the vehicle home. You have explained this already."

"Glade, Glade. Even I know enough about the mechanisms of this world to see that direct human intervention is perfectly unnecessary."

"Oh. You see that, do you?"

"How else did the bubble carry us to the throne room, when it had not been instructed by human voice in a hundred millennia?"

"Still," Glade said tentatively, "because in theory a thing can be done does not mean it can be done by you, or by me, or even by the talented Comhria."

I bent and kissed her carefully, lightly, with friendship. She did not, as I had feared, recoil, but leaned against me for a moment. When she drew back, flushing slightly, I said:

"I have been no more than a puppet, Glade. A marionette wielded by these cryptic, faceless Powers, if that is the true name of the forces working my destiny. I tire of it. They led me to Treet Hoown, used me as their key to unlock the city, sent me to Comhria—"

"Surely you express no objections to this last fact."

"Glade, I do love her. I have loved her from childhood. Wait, I shall make that clear to you in good time; it is not the besotted nonsense it sounds. Yet this one truth remains central: They have sundered me once from my world. How am I to know that They will not do so again if it suits Their purposes?" I was breathing rapidly, with barely suppressed rage.

The quester regarded me quizzically, drawing down the fringes of her hair with the tips of her fingers, curling and releasing it, a tic, or some outward expression of her interior conflicts.

"Xaraf, the Powers are not capricious, I judge. The ways of immortals are alien to us, but not totally inhuman. We know now that legend must be correct, that They checked the War Master at the height of his grandeur and ambition, that They fended off the world's end with Their prophylactic sunlets. I think that you must trust Them.'' She shrugged, dropped her hands into her lap. ''Either that, or turn your back on Their plan and walk away—if you can. If They allow you to.''

''Precisely,'' I said, enormously satisfied that her evaluation so neatly conformed with my own. ''And I attend you now because it will please me to see your quest succeed. You are my dear friend, Glade, my first friend in this world and my true companion. I rejoice that I may *choose* to join you, and be damned to the Powers and Their high plans.''

''Thank you, Xaraf,'' Glade said, but her smile was full of doubt. ''Still, do not be too certain of that. Their perspective must be very long, and Their plans beyond our comprehension. Thinking to thwart Them, my dear, you might well persuade yourself to Their intended path.''

I had seen that logic too, and it made my breast swell with useless rage. I snorted, stared down at the racing earth. Fields of blossoms, violet and yellow, swung gracefully below the bubble. Herds of cattle tiny as specks grazed in lush grass. We were traversing a more temperate region now, watered by wider streams winding their ruddy silver out of the east.

A dark blur appeared at the horizon. Glade pressed her nose to the tinted hull, spun back with a whoop of excitement.

''Asuliun!'' she cried. ''Even from this unorthodox coign I spy the Royal Palace, the old gray ramparts. Home, Xaraf, and with such a prize as none of them ever dreamed of witnessing!'' And she flung her arms around me, kissed me gleefully, and held my hand like a delighted child as we dropped out of the heavens.

Evidently the sphere's wonderful mechanism also distinguished the gray-rimmed outcropping. Obedient to instructions which, perforce, I had left rather general, it slowed as we approached the ancient town, swung in a great curve that carried us into the eye of the sun.

This was at Glade's suggestion. ''In these staid days, who

will be scanning the skies for aerial craft? Still, I prefer to make a diplomatic approach.''

I concurred. Feeble as that sullen orb had grown, its scarlet light would mask the opalescence of our bubble, to casual observation at least.

With the sun at our backs, then, we stared down at the unsuspecting town.

Far smaller than the city of the War Master—hardly more extensive, indeed, than Berb-Kisheh, if memory served me— it was laid out on altogether less authoritarian principles.

Glade pointed, my high guide; I squinted after her finger at an unruly maze of boulevards and mews, merchants' stalls, pretty gardens, antique pavilions, cathedrals, and the muted tints of houses of pleasures.

Almost organic, architecture and disposition followed the natural lie and line of the land, the human-made merging taste-fully with the natural to create a mood of peace, restraint, gentility. It was sweet but stifling, I thought, with nowhere a hint of squalor, nor any breath of passionate intensity. Candid, I said as much.

''I do not think I would care to live in your city while the blood still gallops in my veins. A place to find unruffled calm in one's declining years, perhaps.''

Rueful, the quester sucked her lower lip. ''Oddly enough, I believe I have come to share that sentiment. Once I would have found it unthinkable, the attitude of a barbarian. Now—'' Her hand strayed to the hilt of her energy-lance; I doubt that she even noticed.

''You have developed a taste for adventure.''

She was judicious. ''Our small odyssey has revealed features of my soul which I have been reluctant to concede.''

''This is a fancy, formal way of agreeing with me.'' I laughed, slapped at my knee.

''It is an admission of aspects of an atavism hitherto con-cealed. I do not know if I care any longer to be Sovereign in Asuliun.''

Dryly, I told her: ''You need not accept the post, you know. Come, I grow restless. Shall we descend?''

''Very well. I propose we bring the vessel to earth in the

cover of yonder grove.'' This was a patch of greenery somewhat to the east of the town's chief gate. ''The sentries, while
not excessively diligent, may become agitated if we present
the sphere in a more forthright manner.''

I grinned at her. ''And you might lose the advantage of
surprise when the moment comes for the judging of the quest.''

''Xaraf, the facts slip your mind.'' Her eyes widened in a
show of innocence. ''It is your person, not the sphere, which
represents my most astounding exhibit.''

At my mental command, the bubble swooped sickeningly,
placed us feather-light behind the grove. Markedly seedier of
complexion, we waited for the entrance to nictitate open; I
was holding my gorge down, and nothing droll came to mind.

Rosy light slanted in, then, falling through the trees. A soft
breeze carried delicious odors of soil and leaf and blossom,
scents I had almost forgotten.

From here, the gray walls of the town were hidden in foliage. Faint sounds of human activity came to us on the breeze,
but apparently our arrival had provoked no alarm. Presumably, therefore, it had gone unnoticed.

''It is a pity the sphere could not accommodate our steeds,''
Glade said.

Leaving the animals, so faithful in their service across the
ghastly badlands, had saddened the quester more than I would
have expected. Comhria had found stables for them, ample
feed from automatic machines, but none of this truly replaced
the grassy agistment the beasts had earned. But it was not
primarily justice for the horned horses she thought of now.
''Vanden's casket deserves more noble handling than we two
can manage between us.''

I bent my back, helped her raise the heavy silver box. Quietly I told her, ''I do not think it unseemly that he should be
borne home on the shoulders of his companions.''

We lowered the casket from bubble to ground. The entrance
closed, sealed to an imperceptible seam. I framed a wordless
mental command. Instantly, without even a rush of wind, the
sphere soared straight up and was lost from sight. At the edge
of black space it would hover, dormant, until I recalled it.

If Darkbloom had seen me perform that spell, I told myself, his skepticism would be impaired forever.

By the time we emerged on the wide, worn road which wound out from Asuliun's main gate, our shoulders were bruised and aching. Sweat stung my eyes, plastered my long hair against my forehead. Alamogordo, silent and brooding, banged at my back, until I stopped finally and tightened its strap; now I was strangled.

Ahead, standing open and friendly within the great granite walls, the metal grilles of the city gates held high the proud fluttering cognizances of Asuliun's families.

A footman ran forth at our approach.

"Welcome, travelers," he cried. "Kindly state your business, and pass within." The ferocious pike he brandished was, it seemed, merely decorative. "Why," he blurted then, taken aback, "it is the Merchant Glade Resilience, returned from the quest! Greetings! But where is your baggage, your steed? Let me help you with that box—I warrant it contains some wonder that will astound our ruler."

Glade gave a weary sigh. "Greetings, Bengsun. Be a good fellow and fetch us a coach. No other assistance is necessary."

"Madam." The sentry ran off, after a few steps stumbled, returned sheepishly. "I nearly forgot. The princess requests your presence at the Palace on the instant of your return."

"The coach, Bengsun. Inform the Palace of my arrival, but extend my regrets. I fear I shall be delayed."

The sentry looked appalled. "But my lady—"

Glade's eyes squeezed closed, stayed shut a long moment, opened to pierce him. "The casket we bear holds the bones of my companion Vanden Tenderness. We go immediately to his family's demesne. The Lady Aniera must wait."

"I see. Of course." Chastened, the sentry ran off ahead of us, disappeared at the gate. So, in our turn, did we.

The sun's red ember was well into the west when finally we climbed the broad steps ascending to the Palace in Asuliun. Strange shadows, soft and sharp entwined, bent and stretched and bent again, ahead of us. Rose light and white painted our formal robes curiously.

Against custom, I had retained my surly sword. The two liveried attendants who accompanied us had drawn attention, delicately, to the irregularity. I had been adamant.

How odd, I thought now, stepping with care to avoid falling on my face. What had become of my vow, sworn all solemn before the shrines of the Lords of Life and Darkness, of Light and Death, that I should cling so stubbornly to a killing weapon?

It was incalculably strange. Once only had I taken a human life, and that in another world, albeit my own world. Yet I sensed that it was this world which had changed me.

I have not killed again, I told myself, but I have become an amok. A berserker. A machine primed to run wild, out of control, as Mathketh was undoubtedly poised for mayhem and apocalypse, waiting in its turn only the word of release from the Powers Who had penned it to its citadel. Who penned me? Whose word would trigger me?

My sense of guilt had become numbed, for all my maundering. Dimly I recognized the fact, and there was nothing I could do to remedy it. Darkbloom's advice was a universe away, perhaps in the cold stars. Darkbloom could not be dismissed as negligible: He had sent me dreams of this world, of my love Comhria. But he was beyond reach.

I felt that I was no less damned than my absurd, frightening sword.

We passed into a chamber rich with leather and deep-grained wood. An old man rose from a tall, chastely decorated chair, came forward with his arms extended toward Glade. Bowing, the servants returned to their stations.

"Resilience, how charming to see you returned safely. It is providential, indeed, that you are recalled, if in tragic circumstances. Permit me to offer the condolences of the Royal House upon the loss of your brave companion."

He released her hand, bowed briefly to me, addressed himself again to Glade. "And now, if you will forgive my untoward haste, the Lady Aniera would be pleased to see you in private audience. I will arrange for a young person to show your friend the gardens.''

Glade cleared her throat. ''Sir, I have reason to believe that the Lord Xaraf should also be present during the interview. He is a deputy of those beings known in legend as The Last Scientists.''

The barest trace of emotion flickered in the old gentleman's face: It could be read as annoyance yielding to incredulity, ending with delighted amazement; all these, as I say, registered by a temperament given to nuance and cool diffidence.

''I am honoured, sir,'' he told me. ''My name is Hernedral Day/Twenty-two Month/Four Repose. Know that I am Episcopal in Asuliun, and presently Regent to our ruler. Please follow me.''

Sconces tipped with elaborate light-crystals cast a subdued, graceful glow in the winding hallways. Matching the pace of the old man, we had time enough for reflection. Vanden's family had told us already of the dismal results of the quest. Seventeen had responded initially to the challenge. Glade was not the first to return, as we had expected, but the last. Three, not including Vanden, were known to have perished. The remainder had returned to Asuliun before ten days had passed.

Something was awry with the spirit of these folk. Such prizes as had been borne back, exciting though they seemed to the citizenry, were paltry—a prancing homunculus, statuary of jade and gold dating back to the era of starflight, a calculating mechanism in the form of a waterfowl—a meager congeries of triviality.

I asked myself, Where is their heart? A voice frosty and offended answered from within me. Their silks, their fine stone dwellings, their soft living, it informed me, have robbed them of their virility.

It was my father's voice, of course. Still, it was hard to dispute the indictment.

The Episcopal halted, opened a wooden door bound and studded in brass, ushered us into a softly lit chamber hung with pleasant brocades.

''The merchant and quester Glade Month/Five Day/Eight Resilience, and the Outworld Lord Xaraf, my lady.''

Aniera Arina Argaet (whose birthdate and essential characteristics were suppressed, I took it, by her high office) tilted her head and viewed us haughtily. The effect was not at all diminished by the fact that she sat in bed, leaning back against a pile of cushions.

A ruler who lolls in bed? Decadence!

Startled, then, I saw that her white, pinched features possessed the pallor of illness. A mortal sickness held this woman close to the edge of death.

She caught her breath painfully.

"Yes," she said, "the last of the questers. Enter, gentles. Make yourselves comfortable." Her voice and manner conspired to make the gentle rhythms nasal and supercilious.

"My lady!" Glade was shocked. "I did not know. I ought to have come—"

"Your priorities were correct, Resilience. It was with regret that I heard of your companion's demise; you have given his family comfort and honor in their grief. Here, sit, sit. Come, Repose, find them chairs."

The old gentleman indicated, with a hint of long-suffering, the handsome seating at the sides of the bed. We sat, me hitching at Alamogordo's inconvenient length.

Aniera Argaet folded her thin hands across the linen which covered her breast. "Now, tell me quickly of your quest, for my physicians insist most intemperately that I should not overtax my strength." She uttered a bitter, derisive laugh.

With lucid brevity, Glade recounted her summonsing at the behest of Alamogordo, presumptive instrument of the Powers; our meeting in the Forest of the People, and her part in extracting me therefrom (neither diminishing that brave tale, nor embroidering it); the manner in which we were led to Treet Hoown, and our adventures in that place. When she described our means of transport to Asuliun, the sovereign's eyes gleamed with surmise.

"This sphere? Where is it now?"

"Xaraf is its master, my lady. I had planned to have him summon it dramatically during your adjudication of the quests."

A flush flickered in Aniera's cheeks.

"An aerial vessel!" she said breathlessly. "The lost city, a man conceivably from the stars, the fabled Powers Themselves! Wonderful, Glade, wonderful! I had thought myself surrounded by creatures with water in their veins. Perhaps I need not die after all."

"My lady?"

"Hernedral," she said faintly, "I grow weak. Tell them what must be done."

The white-haired Regent stepped forward, sat carefully beside Glade on a leather couch worked with images of wild flowers. He played out no preamble.

"The Lady Aniera is dying, gentles. A wasting disease ravages her vitality. Only the potent force of her will sustains her. The illness is exceedingly rare, and has no explicit cure. Once, perhaps, in the days when humans were like gods, a specific was known; if so, it has been lost, and all reference to its whereabouts with it."

"Ah!" Glade tensed. "I see. This was the motive for announcing a quest."

"Indirectly. A single nostrum for the disease has been found by our antiquarians, or at least the possibility of such a nostrum. Who in the gray city, though, was bold and enterprising enough to apply it?"

"Water in their veins," Aniera repeated. Her eyes were closed; she gasped; against the pillows her face seemed drained of that vital fluid whose thinning she diagnosed in her race.

Glade was brisk now. "Give me the details as you know them."

"The task is formidable but not, perhaps, impossible. Beyond the mountains to the south, many thousands of leagues distant, a region exists known in legend as the Well of Rejuvenation."

"I have heard of this locale. As I recall"—and Glade smiled tightly—"it has also been called the Haunt of Monsters."

Hernedral acknowledged this gruesome fact. "As well as these tutelary monstrosities, a certain unusual life-form is said to dwell therein. This is a creature capable of symbiotic union with human flesh. Once implanted, the animal derives nourishment from its host's life cycle. In gratitude, it protects the host from every kind of illness—including, it is rumored, the deterioration of age itself."

For the first time I spoke. "This was the War Master's dream."

"No records pertaining to the Haunt of Monsters can be found which are older than sixty thousand years," Hernedral stated. "Aji-suki-takahikone already lay in stasis at that date."

"Could the symbiote have been fetched here by beings from the stars? Beings like Xaraf?"

"If so, the star was not mine," I said. "I have never heard the least rumor of such wonders on my own world, except in tales for children. Tell me this: If such a remedy for death is known, how is it that heaven and earth have not been moved to obtain it?"

"Apparently the region achieved its present character long after all facilities for negotiating it safely had been destroyed by time."

"This is a contradiction," Glade said, irritably. "Whence, then, did the story originate?"

"With the star folk themselves, it seems."

"They left this symbiote to taunt us?"

"As a spur, perhaps."

"It has not been highly effective, then," I said.

For the third time, more feebly than before, the sovereign muttered: "Water in their veins—"

"With your flying vehicle," Hernedral added, "the symbiote might be captured."

Aniera forced open her crepey eyelids. "The risk will be great, but the throne of Asuliun will be vacant for you if you succeed. I will step aside, as I announced. I have had enough of power; what I crave now is the recovery of health, and the peace of my last years at their natural pace."

Glade rose, paced back and forth.

"Given accurate instructions, there is little doubt that the sphere could take me to this place. As to the hazards, they can be evaluated only in the light of their exact nature."

I had been thinking about difficulties nobody had mentioned. "Tell me, sir, how is this symbiote to be carried back to Asuliun? Perhaps it thrives only in its specific environment."

Hernedral hesitated. "There is only one way the creature can be transferred, if our records are accurate. That is within the body of a human being. Aniera's agent will have to carry the symbiote in her belly, and disgorge it with the appropriate mortifications upon her return."

I hooded my eyes at that. The same conclusion must have occurred to everyone in the room. The temptation to retain the thing, with its promise of extended youth, would be close to overwhelming. The thought was clearly enough etched into Hernedral's drawn face.

"First we must speak to the antiquarians," I said to Glade, "then to your armorers."

She touched my cheek. "Xaraf, you have done more than enough in coming to Asuliun with me. I cannot permit you to risk your life further."

I laughed aloud. "Why else did the Powers call you to save my life? Surely not that I might bask contentedly while you confront nameless monsters alone. We must see Their plan through to the end, I think. Besides"—and I let my smile become wolfish—"the bubble is keyed to my mind. You need me with you, if only as its captain."

"Bravely said!" Glade beamed. She clasped my hand.

Aniera Argaet gave a gasping sigh; when we turned to her she lay slumped against her mound of cushions, face bloodless, eyes rolled back. The old Regent was instantly by her side, tugging at a tasseled cord to summon the physicians.

"Gentles, wait without. She has passed into coma. Her illness is more advanced than I had feared."

The door burst open. A physician, attended by an apothecary laden with phials of various hues, hurried to the woman's bed.

"They can ease her pain," Glade murmured to me as we went out through the same door. "Let us hope that we can find a cure for it."

A single thought droned like distant thunder in my head, though I did not voice it:

If I were indeed the representative of gods, that was fitting enough. For what we sought now was not merely a cure for a wasting illness, but a remedy for death itself: Surely a task reserved to the agency of the supernatural.

I remembered the *Mysterium Coniunctionis*, remembered the actuality of dying, and I shivered in a convulsion of dread.

SEVENTEEN

Black masses of cloud obscured the mauve sky, looming over the turbulent ocean. In the dense thunderheads, lightning flickered.

Our vessel hurtled high across these vasty waters, the merest bauble.

"I have seen rivers swollen with spring's thaw," I said, looking down through the hull. "Once, I glimpsed the Inland Sea to the west of Nazarokh. Glade, never once did I dream of such immensity as this."

Maps were spread everywhere, pinned down by an energy-lance here, a pot of succulent jam there. In their midst, plotting our path, Glade glanced up.

"It is said that certain races find their livelihood and joy in negotiating the oceans in frail vehicles of wood and fabric. To me, this is an incomprehensible practice. My own people are no less alien to the sea than yours."

"It possesses a terrifying magnificence," I allowed, deeply impressed by the pent fury so awesomely displayed.

"And, unhappily, a frustrating sameness to the untutored eye." Glade sighed. She lifted one bootless foot; a map, released, sprang back to being a sloppy cylinder. "If these dubious charts retain any relation to a reality altered by fifty thousand years, I cannot discern it."

"Let us hope the bubble is wiser than we are."

"My faith weakens. Surely we should have attained the island of the Well by now."

I pointed to the southeast. "Perhaps we are almost there. Do you see?"

"Hmm. A hint of white foam, at best."

Despite the quester's skepticism, the bubble began immediately to check its flight. We dropped toward the dark waters, swinging to the left ("tacking to port" this would be called, I gather, if the maneuver had been conducted in a surface-running vessel) until the island was directly before us.

I found the vista formidable. Half-submerged reefs guarded the shore. Waves crashed and seethed against them, leapt at jagged cliffs, smashed back in wild explosions.

"If this is truly the Haunt of Monsters," Glade said, "there is little wonder that it has remained inviolate. Only an aerial vessel could possibly approach without the sea tearing it to tinder."

More skilled now in the bubble's operation, I directed it to hover at a safe altitude.

We fell from the sky. Little could be seen of the surface proper. Crags and peaks were lost in dense foliage, blue and purple, which somehow resisted the ocean winds. No clearings were in evidence, let alone any structure wrought by the hand of man.

I drew my sword. For a moment I regarded it.

"Alamogordo, despite your delusion," I said, "you have not experienced death, a tragedy reserved for beings of flesh and blood. For all that, it must surely interest you that we go now to search for the secret of immortality."

Once more I heard that deep and doleful groan.

"Human, immortality is of interest only to the living. To the dead its mention is mockery, detestable."

"Sword, how can you speak to me if you are dead? Logic detects your error."

"Leave the wretched thing alone," Glade said, looking at it with pity and abhorrence. "Nothing is gained in taunting it."

"This is cogent advice," Alamogordo said in its awful voice. "Do not speak to me again unless there is killing work to be done."

I shrugged, somewhat abashed, somewhat irritated, and ordered the bubble to the ground.

A tremendous roaring assaulted us, waves coming and going

with a high-pitched initial note dropping rapidly, as if something came at us from the sky; booming; hissing back to start
once more high, plunging, booming. Added to this was the
seething of wind-tossed trees, each leaf a tongue muttering,
each tree a crowd, all together an empire of peevish babblers.

We stepped warily to spongy, sodden soil. Heavy, fleshy
leaves closed out much of the light from the cloud-filled sky,
letting pass only a dim, oppressive illumination. Ropy vines
clung to the slick trunks of these trees, dripping moisture. The
humidity was grotesquely high; my garments were already
starting to stick to my skin.

Glade stared about her, scandalized.

"The place is an absurdity, the invention of a madman."

"Certainly I would rather be in Kravaard."

"Such an exposed island cannot have soil so rich. The wind
ought long since to have stripped it bare. The heat, the luxu-
riant foliation . . . all fly in the face of nature."

The sphere sealed itself.

"We have found the right island, then," I said with a grin.
"The environment of the symbiote can hardly be anything but
unnatural."

Something skittered in a nearby tree. I caught a brief glimpse
of the thing and felt my stomach turn over.

Wet tangled organs writhed in a livid sac; pink-budded tentacles spurted out to seize a bough and catapult the creature to
cover.

Flurries rippled a dozen different trees; half-seen shapes
scuttled through sinuous roots.

The island was rousing to our intrusion.

A deep booming vibration, more profound than the regular
beat of the ocean, shuddered through the ground. Vines constricted around tree trunks like muscles tensing.

Another rumble shook the soil, threw me off balance so that
my right boot sank to the ankle in the soggy muck. I caught
myself and stared at Glade in astonishment.

"The whole island is alive!"

A tremendous crash of thunder covered Glade's reply; her
face was deathly pale in the lightning which flared at the same
instant, the sheet of brilliance etching tumescent foliage against

the sky. A moment later rain was drumming on the thick leaves. Huge drops splattered through the cover, stinging and soaking.

"Back to the bubble!" Glade yelled. "I will risk my life, but there is scant gain in a drenching."

The sphere refused to open.

I tried again, framing the command in my mind. The curved surface remained unbreached. Pale tints swirled placidly on its pearl.

I doubled up with laughter, water streaming down my back, hair in wet ribbons stuck to my forehead, neck, blown in my eyes. My screams of mirth were carried away. I clutched at Glade, throwing my head back, and howled. Her look of drowned fury doubled my hilarity.

"Betrayed!" I cried. "We shall have to swim home."

"Fool," Glade snorted. "Quickly, then. We must prosecute our mission without delay, rain or no rain." She pulled herself free of my weak hands and strode purposefully, head drawn down into her hunched shoulders, toward the hidden centre of the island.

The wind rose, shrieking in the trees. Rain whipped us with its nettles. Thunder in the heavens vied with the waves' thunder as they smashed on the cliffs of the shore.

There was no way we could talk, plan, protect ourselves from the downpour. The intertwining growth we pushed through gave some small cover, but itself made an irritating obstacle to progress. I soon lost my misplaced levity. Vines looped and festooned the close-packed boles; roots hugged the marshy soil, snared our stumbling feet; branches lashed, their leaves gust-torn; the ground itself continued to grumble and shake. A response to our intrusion? Or to the storm? Impossible to judge as we pushed, heaved, gasped, half-drowned.

At least the creatures of the island remained out of sight, though my clammy flesh prickled with the certainty that they scrutinized our every step.

Leaves began to rip away from their boughs, as if we struggled through an accelerated autumn. Color drained from them; they turned yellow, brown, flew in great damp face-slapping flurries, spun and mashed together in the wind, and were hurled up to the sky, flung across the island to the wastes of the ocean.

It was as if the assault of the elements had achieved some bitter, insupportable intensity: The very landscape convulsed in fantastic metamorphosis.

Protest choked in my throat, caught there. I coughed. "Glade, the trees devour themselves!"

Veins red as new blood scored outward through those blue and violet leaves which remained attached to the trees and vines. Cankerous warts burst from the boles of trees, linked by the crimson networks. Under us, the mossy soil heaved in rhythmic jolts, each greater than the last, cracking the knees painfully.

Now the rain redoubled, as that diminishing cover which had protected us collapsed entirely, and literally: leaves shrinking to wrinkled bladders; these curling up, in turn, into hard little knots of glistening gum. Fluid oozed from the warts as boughs withered; this liquid, resisting the rain, seeped down to coat the trunks, solidifying to a scabrous rind.

We were pelted by unencumbered rain. Within minutes, the trees had become a stark forest of jutting spikes, and we, fleas on the back of a porcupine. Underfoot, the spongy earth was hardening, forming a glossy skin to the island sleek as the hull of our aerial bubble.

I looked squint-eyed at streaming Glade and thought of the Forest of the People where I had begun my journeys in this world. There I had sought potable water and found a cat to kill, and so earned the mortifications of Oak-is-Strong. Here the only element in profusion was water, and again Glade was at my side in a trial of courage. No lesson came to me from this meditation. I pulled off my jerkin and wrapped it about my head, blocked my deafened ears.

We ran together through the gray deluge, slipping and sliding in sheets of water which rushed down wherever the ground sloped. Skidding, we did likewise. The antiquarians in Asuliun, in their cautious, pedantic fashion, had offered their belief that the fabled symbiote would dwell at the centre, the Well, of the Haunt of Monsters.

"We were too cautious," I bellowed. "We should have grounded the bubble directly in the centre of the isle."

"What?"

I repeated my useless complaint.

"It seemed the course of wisdom to conduct a preliminary survey," Glade shouted. "Who could have foreseen that you would forget how to open the bubble?"

"Forget?" I was outraged. "It refused me entry."

Glade grinned wickedly. She glanced up at the sky. The onslaught was easing. Missing her footing, she tumbled. I helped her to her feet. We leaned against one another, gasping. Glade smelled of sweat and mud and drenched leather. I hugged her to me; she pushed at me, frowning. I released her. Without a word, she wrung out her hair and gazed around, and we had passed through the moment, though I was pierced by a pang of melancholy.

"At least we have been spared the monsters," she said. "Perhaps the legends were erroneous in that detail."

"Do not depend on it." My clothing was sodden, and wind bit to my bones. "The creature I glimpsed earlier was monster enough. I would suppose that the beasts are parasites upon the vegetation and now share in its petrifaction."

Glade pursed her lips in scholarly surmise. "It would seem that all life on the isle constitutes a single prodigious symbiotic organism. The storm's advent was to our advantage, I think. Without its intervention, the enmity of the entire island would have been directed at our trespass."

"I do not like such coincidence. Is this the work of the Powers? Can They govern the onset of storms at sea?" The idea was unnerving; it spoke of a disproportion between the abilities of humans and those of gods.

"Why not? If They can build new sunlets to shine in the sky, tampering with a thunderstorm should be the lifting of a fingernail."

I mused on that as we continued to pick our way down among the new, wet rock. "Glade, the transformation we see may be our undoing. Surely that symbiote we seek would have undergone the same change. If so, it must be inaccessible."

The quester bared her teeth. Her plain face, red hair slick-capped, had the look of a skull. "Then we shall wait. At the storm's end, the transformation must be reversed."

"And the monsters reawakened."

"Well, shame on you, Xaraf! Shall we not brave the monsters?"

I grinned. Warm excitement dispelled my chill.

"Let us trust the Powers are then satisfied with our efforts, Glade, and relinquish the bubble to us. Otherwise we shall be braving monsters for the remainder of our exceedingly brief lives."

We descended into the surreal forest. The rain stopped. The wind began to die down. High above, the last of the clouds were rushing westward, and the mauve sky had won back a little of its territory.

I glanced over my shoulder. A hint of swirling pastels showed where the sphere hung amid the drab spikes. Beyond the crest of the basin the sea pounded; it was the only sound in the eerie silence which had fallen like a shadow over the island.

We came at last to the lowest point of an uneven bowl. Ahead, cool light lay like oil on a patch of glazed ground.

"Odd." Glade paused. The transmogrified forest was a maze of multiple shadows as the bloody sun and the forward sunlets struck from their differing altitudes. "I saw no such clearing from the air."

"It does not seem extensive. Perhaps overhanging branches obscured it. Nature appears to obey no consistent laws here."

We trod cautiously into this open place. The dying sun looked down on us, flanked by its attendant luminaries. Beneath our feet the earth trembled, as if we walked on a huge, taut drumskin.

"A membrane!" Glade stamped one foot. Booming waves rippled the clearing. "We stand on the upper surface of a giant leaf."

It buckled.

I yelled.

To every side, the forest was reversing its metamorphosis. All the island quaked and groaned. I stared about in alarm.

The rinds of the spiky boles were splitting in great fissures. Chunks of the scaly stuff fell away, stuck absurdly in the bubbling soil, left the boles smooth and damp. Branches budded forth, extending their obscene foliage.

Beneath us, the membrane was softening.

"Glade, the filthy thing engulfs us!"

Up peeled the edges, folding us in a colossal fleshy wave. We were hurled off our feet. The membrane's core sank, thrusting up slimy purple nodules.

Instant reflex saved me, reflex instilled in a thousand hours of repetitive, chafing exercise under Darkbloom's direction.

Falling, I lashed out my legs, caught Glade's flailing left arm in a brutal scissor lock.

A jeweled poniard, a treasure from the Asuliun armorer, came from my belt like a sigh of pleasure, went with all the force of my fist, to the hilt, into the membrane which rose and rose, towering above us like a green, living wall.

The glazed dermis ripped. Milky ichor spurted, oozed; the short blade held. Glade's weight and my own jolted into my one supporting arm then, nearly dislocating my shoulder.

At once the strain eased, as Glade gained purchase with her own dagger.

We were hanging nearly vertical now. There was little light to see by; the monstrous plant blocked the sky. Below us, waiting for our flesh, acrid juices seethed.

Did I dare move? The slightest shock might dislodge us both. I had no choice. I transferred my weight from right hand to left. The leaf tore; we swayed. In one movement I reached to my shoulder, had Alamogordo's hilt, drew sword from scabbard. I felt the great muscles of my back and shoulders writhe, as if two surly dogs fought there beneath my skin. The bright heavy blade came up above my head, and down, in a slicing chop that carved a great flap of green flesh from the membrane.

An animal would have screamed. This thing was utterly voiceless. It convulsed, though, like an animal.

Again I heaved up Alamogordo, struck into the raw opening. White sap spurted, stung my eyes.

Shadows reeled. A searing flash from the forward sunlet

dazzled me. The membrane shuddered. The rim curled outward, questing like a huge extended tendril.

Glade clung ferociously to my legs, strangling my circulation. I felt that I was being pulled apart. A third time I hacked into flesh. And abruptly we were tumbling, head and shoulders thrown down, legs threshing above, toward the membrane's outer lip.

Still the wounded plant was silent, but a weird high howling lacerated the air. The whole island seemed to be squalling as the leaf lashed outward, seeking to rid itself of its tormentors.

Somehow I regained my feet. Glade's energy-lance flew from her hand in the moment of ignition; I danced aside as it sizzled past my ear and sputtered out.

Three times the height of a man above the spongy earth, we swayed and tottered. The edge of the leaf curled short; reeking of some stench like dead eels, the darkness of its crater opened under us. I lost my footing one final time. Alamogordo whirled dangerously in my whipping arm; I released it, saw it flung beyond the crater's edge. And then I plunged into the place where the plant was rooted.

Hardly able to find breath, I staggered to my feet. I was waist-deep in water. Slush tugged my boots. I looked up. Only the faintest violet light penetrated. Thwarted, the leafy membrane had clamped down once more over the cavity it concealed. A horrid claustrophobia overtook me. I found myself sinking to my heels in the stagnant water, dazed and choking, head curving into my breast. Water entered my mouth. I coughed, jerked up my head.

And knew, in a way, where I was.

''Each thing in the world stands in the place of many other things,'' Darkbloom told me once as we fished at the pool of a drying summer creek.

''How can this be?'' I asked, baffled as always by his paradoxes. I thought he invented them to provoke me. ''There is no thing which is not itself.''

To prove this I picked up two rocks from the creek's edge: one a handsome white smooth pebble, the other dark, pitted by time, scored through with a reddish streak. "Are these stones not utterly different?"

Darkbloom surprised me by nodding. At that moment his line jerked with a fish. He drew it in. His kindness to all life did not prevent him from eating that which was no longer living, nor from bringing his prospective food to that condition. There was nothing simple about my mentor.

"Utterly different," he agreed. He mused then, while the stone knife in his old chapped fingers opened the belly of the fish and threw out its thready guts, scraped off its glinty scales. "That is why they are both called 'stones.' "

I thought about this for a time.

"Words are not things," I said finally. "They may be applied over and again to different things."

"True." Darkbloom beamed, hugged my shoulder which even then was burlier than his. "Our memories are frail, our powers of speech limited. What's more, Xaraf, we need this pretense of equivalence to allow us to speak at all. If we had a separate word for each of these objects you call stones, how could I tell you of stones only I had seen?"

I thought again in silence.

"What you meant before, then, was that every word stands for many things."

"Oh, no," Darkbloom said. "Behind the word is the multitude of things, and these in turn reach out like the roots of trees to touch one another, to mingle below the surface of the world, to become each other."

"What are my stones, then?"

Darkbloom said nothing. He cast back his line and watched the surface of the world, or of the pool at any rate, waiting for those finny things beneath it to rise, to snap, to impale themselves. To annoy him, I lobbed my stones into the water, one after another, directly in the place where his line sank from sight.

"Your stones are cries of rage at my fish," Darkbloom told me sedately. "Xaraf, what is this pool? Think of your dreams."

He had been asking me for several months the details of my dreams. At first this interest had pleased me, for there is no delight so piquant and difficult to obtain as the telling of one's dreams to a compliant listener, halting sentences all broken and filled with deep meaning that runs out through the fingers as one tries to recall the exact moment of sweetness, of fright, of silly pratfall which had involved . . . whom? and where? Now, though, I had come to find his inquisitions tedious, irrelevant to the tumbling tales I tried to recapture.

"This pool? I lay in it and the light was red, all bloody. The tent fell in on me and I was choking. A baluchitherium came at me, but I was safe. I don't know. What is it, skinny old man?"

"It is many things, Xaraf. It is sweet water to drink. Home for these fine fishes." He looked slyly sideways. "Your mother's womb, of course, first and last, where you curled up for three-fourths of your first year, where you dreamed and dreamed and return in dream, where you long to return in life too, Xaraf, to its comfort and oblivion."

"Filthy old pig!" I recoiled when I saw at last what he was saying. "Leave my mother out of this, lecher. Perhaps my father did not go far enough when he deprived you of your cods, foul slime speaker."

Darkbloom sighed, as he often did after he had taught me something so important that I went sideways from it clawing and yelping. "Slime? Foul? Is your mother's womb so horrible to you, boy, that you must revile it and me in these astonishing terms?"

That night I dreamed of a tall tower all of brick, bristling with arrows and swords, topped with a cap of gold, and of a cavern in the forest with walls of moss and honey, where I wept until joy soothed my heart and I woke swollen with lust: at first languorously excited; then, remembering, abruptly ashamed; and at last amazed; profoundly, respectfully, intoxicatedly convinced.

"Glade!" I shouted. "Glade! Do you live?"

A black shape moved hesitantly to my right.

"Not by any great margin." The quester's voice echoed flatly in the enclosed womb-space.

A flicker of light appeared, spread into a soft radiance. Glade raised her light-crystal and smiled sardonically.

"Xaraf, our luck holds. Unless I am mistaken, we stand at this moment waist-deep in the waters of the Well of Rejuvenation."

The membrane's massive stalk jutted like a pillar from the lake. Clots of fungus clung to it, deathly pale against its puce striations.

And, attached at water level to the stalk, flagella floating like strands of pond weed, flimsy tendrils trembling toward us as if yearning to embrace us, clustered a colony of tiny, inexpressibly beautiful creatures.

EIGHTEEN

I caught my breath, or it was snatched out of me.

"They are lovely. The legends of Asuliun describe them perfectly."

"Aniera's cure," softly murmured Glade. "We have not come in vain."

She trod cautiously into deeper water, the light-crystal held high. Yellow as topaz above murky ripples, the symbiotes glistered. Their swaying gossamer threads sheened prismatically.

After four lurching steps Glade halted, submerged already to the armpits.

"The slope drops alarmingly," she muttered. "I shall have to swim across."

"Pass me the crystal. I will wait here. Swimming is an art we desert folk have little chance to cultivate." Certainly it was one outland skill which Darkbloom had forborne to teach me; the Wanderers possessed an ancient abomination of water, using a bound dunking it in as a means of testing the demon-haunted.

The quester waded back to me. She shrugged out of her sodden garments, tugged her boots free, handed me the dripping bundle. Noiselessly, then, she sank pale-bodied, tan-featured and -armed, into the brackish water, swam with long, even strokes toward the crater's omphalos.

I watched in trepidation. To my surprise, I discovered that the symbiote's fabled promise of prolonged life held no lure for me. There was something ineffably sordid in that transaction, something so repellent in the idea that my stomach squirmed.

Glade's head bobbed amid dark ripples. She was almost upon the colony of gleaming creatures. I shivered.

A shelf of some kind surrounded the stalk; with a faint splashing, Glade rose out of the water on hands and knees. With no hesitation she reached for the closest symbiote and prized it carefully from the stem.

The cries of the island did not reach us here, in our shadowy cavern. A shrill keening came to me across the pool as she lifted the small animal to eye level. It was an unpleasant whine, a noise to set the teeth gritted.

"They do not relish being disturbed," Glade called. Shakily she laughed; her forced mirth echoed unnervingly. "I wonder how this little fellow will take to being swallowed alive?"

My arm trembled as she said that, sent dancing shadows from the crystal's light. I could feel my heart bumping.

Glade tilted her head solemnly, brought the bright symbiote down to her mouth as though celebrating some dread, archaic ceremony. When she took away her hands, they were empty.

Choking slightly, then, like one who has gulped too large a mouthful in greed or fright, she leaned back heavily against the thick, be-slimed stalk. I saw her breasts rise and fall, heaving in sudden spasms.

She slumped to her knees in the dark water.

"Glade!" I pressed forward. Under my booted feet, the slushy slope of the crater fell away. "Are you ill?"

The quester made no reply, which was reply enough. Her arms lashed, out and back, clawed at her chest. Harsh, whimpering groans came from her throat. In light which was bright above my head but weak at her distance, her eyes seemed to roll and jerk in their sockets like white globes, the pupils contracted.

Blood gushed abruptly from her mouth. She fell face down into curdled water.

I hurled behind me the bundle of clothing in my left hand, bit the cool, dazzling crystal between my teeth, threw myself into the water.

Clumsily, I threshed my limbs in imitation of Glade's easy

strokes. I floated, bobbing, took a foul mouthful, could not spit because of the crystal, snorted more up my nose, wallowed. Beneath my heavy legs I felt nothing but black water. Through my tremendous flailing and thwacking I could hear nothing of Glade.

I sealed my thoughts against terror then, with chilly, remote will.

Darkbloom had chanted often enough with me, chanting over and again the syllables which close out fear and the babbling of unwanted thoughts. I sought that harmony, that Oneness of his doctrine.

My weighted, soaked-clothing-bound legs thrust against the alien element which tugged at them, found a rhythm like the rhythm of my mantra. Stagnant water stung my nostrils; I blew it out, let my head turn to the side, breathed stinky air, bubbled out stale beneath the water, turned again, breathed, while light coiled in rippled streaks, and I was borne up, my limbs drawing me forward, gliding, more bird in sky than fish in creek, with smooth coordination, a grace.

My feet tangled then in slimy roots.

I staggered up into cold air.

Glade floated in the shallow water. I caught her by the shoulders. Curds of blood hung at her lips. Her abdomen was distended; horribly, the bulge moved.

Desperate, I tried to recall the ornate rites of disengorgement described by the antiquarians in Asuliun. Glade's naked belly heaved. She was dying. I had seen women far advanced in pregnancy, their bodies great before them, the pucker of the navel lost, breasts richly swollen with milk: this was nothing like that. It was an abomination. Like a bruise, livid coloration seeped across her dilated abdomen.

There was no time for finesse. I stiffened my fingers, as for the blow which, sent to the heart or throat, kills; brought them high; jabbed down into the jerking bulge.

Glade screamed.

She spasmed, doubled, clasping her stomach, and vomited a thin gruel.

Without mercy, I slapped aside her clutching hands. I smashed another blow into the bruised, twitching mound. The dying woman fell on to her side. Her mouth flew open in rictus. In a torrent of bloody froth, the symbiote came up out of her guts.

I kicked it aside. It sank into muck, like a gorgeous neck-lace all stained with red.

I looked down aghast at Glade, wondering if I had murdered her in my attempt to save her life. She stared up in wordless pain, plucked feebly at my arm as I bent to wash mud and vomit from her face.

"Lie still," I said gruffly. "You may be bleeding inter-nally."

"No," she whispered, and struggled against me to sit up. Failing, she slumped against my arm as I squatted in the clammy, horrible mud. "Listen to me."

"I have to get you back to the bubble," I told her. I lifted the light-crystal, gazed about for something to use as a bridge, a raft, some contrivance to assist us across the deep waters of the Well.

"Damn you, listen. . . . The . . . symbiotes are . . . sen-tient." Glade closed her eyes, gasping. "They . . . observed us. It spoke . . . spoke to me . . . in my mind."

"It is gone now," I told her. "You have nothing to worry about, if I can get you home. Relax, Glade: I will fetch the sphere and convey you to the physicians." Surely the Powers would not be so cruel as to keep the sphere from me in this time of drastic need.

Angrily, Glade cried, "Heed me!" Her throat was rasped and raw. "They knew my . . . body . . . was unsuitable. They tried . . . to warn me. But you . . . Xaraf, it told me . . . you are a compatible host."

"I will not," I said instantly, turned away in loathing.

Her fingernails dug my corded arm. "You can . . . carry . . . a symbiote without risk. . . . And the Lady Aniera . . . is dying. . . ." Her fingers loosened, fell away.

I hunched beside the unconscious woman. Fear rose to choke me. What she proposed was vile. I could not do it. I would not.

Flagella floated in the black lapping water, tendrils lofting light as cobweb. I imagined them tearing at my bowels, sucking the blood out through my internal tissues.

"What do I owe Aniera Argaet?" I cried aloud. "Nothing. What is it to me, if she lives or dies?" I pictured her thin, pale face against the pillows, saw Glade's blanched face in truth, and knew that one had consciously risked death for the other, not simply from a hunger for the crown in Asuliun but out of compassion for the sovereign's lonely pride and need. Each is connected with every other, Darkbloom had insisted. Was this why the Powers had sent me here, if indeed They had? I groaned, and turned to the beautiful animals gleaming against their vegetable host.

I thrust in my fingers among them; they shrilled.

Threads like the legs of huge hairy spiders writhed against my fingers. Shivering, I tugged gently at one of the creatures. For a moment the suction holding it to the stalk resisted, then gave. It came free, squirming in my hands.

I squeezed my eyes tight and took the thing into my body.

A vivid lance of scarlet fire plunged from my rigid jaws to my deepest parts, slashing.

No air. I suffocated, smothered. My lungs seemed to collapse.

A thousand barbs ripped me within, settled in my entrails, butchered my vital organs.

Agonized, I cried out. The blackness and light and shadows rolled away, rolled back.

Insects gnawed at my naked brain, a shrill hungry whine.

And then the fire had surged past, was gone. Billowing clouds of sweet fragrant foam lifted me, in rapture, bore me high as the water had borne me in my mantra-grace, tossed me weightless into a sensuous oblivion beyond pain or joy.

I soared, a snow bird floating over fields of dazzling white, swooped and fell on tilted wing, climbed powerfully into a glory of cold dawn.

Soft breezes stroked my burning, delighted flesh with kisses, drew me fainting and suffused with pleasure beyond the boundaries of physical sense.

My spirit merged in exultant communion with the ageless
entity within my body, and I knew—

. . . I heard—

. . . We—

Glade groaned, resentful. I opened my eyes, blinking and astonished. The quester rested on her elbows, teeth gritted, legs
drawn up to push weakly at the muck she sat in. On shaky
legs I crouched beside her.

"Can you move?"

"I believe so. Help me to my feet."

Once upright, Glade swayed but stood without assistance.
She smiled wanly.

"Xaraf, you have saved my life. Next time, you might be
less enthusiastic about it."

I regarded her lovingly. The symbiote looked at her too
through my eyes. She looked back at us; after a moment she
shrugged, moued her lips.

"Intoxicated as a loon. Wafted up to the Eighth Sphere, is
that it, Xaraf?"

"The experience is . . . indescribable, Glade."

"I'm sure it is. So was mine. Oh, well." She stared across
the black water, swung back with a scowl. "The membrane
has sealed us within. By now, the monsters must be full roused
without. We have lost our weapons. Or are you too drunk to
care?"

"Do not be angry, Glade. You are not to blame."

"No, damn it, but it was my quest and my trophy, and my
body which betrayed me, so I have no right to be furious with
you but I am, Xaraf, I am so furious I could smash your
beautiful face in," and she sat down in the sludgy muck and
burst into tears.

Once this might have made me profoundly uncomfortable;
now I was too dazed. Sympathetic, I hunkered near her and
waited for her to sob out her misery and shock, and when I
judged the time was right I put my arm about her and drew
her into my shoulder, where she tensed, and eased, and shook,
and at last laughed quietly, pulling her grimy face back and
shaking her head, gazing up at me; she gave me a quick kiss,

then, on the mouth, and pushed me away, stood up, shook her wet hair away from her brow, clenched her fists, trod into the slush and examined the dark.

"The prospect is not entirely hopeless," she said in a relaxed tone without turning her head. "If we assume that your power over the bubble has been restored, you can summon it to this spot. Doubtless the membrane can be coerced."

"First we must regain the farther shore," I pointed out. "Glade, I cannot swim."

"You are here, on this side of the pool."

"I do not understand how I reached you. Need impelled me."

The quester shrugged. "Then I shall instruct you. There is no overwhelming urgency, though I admit I am hungry." Reaction trembled through her again; she sat down in the tangled roots. "I trust you are an apt pupil. You may have to tow me across."

Stripping off my own clothes, I examined my body. The hard, flat muscles of my abdomen betrayed no sign of the alien creature buried in my guts. I sought within me for a hint of that odd communion which had washed through me. No response came; the symbiote had integrated itself already into my vital processes, and its sentience was locked away from my probing, as those portions of the spirit are locked away which fetch us dreams.

I slipped back into the unpleasant water.

Glade shouted. Startled, I jerked up my head—and almost sank.

Once again, with no memory of choosing to do so, I was gliding through deep water, limbs stroking with rhythmic ease. Incredulous, I swam toward the glimmering light in Glade's hand, hoisted myself back up on the slimy shelf.

With a certain rueful irony, Glade said: "Perhaps you would care to instruct *me* in the art of swimming. I have never seen any human so perfectly in his element."

Astonished, I shook back my wet hair.

"The symbiote." I stared at her. "Evidently it has lent me a skill I never learned. How is this possible?"

Glade narrowed her eyes speculatively. "You mastered the

trick briefly to reach me before. The creature has simply helped
you draw on that experience.'' She looked away, as though
we spoke of something of which we should both be ashamed.
''The symbiote is not without its advantages. You may find
difficulty in parting with it.''

I dropped back into the water without a word, helped her
descend the tangled shelf. Once in the deeper water, she floated
on her back, fanning with her hands.

Tersely, I asked; ''How shall I carry you?''

''Merely cup your hand under my jaw, and tow me.'' Water
ran into her nose; she coughed. ''What of your garments?
Perhaps I could carry them, though that will be difficult if I
am to hold up the light.''

''Leave them.''

We moved away cautiously, Glade bobbing, her firm chin
pressing my palm; drifted slowly toward the violet rim of the
enveloping membrane. Light shivered strangely as the crystal
in Glade's hand rose and fell.

At the sloping edge of the crater she stood more confidently,
leaning on my arm hardly at all. We waded into the shallows.

On her toes, Glade poked at the boundary between crater
wall and leaf. A thick crust of hardened mucus made an im-
pervious seal.

''Put your shoulder to it,'' Glade said, and did the same. I
strained and heaved, but the muck underfoot gave way, dump-
ing us back in the water. The membrane declined to budge.

''A pity Alamogordo is lost,'' I lamented. ''I might have
hacked us free.''

''No less a pity that I let my energy-lance fall,'' said Glade.
''A touch of its hot fury would have given the plant pause.''
She snapped her fingers, then, and looked at me with satisfac-
tion. ''There is an alternative expedient along those lines.''

Bringing the light-crystal close to her slit-shaded eyes, she
ran a long thumbnail carefully along one lattice intersection.
The device split at once into two unequal chunks, revealing a
tiny intensely bright node.

''Summon the bubble,'' Glade said with a grin. ''We may
have to debouch rather rapidly.''

I focused briefly in command, but had no way of knowing if the machine was responsive. "What is your plan?"

"Watch and learn." Detaching the lesser fragment of sharp crystal, Glade scratched with its edge at the membrane. The dermis was thick, glazed, resisting her attentions. A small section shredded free.

"This might hurt our eyes," the quester warned. She flicked a control embedded in the broken crystal, jammed the bright node into the plant's raw flesh. Her hand jerked back instantly; she yelped with pain.

The hot crystal fused itself into the membrane.

"Cover your face, Xaraf!"

All the energy of the thing went into the leaf in one incredible gout of burning light.

The membrane convulsed like a fire-stung baluchitherium, ripping free of the crater wall with the sound of a great dead tree splitting. Pink light poured down from the sky as the leaf lashed upward. Oily smoke fumed and boiled from the deep scar in its green flesh.

And I was leaping, heaving myself by my fingernails to the spongy soil beyond the crater. I spun, one hand maintaining my hold on the earth, the other reaching for Glade. I caught her arm, hoisted her wrenchingly out of the Well of Rejuvenation. We rolled, gasping. Down crashed the membrane like a king's tent blown high in a desert storm and brought again to earth in one terrible gust, like a roof of timber and tile shattering about us in an earthquake, like a dying steed falling on a thrown rider. The earth shook in its paroxysm.

I looked about, grit in my mouth. The sphere hung ten paces distant, glowing benevolently.

Blue foliage trembled on dark glossy branches as, behind us, the wounded membrane flailed, shaking the island.

I lifted Glade across my shoulders and ran, nude and unarmed, hysterically aware of how vulnerable, how utterly exposed we were.

The whole forest burst forth, then, to position in our path a bestiary of horrors.

Hideous things flopped from the trees, things that squirmed and lurched and scuttled, gouged the soil with talons.

Bodies ridged and wet as flayed muscle dragged sacs along trails of slime, slapping the ground with tentacles obscenely, pinkly, mouthed.

The Haunt of Monsters was truly named. My gorge rose as the things scurried in all their nightmare variety to block our path to the sphere. I ran for the cover of trees, and vines coiled and struck at us, spurting droplets of astringent poison that, splashing, burned my skin.

A jolt threw me off balance. Something had dropped on to Glade's back, had wrapped pseudopods about her neck, strangling her. I staggered, let her torso slip from my back. Glade fell crookedly to the ground, screaming hoarsely, slapping frenziedly at her throat and back. I rolled her over, scraped the thing off. It humped and hunched, aimed a quivering needle as long as my arm at her spine as I pulled her up.

I howled with rage, caught the needle as it struck, wrenched sideways with a powerful jerk that ripped it, bleeding and pulpy at its base, from the monster's body. With its own bony spike I slashed its sac, and tore the slackening tentacles from black-faced Glade's throat.

She vomited again, dark bile. When she attempted to stand, her legs gave way.

The sphere was five paces away; it might as well have been five thousand. I stared about me wildly.

Alamogordo's hilt jutted from the soil, half the sword's bright blade buried.

Talons stropped, cut at me. The alien things closed in on us. I crouched naked over my unconscious friend, the long bloody needle in my fist, and prepared to die.

Fire seared my nerves.

My senses spun, accelerated. Power gusted in me like a hurricane.

I threw back my head and howled like a wild beast. I moved faster than a man can move, attained my battlesword, grasped its lovely hilt in both hands, drew it suckingly from the marshy soil, heaved it whirring around my head, blurring, hacking: killing, killing, killing.

* * *

After a black infinity, the sword fell from my bruised hands.

Staggering, I hoisted Glade on my bloody back, stumbled through lumps and mounds and shreds of sundered meat.

The bubble's entrance dilated. I pushed Glade inside, leaned for a moment against the opalescent hull, surveyed the carnage I had made.

Those might have been men, I told myself.

It is true. I am an amok, a berserker.

Horror shook me. Once again I threw back my head, hands clenched at the edges of the bubble's entrance, and cried aloud, a long, desolate wail of bitterness and despair.

Alamogordo lay like a discarded skewer on a butcher's bench. I went to it, reeling, snatched it high with arms weak as a child's. The power borrowed from the symbiote was spent, all of it.

"I repudiate you," I bawled. My voice was strident, unconvincing even to me.

"No," the blade told me, terrible as a god. "I am damned, but you are in Hell with me. And I am no more than your weapon. Who is the killer, Xaraf?"

"These would have killed me!"

"You came here to steal their treasure," Alamogordo said. "You are a thief and a murderer."

The woman made me do it, I caught myself thinking; it was the symbiote itself which propelled me; you are the weapon which made it possible. I uttered none of these absurdities. But I took the sword anyway in my hands and with my last strength swung it around my head until it shrieked in the air, and when it contained all my remaining force I let it fly free, so it spun like a bloody, shining, half-transparent salver, and fell like a stone into the heart of the Well, where it vanished from my sight and my hearing and my raging, self-destroying heart.

I crawled into the bubble then, every fiber of my body numb with pain, and ordered the vehicle back to Asuliun.

Up it floated into the scarlet sky, northward, and I let myself too, at last, slip free.

NINETEEN

Liquid splashed my face, ran freely about my lips and down my neck.

I groaned, pushed myself up on one elbow. The blur above me shifted, came into focus. Glade was gazing down anxiously, an unstoppered flask in her hand.

"Xaraf! You lay so still I was half convinced you would never move again."

I snatched uncouthly for the flask, gulped its bright contents thirstily.

"When I last looked," I said then, "you were the one who simulated a corpse. Where are we?" The muscles in my hands were swollen and mottled. "Gods, from the clamoring in my belly I could swear I had not eaten in a week."

The quester rummaged in the trunk prepared for us by the Palace staff before we set out for the island. Here was a long loaf of crispish-crusted, mealy bread, three or four roasted, severed fowl, a container full of dark salty olives, other treats whose odors went direct to my salivary glands. My mouth rushed with hunger; I seized items up without discrimination, ate with furious appetite, eyes bulging.

"You need not save any for me," Glade remarked.

"Urmph," I protested, waving a greasy hand. Admittedly, the provisions were vanishing with prodigious speed.

She smiled. "Truly. The aches in my belly have eased, thanks to a potion, but the very thought of eating fills me with dismay." Tapping the forward bulge of the hull, she added: "We rapidly approach Asuliun, which is why I awakened you. Incidentally"—and she bent to the trunk again, tugged out a length of striped fabric, surely a sleeping sheet—"clothing is *de rigueur* in the city," and indeed she was wearing just such an improvised garment, wound high about her breasts, falling free to make a toga. "But tell me: how is it that you are the diner and not the dined-upon? I should have expected that we would be half-digested already by that misbegotten horde of fiends."

I licked my fingers clean, appetite abruptly gone. Somberly, I told the quester what I could of that explosion of whirlwind ferocity I had become in the timeless void of slaughter.

Glade nodded gravely. "Little wonder you were famished, Xaraf, that you lay here slumped in exhaustion. The symbiote must have drained every reserve in your body to combat a mortal threat otherwise insurmountable."

I curled my lip in distaste. "I shall not regret being relieved of the thing. It is like being in the possession of a demon."

The bubble slowed, drifted toward the ground. Asuliun was spread out beneath us, green and gray, ramparts warm with a tinge of crimson.

Glade gave a sudden harsh cry. She pointed to the foreshortened battlements of the Palace. From its tall mast, a black guidon stood out in the breeze.

"The Royal Flag of Mourning!" she cried.

"The Lady Aniera?"

Glade slammed a fist into the yielding substance of the hull. I saw that she was no more truly recovered from the stresses of her exertions than I; she was close to tears of frustration.

"Poor, frail Aniera. Fate has cheated her in the moment of deliverance. Her stubborn spirit surrendered one day too soon."

We sank gently into the wide courtyard at the front of the Palace. Startled dignitaries all in black and scarlet peered in censure at us, or averted their haughty gaze from this rude intrusion into public and private grief. I watched them file solemnly up the broad steps, let my eyes drift back to the grim banner snapping high above the battlements. It seemed to me that neither Glade nor these scandalized burghers understood what that flag made her.

"Glade," I said quietly, "if I understand the terms of your quest, surely *you* are now sovereign in this place."

She bared her teeth. "Not so. The quest is automatically void.

Hernedral Repose, our Episcopal, is confirmed as Regent in Asuliun; his obligation is to conduct a lottery for the post."

I was incredulous. "You dice for the crown?"

"We are radical thaumatocrats," Glade said carelessly. "The Fates may intervene through many processes; a full-dress quest is only one method among many, and hardly in favor in these drab days."

Comhria Chtain's bright, joyful image flamed in my mind, as if she stood beside me in a beam of brilliant sunlight, the sun of my world and not this, not this tedious, guttering ruin. I put my arms around Glade, looked down into her studiedly impassive face.

"I am sorry, Glade—"

"It is without significance."

I shook my head. "My obligations, I judge, are now discharged, and yours too, I think. Let us seek more formal apparel and pay our respects to the Lady Aniera."

Glade's voice was woeful. "You will wish to return immediately to Treet Hoown."

"I cannot deny it."

The face of the quester-no-longer filled with unashamed distress. She freed herself from my arms. "Xaraf, nothing holds me here. The sedentary ways of Asuliun, under some hapless random ruler, some shopkeeper or sculptor . . . they will destroy me, Xaraf. Allow me to accompany you. Perhaps in the city of the War Master sufficient spirit remains to spark this tired old world to a final glory of adventure before the sun expires."

Surprise and delight caught me, and I heard my own laugh ring in the bubble like a great bell set gonging.

"Indeed we shall, Glade! Ah, friend, let us send the world shouting in one last drunken—"

I broke off. It was as if most starless night had fallen at a word. The swirling pastel hues of the hull were gone, darkened to ebon opacity. We were locked in a bubble of gleaming blackness.

Sparks cascaded between us then.

Over our heads, stinging our hands and feet, tingling in legs and cheeks, sparks spun and swept.

Rank as a cat from the Forest of the People, in motes of fire, the eagle-headed beast stood with us in the vehicle.

Glade shrank back in terror. I stood my ground, and the scattered runes of memory tumbled together, well ordered now and implacable.

"Goldspur," I said wearily. "What heartache do you come this time to convey?"

The gryphon's tongue darted in its beak.

"Greetings, Xaraf Firebridge. I bring the greetings of the Powers, and to the merchant Glade Resilience also." It sat back delicately on its haunches, ruffling up the green-gold feathers of its furled wings.

"So Mathketh was correct in his surmise," Glade said softly. Gravely, she bent the knee to me. "Xaraf, I knew you to be no ordinary man, but I had not guessed that I journeyed with a deputy of the hidden gods of this world."

My face was aflame. "Glade, my friend, stand up."

Her tone was remote with wonder. "The Powers graved the map on your sword, then. It was They who guided us to Treet Hoown."

"And then snatched the memory of it from me," I said resentfully.

"I cannot plumb Their motives in withdrawing the truth from you, Xaraf," she said, still wide-eyed, bright-eyed, "but who dares question the gods?"

"They are not my gods," I cried. "I revere the Lords of Life and Darkness, of Light and Death, not these inept sun-kindlers."

"The sun?" Excitement quickened Glade's voice. "The sun is dying, Xaraf, and all the world with it. Is this your mission? Can it be that you are to be instrumental in reviving it?"

My gloom deepened as her feverish vivacity glowed higher. I had voiced this speculation before, to Alamogordo. "Is she correct, Goldspur? Is this ludicrous burden to be placed upon my shoulders?"

Amiably, the beast said: "You continue to surprise me, dear boy. You appear to have broken the posthypnotic amnesia without benefit of my verbal key."

I sighed. "Gryphon, I am in no mood for esoteric pleasantries. Deliver your message and allow us to go on our way."

Yellow eyes, at once genial and feral, swung from one of us to the other.

"I come to fetch you to the Keep of the Powers, Xaraf."

Blood rushed to my face. "Comhria!" I cried, but Goldspur continued placidly as if I had not spoken.

"Your period of instruction is at an end. The Powers judge you fully equipped to cope with the dangers threatening your own world, and Their energy wormline. You will be repatriated at once to the past."

My motives fought to a deadlock within me. All my life, it seemed to me, I had been walking steadily toward Comhria Chtain. She was my destined love, my other half, my true wife, my goal. Yet my father and his people, *my* people, Firebridge, the Wanderers, the lame, tame cityfolk of Berb-Kisheh who had given us my mother and a quarter of my cousins, all the world I knew needed me, needed my knowledge and the strength of my arm. For all Their cynical indifference, the Powers had indeed rehearsed me splendidly to combat sorcerers and ghouls.

Yet I had cast Alamogordo back into the deeps. I wanted no more of such murder. Darkbloom's teaching was right, as it had been always.

I uttered a groan, turned away to stare at my inverted reflection in the black gleaming concavity of the bubble.

Mastering her fear and adulation, Glade stepped forward.

"The past? You mean that Xaraf's world is not, after all, anchored in the sky, but buried in our own obscure history?"

"How keen your mind is, merchant." The gryphon's claws glinted and retracted, with a ratching sound. "Xaraf's world has been dust for a million years."

"How, then, can he be returned to it?"

"My immortal masters have conquered Time, and guide the borrowed force of the young sun into the belly of this exhausted star, readying its reignition. The Powers bend Time's fabric to Their will. Xaraf will walk again amid the tents of his people."

"And I?" Now that Glade saw what was afoot, minute by

minute there was less of her instinctive obeisance, and more of that astute self-interest I so admired. She put her fists on her hips, leaned forward so that her nose was a hand's width from the gryphon's cruel beak. "What disposition do the Lords of the Evening plan to make of me, now that I have helped school your agent, much against his will, I do not doubt?"

Goldspur rose, arrows of fire gliding gorgeous in its wings.

"You are an atavism, merchant. Your soul hungers for adventure in a bland world. The Powers offer you hazard such as no human has known since the passing of Earth's dawn."

The beast smiled, a daunting yawn of its sword-sharp beak. "You are splendid companions, you two. Each augments the talents of the other. What say you, then, Glade Resilience? Shall you leave us now and submit to the lottery? Or shall you dare the past?"

Glade's mouth opened; sly, its timing wicked, the gryphon spoke again before she could utter a syllable.

"You should recall, of course, that the advent even of storms at sea is no more than the lifting of a fingernail, to the Powers. And you, as we all know, were the rightful victor in this quest just completed. I have little doubt that the fall of chance will nominate the correct candidate for the crown in Asuliun."

Glade swallowed, hard. I heard the sound of it as I stood in silence, scowling.

"A novel choice," she said shakily. "Exile and adventure, or sovereignty by supernatural malfeasance." She hesitated, glanced sidelong at me. "Xaraf, though, has his own priorities. The Lady Comhria Chtain awaits him in Treet Hoown."

I shall voice my own grievances, I started to say, but stifled the rebuke.

"Did you not just complain that a life in Asuliun would stifle you?" I said. "Would it alter your prospects so much, to stand at the head of a citizenry hardly more vital than the sleepers in Treet Hoown?"

"Not while the dying sun flickers out overhead," she admitted, knotting her fingers together.

"Well, then," I growled, "let us go to the Keep, Gold-

spur.'' I did not disguise my bitterness. ''We must not delay
your Masters' plans with our petty quibbles.''

The gryphon padded forward, its gaze softening, and placed
one huge furry paw gently on my tensed forearm.

''Xaraf, the Powers are not so heartless as you imagine.
The enterprise in which you reluctantly share is of the largest
moment. What could be more important, as your companion
has seen, then the revival of Earth's dying sun?''

The gryphon lowered its paw. ''Not the Powers' whim, but
destiny, has imposed itself upon you.''

The bubble's hull lost is ebon sheen. I had a moment's
dizziness. No longer in the square of mourners, we lofted light
as a dream high above the gray paving stones, afloat in the
purple melancholy of evening. A handful of loiterers stared up
like inquisitive insects.

''Trust me, mortal,'' the beast said. ''The Lady Comhria
shall be appraised of your duty. If you survive your momentous destiny, you shall doubtless find her waiting for you.''
To Glade it said: ''With the sun renewed, the crown in Asuliun will be a prize worth owning.''

I threw back my head and laughed in incredulous admiration.

''How devious immortals are, Goldspur, and how transparent. Always they manage some poignant incentive to draw us
on. Well, it is enough. It is more than most men know in the
false freedom of their lives.''

I raised my head with some pride, put my arm about Glade's
shoulder.

''Yes. Take us to the Powers.''

All the pearly hull sparkled in a rain of fiery sparks. A
dancing net of tiny stars etched Glade and the gryphon, and
me too, I suppose, and the dark came and went behind our
open eyes, flinging us at the waiting gods.

From the high thrones, four Beings gazed down upon us.

Night was everywhere, utterly black and remote beyond the
crystal dome, splattered with the pale points of stars. Incense
came to my nostrils, pungent and brisk. Glade touched my
right arm lightly. Goldspur was gone. I looked at the Powers.

One was young, pale, exquisite: Jesrilban Julix.

One was hard, burly as a warrior: Ah Balmorq.

One was frail, pink and white with years: Eis Creid.

And a fourth was a woman of middle years, relaxed in her gorgeous throne, garbed in robes that draped her with sheening darkness. I had never seen her before, and I knew her instantly.

"Darkbloom," I said, before the shocking absurdity of my words could still my tongue.

"Flowers of Evening," she corrected gently. "Hello, Xaraf. How glad I am to see you safe and well."

Glade said tensely: "What is this? I took your mentor to be an old man."

"So he was," I said, and the words hurt my throat. I swallowed. All my body was cold and wet. "Yet this is Darkbloom, Glade. I know it."

"Come," Julix told us imperiously. "Approach us. There is little time to be lost in idle chatter."

"Go easily, Jesrilban," said Flowers of Evening, placing a hand on his wrist. "This boy is my charge, and I will not see him harassed."

Marveling, I went forward by halting steps. "You *are* Darkbloom."

"I was, Xaraf." She stared piercingly at me, into my innermost soul. "All your life you have pestered me with questions, boy, and I have spent a good part of my time among the Wanderers answering them. Be warned. This is no longer the time for questions. Keep a guard on your curiosity. We deal now with the mysteries of Time."

I shivered, not understanding, feeling in my bowels how completely serious this warning was.

"Darkbloom," I said anyway, "you have troubled to fetch me here. This must be because you desire my service. How may I serve you if I may not ask your will?"

"You have a task. You will know it when it confronts you, for I have prepared you well."

A swelling mood of bitter repudiation rose in me.

"As you prepared Comhria Chtain to love me, with false memories?"

"Were they false?" Flowers of Evening teased me, her

smile as feminine in that moment as ever Darkbloom's had been masculine. My certainties were crumbling and reeling. I reached for Glade's hand, felt the sweat in her cold palm. "Do you not share these dreams of childhood?"

"Because you planted them in my mind, and hers, and nourished their growth."

"This is how all memories grow, if you think the matter through." Once more I heard the authentic irritating voice of Darkbloom the dealer in paradox and confusion.

"You spoke of a task," Glade said. Her voice shook. I realized how appalling this hour must be for her as well; these were the gods of her world. She had never laid her head in Darkbloom's cold ashes, or hoisted great stones on her back at his behest, or parried whimsies and speculations through the chill of winter.

"I did. Glade Resilience, you may adopt this task for your own as well, out of friendship for Xaraf Firebridge, or from your love of adventure, or for whatever reason suits your temperament; or you may abstain, and we shall return you instantly to your city and its lottery. The one thing you must not do is ask for the details of this task."

"And if I insist?" Glade's cheekbones were pale with anger. "It is the basic right of all consciousness to act only from a responsible estimate of the case before it."

The Power Eis Creid laughed, a wheezing exhalation of pleasure.

"Of course you may *ask,* my dear. Flowers of Evening is making a somewhat different point, to wit: by the nature of the case, you shall have no answer."

With tight lips, Glade lowered her head, turning her face away. I looked from her to Darkbloom, sitting easily in her high seat.

"Once I made you a vow," I told my mentor, "and broke it. That was to my great shame. Now you give me the chance to make atonement for that lapse. You were my dearest friend, Darkbloom." I found that I was standing at the very foot of her throne, gazing up into that placid, changed face. "I shall do as you say. But I would ask you to spare Glade this burden."

"You offend her by this request," Balmorq said in his bass rumble.

Perhaps Glade had been on the verge of rebuking me; instead, she turned heatedly on the immortal.

"Xaraf expresses his care and concern in these words," she said. "It is a great deal more than I see in any of you. Are you so mighty, so elevated above us, that you use human beings as your tools without a hair's flicker of conscience for our special worth?"

"What you say has its truth," Flowers of Evening admitted. She frowned. "Your individual lives are so fleeting that for the most part we find it almost impossible to value them." She paused to regard us, leaned forward. "This is not necessarily so, however. As Xaraf can assure you, I have spent part of almost every day of his life in his company. I love him, Glade Resilience. Believe it or not, I probably love him even more than you do."

Glade scowled, and would not meet my eyes. "Have it your own way."

A beautiful gonging tone sounded through the chamber, and a bank of lights lifted from the flooring.

"The Matrix is activated," Jesrilban Julix said imperatively. "We can delay no longer."

"You are right." Flowers of Evening stood, came down from her throne. She reached into a place I could not see well, a flickering translucence in the air, and drew forth something heavy and bright and graved with mysterious sigils. "Xaraf, you abandoned this friend too soon. Here, take back your sword, and keep it by you in this time of need."

I looked at the mad blade with a surge of pity that surprised me, and kept my hands by my side.

"Alamogordo," I said.

"Do you come to claim me once more?" the sepulchral voice asked.

"You represent something in myself which I repudiate, which I wish never again to claim," I said. To Flowers of Evening, who held the massive thing with absolute ease and grace, I said harshly: "You taught me in all those days of our life together to deny the violence in me. You reproached me when I joined my kin in practice with weapons. Why do you tempt me now?''

"What use is a vow when it cannot be put to the test?"

"I was faced by that test, more than once. Each time I failed."

"So now you skulk away from temptation? This is not the path to victory, Xaraf."

Abruptly, like a wash of light, I saw what he was telling me. With a sigh that shook my chest, I reached out and took the sword from her, one hand grasping the hilt, the other cradling the lovely, murderous blade.

"I think you will die soon," said Alamogordo, "and join me here in Hell."

"Perhaps you are right," I said. "Glade, do you wish to do as these heartless beings ask?"

"If you wish my company, Xaraf, I will come with you."

I placed the blade at my feet and held out my hands to her.

"Thank you, my friend. I will be very glad of your company."

"Then let us go, with no questions and no hopes."

"Goodbye, Xaraf Firebridge," Flowers of Evening said. She came forward and brought my matted hairy head down against her unlined brow. Calm and love flowed from her hands. "I thank *you,* too, my dear."

Goldspur took us from the crystal night, to baths and sleep, to food and clothing, and then led us, Glade and me and my poor demented sword, into the black place all scored with runes, the Matrix of Time, and cast us a million years backward into a history which hung (though this reality was beyond our intuition) precisely upon those choices we now faced.

TWENTY

Once, Darkbloom filled my nostrils with burning fumes to put me in a reeling trance. At the centre of my vertigo, though, I found a still, quiet place, and he instructed me as I sat nodding there.

"Go back to your mother's womb," he told me. "Return to the moment of birth. Experience once more the struggles you endured in coming out to us, the effort of birth, the pangs of leaving and the bold savage joys of arrival. Draw in once more your first breath, and scream with the rasp of it in your wet lungs. Do it, Xaraf, now," and with each jolt of his chanting voice I felt the pulsations on my flesh, caught a blurred glimpse of the dim red light toward which I strained, howled with the bruising pressure on my head, my tiny arms, the useless kicking of my legs, the dragging at my belly where my mother and I were linked by a coiled rope—

It was like that, pushing back through Time to my origins.

Glade came at my heels, like a twin, and my ears reverberated to her groans.

Alamogordo was a burning brand across my back. A kind of lamentation rose from it, less words than the droning babble of a child in inconsolable misery.

It is hard, being born.

"My reverence has been extinguished," Glade said, panting. "I do not trust Them. Why are They doing this to us?"

To my astonishment the sword answered her, speaking thoughts from my mind, skewed to its own delusion.

"This is birth. We are being reborn. Perhaps in this way we can be cleansed and saved from hell."

Until this point I had not realized that we could converse. I had struggled almost mindlessly. Now, in the heaving redness, I sought words and with those words tried to capture the ideas which words all too easily obscure.

"Alamogordo, you are correct, I think. Cling to this notion. When we break loose of this horror, you will be free entirely."

"There is much you have failed to tell us," Glade said reproachfully.

"There is much I have not understood myself," I said, defensive in my own cause. "The relevance of much more has not until recently been apparent."

"Now that it is, you might divert us, at least, with an account of them."

So I did. Struggling in the birth canal of Time, almost blind, half-lost in fantasies of infancy, half-mad in the terror of our passage, I told my friend and my weapon all I could remember of my curious upbringing: of Darkbloom, and my father's maiming of the interloper; of Firebridge Tribe and its ways; of my mad mother and her besotted attendance on the wounded priest; all of it.

"Xaraf, you leave so much out."

"Of course I do," I cried angrily. Red moist everywhere. "Shall I tell you of my first kendo stick? The third worm I ate, testing its taste? The last shit I took—"

"Why was Flowers of Evening in your camp all those years, Xaraf?"

"He was a— Why, where else could—" I stumbled. Incredibly, I had never asked myself that simple question. What I knew of my own world was segregated, somehow, from my grasp of this one. Yes, I had come finally to believe that the world of the dying sun was ruled by gods, or by Beings close enough to godhead. Yes, I could even accept that one of these Beings had tarried in my world through the duration of my life, and doubtless (though I did not know where, or to what end) for years prior to that. And it had not occurred to me to link those fragments of knowledge, to ask the question which astute Glade now had posed:

Why had Flowers of Evening wasted her immortal years

under the guise of a mutilated shaman, in the shadow of the Black Time, shivering at the foot of the chilly glacier of a small insignificant valley in the south of the world nine hundred thousand years before she came to the world of the Dying Sun?

With a consciousness of how thin and boastful it sounded, I said: "To teach me, I suppose."

"Teach you what? The Open Hand, as you call it? The way of the coward, in a time when terror is about to descend on your world, if the news your father bore is true."

"That was only part of Darkbloom's instruction." I was hurt. "And it is hardly cowardice to face one's foes without weapon in hand, with only the force and wit of one's training."

"Yet she returned Alamogordo to you."

"That I might refuse its use."

"This is metaphysical gibberish." Glade sounded tired and out of patience with me, with her efforts, with her life. "You tell me that she instilled dreams into your mind, dreams of Comhria Chtain."

"And the tongue used by the people of Treet Hoown."

"The same language employed by the Powers. Why is this needful, when my world, Comhria's world, does not lack for translation devices?"

I mused on that, and could find no answer.

The blade found one, however: "So that you might speak face-to-face with your enemy when you meet him."

Glade pounced. "Who is this enemy? A vapor of dreams, a mishmash of antique mythology and the babblings of your unconscious mind."

"My brother," I heard myself say. "What more can I add, that I have not said already?"

"Damn you, Xaraf, think this through! Whose son are you?"

My pride flared. "I am the son of Golan Firebridge, and do not question it!"

"How should I do that? And was there not another involved in the process?"

"My mother, of course. Neeshyaya Yubka, the crazy woman from Berb-Kisheh."

"Xaraf, you do your mother less than justice. Shame on you for that impiety. I have noticed it before as you spoke of her, that you diminish and mock her, yet I think that she is the one person who truly loved you for yourself among all those men and women in your filthy primitive tribal pesthole."

I tried to turn, to strike her for her impertinence, and could not; the walls of the tunnel pressed me, squeezed my scalp, closed my eyes with red. My fury mounted and spittle ran from my clamped lips. I strangled and choked, and said at last, "Her name means 'petticoat' in the old tongue. She was a worthless creature, Glade, a fool, and I am a mockery as her son, restricted to the outskirts of the camp, glad even of the scraps of company I can find in the ashes of the foul shaman Darkbloom." Snot ran into my mouth; I sniveled.

"Damn you, fool, Xaraf, wake up, keep your mind whole!"

Her tone lashed, it bit, it struck me with barbs. I jerked open my eyes as I had done when she called to me under the tree where birds fell to eat my flesh.

"My mother, yes," I said clearly, angrily.

"That is better. Xaraf, there was another, as you tell the tale."

" . . . Darkbloom?"

"Of course."

I saw it in my mind, then, as I had heard it in scraps and pieces of leering gossip: the rancid old man hovering over the half-naked body of Petticoat, her belly swollen with the last of Golan's seed, the last and most scorned of his children before the wild boar most eerily gored his loins a month after he had worked the same mutilation on the shaman; Darkbloom's muttering and passes and herbs—

And then from deep within me I called up a profounder memory, a memory of the place which preceded the place my present captivity mimicked: the womb, the whirling light in blind eyes, the voice of Darkbloom, deep through the waters, speaking and singing and drumming, drumming.

"Darkbloom was my father?"

"In a sense, I think."

"And so my enemy is another man shaped in another womb by this cruel god who could not leave us to become what the Lords of Life and Darkness decreed in the stars. . . ."

"Nothing is decreed in the stars, Xaraf. Surely you know this by now."

"Everything is decreed, it seems to me. Everything."

We went on, then, through the millennia which peeled away before us like waves of veined, pulsing, pressing muscle and fat and flesh, carrying us with its contractions into the battle which, I saw now, I could not avoid.

At length, Glade spoke again.

"I think you are a courier, my poor dear. A vessel. A living container."

Some tendril stirred within me. I had forgotten the creature which extended its cilia through my heart, my bowels, my lungs, breathed with me, heard and saw with me, lent my arm the power of a murderous lunatic. A shiver caught me.

"The symbiote?"

"It is immortality, Xaraf. Darkbloom was dying. I think he made you, trained you, so that you might fetch him the stuff of life."

I pondered that extraordinary conjecture. A deep welling response had flooded me as she uttered it: an affirmation, a desire to die if need be for my teacher, love so rich and over-powering that my mind all but ceased to function. Blurrily, I brought my hands to my face and touched my wet eyes.

"How can this be, Glade? Already Darkbloom is back in his own time. Her time. Gods, I cannot deal with this confusion of name and sex and time—"

"Flowers of Evening is young, rejuvenated. She is Darkbloom after your miracle of mercy." This was bitterness so stinging that my dazed emotion sharpened, became an insistence that my teacher should not be traduced.

"Glade, if that is where I go, I can imagine no happier task in all the world for my duty. Everything good in my life is due to Darkbloom."

She was silent, and the sword said nothing, and we went on, as if sleep had been taken from us forever, along with hunger and lust and everything human but anger and love, overwhelming dedicated love.

Light budded, blossomed, burst, dazzled me. A gust of freezing wind tore the sweaty hair from my eyes. I cried aloud with the cold and shock, and stumbled into snow.

The light went out, like a doused fire. Poised, I waited, hand on my sword's hilt for a moment, before, in revulsion, I forced it down by my side. Pale moonglow spread across the crisp snow of the high valley above Rezot-Azer. A huddled figure wrapped in blankets and mourning rocked, keening, across a funereal form molded all in packed snow.

I cleared my throat in warning, stepped toward the figure. Slowly she raised her head; the pitiful, desolated keening never ceased. The sound set my teeth on edge.

At my back, Glade activated a light-crystal. Shadows went deepest black, human features stark and exaggerated.

The woman's gray hair was knotted as a widow would knot her tresses, among the Wanderers, and covered with the bleak headdress called for by the rites of Firebridge. She turned her eyes to me, red-rimmed and bloodshot in the hard light, old eyes wrinkled and confused in a face ill-used by the elements, though she was barely more than half the age of Glade.

"What are you doing here, Mother?" I said as gently as I could.

She gave a rasping sob, and then cloaked herself in her sorrow's dignity. "He said I must await you here."

My forehead prickled with dread. I went down into the hard snow on my knees, and reached roughly into the icy package of dead human meat beside which Neeshyaya Yubka Firebridge sat in her grief.

His head was twisted horribly. Blood had hardened in thick ropes about the wound, spilled down his breast, congealed in his ragged beard. The sword or battle-ax which had done this thing had hewed his head almost wholly from his body, so that it lay attached only by the threads and bones of the spinal column.

I drew in a great shuddering breath and sent it out in a cry, a howl of bitter fury.

"Who did this?"

"Your brother Jopher, your cousin Yharugh, other men, the priests."

I bared my teeth like an animal.

All his body was slashed and butchered with insane, cruel strokes, his arms half-severed from his shoulders, his belly rent open, his thighs and calves hacked by ax and blade, the flesh broken and split and black with blood in a hundred places where they had kicked him and beaten him with sticks, stoned him probably, and then mutilated his already-castrated corpse.

Drenched with tears, I lifted dead Darkbloom in my arms and hugged his cold body to me, mumbling and crying, aware of nothing but my grief and his loss, anger held back for a moment by the whirling blankness that came and went, my love spilling from my heart to warm him back to life.

He lay inert in my arms, and slowly I grew to an awareness of the world, the snow and the slush of it where I crouched bent across his cadaver, Glade speaking to me clearly and carefully, and my mother's broken voice, both of them telling me what I must do.

"Why did they dare this murder?"

"The wizard your father fears falls upon the lands of the North. He comes with fire and storm. They blame the outlander."

"My enemy," I said. I hardly knew what I meant. I spun upon her like a wolf. "Woman, did my father, Golan Firebridge, have any part in this?"

She shook her head.

"Xaraf, he said you carried a charm of life and death. He told me that you must keep it to aid you in your battle with your brother." I thought for a moment it was my father she spoke of, but all her thoughts were fixed on Darkbloom. "Do not keep it, Xaraf, my dear, my son, I beg you. Use it now, for the sake of pity," my mother implored me. "If you can fetch him back, use it."

"She is correct," Glade was saying. "The symbiote might reverse even the process of death, if it can be introduced into the corpse before putrescence has set in. The cooling of the body is a favorable circumstance." I heard a return of that bitterness in her voice. "Of course, we know already that this rescue has succeeded, do we not, my dear? How else should Flowers of Evening have returned to guide you in your quest for the thing which finally you would bring back to this moment of melodramatic theater?"

Shaking, half-blind with tears, I let the body of my mentor back down into its catafalque of ice and stood up, backed away, denying the tug of devotion and sacrifice which drew me toward him.

In a high, hard tone I cried: "Do you understand nothing? I must leave him dead, or all this is in vain."

"You cannot leave him dead, for we have seen him alive."

"Have we? Do we know that the moment when we spoke to Flowers of Evening was later than this one? Perhaps it was earlier. Would she not have given us warning, if this horror had lain in her own past?"

Alamogordo spoke then, and his voice, for the first time since madness occluded it in Aji-suki-takahikone's chamber, was free and sane.

"Xaraf is right, Glade Resilience. More is hinged on this moment than the life of one immortal. Consider: you asked why Darkbloom spent so many wasted years in this wasteland. If he lacked the symbiote which lent him immortality (and how could such a disaster have come about, except by conscious decision), why did he not simply return to his own time and obtain relief from his temporary mortality? Is not the answer obvious?"

Glade and I were silent.

"He *could not* return," the blade said remorselessly. "His path was blocked."

"Ours was not," I objected.

"Two great forces may oppose and neutralize each other and have nothing to spare for a third which might tip the balance."

"I am that third?"

"You were," Alamogordo said with a measured intensity far more penetrating than the mad ranting which earlier had seemed so awful. "No longer."

"Because Darkbloom is dead," Glade said, her voice no louder than a breath.

"Yes. The opposing force is now unbalanced and will have its way unchecked, unless Xaraf takes his mentor's place in the battle."

"You must abandon this battle," my mother cried, desperate. She tugged at my arm, pressed her face against my breast. "He is dead and you can revive him. That is all that matters, my son. Do it, forget your foolish talk of battles. That is the nonsense your father spends his life upon, and it has brought us nothing but misery and waste. Fetch him back, Xaraf!" She looked up at me, so much taller and physically stronger than her, forced me to meet her wept eyes. "And if love is not motive enough, do not turn your back on your debts."

"I must," I said, and left Neeshyaya Yubka and my true father hunched there in the icy snow, walked on legs that hardly held me, and went back, Glade following reluctantly, to the place where white fire would blossom and bear me to my enemy.

This time I walked into an endless void without light. Glade's crystal faded with each step we took, as if its power was being drained from it, and went out. I peered blindly. A hundred voices murmured indistinctly, a thousand, an untold number of whispering people in the darkness.

Glade, I said. No sound came from my throat.

I reached behind me, panicked, and caught her outstretched hand. I drew her close to me.

He was somewhere ahead of me, my enemy.

I sniffed like a dog bred for tracking, breathing the dusty air. Yes, I found his scent there, an odor I knew from dream, a smell of the earth, of moist clods thrown up to view by the pounding hoofs of a baluchitherium, sweet and dark.

I turned to follow his spoor, Glade following, and all the voices of the dead and the unborn muttered their inscrutable conversations in my ears.

In the sky, colossal sheets and veils of pastel luminance swirled, hanging like folded clouds against the deep blue of late twilight.

A hot blue-white spark spat into the steaming soil, and a tremendous crack of thunder left me truly deaf for a time.

People such as I had never seen (soot-skinned, row-haired) were scattering like chickens at the coming of a fox. A second firebolt lashed instantly in the wake of the first, searing an image in red on my blinking eyes.

Trees soared around us, vast-leafed and flowered. I wondered wildly if we had been returned to the Haunt of Monsters, but this air was thick with moisture, and it lacked the near or distant thunder of waves. Only true thunder, or its brother: A third seething jet of hot light crashed between earth and heaven, and the wicker huts of the running black men and women burst into flame, shot into the heavy air smoke and coils of burning rushes, timber posts, stored grain, dried meat, all the stuff of a village.

I heard a baby screaming as it burned, and saw its plait-haired mother run into gusting red and yellow flame.

"He is killing them like insects," I said, revolted. Since childhood I had been raised to a communal belief in rapine and slaughter, but this brutality was somehow too barbarous even for the imagination of the storysingers of Firebridge.

"And he sees us," Glade cried. Her arm pointed high, to the flaring aurora.

Black and vast, a bird half the size of a baluchitherium was stooping on us, its dreadful claws extended, wings raised.

Whooping in a saddle of bright metal at its thick feathered neck was a man all wrapped about, like his appointments, in gold and silver.

His right hand lifted from the falcon's neck and lightning came down his fingers, a blinding boiling drop of light that fell ahead of them, singing in its stink of smashed air, plunging into the midst of the cowering warriors who crouched pathetically vulnerable beneath their woven shields and their wooden spears.

I took Alamogordo from its sheath then, in a reflexlike instinct, and lifted the blade high.

Light ran about it. A shockingly bright pulse of blue radiance jolted down its length, arced the tormented air to strike the stooping hawk in the plumed flags of its extended legs.

I heard its scream, and his yell of joy.

"You come! You come!"

The bird staggered in high air, wings cracking down, head dropping to bite at its burning limbs. My enemy stood high in his saddle, leaning back in the wind, and tugged brutally at the reins bolted into his steed's beak. Their breaking fall passed beautifully, terribly, back into control; the bird hung in the air, wings beating rapidly, hovering above us.

"I knew you would come if I provoked you," he called, his voice like the clear cry of a bird speaking the language of the Powers. "Thank you. Now I can abandon these distasteful trivialities and contest a foe worthy of me."

"Come, then," I cried back. My voice came from the depths of my chest, and it rang in the burning clearing like a deep bell.

The falcon's huge pointed wings struck the air.

They dropped from heaven.

I waited for the fall of night, for I had been taught that it came suddenly and all at once in this Northern tropical land. Yet twilight went on and on. I saw then that the light was all from those shimmering pearly flags slowly curling above us at the sky's extremity, and I knew that they were his work, and I was so afraid I wanted to vomit, to turn my back on my enemy and run for the forest of dark trees, to dig myself into a hole in the soil and hide from his wrath. I did none of these things. I waited as he dismounted, and I watched in terror and incredulity both as he came toward us, his head helm-protected in plates of gold, taller than me as I was greater than a child, his shoulders and breast gleaming with soft light as the scales of his armor took it and threw it back, his great legs striding in greaves all of copper and bronze, and his tail (his *tail!*) lashing behind like the tail of a gigantic lizard.

"How wonderful. The new, improved model," he said, regarding me with satisfaction.

I allowed my blade to drop, let its tip bury itself in the soil, leaned on its hilt with both hands so my shoulders bunched and the muscles of my upper arms pressed hard against my sleeves.

"Who are you?" I said, and I think that even then I knew.

My mouth was dry, my eyes darted, sweat was cold on my back and belly.

"You know me, Shadow," said my brother. "He has taught you that much, I am certain." He halted a stone's throw from us and placed his four-fingered hands negligently upon his thick waist. The visor of his helm opened and closed like an animal's muzzle, like a beak; his tongue flickered like a serpent's.

A wave of weakness and cold passed through me. Darkness flooded the twilit clearing. I forced it back.

I could no longer deny the appalling truth of what I saw. My enemy wore no armor. This was his body: the gorget at his throat, the gauntlet, vambrace, couter of his powerful arms, the bulging pauldron at his shoulders, the cuisse and greave of his legs, the taloned claws of his monstrous feet, all his flesh and scale.

"You are Dragon," I said, and my voice broke.

"I am Apepi, the Serpent of Night," he said in a great musical voice. "I am the First and Last of the race of Men who should have ruled this world, if your master and mine had not gutted the sun in his greed. I am *dragon,* yes, I am *lung,* I am *tatsu,* I am the first son of the Earth and the father of the world which shall come when I have taken you, frail stupid human, and broken you, and fed your carcass to my steed." He lowered his burnished head and laughed, looking at me with eyes like jewels. "But I still haven't told you my name, have I? You can call me Faust, if you like.

"Better still," he added, "call me Galahad."

TWENTY-ONE

"Liar!"

I am certain that my cold face was dirty-white as old snow.

"Oh, dear." My enemy raised one elegant, taloned, jointed finger to his mouth, peeling back those reptile lips, and nibbled on a claw meant for disemboweling. "Did you suppose *you* were the hero? Have I spoiled your innocent illusions?"

"He sent me to stay you, dinosaur. I am your master. Hear this warning once only."

"'Dinousaur!' How acute of you, human. Plainly, you deserve a measure of respect." His tone lashed, then, poisonous and full of spite: "Or are you so ignorant that even the utterly fantastic seems perfectly mundane to you? I think that must be the way of it."

"You are a genetic restruct from the Black Time," I told him. "The dark wizards of that age created mockeries like you for their sport."

He threw back his lovely head and laughed without restraint.

"Excellent! You will provide me with endless amusement. 'Restruct' indeed. Ah, if you but knew. The millennia, the eras, the megayears, you damned simple narrow fool."

Glade said: "He made you so long ago?"

"The Cretaceous," the dragon taunted her. "Do you know that term, that piece of human scientific mumbo-jumbo?"

"I know this much," she said cruelly. "That was when the world-island cracked and split apart, and most of its creatures died, yours among them, like snails crushed by a boot."

He pounced forward so swiftly that I could not raise my

blade sufficiently to intercept his blow. The wicked metal-bright club of his left arm swept across Glade's face and took out of her cheek four deep scoring strips of living flesh which peeled bloodless down from her chin when his claw came out of her skin to fall like a bar of gold, to hover at his breast awaiting my own blow. Shocked, Glade made no cry. Beads of blood started then, hung against her white face, ran in four trickles to drip from the long shreds of flesh.

"Kill him!" shrieked Alamogordo in a murderous whistle which convulsed my muscles and brought the blade out of the earth and into the air, curving like death itself. "Kill the fucking filthy bastard monstrosity!" but already he was away, tail cracking with threat and rage, and almost in the same moment settling just beyond my reach, without the remotest sign of fear, into a defensive pose I recognized, a posture I knew in my deepest bone and sinew because Darkbloom had taught it to me at the age of ten and each evening for five years compelled its practice until it was instinct in me.

"So. Has Flowers of Evening changed his tune?" he asked mockingly. "Discarded his cant about the Forceless Way? I'm shocked, truly. I hardly expected to meet a disciple of our creator clutching a weapon in his Closed Fist."

I watched him grimly, lips tightly clamped. At my left shoulder Glade stood with her energy-lance alight and sizzling, still uttering no single sound of pain or rebuke.

He was a terrible great animal with the eyes of a wise human. I knew that this was no place to confront him, for it was his chosen territory, the landscape he had terrorized for months or years and must know better than any high-country Wanderer could.

"Follow," I hissed to Glade, and went crabwise toward the place of white light.

"Ah, a joust in the corridors of Time! Delicious. Or is it a chase, a game of mouse and Dragon?" He came forward with his stilting steps, pressing us as if this had been his plan from the outset. I was struck instantly by the realization that the voids between time and time must surely be his native landscapes as well, more so than this tropical nightfall, but it was too late to alter our path.

Light flared at our backs, shining like the sun from my raised blade. I heard the singing of its energies, the siren call which had lured me in the icy fields of Kravaard when I had stumbled lost into its gate like a spoiled child in my resentment and ignorance, a murdered man's grinning head jouncing at my belt as his blood ran into the coarse fabric of my garments.

At its boundary, where the air cooled suddenly and the light underwent a subtle shift, I spun on one foot and took Glade's right arm with my left, sword high, and leapt into the place outside history.

And my enemy was there with us, then, in his sweet stench of opened soil, the rasp of his scales as limbs slid sinuous and powerful in the slow eye-luring motions of the Open Hand, the hiss of his breath, the bright points of light in his arrogant eyes.

"Go," he said, taunting me. "Go, run. I will hound and harry you down the days and down the nights, down the arches of the years, until I sound the trumpet from the hid battlements of Eternity."

His baiting sent my hackles up, flooded my face with blood; I felt the veins tighten in my arms and temples; and could do nothing but what he had predicted.

With Glade at my heels, I turned and ran.

We were in NoWhere and NoTime and it was not like headlong flight from the pursuit of an enemy into forest or rockscape. It was, of course, like dream, though like none Darkbloom had sent me in preparation; or nightmare; or better yet, like drunkenness and its aftermath. We ran into dizziness and night that never lightened but only grew more oppressive, its coolness shading into cold, into gusts of icy wind, into frozen blackness.

He came after us, my dragon-brother, with loping ease, laughing.

Glade's energy-lance had flickered to red coal as we passed into this terrain of madness, and the blue flame of Alamogordo licked in the gloom like witch-fire, without yielding useful warmth or illumination. I found no stars to comfort me, not even the evil stars in their fractured patterns which eased the night misery of Glade's world, Comhria's new home.

Her face, my love, my true woman, in that darkness filled my mind: pale gold, and golden bronze of her hair.

I knew bleakly that I would never again see her, that the towers and dry courtyards and dust-filled cataracts and canals of Treet Hoown were lost forever to me, as they had been lost to all the world for a hundred thousand years under their cloak of invisibility, as they had been lost in the dementia of their vile master; I thought that now she was free, and I was lost, fleeing from a creature who could not exist outside the madness of sleep or the feckless whimsy of the surgeons of the Black Time, or the intervention of one nearly enough a god to make no difference; with awful bitterness, as I ran, as my brain labored in its search for some tactic or salient whereby I might use all my force against the dragon, I thought of his creator and mine, of Darkbloom, Flowers of Evening, god, sun-thief, pacifist shaman, and father of killers. . . .

We crashed out of NoWhere into SomeWhere:

Stars were bright fish drifting in a midnight sea, and we floated in their midst in a crystal bubble the equal of that dome which held the thrones of the Powers in the time of the Earth where the sun was dying.

Here, as I swayed and stared, the place in the heavens where the sun should be held neither a tiny circle of hot yellow-white nor a bruised ember looming across a quarter of the sky. The object which hung there was greater than either, and less: a globe of dullest red which filled half the universe, nearly invisible, an emanation of heat, it seemed to my astonished and battered senses, rather than light, all swept about by veils and ropes of blackness.

"It is not dying," the dragon told us.

He stood at the far diameter of the chamber, poised behind the glassy console of a light-daubed machine. His tone held a curious melancholy, yet it contained, as well, a note of vibrant pleasure, of impersonal triumph, bespeaking not that arrogance which earlier had filled me with a desire to bring him to his knees, but some nobler emotion which caught at my throat, disarmed me, sent my gaze away from him into contemplation of the vast deep burning thing beyond us.

"It is the sun, yes," he said, "but it has not yet been born."

Transfigured, Glade said very quietly, "Flower of Dawn."

That helmed head went up sharply, and then he put his four-fingered hands together in slow applause.

"Apt! A cogent likeness, my human lady." Gallantly, he bowed. "You are droll."

I lacked Asuliun's tradition of half-lost moldering sciences and so failed to comprehend what they were agreeing upon, save the lunatic assertion that this tremendous ball of warm cinders was somehow the sun, or its unfruited seed.

"Where is this place?" I said hoarsely, tired of poetry, feinting, the incomprehensible. "Are you saying that we witness the kindling of the sun?"

"Precisely. We dangle on the hook of our Fisher King's wormline."

"Speak sense, dragon."

"Shall I speak in the babble of children, then? Very well." He came forward, all his menace in exquisite abeyance. I waited for him to approach near enough for me to take action, so swift and berserk and governed by my sword and the symbiote that he would find no signal in me to warn him of it. "The sun which warms our world is a great furnace, burning under its own weight—"

"If the sun is a fire," I said, temporizing, watching everything about him, stance, breathing, the places and ways in which his weight pivoted, "why does it not consume itself and die, as fires must?"

"Oh, babykins is a clever babykins, eh? Because its fire is a special fire, fool, the fire which burns in stars and would eat the world in an instant if the world were flicked by the edge of the flame of it."

"Yet the Powers draw their strength from that flame," I said, half-remembering. "As you claim to do, I think." I could not leap the gap; he would not approach further, but loitered, claw-tips tapping.

"I will tell you simply, fool, and you will not understand because your mind is the mind of a vicious beast which lives to maim its own kind and every other."

Now the dragon's voice was closer to shrillness than I had yet heard. It pleased me to see him provoked, though my flesh itched with his nearness.

"Yes: Listen to me:

"The void in this ancient epoch is full of dust and fumes and young stars which burn like twigs, cracking and exploding and sending their shocks into the dust. Rich and hot, the dust draws together under its own weight, heats and swirls and catches fire, and burns in this simple fashion for a million years."

Golden, his arm swung outward to the cool gigantic pyre beyond the bubble.

"Soon, that mass of hot wind and smoke will aspire to a condition of still more noble heat and brightness, with the very fragments of its dust crushed together by the pressure of its present flame, and then we shall see a true star born, though it will take nearly four thousand million years to reach its maturity."

"Where is the world, in your fairy tale?" I asked.

"Why, at this moment it is spinning in the ring of dust which clings to that dim smoke outside our window. Soon it will gather itself together and roll like a hot dumpling about its oven, and its crust will set about it, a tasty morsel, and in another few thousand million years life will come creeping to its cloudy seas and turn the sky to pure glass, and out will creep the beasts and the ferns and the finned things of the water and the feathered things of the sky and the dinosaurs, ah yes, the lovely reptiles, for one hundred and sixty million years they will come and go upon the face of the deep and the land and make ready the place of my people, my people, my people, and a foul fool god from a shit-stinking future will reach back his wormline at the moment of their birth and poke it into the sun and suck out the light and heat, all he wants, all he can chew of it until he vomits with his gluttony, and a great darkness and chill will fall upon the world and we shall die, the food we eat will die and we shall die, and none shall there be to grieve for our going for of all our vast number I alone have been gifted with the poison of knowledge and thought, blown into my nostrils by Flowers of Evening, in the womb of my animal mother fetched out of the ignorance of all my people and shown the world, to have it snatched from me for the sake of an unborn race, a species of small hairy murderous monkeys scurrying between the legs of their betters while the gods drain away the heat and light which nurtured our world, my world, the world of the children I would have made and watched over and loved and given to the world and all the world to their care—''

He was screaming, a torrent of bereavement, and if I did not grasp more than one idea in ten, still the sinew of his anguish reached me, the melancholy of his tribulation, and I could not have looked away from his ferocity if the crystal bubble above our heads and beneath our feet had split open to the void and spilled us into its endless hunger.

He fell silent then, and in the silence I heard Glade's whisper:

''Oh, how beautiful! Xaraf, look at the sun.''

I took my eyes from the dragon and glanced into the darkness. And caught my breath.

Where the vast dim cloud had hung, a sphere of warmly glowing yellow-pink was shrinking, brightening, within a spinning garland of rainbow-frosted jewels, a ring of turbulent light which splintered as we watched into a hundred separate braided rings, crossing and recrossing, coalescing and colliding, contracting into fine circles of starlight girdling the new sun.

A world-filling flash of light scratched my eyes like a hot needle. I flinched from it, covered my face.

''The sun has ignited,'' the dragon said.

The haze of dust which had troubled the circlets of light was gone, puffed away in that cosmic shout of brightness.

Our bubble fell toward one of these rings, I saw, swooping like a hawk on its prey under the direction of its captain who stood now gazing at our wonderment almost as if he had brought us here for no other purpose than to crack our minds with this beauty.

"Does this truly happen as we watch?" Glade asked him.

"We pass through time at an accelerated rate," he told her. "I have set the ratio at two hundred million external years for each minute we experience."

"Why? Why do you bother, if you mean to kill us?"

"Let him try," I growled to her. To him I said: "Come closer, reptile. Are you afraid?"

"I shall not kill you, stupid humans. Unlike this faithless son of our father, I have sworn to preserve life and mean to keep my oath. Unless, of course, he forces his death upon me in self-preservation."

"You showed little respect for life when you rode your bird and sent lightning among your victims."

"Their existence is an illusion. Soon it shall all be a vapor."

Glade's frightened glance showed me that she deemed him deranged. "Why do you show us this . . . this beauty?"

Pride roared in his voice. "Because I am its custodian. Because it was given into my charge by Flowers of Evening. Because I would have you understand some tiny part at least of his treachery and cruelty, before he and all his world are dispelled forever."

"Xaraf and I are part of his world. So too, surely, are you."

"In this bubble, we stand outside gross causality. Never fear, little humans, no harm shall come to you two. I mean to keep you for my pets, my witnesses."

Now the jeweled ring beneath us broke apart into tumbling stars which merged as we watched into whirling globes of light and dark, and these thunderously came together until a single world lay below us, the size of an open hand at arm's length. It dazzled, a great pearl, reflected the yellow shining of a sun almost recognizable as the sun I had always known.

"This is the world itself?" I said.

"All wrapped in its cloud and its heat," the dragon told me. "Even at the rate we skip through time, it will be some minutes before the crust firms under those deep clouds."

The brief piercing flare had cleansed the blackness of its veils of dust, and I saw for the first time that the stars themselves were moving. Behind the bright disc of the Earth, the fixed stars crawled across the blackness in various directions, like bugs on a tent.

I tried to make sense of what he had told us. Two hundred million years passed with each minute? Such numbers were entirely beyond my experience or comprehension; until this moment the most appalling number I had been required to cope with was the single million of years which separated my era from Glade's, Comhria's, Darkbloom's. Now we soared through time at such headlong pace, if the dragon was honest, that the gulf of a million years was leapt in less than the third part of one second.

Mere physical threat seemed totally banal; I could not believe that my enemy would use our bemusement for so paltry an end as distraction while he killed us. Even so, I kept my eye on him and my grasp on Alamogordo's hilt.

"Ah!"

The brilliant cloud obscuring the surface of the world was gone, in a breath. We looked down through a frosty haze at blue and brown. In my ignorance I could make nothing of this, but Glade stared in fascination.

"I see no clouds."

"An optical illusion. My machines are sampling the visual spectrum thirty-three times each second. Every frame we observe is separated from the last by a hundred thousand years. Cloud patterns are ephemeral; they show only as a pointillist haze. Ice masses, though, as you see—"

The world was abruptly white at its upper pole. The dun-brown of a continent which had touched that polar region was swallowed up in glaring blue-white. For several minutes we gazed on a world in endless winter where the edge of hard white crept now lower, now higher on the land, and the land itself crawled across the face of the world. Suddenly the ice was gone again.

"Oh. Oh." Glade's voice had the remote, furry sound of one who sits very drunk beside a camp fire, seeing the secrets of eternity. "This is Darkbloom's work."

I looked at her, puzzled. The dragon nodded.

"The wormline intrudes into the solar core on average every two hundred fifty million years. For fifty or a hundred million years it withdraws one-tenth of the energy from the convective mass and translates it forward in time to the heart of the dying sun.''

''And this larceny brings on ice epochs?''

''When the arrangements of the continents are so disposed for permanent glaciation at one or both of the poles.''

Glade shook her head, laughing in a strained manner.

''This is impossible to credit! It would make Flowers of Evening the architect of all life on Earth.''

I was shocked. ''Glade! That is the province of the Lords of Light and Death.''

''Light and death indeed. If Darkbloom has ordained the measure of heat which reaches the world, he governs the great cycles of speciation and dying, the rise and fall of the living and the dead.''

''Now you start to understand,'' the dragon cried to her.

Beyond our crystal bubble the world continent was breaking apart once more; ice came and went; four continents crept apart from their ruined parent and sunned themselves.

''The Powers reach into the history which formed Them and Their ancestors and remake it to Their taste,'' my enemy told us. ''In Their monstrous arrogance They foreclose the history of every competitor. If the Earth is the Mother of life, They are the envious heirs who murder in the cradle every other child of that mother.''

A new world-island formed itself at the Earth's edge as oceans opened like slow toothless jaws, and squeezed shut: by now I was beginning to learn the interpretation of these patches of brown and green and blue and white, the bright blue-white of the ice.

''Pangea,'' said Alamogordo, and I jumped.

''What?''

''We cannot be more than two or three hundred million years from home,'' the blade said. ''That gigantic continent is Pangea. It is a killing ground for species which enjoyed the shores and rivermouths which are now crushed into its dry interior. Wait a little, though.''

I listened to the carefully enunciated voice as if I were in a state of trance brought on by Darkbloom's burning herbs.

"Yes, you see? It leaves the southern pole, it cracks across at the equator into twin continents, Laurasia and Gondwana."

The world hung in a void of dancing, shifting stars, and on its face the land itself, the solid landscape of mountains and rocks and trees and flowing rivers and animals, and for all I knew people, flowed like softening ice on a puddle.

"Now these in turn begin to splinter. Africa and South America, joined, break free of the Antarctic iceland. The Atlantic Ocean rifts North America from Eurasia." The sword's tone altered, giving way to something like joy. "I had never expected to see such a lovely thing as this. Thank you." Did it speak to me or the dragon? I could not guess.

I heard my enemy's cry of grief.

The sun dimmed to a red glimmer.

His hand flashed to an illuminated control, and beyond the crystal the image froze.

With blurring speed he came, lifted me, sent me crashing across the chamber to fall bruisingly into the transparent wall.

"This he did! For you, for you! I wish I might kill you now, but I gave my promise and I will not break it."

Shaking with shock, I crawled across the floor. Alamogordo lay some distance from me. The dragon crouched, eyes bloody with rage, allowed me to reach it. I snatched it into my hand, rose tottering.

"What are you saying? Did? He extinguished the sun?"

"Xaraf, this must be the Cretaceous boundary," Glade said breathlessly. "A deliberate culling?"

His arm struck the wall, which shivered in a high, keening note.

"You see how the sun stands. He was not satisfied to plunder those epochs which were free of life. He came down from this place and reached into my mother's uterus and constructed me, and then he brought me here that I might witness what he would do to my world. And then he turned off the sun and waited while the great saurians died and died and died. And when that was done, he gave me his immortality and the mechanisms of the wormline, and made me his regent, his gardener, his trustee."

Incredulously, Glade said: "He gave up his symbiote to you?"

"It is the mark and measure of his insolence, this mammal god. Yes."

"You betrayed his trust," I said.

"His trust? I stood in his path, and smote him. I sent him like a beggar into mutable history and blocked his gate against him, and drained the stolen energy of his wormlines to my own reservoirs, and waited for him to build a new champion." He smiled, a terrible thing to see. "Now you come, frail pale worm, and I rejoice at least that I shall have you beside me when I watch him die, and to witness the justice of history returned to its path."

"Your desire is cheated," Glade told him. "Darkbloom is dead already. We have seen his corpse."

He laughed. "A dead god is easily revived. Worm, you carry within you what is necessary, do you not?"

I pictured the wretched bloody corpse and my huddled mother. Had I met her request it would be Darkbloom who now confronted my enemy. I smiled, and all my body felt alive.

"Alamogordo," I said, "has this vessel a mind like yours?"

"Naturally."

"And you can speak with it?"

"It is loyal to its master, and cannot be contaminated."

"Reconcile yourself," the dragon told me in a mellow voice. "You are in my custody." His hand moved across the glassy console. The stars recovered their flight, but this time in the reverse sense. I blinked as the sun came on.

"You take us back to the beginning?" Glade cried.

"No." Again he gestured; again the stars ceased their agitated movement.

A tremendous construct floated beyond the crystal bubble, like a trellis made for growing grapes in the spring sun, if grapes were moons.

On the world's face, smoky haze curdled into whirls and knots of white.

"The evening of the dinosaurs," Glade said somberly.

"Their morning," he said, denying her with effortless confidence. He approached the dome, looked on the world he meant to remake. "I shall go down among them like a god and work in them the changes which the mammal worked in my genes. I will be Osiris, teaching them all things, and no Set shall rise up to hamper my governance."

I lifted the sword to my lips.

"Can you learn how to open the dome?" I whispered.

"The air would be spilled. Glade would perish," Alamogordo told me, aghast, aloud.

"Do this thing," I said.

The bitter, horrified look of betrayal on Glade's face stung me to the heart. A clanging racket of alarms sprang up, and a hissing wind.

The dragon turned, ran for the glassy place of lights.

I was running too, and the sword cut the gusting air to strike my enemy's shoulder, laying it open; blood jetted from meat red as any man's.

He spun back, brought up his left leg and caught me in the belly. His four-fingered hand (one thumb, three brutal claws) stabbed again at the mechanism which organized the vessel.

The wind stopped. I came at him again, and he stepped aside with the speed of Darkbloom and my blade cut only the back of his left arm.

I could hardly believe what I saw. The wound at his shoulder had closed, like a soft mouth, and was crusting with heavy scab as he turned again to the block of glass.

I retreated once more to Glade's side.

"You shall not harm my witness," he said with cold anger. "If you insist on your wretched heroics, let us face one another in a field suitable for contenders gifted with the privilege we have each stolen from our creator."

A line of brilliant crimson looped an ellipse against the crystal at my right hand. Another blinked into being behind him.

"Pass through," he said, looking away from me with disdain, "if you dare."

It was an insane challenge. How could I trust him? I might step beyond the wall and find myself locked out in the teeth and jaws of the uttermost void.

Yes. But he was my brother and my enemy, and I was his,

and this moment had surely been ordained from the ends if not the beginning of time.

"I will fetch you his head, Glade," I told her, placing my arms about her and kissing her mouth. He would not harm me now.

"You have sworn not to kill him, Xaraf."

"If I do not kill him, Darkbloom is dead."

"And Comhria never born." Her gaze was brittle.

"Yes. And Firebridge; Ren and Hahn and Vanden, all Asuliun, and the curse of the Black Time, and every part of the world we ever knew. Would you see these slip away uncontested?"

"Come," cried the great beast. "Step forth now, with your weapon or without it."

"To your death," I cried with equal voice. "To the victory of our father."

I came out through a blurred opening which gave before me, closing on my garments and hair with the slightest sucking sensation; and I looked down at the entire world swirling and swept with cloud.

Stars swung slowly in the night like firebugs flying about my face.

I took a step, and another. Each surface tilted from its neighbor, yet as I went from each to each I seemed to be standing vertically, lightly as a dream, so that I made my way like a fly without fear of tumbling into the void.

The struts and beams of the wormline engine extended forever, it seemed, dwindling into distance and invisibility, small dark squares bonded together into large panels. It was not meant for climbing. I had trouble finding purchase for my feet, though I skimmed lightly as a bird, my shirt billowing.

In my right hand I held Alamogordo, its bright blade, englyphed with the map of our ancient trek to Treet Hoown, covered in small discrete droplets of blood red as blossoms. Already, though, these were boiling off into the emptiness through which, not breathing, I went, my flesh sealed somehow by the action of the symbiote into a stiff armor against the dreadful cold and airlessness of the high reaches above the world.

Moisture puffed into light, froze, vanished. My enemy stood ahead of me, weaponless, protected only by the armor of his gold and silver scales and the symbiote grown through his flesh like the branches of a tree.

Only then did I recall the dream of my childhood: the garden where a 'stranger whom I yet knew used a rake to comb out the branches of a tree similar to my own.

In that dream I had asked if such trees could be transplanted into my garden. He had insisted that this was so and promised to show me how the planting was done in another garden.

I saw now that he had lied in telling me this, for the planting was the life of his reptile world in the garden which Flowers of Evening had prepared, and his gardening would call for the uprooting of all the stock of humankind.

He came toward me in the emptiness like a demon, half illuminated by the hot sun, half in shadow so deep I could see nothing of him.

Why had Darkbloom given me that dream?

If my mentor was doomed to death, death in the way of mortals, never to be returned, why had he shown me a false dream? Why indeed had he sent me forth with a sword he forbade me to use, when he might simply have ordered me to lay the symbiote in his dead mouth and dealt, in his own rejuvenated and undeputized person, with this other, this insurgent son of his?

I felt the reverberating impact of the dragon's clawed feet upon the struts. I saw one eye flash red, a taloned hand moving with grace through the passes of the Open Hand.

There was no air between us to carry any offer of surrender or peace.

This was not a disappointment to me. I wished only to kill him.

His mouth and nostrils, I saw, like mine were sealed by the action of his symbiote, like the perfect scar tissue which closed the dreadful wounds I had dealt him. He moved like a statue brought to life, as I did.

Without warning of any kind, with all the strength of my

legs, I flung myself at him then, flying truly, at last flying, his own grim falcon turned against him, and my long wicked sword went ahead of me to spit him and open his vitals to the searing cold.

He crouched back. I could not change my leap. His hands came up, struck aside the blade with a blow so swift that it blurred.

Alamogordo spun length over length into the black void, and was gone, and even the terrible shriek of despair which I know he must have made was lost to my ears in that place where no cry may be heard.

Animals of legend marched in the sequence of my enemy's blows, and mine.

My head cracked back against metal, suddenly, sickeningly, and when I regained consciousness an instant later I knew beyond argument or clutch of hope that my life was at his disposition.

The dragon lifted his hands over me then, his open hands, raised them high above his helmed head.

Lightning sparks poured from his fingertips, from his reservoir of stolen sun-stuff . . .

. . . expended themselves contemptuously into the empty waste.

I shuddered and struggled to regain my balance. Humiliating as a slap in the face, as spittle cast at a foe, he would not use his energies to best me.

There was no call for them. He had mastered me by right.

I cowered, and he picked me up as a man might hoist a tired child, and in that manner we passed back through the puckered entrance to the crystal ship, the last and first woman, and the ruin of the gods.

Where I am now, people frown on murder. Even now, after all these years, it sometimes makes me feel I wander in a dream.

They do not approve of killing others for revenge, profit, or whim. They settle their scores by the methods I once imagined my old teacher had invented.

Can these cloned and gene-shuffled children of my great

enemy really live without honor and mayhem? I used to provoke Darkbloom with my scorn. Now I see he was correct,
but I still do not pretend to understand it.

They know rage and lust, like the men and women (and the
mocking children, for that matter) of my own lost tribe, my
own forever lost people. How do they manage without killing?

They contain themselves. They hold their tongues. They
back down. Conciliate. Smile. Offer gifts to those they despise. Somehow they deal with their most powerful impulses
without losing themselves in a ruinous tempest.

Often they seem merely pallid to me.

At other times, when I watch their cool reptile restraint, I
am awed by their courage.

There are criminals here, as everywhere. Are they slow to
kill? It seems so. What stays their hand, as Darkbloom's pledge
did not ever truly stay mine? Is it merely the fear of consequences? Even yapping curs are richer in spirit than that.
(There are no dogs here.)

Even so, surely it takes bravery to trust individuals you do
not know. These people, without a qualm, place themselves
in the hands of those whose names are a mystery to them.

How can you gauge the intentions of one whose ways might
well be as sinister and dangerous as your own reflections in a
lying pool?

Certain exceptions are allowed. There are lists written down
in books. They like to refer to the records before they do
anything irreversible.

That is how they are.

Glade's children and mine look out from the open prison
which my immortal enemy has allowed us, in his benignity,
and they see nothing at all strange in any of this. It is their
world too, a world without kittens or baluchitherium restructs,
lacking tribes, and machines which speak, and great boasting
and great anger.

Except *his* anger.

I search with an unslakable hunger for the weakness of the
dragons, and I think perhaps that is it.

Their god-emperor is, first and finally, the child of a true human god. He will never break the cord which binds him to Flowers of Evening.

One day she will send him a call from the echoing voids of her nonexistence and he will answer to it with his long delayed duty.

Or that may be my delusion merely, the wistful foolishness which keeps me by my own camp fire instructing my grand-children and their children in the secrets which Darkbloom taught me: guile, mystery, the Open Hand, and always, always, the song (now that Glade is no longer here to weep when I tell it); the song of lost Treet Hoown and its lovely mistress, mistress of my dream.